HARRY
KAPLAN'S
ADVENTURES
UNDERGROUND

Books by Steve Stern

Isaac and the Undertaker's Daughter
The Moon and Ruben Shein
Lazar Malkin Enters Heaven
Harry Kaplan's Adventures Underground

for children

Mickey and the Golem
Hershel and the Beast

HARRY

KAPLAN'S

ADVENTURES UNDERGROUND

Steve Stern

TICKNOR & FIELDS

NEW YORK 1991

For information about permission to reproduce selections from this book,
write to Permissions, Ticknor & Fields, Houghton Mifflin Company,
2 Park Street, Boston, Massachusetts 02108

Library of Congress Cataloging-in-Publication Data

Stern, Steve, date.
Harry Kaplan's adventures underground / Steve Stern.
p.   cm.
ISBN 0-89919-724-8
I. Title
PS3569.T414H37   1991   90-21622
813'.54 — dc20   CIP

Printed in the United States of America

BP 10 9 8 7 6 5 4 3 2 1

For Lizabeth Smith and her Ladies

and for Kathy the Brave

It wasn't a dream, it was a flood.

— *Frank Stanford*

I

One

During the spring of the flood I took up with a couple of colored boys down on Beale Street. I was fifteen years old and my father had recently plucked me out of a book to put me to work in his pawnshop. Of course I would have preferred to remain in the exotic landscapes of my reading, in the muggy jungles and pastel deserts and the remote mountain fastnesses where you lived forever, along the moon-drenched, hoof-beaten highways and the bounding mains. But when I saw the way that the swollen river had transformed the city, which I'd never paid much attention to before, I began to have a change of heart.

The water had risen to the height of the rockbound bluff, inundating the levee. The low-lying cotton warehouses were swamped to their second stories, stranding the pin-striped classers (who dispatched their porters in washtubs to fetch their lunch) in marathon poker games. The paddle-wheeled excursion boats bobbing high above their customary stages, their pipe organs blowing bubbles, looked from a distance to be floating in midair.

The river itself, having climbed the levee as far as Front Street on its east side and spilled over the Arkansas bottoms on the west, was broadened to the width of a sluggish inland sea. Outhouses, church pulpits, windmill propellers, suites of parlor furniture, and the bloated carcasses of cows rode the current. Whole families were regularly washed ashore. Clutching soggy bundles, questionable heirlooms, and mildewed children on tethers, trailed by attenuated shadows and wet dogs, they squatted in the public parks and wagon yards. They huddled under the department store awnings and theater marquees along Main Street. In the hot afternoons their shrunken garments sent up threads of steam, which made them appear to be smoldering or about to evaporate.

But what I personally couldn't get over was how so much of my papa's own Beale Street was under water. The surrounding Gayoso Bayou had backed up, overflowing its banks, so that it washed into the basin of the block between Hernando and Third. Now, in place of trolley tracks and asphalt with the cobbles showing through, there was a rippling, sun-splintered lagoon. Back and forth across it in an unending poor man's regatta, the Negroes ferried themselves in wooden skiffs.

My family had been in the South just a little over a year when it happened. We'd come down from New York City when my father, after the failure of half a dozen business ventures, had claimed a sudden attack of wanderlust. Mild-mannered, good-humored, and slight behind nickeled spectacles, his six feet diminished by posture like a question mark, Papa had never had any prior history of such complaints. At least not to my knowledge. So far as I knew, despite all his pipe dreams about far-flung commercial concerns, he'd always been a confirmed homebody. From the familiar headquarters of our dingy duplex apartment in Brighton Beach, he kept his head thrust firmly among the clouds. This was what he was known for; though my grandfather, who was hardly one to talk, sometimes accused him of keeping his head stuck in less ethereal places.

Then one afternoon, when no one had asked him, Papa took

it on himself to declare, "Brooklyn ain't America!," jerking his thumb toward a window overlooking a street where Yiddish was still lingua franca. Propping his glasses on the slope of his forehead, he covered his eyes with one hand and spun a standing globe of the world with the other. "Round and round she goes," he chanted, a carnie at a wheel of fortune no less. He was always the kidder, my papa, though games of chance had never really been much in his line. In any case, with a skidding forefinger he eventually stopped the world; he uncovered his eyes to announce that fate had designated for our new home a place called Memphis in the state of Tennessee.

I might have pointed out that the finger of fate had actually come to rest somewhere in the vicinity of the Outer Hebrides, but I wasn't fooled for a moment by this phony random selection. I knew, as who didn't, that behind it all was my father's relocated older brother, my well-heeled if somewhat shady Uncle Morris. Despite the lean years for almost everyone else, Uncle Morris, following instincts he proclaimed as surefire, had made a killing down south in real estate. That was the story, and it had kept him virtually out of touch for almost a decade. Then shortly following the death of his chronically ailing wife Nettie (whom scarcely anyone seemed to remember), he began to find frequent excuses to make trips to New York. On those occasions, professing a slavishness to the sacred idea of family, Uncle Morris would invite us all to come to Memphis and share the spoils.

"Solly Solly Solly," he would grieve, clucking his tongue over the crumb-strewn oilcloth of our kitchen table, flapping his jowls and flicking cigar ashes onto his plate. "When are you gonna get wise?"

Then he'd repeat his standard lament about how my papa was wasting his talents (what talents?) in the ghetto. He should come already to the land of the honeysuckle and the mockingbird, where his fortune was waiting to be made. "The family should be together," he would solemnly intone, insisting that

5

he meant it from the bottom of his heart — a place I imagined as full of extinguished cigar butts. "Mama and Papa can enjoy a temperate climate in their sunset years, and Mildred here" — he leaned across the table with his labored breathing to pat my mother's hand — "Mildred we can make into a lady of leisure."

This gesture on the part of my uncle always sent my mama — not a bad-looking woman if you liked them in the full-figured department — it always sent her into fits of tittering laughter, which wasn't ordinarily her style. Generally speaking, my mama was quite a sober person, the firm set of her lips perhaps compensating for the careless curve of my father's smile. But a touch from Uncle Morris and you'd have thought that the brother-in-law had started in munching her fingertips, or worse.

In fact, it was common knowledge among the Kaplans that my mother had been courted by both brothers in their youth. How she finally wound up with Papa was a question I'd heard my mama ask herself aloud more than once. It was a way she had of trying to needle my father out of his dreaming, though you had to wonder how much of it was actually in jest. You wondered if — when she compared the portly Morris with his much vaunted assets to her spare and feckless husband Solly — my mama sometimes had honest second thoughts.

Occasionally Uncle Morris would bring along on his visits his mousy daughter Naomi, and everyone would always try to throw us together. She was a droopy-drawered, goggle-eyed dishrag of a girl, my cousin, shy to the point of affliction, and I for one had never been moved to draw her out. Over the years of what I'd assumed to be a mutual hostility, we'd exchanged no more than a token couple of words. Hello and goodbye, with maybe a sortie as far as gesundheit, comprised the bounds of our intimacy. That the two bookworms would at last have some time for each other, this was one of the pros (there were no cons) in my uncle's relentless argument for our moving south.

Needless to say, such a proposition sounded to my ears less like a promise than a threat.

Anyway, with his avowed faith in his current enterprise and in the one that followed after its failure, with his insistence on the wealth of opportunities that lay close to home, it took a while for my father to see the wisdom in his brother's advice. It took the collapse of a series of mostly imaginary business ventures (a telephone pollstering service, a mail-order toiletries outfit, an independent, not to say unlicensed, investment-consulting and brokerage firm) before Papa allowed Uncle Morris to call his bluff.

At the announcement of the family's exodus, Grandpa Isador, for whom any change was a change for the worse, carried on in the way that we'd come to expect. "A shvartz yor!" he moaned, wringing his hands, making as if to pull off his face by the fringe of his wispy, yellowing beard. He complained that his son was as good as delivering us into the hands of Cossacks; he opened his Scriptures to the riot act. It was the same performance he'd given whenever Uncle Morris suggested that he and my grandmother come south for their health.

Though in their case, given my papa's perpetually empty pocketbook, this was maybe not such a bad idea. After all, why remain in humble circumstances with a poor son when the rich one was extending an open invitation? Not that my uncle had ever exactly stipulated that the old couple live exclusively with him, an omission that may not have been lost on Grandpa Isador. So it's possible that, as much as he disapproved of my papa, my grandpa disapproved of Uncle Morris even more. But then he'd always asserted that, having already crossed an angry ocean, Brooklyn was as far from Byelorussia as he intended to budge. The rest of the country was anyway infested with pogromchik wild Indians.

Meanwhile his wife, my adamant Grandma Zippe, as usual expressed no emotion whatsoever beyond her frozen, all-purpose frown.

My mother, however, surprised us all. Despite a strict allegiance to her mah-jongg circle and her active Hadassah involvement, for all her traditional hard-headed skepticism with respect to her husband's schemes, she seemed perfectly amenable to his latest big idea. She even went along with the pretense that the idea had originated with him. For his part, Papa behaved as if he were almost disappointed that his wife hadn't bothered to show more resistance to the move.

As for me, I suppose I might have put up a fight if I'd given it much thought; I was after all being torn from the bosom of the only home I'd ever known. Still, it would have been hard to get sentimental over our cheesy apartment, located as it was a few blocks from a beach that, even in the middle of my second decade, was mostly a rumor to me. Besides, in those days I had other priorities.

I was living in books, so preoccupied with my reading that I could hardly remember having ever done anything else. I was out of reach, immersed in the picturesque pages of John Buchan and H. Rider Haggard, Edgar Rice Burroughs and Baroness Orczy and Captain Marryat. With hungry (if myopic) eyes, I ate up *The Prisoner of Zenda;* I was absorbed beyond recall into the depths of *Ardistan and Djinistan,* hopelessly abandoned to *Propeller Island* and *The Lost World.* From painted howdahs and the hollow trunks of baobab trees, from behind a taffrail or a gaslit lamppost, or from under the grid of an oubliette, I might spy now and again upon the antics of my family. But the haunted escarpment and the vaulted catacomb, the uncharted archipelago in its peculiar wrinkle of time, these occupied the foreground of my attention. So why should I care which corner of the material planet the Kaplans might decide to call home? Brooklyn, Memphis, the Outer Hebrides, they were all the same to me.

In Memphis we took an apartment that Uncle Morris had found us above a little bakery on North Main Street. A cramped and shabby two-bedroom affair, it was not so unlike our vacated shoebox in Brooklyn. It had the same rolling floorboards and musical plumbing, though added to these standard features was a dusty skylight the color of beer. It was situated in a clamorous downtown neighborhood that everyone, for some immemorial reason, called the Pinch.

Perched atop the bluff a stone's throw from the river, North Main Street was wall-to-wall mama-and-papa shops, each of them crammed with hustling Jews. And every one of those merchants was getting the hell out of the Pinch next month, next year, just as soon as business improved. In fact, but for the dank humidity that turned your lungs to wet cellophane and the summer heat that drove families to sleep on their tenement roofs, but for the way the weeds and toadstools sprouted from telephone poles and grew out of cracks in the walls, we might almost have been back in Brighton Beach. Never mind the corners enshrined with Civil War cannons and plaques commemorating victims of various plagues; the gunsmiths and feed emporiums and storefront Pentecostal missions; the truckloads of yokels dressed for blood sports. In any case, there were enough starving cobblers and piecework tailors around to keep Grandpa Isador from perishing of homesickness.

There were also enough similarities with home to calm my father, whose pioneering spirit had not survived the train ride down. The miles of monotonous flatlands, littered with tarpaper shacks amid boneyards of eviscerated automobiles, had taken their toll on his enthusiasm. When the shoeless families on rural platforms — their eyes like old money — peered into our coach, he sank into his collar until he was practically headless. Just outside Memphis he was still twisting around in his seat as if he thought it might not be too late to turn back.

Not until we'd left the station and taken a taxi to North Main Street did Papa begin to breathe easier. He even screwed up his courage enough to make a wisecrack. "To the ends of the

9

earth we came to see a potato knish?" he quipped at the sight of shops with Hebrew characters scrawled on the windows.

About to introduce us to our new apartment, whose homely virtues he'd already begun to recite, Uncle Morris had taken offense. "So maybe you expected the ladies with their hoop skirts and the darkies singing hymns?" he wheezed. "Maybe you want egg in your julep?"

Wistfully lifting his caterpillar eyebrows like he wouldn't have minded, Papa said that he hadn't meant to seem ungrateful.

"Sol-ly!" Uncle Morris was suddenly all consolation, slapping his brother's back as if to encourage a belch. "Give it a chance." Then he winked at my grandparents, who'd been deposited along with the luggage beside the curb. (It had been decided that, for the time being at least, they would be more comfortable on North Main, as Uncle Morris's place was currently undergoing repairs.) He chucked my mother under the chin and waved a gesture that seemed intended to make the drab tenement building disappear. "Give the business a chance, and before you know it our Mildred'll be mistress of a grand house on the Parkway."

The business in question was a pawnshop that my uncle had repossessed, merchandise intact, from its hapless former proprietor. He was turning it over gratis to my father, lock, stock, and cash drawer, as he liked to say, with no strings attached.

"Please don't thank me, Solly," he kept protesting, though Papa was clearly of a couple of minds concerning his brother's largess. "It's a mitzvah for me," he insisted, my pious uncle, rolling his eyes whence cometh his reward, clearing his throat like a trumpeting pachyderm.

The shop was located on Beale Street, a place that inspired all kinds of gossip and hearsay. It was there, as Uncle Morris had promised, that my father would find the local color he'd missed on our arrival in the Pinch. It was the street where the shvartzers came to make their crazy music, to kick up their heels and generally misbehave. But the nearest thing to music at my papa's end of the street was the creaking of hinges on shop signs and the jingling of tills. The only musicians were the poor shnorrers, down on their luck, who came in to hock their broken-necked ukeleles, their mouth harps that sounded like breaking wind. So maybe the fabled Beale Street began a little farther down the hill, down past the colored park on the other side of Third. But that was a section of town toward which the merchants on my father's block seldom had occasion to go.

Not that the street was a source of any special curiosity for me. I was no more interested in the locale of my father's business than I was in the business itself, though I could appreciate that it was something of a heroic departure for him. Despite his ill-fated succession of careers, my papa had rarely been called upon to face the public. Now, with a windy bravado that fooled no one, he attempted to infect the rest of us with his bogus optimism. Again and again he repeated his resolution to make a go of it. But it was clear that the strength of his own conviction depended on the family's endorsement; and at the least excuse he would try to inveigle us into coming down to visit the shop.

There was the evening, for instance, when he had everyone down to Beale Street for the maiden illumination of his sign.

"Give a look," my papa had nudged us, ducking inside to plug in an electrical cord. There was a burst of scarlet neon over the door, whirring like a horde of locusts, spelling out our name in lights: KAPLAN'S LOANS. Back on the street Papa lifted his face so that it was bathed in the flush of his sign. Then, like a knight raising a visor, he ceremoniously pushed back his spectacles.

"This is the work I was born for," he declared. It was what he said at the commencement of all his disastrous pursuits.

You could only shake your head, but did I worry? After all, I had my own concerns. In my alcove over the unpaved alley that separated our building from Petrofsky's market, I'd kept on reading. Lately my specialties were the kind of stories that began in hidebound studies appointed in glasses of claret and mastiffs asleep by the hearth, and ended up in a godforsaken wilderness amid quicksand and dinosaur bones. I liked unlikely heroes who left their cozy digs to investigate a tap on a windowpane, only to be waylaid by adventure for the next half century or so. I liked it when they stumbled downstairs into prehistory, or fell through a revolving bookcase into a subterranean stream that led to a kingdom of thieves.

Sprawled across my hide-a-bed, I would hold an open book like the helm of a ship. Or sometimes like a sprung steel trap or a pair of wings about to flap and fly away. Nothing short of the boldest illustrations — I'm talking flashing gold sabers and crimson sails — could distract me from my regard for the printed page. Not the kids at the Market Square School with whom I wasn't too popular, owing I suppose to my Yankee accent and my habit of keeping to myself, but did I care? They didn't bother me any more than did my righteous grandfather, who would have had me visit the ritual bath for handling unsanctified texts. ("Chozzerai!" he'd lament at the sight of me poring over my sagas, then stick a finger down his throat.)

From virgin whiskers I might scratch my pimply cheeks till they festered, but my concentration remained unimpaired. Neither shmeikeling shopkeepers nor clattering streetcars, not church bells or factory whistles or steamboat calliopes, or the cries of newsboys announcing no end in sight of hard times — nothing could turn my head away from the stories that had turned my head.

Once, however, my father had caught me off guard with a chance remark. A real card who read the funny papers if he read anything at all, he managed to strike a nerve.

"Haven't you heard, boychikel? Books'll make you blind."

This sounded vaguely insinuating, as if when he said "books" he really meant something else, "books" being a code word for the unspeakable. Then I told myself: Hold your horses. What did I have to feel guilty about? Nothing at all. So why was I suddenly blushing as if I'd been caught at some shameful practice? All of a sudden I was embarrassed to find myself, at the relatively advanced age of fifteen, still hostage to boys' adventures when I should have already outgrown these silly tales of voyaging princes in disguise. It was maybe time I should begin to put away childish things in favor of more high-minded pursuits.

From the red sandstone library on Front Street I started lugging home thick volumes with no illustrations. The drier the topic, the finer the print, the yellower the page, the more sophisticated I felt. I tried books on a wide range of subjects to broaden my interests — from marketing strategy to parliamentary procedure, insect lore, oral hygiene, and agricultural reform. Books with titles like *Systems of Statistical Mechanics, The Future of the Federal Whatsis,* and *Principia Youtellme.*

My idea was that a saturation diet of deadly boredom would accelerate the process of maturing. It would make me the serious person that I had taken it into my head I wanted to be. But anxious as I was for results, I lacked the heart for this particular method. A club from whose membership I would've been restricted even if I was old enough to join, the books conspired to snub me, their big words obstinately refusing to turn into heroes or foreign parts.

As a compromise between my accustomed frivolous fare and self-inflicted tedium, I took up reading poetry. I read it aloud like a haftorah offering, safe in the assumption that it wouldn't make sense to me anyway. But while I was in no immediate danger of acquiring a taste for the stuff, its substance wasn't entirely lost on me.

I noticed, for instance, that poets went in for a wide variety of concerns. You had your hearts and flowers, your silvery beams and assorted la-di-da, but there were other things as well: the odd voyage of a ghost ship into waters that spilled off the map, treachery and mortal combat and desperate characters with too much full moon in the blood, gypsy daredevils and sorcerers who resided in caves of ice or languished in towers with mile-thick walls. And then there was this business of what poets called their muse.

As best I could make out, a muse was a species of phantom lady who inspired you to feats beyond your ordinary means. Under her auspices a nebbish might prevail against overwhelming odds in pitched battle. An illiterate could compose three-handkerchief dramas, a bumpkin with no sense of direction travel to hell and back to fetch her souvenirs. While I wasn't exactly certain I would know a muse if I saw one, I began to think that, weak-chinned and four-eyed though I was, I might like one of my own. And as long as I was in the business of wishing, I might as well cite her specifications to order.

She would be ample of breast and hip, my muse, bare of shoulder, platinum-haired, azure-eyed, and ruby-lipped, wearing a diaphanous gown with (God help me) nothing on underneath. In the small hours she would glide into my alcove, whispering with cinnamon breath, suffering me to touch the hem of her garment, which had risen on the wind above her knees. Then I would be transported instantly to someplace out of one of my books.

Sometimes I half suspected that the ticket was to get off your tush and actively seek your muse. But where would you look in such a jerkwater town as Memphis, such a far cry from its namesake on the Nile? It was a dingy city without a trace of class, with never the hint of a hanging garden or a necropolis, a city where no self-respecting muse would hang her hat. There was just nothing here to excite the curiosity, and since my regimen of boredom had more or less backfired, I was beginning to feel a little restless.

It was around this time that my father invited me to come and work in his shop, an invitation hardly even deserving of an answer, since in those days Papa himself took every opportunity to play hooky from Kaplan's Loans.

"Thanks anyway," I had muttered without bothering to look up from my book. Fallen back on old habits, I was belly-down on my hide-a-bed, reading the rattling tale of an ace cricketeer who is also a crack second-story man. But as Papa continued to stand over me, I experienced another twinge of the shame he'd caused me to feel a few weeks before.

Ordinarily Papa would have shrugged and walked away. That would have been in keeping with the unwritten pact between us, whereby we observed a mutual lack of interest in each other's affairs. He never interfered in what he referred to as wasting my formative years in Cloud-Cuckoo-Land, and by the same token I never accused him of squandering the family resources on his crackpot careers. But on this particularly mild March afternoon, my father stood fast, so that in the end I had no choice but to look up at him.

He was peering at me over the rims of his glasses, his usually bemused smile inverted. His feelings, it appeared, had been hurt. This was not an entirely new development, given how temperamental he'd been since coming to Memphis. In fact, for all of his sanguine talk talk talk, it was clear that he was still unresigned to his latest occupation. I suppose it wasn't so surprising, considering the way that the pawnshop had flushed him out, forcing his reluctant public exposure. As a consequence, trying to wean himself from the apartment while at the same time unable to keep to his shop, Sol Kaplan was neither here nor there.

"So, Mr. Diligent," he persisted now that he had my attention. He was keeping up a front of being sociable, rocking back and forth on his heels. "What do you do with your afternoons? Still with the reading?"

I had to fight the urge to deny what was perfectly self-evident. "How did you guess?"

Papa stopped his rocking and stiffened, lifting a trigger finger on the verge of warning me not to get fresh. Then, perhaps remembering what a dud he was for scolding, he relaxed, or rather deflated, into a crestfallen sigh. "Harry," he nearly implored me, "come down to Beale Street, why don't you. You'll learn the business, you'll be a mensch. Ain't it time you took a gander at real life?"

Under my breath I said to him, "Give a listen to the voice of experience here." I hadn't actually meant for him to hear me, but I could tell by the way he hung his head that he had. I wanted to tell him I was sorry, I'd spoken out of turn, while on the other hand I couldn't help thinking, Some macher, some big man of commerce. One of his boondoggles finally boots him outside the family circle, and what does he do? He tries to drag the family along with him.

He had already made his appeal to Mama, who had lately begun putting on airs — she'd declared that a pawnshop was no place for a lady. He'd even tried drafting Grandpa Isador out of retirement, an old man who'd beaten himself batty over a cobbler's last for half a century. (Grandma Zippe had naturally been regarded as a lost cause.) And now, as a last resort he'd set his sights on yours truly.

Well, it wouldn't work. Nobody was going to tear me away from what, in a desperate effort to lend dignity to misspent time, I'd begun to call my studies. My extracurricular field of endeavor. Nevertheless, I'll admit that it gave me a royal case of heartburn to see my dewy-eyed papa looking so all alone.

Two

Once he'd succeeded in suckering me into his employ, my father was at a loss to tell me exactly what I should do. Except for the times when he had me assist him in his ongoing inventory, I was left pretty much to my own devices. This confirmed my suspicion that I'd been imported from North Main Street for no better reason than to keep him company.

Every once in a while, between customers, he might take me aside to explain some of the finer points of the business. Then he would make a show of grooming me to take over someday, assuring me that if I played my cards right, this whole heap of rubbish could be mine. But despite his whispered disclosures concerning foolproof methods of separating base metal from gold, of measuring the grade of a precious gem by the degree of its luster and so forth, Papa never offered me a single practical demonstration. Words he must have picked up from his colleagues along the street — like "touchstone," "nitric acid," "avoirdupois" — he pronounced the way someone else might say "hocus-pocus" or "Shema Yisrael." He cracked his knuckles like a concert pianist before pressing the keys of his Gilded Age cash register, and stroked the bill of his leather eyeshade like an admiral on a bridge. But it was ten-to-one that he was making it all up as he went along.

It was all an act to prove the shopworthiness of his new public personality — that's how I saw it. It was a performance that, for the purposes of authentication, required an audience. And since his customers had to be counted as more or less a part of the act, this was where I came in. So you had to hand it to him, my stagy papa — he could certainly talk a good pawnshop. Nor did I ever see him as fragile at Kaplan's as he'd appeared that afternoon when he recruited me from North Main. But who did he really think he was kidding? When it came to real life, Kaplan's Loans had more in common with make-believe.

Sometimes, if I got fidgety enough, I might be moved to take a little initiative. I might wave a feather duster over the green-tinged glass of a display case or the battered bell of a trombone. This earned me the attention of my papa's puller Oboy, who once or twice had left his post in front of the shop to instruct me in the use of dry mop and broom. Clearly not delighted with my presence on the premises, the runty little shvartzer tolerated me with a stiff impatience. It was apparently more than his job was worth to have to put up with the unskilled likes of such as me.

A legacy (as Uncle Morris put it) from the previous owner, the pint-sized Oboy sat astride a tall, three-legged stool on the sidewalk outside Kaplan's Loans. His pinched face, hatched with deep wrinkles like ancient characters on muddy parchment, was perpetually deadpan in the shadow of his nautical cap. The other pullers on Beale Street were smooth-talking jokers in eye-catching outfits who would accost a potential customer just short of assault. They would detain him on the pretext of, say, scrounging a dip of snuff, then hustle him into the shop for some bargain reserved for his exclusive patronage. But not Oboy, who kept mostly mum.

If he spoke to me at all, it was in brief, gnomic utterances, nuggets such as: "It ain't a flo wax mo better'n elbow grease." This kind of advice he croaked in a froggy voice whose tone I didn't think he should have taken with the boss's son. So maybe he resented the way I'd begun to usurp some of his duties — not that I could even have told you what his duties were, since they were every bit as vague as my own. Resentful or not, you'd have thought from the way he behaved that I was distracting the puller from more pressing concerns.

He sat on his stool like a watcher in a crow's nest instead of a professional shmoozer there to entice the passers-by. In his lumpish rigidity he put me in mind of a stone monkey in front of the ruined temple described in *The Lost Jewels of Opar*. He was more like the guardian of the shop than its employee.

And I was the license that Papa'd required to abandon himself entirely to the ritual of running his pawnshop. To the bizarre items of merchandise that had begun to fill his shelves, my father now gave his undivided attention. The only reason I didn't feel more out of place was that my afternoons in Kaplan's weren't so dissimilar from afternoons in my alcove above North Main. Nestled under a musty rack of topcoats that hung in the plate-glass window, I would bury my nose in a book. Virtually concealed from the rest of the shop, I made myself at home, though the noisy procession of customers, which seemed to increase by the day, put even my powers of concentration to the test.

En route to some volcano island on board a shanghaied junk, for instance, I might be rudely recalled to Beale Street by the chimes over the door. I might get sidetracked by some colored tailor in fire-engine-red suspenders, boasting the magical properties of a broken sewing machine. Or some blowsy, russet-faced auntie, hitching up several layers of skirts to detach a homemade wooden leg, explaining as she clunked it over the counter, "I be's tired but it still want to dance."

So maybe I liked the business of furtively parting the coat-sleeves, like leaves in a hunter's blind, to spy on a gambler twirling a key chain. Observing without being observed, I would watch as the gambler grinned hugely so that my father could appraise the diamond set in his gold-capped tooth.

"An unusual cast for a solitaire," said Papa, making professional noises that who could believe. "Seriously flawed in the center, but the crown facet — oy, what a fire!"

Later on I might watch him give the nod to a hearing trumpet posing as the speaker on a gramophone. He'd make a "hmmm" like a sage physician as he assessed an asthmatic squeezebox, a telescope with a missing lens, a set of worm-eaten Indian clubs, or a pin-bristling voodoo figurine. If ever Papa objected to an item's quality or questioned its authenticity, it was only for the sake of form. Take the case of the crooked old party with the patent-leather face who came in proclaiming, "This am the riginal same coat whooch I wo when the marsah have made I'n the wife to jump over the broom."

"Uncle Joshua!" Papa clucked his tongue as he fingered the tatty material. "What you're hocking is you're hoken a tchynik." But he took the coat anyway, in appreciation of its sentimental, if not historical, value, while the old man stood blinking as if the Yiddish for bunkum was a gentle rain in his face.

From the amount of worthless merchandise that he so indiscriminately took in, you'd have thought Sol Kaplan was running a junk shop instead of a loan. He was becoming the curator of a seedy dime museum, of a sort that even P. T. Barnum wouldn't have been caught dead in. On the other hand, I'd begun to think I wasn't the only member of the family who was a pushover for a good story.

Because Kaplan's Loans was turning into a regular clearinghouse for tall tales, its proprietor swapping cold cash for the moonshine that his clientele carried in. The rusty weapons and nameless musical instruments, the two-headed sheep embryos in pickle brine, the Rube Goldberg inventions, the homespun clothes, the encyclopedias eighty years out-of-date — they were merely thrown in for good measure. They were mementos of the exotic places the stories came from, places that lay, by my reckoning, somewhere to the east of Third Street in a district that had begun to arouse my interest, though I didn't let on. While my father continued to pretend that he was a serious pawnbroker, I kept on pretending to read.

The rains came to Beale Street at approximately three in the afternoon on a Saturday toward the end of March, after an unseasonably muggy couple of days. I recall that I was busy for a change, assisting Papa in the never-ending inventory of his stock. This was how he occupied himself in the interludes between customers: he checked and rechecked the merchandise that he already had almost by heart, cross-referencing recent acquisitions against the ever more elaborate entries in his multiplying account books. From the high solemnity with which he called the roll of his purchases, he might have imagined himself a recording angel. He was judging what did and did not belong (what didn't belong?) to his kingdom come of vintage junk.

As usual he was taking his time, incapable of citing a flatiron or a butter knife without relating all he knew of its intimate history. It fell to me to hold the ledgers, entering any new additions and correcting him on the rare occasions when his memory was imprecise.

"Item," he would pronounce, a forefinger lifted as if to test the wind, "one pair of trousers, gray worsted with shiny seat, custom-made by Mose the tailor for the world's first colored millionaire. This is the one that helped finance Mr. Crump's campaign before Mr. Crump had him run out of town." Or, "Item, one shotgun with sawed-off barrel, once owned by Jake 'the Milk Snake' Miller, a protégé of Machine Gun Kelly, Memphis's own native son. His poor mama that don't look so

·

21

good was in just this morning with this item, one silk camellia in cracked bell jar, once worn behind the ear of . . .''

A new entry, this one required my taking dictation, something to do with a lady singer in some legendary somebody's legendary band. "Do I have to write all of it down?" I asked, though of course I knew better than to ask. But hadn't I humored him enough for one day?

Papa peered at me sharply, allowing his glasses to fall from his forehead and travel down his rostrum nose. This meant that he was shocked by my lack of manners, that I should have interrupted him at his holy office. It was about as far as he ever went in the way of expressing displeasure.

I sighed wearily and rolled my eyes toward the window, where Horatio Hornblower was gathering dust on the sill under the rack of coats. That's when I saw how the world beyond the window, as if to second Sol Kaplan's annoyance, had turned to darkest midnight in the middle of the afternoon. The sidewalks stood eerily vacant of weekend strollers, the dead-silent streets keeping the secret of where they had gone. The bass throb of my heart began a countdown that reverberated in my ears. Then it came, like a sound you might hear when an ocean liner collides with an iceberg. It was the sound of the sky cracking open.

What followed was a tropical deluge such as you'd live a long time without seeing in Brighton Beach. It was a storm so furious that I expected the swaying lampposts to be uprooted at any moment and blown away. Even the immovable Oboy, who'd braved the squall's initial force with the resignation of a ship's figurehead, had at last to surrender and carry his stool indoors. Then, for an indefinite time, the three of us stood in the window, having shoved aside the hanging coats to watch the rain come down.

Sometimes it fell at a slant like a hail of arrows; sometimes it was whipped by an angry gale into a frenzy of beaten sheets.

The plate glass would shudder its accompaniment to the thunder, the branched lightning performing its sudden alchemy, and for a split second the shopfronts were transfigured into a solid-gold replica of themselves — a commemorative coin of a storm-ravaged street stamped white-hot into my mind.

The gutter backed up and foamed like a boiling moat; it ran with white water carrying fish heads and fruit rinds, a tape measure, a whisk broom, a terrified cat with its talons fastened to a whirling picture frame. Other things flashed by too fast to identify, nondescript objects fallen out of the burst bellies of clouds. There were items that scooted in flight down the pavement with no assistance but the wind: a potted rubber tree overtaken by flapping newspapers escorted by a rolling barrel hoop, an empty rain cape wrestling with the turbulent air. Meanwhile the awning along the front of the shop had filled with rain like a berth, spilling over until the interior of Kaplan's was a cave behind a waterfall.

I don't know how long we stood there watching. How could I when there was no distinguishing night from day, and the clocks in the shop, if they worked, were all set at random times? Eventually the storm seemed to have spent its original violence, subsiding into a persistent, still relatively savage downpour. At some point the power had failed, and in the darkened shops over the road you could see the flashlights darting like fireflies. Then the flashlights began to go out as the brokers and their help started to emerge. Some dashed madly while others groped with their coats over their heads, scattering in various directions toward home.

The first among us to utter a sound, my papa felt compelled to offer the odd remark: "What do they think, that they're swimming upstream to spawn?" But as the evening wore on with no letup in sight, even Papa had to admit, "Well folks, it looks like business is kaput for the day."

Still nobody budged. We continued bearing our silent witness to the torrents, listening as the heavy furniture was re-arranged on high — while I wondered if my father was thinking what I was thinking: What was to keep us from staying the night in the shop? Honestly, the place had never seemed so snug, especially since Oboy had lit a couple of kerosene lamps. We had plenty of provisions, zwieback crackers and soda and even some salt-cured sidemeat (albeit a little green) that Papa had conceded to make a loan on. We had lamps for reading and hammocks that you could hang and curl up in, like sailors who've come through a typhoon. What was it they said, any port in a storm? I was about to present my case when the telephone rang.

Papa removed the receiver, and I could hear through the static — even from several paces away — the shrill, demanding voice of my mother. She was jabbering about something that my father, holding the phone at arm's length, couldn't have caught any better than I. Nevertheless, after a few moments he interrupted her to assert, "You're so right, Mildred, it's time we came home." Though once he'd hung up, he was as irresolute as before.

"What do you say we make a break for it?" he submitted at length, with an enthusiasm you could see clear through. "Now's as good a time as any." He even went so far as to take some umbrellas out of an elephant's hoof, dispensing them as grimly as if they were life jackets. Not that anyone seemed inclined to take the first step toward the door.

"Nu, Oboy?" Papa meant to sound breezy despite a quavering in his voice.

A character of few words, like I said, Oboy could speak volumes with the knitting of his deep-etched brow. "My mama didn't raise no fool" was what he was saying, if I read his configuration of wrinkles correctly. Or did he hesitate because, for all I knew, he had nowhere else to go? Come to think of it, when had I ever seen the pawnshop when the puller wasn't around? Oddly enough it made me nervous, Papa's sending him away — like it might be some violation of the lease.

Nor would it have surprised me if Oboy simply refused to leave, if he had carried his stool back onto the sidewalk and sat there defiantly, taking whatever the weather could dish out on the chin.

But in the end he croaked without an argument, "Yassuh, Mistah Solly, I see y'all tomorrah." Mindful of opening the umbrella prematurely, he made for the door. As I watched him struggling under a streetlamp like a wirewalker losing his footing, I half expected the stunted puller to be taken aloft. The storm would disperse him over rooftops like a seed. But instead the wind turned his umbrella inside out, tugging him down the sidewalk as if he had a wild thing on a leash.

No sooner was he out of sight, however, than Papa began to dawdle again. From the way he was behaving, you'd have thought he was a captain torn between saving himself and going down with his ship. Stalling for time, he puttered around, transparently jaunty, starting to sing to himself as he oiled his cash register keys.

"On the road to Mandalay," he sang in a false baritone, "where the hmm-hmm fishes hmm . . ." This as he stacked his ledgers. "And the dawn comes up like hmm-hmm . . ." He'd turned to a coatrack, lifting a sleeve to blow off the lint; then he lingered as if he'd taken the hand of a friend he might not see again. Until now I'd been no more eager than he was to step outside, but I found I was growing impatient with Papa.

We were going, we weren't going — the suspense was getting to me. Once I'd turned my thoughts toward leaving, though, I began to become a little excited. The prospect of making our way back to the Pinch in a squall smacked of high adventure, or as close to it as a Kaplan was likely to come. Giving up on Papa, I decided to make the first move myself. I opened my umbrella, enjoying an act that flew in the face of superstition.

"Are you coming or not?" I put the question to Papa and received for an answer only his deferred big finish: ". . . Out of China 'cross the hmmm." On that note I was out the door in a howling blast of rain.

It was my conviction that my father would never allow his only son to negotiate such a gullywasher on his own. But by the time I'd toiled up the hill as far as Second Street, I wasn't so sure. Drubbed by the elements, soaked to the skin through my flannel knickers, I was already beginning to think I'd had enough. I was about to turn back when I saw him coming. He was ducking from awning to awning, aiming his umbrella into the wind as if he meant to poke out the eye of the storm.

I waited for him to catch up with me, and together we huddled in the doorway of a pharmacy at the corner of Main Street and Beale. When the streetcar appeared, it struck me that a streetcar might not have appeared, since the power was off all over the place. But there it was, which now seemed slightly miraculous. It was concentrating the rain in the sweep of its headlights, churning like a steamer up the washed-out thoroughfare.

On board the passengers were as chummy as if they had in common being snatched from the jaws of certain disaster. They wore yellow slickers and peaked caps made out of newspapers, some of them carrying frightened chickens from the market. So they could face one another, they'd reversed the convertible wooden seats. They burlesqued the thunder and told corny jokes to which the stock response was always, "You're all wet!" A couple were trying to inspire the rest to join them in spirited song: "Oh Noah, he built him, he built him an ark-ie ark-ie . . . ," but they were drowned out by the drumming of rough weather on the trolley car roof.

For all we could see through the windows, draperied in

streaming lights, we might as well have been making the journey by submarine. Were it not for the good instincts of the conductor — he shouted "Commerce Street!" with a fervor better suited to "Land ho!" — we would never have known where to get off.

During the short sprint to our building, buckets were dumped on us. We drooped from the weight of our saturated clothing as we slogged into the passage, leaking rivulets that cascaded behind us down the stairs. On the landing, pausing pointlessly to wipe my glasses in a wet handkerchief, I noticed that Papa was doing the same. He was such a sight, with the rain dangling in beads from his earlobes and nose, that I had to laugh. So maybe I looked similarly ridiculous, because Papa got tickled too. He laughed, shaking off raindrops, pointing a finger first at himself and then me, declaring, "Ain't we got fun!" It was bracing to think that my father and I had shared an actual escapade and survived to tell the tale. "Out of the storm we came," he proclaimed in mock triumph, knocking on wood, "but at least we ain't orphans, eh Harry?"

We were still in stitches when the apartment door opened and Grandpa Isador met us, babbling woe. "Ek velt!" he bleated, wringing his hands in the scrubby bib of his beard, which I'd have sworn had turned a shade whiter in our absence. Behind him Mama, not ordinarily given to indulging the old man's outbursts, looked on dolefully.

"For such a greeting we defied the hurricane?" complained Papa. His lightheartedness should have been enough to dispel whatever anxiety the family might have had on our account. But in the midst of his efforts to calm Isador's hysterics, I saw in my father's altered expression that he'd sniffed what I had also begun to discern. The long-standing fishy odor of our apartment, whose source — it was no secret — was Grandma Zippe, had become almost unbearably ripe. What's more, her cushioned chair by the window was empty at an hour when she was normally seated there. This led to the conclusion, confirmed by my mother, that the old lady had taken to her bed.

I knew I should have felt more alarmed by the news of her illness, but the shameful truth was that for some time now my bubbe had been little more to me than part of the furniture. And as far as I could tell, the indifference was mutual. Of course there were still moments when you might almost think she was conscious of my presence: an eyelid might flicker as if to hint at some private understanding; but I was satisfied that this was nothing but a tic. There were occasions over the years when she'd gone so far as to thump the table, admonishing the fussy eater, myself, to eat his zoop; and sometimes, when I was out of sorts, she found the wherewithal to pronounce the dread word "Cristiyer!" — the signal for Mama to bring out the enema bag. But these, I was sure, were only reflexes left over from more vital days.

If I'd tried, I guess I could have jarred loose some long-lost memory: the old woman rolling up her sleeves, say, to punch the lights out of a hill of risen dough. I might have recalled how the ensuing cloud of flour powdered her cheeks and made her sneeze. I might have reached back in my mind to a time when she was stuffing derma or humming a freilach or decanting tea from her tarnished copper urn. But the samovar with its gilded dome and ivory-handled spigot, shlepped all the way from the Russian steppes, had stood empty now for a decade or more, and Grandma Zippe seemed to have dried up along with it.

She had never, to anyone's knowledge, suffered a stroke or any other ailment that would have left her terminally indisposed. The doctors had given up on locating a specific disorder. It was just that, at some point in her mature years, she'd retired from an active involvement in life, commencing an early rehearsal for the long stillness to come.

"Mrs. Sitzflaysh," as Grandpa Isador called her, she'd done nothing for years but mark time beside her copper keepsake, adding fuel to her husband's lamentations. On occasion the old man had been heard to grumble, "I ain't her husband no more. She's the bride of that empty jug."

It was a gripe that raised in my mind the question of the chicken or the egg: Which came first, Zippe's clamlike withdrawal or old Isador's breast-beating distress? Was my grandmother's incapacitation the cause or the effect of my grandfather's Torah-thumping otherworldliness? Because, when he wasn't trussed in the thongs of his tefillin, a hostage to piety, my zayde was chasing through moldering texts after the rumor of the Holy Shechinah. This was the elusive female aspect of the divine.

He pored over glosses on commentaries relating the finer points of a dialogue between Daniel and a scholarly lion; he split the hairs that Delilah had snipped from Samson's head. They were activities that, when all was said and done, might make a person no better a companion than an empty samovar.

All day long she sat beside it, staring steely-eyed out the window, her puckered face in the hand-painted babushka like a pitted prune in a sling. In the evenings she rose briefly as Mama turned her chair to face the living room. But beyond the necessary, beyond her involuntarily blurted "Feh!"s and her spontaneous gestures against the evil eye, she never stirred.

Then there was the business of her odor. Nobody could say exactly when it had started, so long had the odor pervaded our household, but it was generally agreed that it dated from around the time when Grandma Zippe sat down for good. So maybe it had attached itself to her back in her ambulatory days, a stray aroma that had followed her home from the market. It had found in her once bustling person (for reasons who could say) the perfect host, and invaded the somber privacy of her shirtwaist. It had hung its wreath so heavily about her shoulders that she gave in at the knees.

For a while the smell seemed impersonal and unlocalized. It

was possibly something rotting in the icebox, which Mama scrubbed as she did everything else, in a deodorizing passion. But as the reek became stronger, it left no doubt as to its point of origin; and unlike my grandmother's forbidding presence, her fishy smell was not so easy to ignore. You might almost have said it had a personality all its own.

Naturally we learned to live with it, but every time you adjusted to the latest level of fetor, it seemed to have been turned up a notch or two. Full-bodied and dense, with a richness that brought tears to the eyes, it scented our clothing and flavored our meals. It caused otherwise decorous guests to hold their noses and whisper "Pee-yoo." It soiled the air with an olive cast and filtered into your sleep, giving you troubled dreams of stagnant seas. While every measure was taken to ensure that my grandmother was antiseptically cleansed and disinfected, nothing worked. No amount of sitz bathing the old lady in aromatic bath salts or soaking her garments in lye, no rings of pink-smoking germicidal smudge pots — nothing had succeeded in purging our apartment of her odor.

It was hoped that she might lose it during our move to the South; she might leave it where she'd found it in our old neighborhood by the sea. This was a point that Uncle Morris had had the doubtful taste to raise more than once. But the odor had traveled well. In fact, owing perhaps to the oppressive humidity, it had become even more exquisitely intense. And now that it was nearly unbreathable, we understood how it had been all along the smell of her dying.

Three

By the close of the weekend the rain had sown its wildest oats, settling down into a permanent pelting gray monsoon. It was a fitting accompaniment to the prevailing gloom of our apartment. The silver-haired Dr. Seligman, a little vague as to actual causes — "At her age it's always a combination of things" — had assured us that my grandmother's passing was only a matter of time. At this stage of her illness the hospital would be a needless expense, he'd said. Why put the old lady through the ordeal when she could be made so much more comfortable at home?

Over corn flakes on Monday morning Papa told me not to bother coming down to the shop after school. Business was going to be slow thanks to the weather, and I could make myself more useful at home. But I surprised myself by arguing that I would rather go to work; in the apartment I would only be in the way. Already the place was filling up, somewhat vulture-like, with Mama's friends from the local synagogue auxiliary. Offering a token assistance invariably diverted by gossip, they doted more on the visiting doctor (a bachelor) than on the failing patient herself.

Meanwhile Grandpa Isador, a tallis draped over his head like a cloth draped ineffectively over a canary cage, warbled prayers as unrelenting as the rain. Uncle Morris came and went, preceded by a paunch that strained the limits of his corsetlike waistcoat, blustering all the while as if he believed that God could be bribed. His stale cigar competed with the carbolic acid and atomizers of cheap perfume, deployed by the ladies in their futile efforts at fumigation. Compared to all this, the pawnshop was a regular safe haven. And it wasn't fair that my father, with whom I'd endured a trial by hurricane, should keep the benefits of his sanctuary to himself.

She died toward the end of the week. I knew it even before Dr. Seligman, sloping out as I entered, gave me his sympathetic cluck of the tongue. I knew it before I saw Mama being fanned by the Hadassah ladies as they coaxed her to take a cup of tea. I knew it the moment I opened the door and for once my stomach didn't churn or my eyes smart from the smell. For once you could inhale the fresh challah that the Ridblatts were baking downstairs. You could identify garlic and orange pekoe, molasses and rising damp, all the odors that had surfaced since their yoke of oppression was lifted. Whatever the corruption that had occupied old Zippe's brittle anatomy, it had finally fled. It had escaped, presumably along with her soul, into the great out-of-doors — which smelled, as I'd sniffed it on the trolley ride home from the shop, unmistakably of fish.

When I came in, my mother excused herself from her ministering ladies to ask in an accusatory tone, "Where's your father?" The question was of course rhetorical, since where else would he be but in the pawnshop, where I'd left him not half an hour before. Nevertheless, she succeeded in making me feel guilty by association, as if I might be covering up for something unseemly. As if, instead of attending to business, my father and I had been lying doggo, afraid of facing the music of Zippe's inevitable end.

In the midst of gloating over my discomfort, Mama suddenly

unsmirked her lips. She rolled her eyes and slapped her fore-head theatrically, maybe for the sake of the ladies, then recalled aloud, silly her, that in her shock she had forgotten to phone her husband. It was not an oversight you'd have expected of Mama, for whom the telephone was ordinarily an extension of her arm.

Uncle Morris (had she telephoned him?) was already at hand, saying "There, there" as he escorted Grandpa Isador out of the sickroom. Leaning on his stout son, the self-appointed rock of our family, the old man was weeping buckets. Between wrenching sobs, he managed to insist on the traditional exequies: the body sponged in Jordan water by tenth-generation lavadors, laid out on the floor facing east with six-foot candles at either end. It must be interred without a coffin, in a sailcloth winding sheet smeared with Jerusalem mud. To all his demands Uncle Morris responded with approving nods of the head, which he alternated with conspiratorial winks at my mother.

Changed out of the rumpled clothes that he'd slept in all week, old Isador had wasted no time in donning the accessories of mourning. He was wearing the silk-trimmed caftan that reached to his knees, below which his legs were bare but for his gartered socks. On his head was the molting fur shtreimel that Papa used to say was standard issue at the Wailing Wall. For a hat, he said, it had a lot in common with the rotary brush of a chimney sweep. But Grandpa Isador was obviously convinced that mourning became him. Moreover, so absorbed was he in his tearful vision of the perfect funeral that he failed to notice the arrival of the undertaker, Mr. Gruber.

This was the less surprising, as the long-faced Mr. Gruber was anyway almost invisible with unobtrusiveness. With a knack for being present without occupying space, he seemed to hover above the carpet as he conferred with my mother. Then, turning with a barely perceptible nod, he stage-managed the two assistants who had furtively followed him in. Identified by armbands as members of the synagogue burial society, they slouched toward the sickroom with an empty litter. Moments later they reappeared with a sheet-covered burden, Zippe's habit of a gray serge shirtwaist folded neatly on top. Mr. Gruber held the door as they departed, closing it behind him with a regardful click. It was an operation that would have served as well for robbing a grave as for lawfully removing a body to prepare for interment.

Now that most of the evidence of my bubbe's occupancy had been spirited away, her absence from the chair next to the samovar made the room feel somehow askew. The emptiness surrounding her chair was almost palpable. Not that I actually missed my grandmother sitting there by the window; it's just that it seemed easier to think of her being alive now that she wasn't.

The next thing I knew, the place was swarming with neighbors, their faces benign with solicitude. They had come bearing covered dishes of cholent and steaming compotes, trays of assorted nosherai. There were cold cuts and golden kugel, almond cookies in drifts of powdered sugar, milk bottles filled with bathtub shnaps. With every gift they contributed to a medley of aromas that turned our once malodorous apartment into a culinary nosegay. What I couldn't figure, though, was how word of Zippe's passing had gotten out so fast, unless the Pinch had a sixth sense about such things. Or was it that you only needed a sense of smell? In any case, the neighbors quickly made themselves at home, beginning to behave in a way that I wasn't sure was altogether appropriate to the occasion. For all their protestations of sympathy and heartfelt condolence, our guests seemed more in a mood for celebrating than paying respects.

In no time their faces had dropped the solicitous formality. The ladies were recommending beauticians, swapping tidbits about the indiscretions of film stars; they sniped at absentee members of their mah-jongg circle until said members arrived. Conceding that business was universally in the toilet, their husbands got down to cases. They told indecent stories about the exploits of Yudl the peddler, slapping backs with a hardiness that launched more than one macaroon. Our apartment — with its piebald carpet and tacky apple-blossom curtains, its tallow-encrusted candelabra on the sideboard, the faded print of a shepherd playing his harp at the foot of a king — had taken on a frankly festive atmosphere.

At last my duly summoned father appeared at the door. He was met by Uncle Morris, holding old Isador upright with one arm, squeezing Mama's hand with the other. When he managed (without letting go of the others) to draw Papa into the circle of his embrace, it was like a bid to become literally the family's sole support.

"Solly," he sighed, his cigar shifting from one corner of his mouth to the other, "she was a woman in a million, an institution, our zelig mameh." My father allowed himself a sorrowful nod on his brother's shoulder, then cocked a brow as if trying to match the words against his memory. "It's like it says in Talmud," continued Uncle Morris, a philosopher no less, "life is dreck, but what can you do?"

This was the cue for Grandpa Isador to try the full range of his anguish. Inviting martyrdom or admitting envy, who could say, he let loose a cry that stopped conversation for the space of a syllable or two. "It should have been me!" he groaned. The tears swelled to freshets, overflowing the troughs beneath his eyes, following well-sluiced courses down his hollow cheeks. Several representatives from the liars' bench in front of Jake Plott's barber shop, themselves done up in their most chapfallen gabardines, gathered round him to commiserate.

Meanwhile, set adrift by Uncle Morris, my papa looked a little unsteady on his feet. In fact he seemed uncertain, in the face of our packed apartment, as to whether he'd even entered the right place. He was fiddling with his bow tie like he was trying to crank a propeller, having a hard time choosing an attitude suitable to the circumstance. It was as if, since Isador had a monopoly on grief and Uncle Morris had cornered the market in consolation, there was nothing left for him to do. All the same, by the arrival of the next wave of neighbors, Papa appeared to have determined a proper line of behavior. He greeted the guests as if they were bringing their covered dishes to pawn.

From my spot beside the hat tree, I decided that I'd seen enough of the proceedings to get the general idea. No one was paying me much attention anyway, apart from the occasional consolatory mussing of my hair. So I was headed for my alcove, where I would shut the double doors and slip between the covers of a book. In seconds I would have swapped the tummel of North Main Street for the clangor of scimitars, the echoing reports of service revolvers in the Khyber Pass. But on the way I happened upon my cousin Naomi. She was wedged between an overstuffed cushion and the raveled arm of the sofa, looking as if she'd been dumped from a considerable height. She must have been there all along.

Her dress of faded violets served as camouflage against the threadbare floral fabric of the sofa. It drooped from her shoulders like it could have been still on a hanger; from the closet to my cousin, the dress had scarcely acquired a dimension. Her magenta beret was tilted at an angle that you might have called rakish on somebody else, though on Naomi it was only lopsided. An ice pack would have achieved the same effect. Then there was the business of her sullen eyes, too large for her narrow face to ever grow into. This was probably why she tried to conceal them behind a fringe of stringy bangs, which, had they been any longer, would have lapped over her nose like a wave around a fin.

She was a sad sack all right, my nebbish cousin, and I'd always tried to avoid her like she might be contagious. Having shown myself proof against the family's best efforts to encourage our friendship over the years, I saw no reason to let my guard down now. But maybe in deference to our common loss, I ought to let hostilities rest for a spell. I paused and gave Naomi a sort of smile, then waited for her to make the next move, until I'd digested the fact that it was still up to me to open.

At length I asked her above the noisy company, satisfied that the question was as neutral as they come: "When did you hear?"

She looked up from an intensive study of her lap as if I'd clashed a pair of cymbals in her ear. "Wha?" was all she said.

It made me want to tell her I was sorry I'd bothered her, forget it, a mistake. It made me want to screw up my eyes and flap my cheeks, or at least suggest she zipper her still-parted lips before the flies got in. But instead I was civil enough to repeat the question.

"Hear what?" wondered my cousin, still at sea.

That tables have legs, that birds can fly, that Joshua blew his bugle and Wall Street collapsed. Was she deliberately trying to make things difficult, or could it be possible that I was the first to inform her that something was wrong? She was said to be some kind of a whiz kid at the private school she went to, a straight-A student who did algebra backwards and could recite the whole Constitution in her sleep. But you couldn't have proved it by me. Still, for the sake of our blood relationship, which I guessed ought to count for something, I resolved to give her the benefit of the doubt.

"You know," I submitted hopefully, "about Grandma Zippe."

"Oh." She nodded.

Had I missed something? Ordinarily I'd have been happy to let it go, having no doubt gotten what I deserved. This was what came of your good intentions to try and touch base with your cousin. But now that I'd put my foot in it this far, I couldn't help feeling that some principle was at stake.

"So when did you hear?" I persisted.

Naomi slumped down farther into the sofa, tugging at her beret until it covered her ears. She tucked her chin against her chest in an attitude suggesting that she didn't like to be bullied. Stirred by the ceiling fan, her inky bangs (which made me think of a cyclops's eyelash) fluttered petulantly. "Sometime, I dunno," she mumbled into her collar.

It was just this type of contrariness that made you want to press her for details. You wanted to demand to know precisely what she'd heard and where she was when she heard it — while shouts went up all around that you were hounding the witness. But I'd had enough of my cousin's conversation to last me a lifetime and, shrugging, I started to walk away. She could sink into the sofa till it swallowed her for all I cared. In future I would sit on it smugly, never letting on how Naomi, mysteriously vanished, had become part of the decor.

But I stumbled, hung up on whatever was snagging my left leg. I turned to discover my cousin, her eyes still meditatively downcast, clutching the elastic bottom of my knee pants. My first thought was not rational: She wants to take me with her. Like the nymphs that dwelled (according to my grandpa) under the waters of the mikveh, she wanted to drag me down.

I was about to give some audible expression of my horror when Naomi — using her free hand to part the veil of her bangs — looked up at me to inquire, "Do you think they were ever in love?"

It was my turn to say, "Come again?"

"Zippe and Isador. Do you think they were ever in love?"

The note of desperation in her voice made me want to jump clear of my skin and bolt without a backward glance. I whipped my head left to right, half looking for help, half hoping that nobody saw my predicament. I hoped I wouldn't have to leave my pants in her hand.

Without pausing to consider, wanting only to put an end to a game I hadn't asked to play, I blurted out, "Yeah, I guess." A stab in the dark, it must have nevertheless been on the money, because she right away let me go. I shuddered to think what might have happened had I answered in the negative.

I backed up slowly, in case Naomi should make any more sudden moves, then wheeled about and made a beeline for my alcove. Closing the doors, I drew aside the dimity curtain to make sure that she hadn't followed. Still in a slump, she was shoved even farther into her corner by a pudgy couple who'd commandeered the rest of the sofa. They were wolfing down food as if in competition, each playfully stealing forkfuls from the other's dish. Despite them, however, my cousin had returned to her prior state of contemplation.

All around her, guests were partaking of the general conviviality. They dipped their noses, frosted with powdered sugar, into spirits-laced cups of tea; they tossed meatballs into the air and caught them in their laughing gobs. They elbowed their way to the table, which sagged from the weight of its bounty, falling into impromptu waltzes as they maneuvered to get by. Only where they clustered around the members of my family did they moderate their horseplay, trying to keep in check an otherwise irrepressible bonhomie.

Holding court beside a standing lamp, my grandfather had attracted the largest audience. He was narrating his sorrow to a bunch of alter kockers who appeared to be saying, at proper intervals, "Amen." I watched his crooked fingers with their tufted knuckles tenderly sculpting the air, fashioning it, I was certain, into a likeness of his lost Zipporeh: how she blushed in her maiden ripeness, carrot-haired in a hay-scented pinafore, modestly wringing a kerchief or the neck of a chicken, blowing a kiss through lips stained a feverish pink from beet soup.

By next morning the rain, which we'd come to accept as a fact of life, had finally played itself out. The sky above the alley was like the skin of a pearl-gray balloon, bulging copper at the place where a thumb was pressed against it from the other side. That was the sun trying finally to shine through.

According to the custom of a house in mourning, I'd slept with the window cracked open. Now, as I poked my head out, my cheeks were bussed by soft breezes, my eyes stunned by a riot of unruly colors. When I put on my specs, the colors resolved themselves into wildflowers spilling out of fissures in the brick walls. Lush weeds sprouted from puddles, and creepers slithered out from under stones. They twined about the axles of an overturned soapbox racer and the rusty barrel of a popgun; they spiraled the mimosa until its trunk looked like a jungle barber pole. There were sprays of pink and white blossoms, like uncorked bottles of floral champagne, and air so fragrant it made a harp out of your nose hairs. Suddenly it seemed to be spring.

Then Papa was at the foot of my hide-a-bed, which he'd already begun to fold up, announcing that I should forget about going to school. "Get dressed already," he charged me, "we're burying your grandma today!"

I suppose that he meant this respectfully, but in my drowsiness it sounded for all the world like Papa was declaring a holiday.

I got out of bed and shuffled down the hall to the cardboard wardrobe to reclaim my old bar mitzvah suit from mothballs. Opening the door, I released a heady smell of camphor, a smell with character, as if I'd set loose a captive genie. But the camphor promptly met its match in another decidedly unfishy aroma, the coffee that Mama was brewing in the kitchen. I could hear her humming (since when did she hum?) a peppy rendition of "A-Tisket A-Tasket," Papa gargling accompaniment from the john across the hall. Moments later he passed by on his way to the kitchen, ostensibly seeking help with his tie, while his eyebrows performed a sort of hubba-hubba dance.

Then, was I dreaming or did my mama squeal coquettishly, "Solly, shame on you!" It was a morning that seemed to admit, beyond reinstated aromas, the revival of a lost sound or two.

Even Grandpa Isador, despite the sag of his woeful features, looked almost waggish this morning in his miniver hat. You might have taken him for a species of ghetto Davy Crockett — whom Papa, the chozzer for local lore, had told me was a patron saint of the town. As we headed out the door, I had to remind myself that we were going to a funeral, not embarking on some lark of a family outing.

We went down to North Main Street, where the wind from the river had a brisk, maritime quality — like it had traveled all the way up from some island in the Gulf just to tease your hair. The shops sported their pyramids of moisture-spangled produce, the racks of irregular pants, the solitary shoes intended to discourage thieves. The rain-washed windows were grease-penciled in freshly slashed prices, in certifications of strictly kosher. The awnings flapped like barbers' bibs. But the businesses must have been manned by skeleton crews.

This I assumed from the caravan of droning automobiles that was stretched for several blocks along the curb. The street was backed up bumper to bumper from Auction down to Commerce, as long as the gangster cortèges that used to pass through Brighton Beach. Every vehicle was stuffed to its rumble seat with a well-scrubbed North Main Street family in their Shabbos best.

I doubted it was Zippe's popularity that had brought them out in such numbers, twice in as many days. I knew that the Orthodox cemetery was located in the woods to the south of town, a place said to be ideal for picnics and strolls. So you had to suspect that, where yesterday she'd served as an excuse for a party, today Grandma Zippe provided an opportunity for a community excursion. But that's not what it looked like. What

41

it looked like was a neighborhood that had turned out en masse to give my grandmother a send-off in high Pinch style.

At the forefront of the line of cars was Mr. Gruber's pride and joy, a regular jewel box of a hearse. It had polished brass sidelamps and chromium everything else: hubcaps, S-handles, ornamental winged diety on a louvered hood. It had windows like an oversize fishbowl through which you could view the anomaly of a rough-hewn wooden casket. This was the single concession to the traditional affair that old Isador had envisioned; it was a compromise between no coffin at all and the grand sarcophagus that Uncle Morris claimed he could get at cost. In the bed of that fancy hearse, however, the knotty pine looked like it was incubating, about to transform itself into something worthy of such a vehicle.

Parked directly behind the hearse was a freshly waxed Packard limousine, its elliptical rear window framing the unhappy face of my cousin. She looked all the more pained for having twisted her neck a good hundred and eighty degrees to peer out. How was it, I wondered, that on such a pleasant morning Naomi could still manage to look like the victim of a kidnapping? Like she expected that you should personally arrange for her rescue — but from what? Just seeing Naomi was enough to put a crimp in your day, let alone the nuisance of having to unstick your own eyes from her sullen tarbaby stare. It took the sudden outbreak of a ruckus in front of the storefront funeral parlor to break the spell.

A discordant delegation of worried-looking neighbors had burst forth from Mr. Gruber's crêpe-hung door. In their midst was Uncle Morris, puffing portentously and clenching his chubby fists, flapping his jowls. Despite their strident efforts, neither Mr. Petrofsky the grocer nor Sacharin the fishmonger, Alabaster the tinsmith or the otherwise internally battling Mr. and Mrs. Rosen, could appease him. He was threatening to have the undertaker's job. When he saw my family approaching, Uncle Morris held his hand up palm-forward like we should cease and desist.

"Keep your shirt on, Solly!" he cautioned my father, who had yet to say a word; meanwhile my uncle's own sweaty shirt-front was bunching out of his vest. "Everything's under control," he assured us, groping at his breast for his heart or a monogrammed hankie with which to mop his brow. He would have us know that he was phoning certain parties who had their own way of taking care of business. Pressure would be brought to bear on the office of the mayor himself, we could count on it. Don't worry, the place would be drained by noon.

Good-naturedly, as if they were playing a game that he thought he might like to join in, my papa asked if someone would please tell him what was going on.

Everyone spoke at once, fracturing the morning's tranquillity with a babel of cross-purposes, until Mr. Gruber interceded, stepping forward to hush them with his imperturbable graveside manner. His eyes were demure, his bald spot (when he bowed) a yellow egg in the nest of his oily hair.

"The cemetery is under water," he patiently explained. "I been to the site myself. The headstones look like bell buoys. You can't bury no Jews there today."

On my mama's arm Grandpa Isador let go his most blood-curdling "Vay iz mir!" He tore the lapels of his caftan, leaving them to hang like a pair of vestigial fins. Some of his cronies from Jake Plott's shuffled over, but instead of offering conventional words of comfort, they joined my zayde in his moaning desolation. Think of an Old World version of barbershop harmony. The rest of the neighbors, competing with Uncle Morris's renewed fulminations, jockeyed for openings wherein they could offer advice.

"Consult the rabbi!" called out some greenhorn, probably from force of habit, since the Market Street shul had never been able to support a full-time rabbi. There was a recommendation that the body be cremated — this from Mr. Loewy the jeweler, a man known to consort with freethinkers in the Green Owl Café. Immediately he was shouted down. Then came a suggestion concerning the Reform cemetery, which was situated in a suburban setting on high ground. Maybe under these circumstances they might agree to make room . . .

At this Grandpa Isador came alert. Miraculously rearing up on his fallen arches, he bellowed, "Hab rachmones! My wife you would put in unhallowed ground?"

Mr. Gruber, who had only to open his mouth to create a lull, submitted that things could be worse. After all, at Mr. Kaplan's insistence, the deceased had been prepared against decomposition, and could thus be stored indefinitely in Gruber's establishment for a mutually acceptable fee.

Snarling at the undertaker, Uncle Morris turned to defend himself, explaining (while Mama covered Grandpa Isador's ears) that Zippe hadn't exactly been embalmed. "This is strictly according to Jewish custom. They use Diamond kosher salt or something." Then he turned back around to give full vent to his outrage over Gruber's seeking to make a profit from our family's misfortune. Working himself toward a stroke, he wanted to know who was in charge here, Morris Kaplan of the Parkway, a fully assimilated and well-connected man of business, or this moldy, two-bit, North Main Street Litvak shmuck? As he ranted, my uncle strangled the balmy air.

All along the procession of cars there were honks and heads leaning out to demand we get the show on the road. Having given up on a practical expedient, the neighbors in front of Gruber's had begun to argue among themselves. They were debating what motives the Lord might have had for inundating a graveyard. It was at that point that my father chose to come forward and tug at his brother's sleeve.

"Never mind, Morris," said Papa, still chipper under the influence of the vernal morning. "Tell you what I'll do." It was a voice I'd heard him use in the pawnshop, its tone implying satisfaction guaranteed. "I'll . . . ," he began, then abruptly left off. He must have sensed that all eyes were upon him, that it was presumptuous of him to volunteer a solution when it was Morris who made the decisions around here. Or was it just that he'd opened his yap without any real solution in mind? In either case, having stuck his foot in it, Papa looked at a loss for some graceful way to pull it back out. "I'll . . . ," he tried again, and fell silent.

Just then the sun broke through a bank of khaki clouds for the first time in a week. Coming into view, it struck the lenses of my father's glasses, which blazed like a pair of molten medallions. At that moment, with everyone shading their brow against the brilliance of his spectacles, my papa might have been something other than he was. He might have been great and terrible — a renegade high priest from the continent of Pellucidar, say, with deadly ray-beam eyes.

"Tell you what." He was having another go at it, this time in a remarkably even voice. "I'll keep our mama in my shop till the water goes down."

As suddenly as it had appeared, the sun was gone again, leaving Papa in a state of blinking chagrin. Nervously he removed his glasses and breathed on the lenses, clearing his throat like he might have spoken out of turn. He chuckled, it was only a joke: that's Solly Kaplan all over, always with a line. But nobody was laughing. Instead, with pulletlike jerks of the head, they were looking from one to another. They were shrugging nifter-shmifter, so why not, waiting for Uncle Morris or anyone else to point out the obvious flaws in Papa's plan. I don't know who was more astonished, my father or the rest of the street, to discover that he'd been taken seriously.

Four

As Papa and I rode down Front Street in the plush-upholstered cab of Mr. Gruber's smooth-running hearse, I saw for the first time just how far the river had risen. The old paint-chipped, cast-iron classing houses that lined the eastern side of the street were hidden behind tall stacks of cotton. This was cotton salvaged from the deluged warehouses at the bottom of the bluff below. Precariously balanced, the bales formed a bulwark of chalk-white palisades, which overlooked the pools of prune-purple water down the slope where the levee had been. To the west the drifting plain of what they call the Big Muddy had no visible bank at all. In fact, there was no horizon to let you know when you were sailing out of the navigable (if hazardous) gunmetal currents into the unmapped gunmetal skies. Only a stranded stubble of unsubmerged trees marked the spot — rest in peace — that once was Arkansas.

The foot of Beale Street was also under the river, which lapped now about the pilings of the Illinois Central Railroad overpass. On top of the elevated trestle a gang of scruffy truants were dangling their skinny legs, pointing at a floating silo that rolled like a lolling leviathan under a flock of barnyard fowl.

I recognized a couple of them from my school, snot-nosed shaygets hooligans who mocked me for a Yankee or a Yid or a four-eyed bookworm if they spoke to me at all. Among their ranks was also a wild Jewboy or two, from whom I'd received much the same treatment, not that I had any use for the lot of them. Friends had always been a commodity that I could mostly do without, thank you very much. They were forever goading you to join them in their pointless games and explorations when you had much better things to do. So maybe it was just that I happened to be wearing a suit on a morning when bare feet would have been more in the mode, that I somehow resented my exclusion from their tomfoolery. Then I had to remind myself that while they were wasting their time, I was involved in an important, even sacred, commission.

As we rounded the corner into Beale, my papa, who'd been thoughtfully silent ever since we'd left the Pinch, looked back to observe, "It's like the view from Mount Ararat after the ark runs aground." This was untypical of his off-the-wall remarks, which didn't ordinarily include references to the Bible.

We were headed up the hill toward Main Street in time to meet a convoy of gear-grinding trucks coming down. To the rattling wooden tailgates and running boards of these trucks, their beds piled high with bags of sand, dozens of colored men were clinging for dear life. Some of them were wearing the county-issued striped pajamas, while others were dressed nattily in seersuckers, level straw skimmers, and spats. Armed police in dark glasses and mud-spattered spit shines, poised like they were squiring dignitaries, drove their motorcycles on either flank. Bewildered, I turned to ask Papa what he thought was going on, but got only this curt reply: "Mr. Crump decided to build a pyramid — how should I know?"

He seemed frankly a little on edge, my papa, constantly looking over his shoulder as if to make sure that we'd made a clean getaway. Like he wanted to reconfirm that the funeral cavalcade had not followed us from North Main Street, calling more attention to our enterprise than it needed. Of course I was also relieved on that score, glad that we were on our own again and that Mama and Uncle Morris had volunteered to stay and look after Grandpa Isador. Moreover, I was pleased to have been elected, even though I hadn't asked, to ride shotgun (so to speak) on my grandmother's next-to-last journey. Honestly, I didn't know what had gotten into me lately — that instead of sitting alone with a book, I should be hanging out the window of a murmuring hearse, determined not to miss a single detail of this unusual day.

We crossed over Main Street and started down the long hill into the pawnshop district. That's when we were presented with the sight that caused even the unflappable Mr. Gruber, suddenly sucking in air, to miss a gear. From Main down to Third, the street was still business as usual: the pullers lolly-gagged among the show racks while the eye-buyers swarmed the sidewalks, golden balls dangling over their heads like King Midas's apples — the whole place with a sharp, freshly minted clarity in the aftermath of the rains. But just below Third Street everything was changed. Stranding the row of garish old build-ings on the right-hand side of the street and pouring over into what you could call the sunken gardens of Handy Park on the other was a sizable body of water. Its coppery surface, ruffled by the wind, was even further disturbed by a crazy flotilla of wooden fishing dinghies and skiffs. Gliding and colliding back and forth across the water in helter-skelter navigation, they looked like aquatic bumper cars.

What floored me the most, however, was not the mere fact that Beale Street had been so outlandishly transformed — this you could sort of explain. What knocked me for a loop was how natural everything looked. The startling existence of the water seemed to have erased the memory of the original thorough-fare. One glimpse and I could hardly think back to a time when that crowded lagoon hadn't been a regular feature of the local landscape.

As I was leaning a bit too far out the window, Papa reeled me back into the front seat by my coattails. "Our catastrophes," he sighed, "they're the shvartzers' holidays." This was maybe his effort to restore a sobriety more in keeping with our solemn errand, though I could have sworn I saw the good humor beginning to tug at the muscles around his mouth. And his eyes blinked the suggestion that, on such a strange day, who could help behaving like shvartzers?

Mr. Gruber pulled his hearse to a puttering stop alongside the granite curb in front of Kaplan's Loans, and there sat Oboy with his back to the iron lattice. In place of his stool, which must still have been locked up inside the shop, he was perched on an upended Kickapoo crate. It was a pointless fidelity, of course, since Kaplan's had been kept closed for the funeral — though I didn't suppose that Oboy had been informed. And besides, when does a wooden Indian leave the cigar store? He was sitting, as usual, with his canvas cap pulled low on his leathery forehead. Gazing in the direction of the outsize puddle down the street, he looked like someone scouring the horizon for dry land.

He remained in that frozen posture until after we'd stepped out on the sidewalk, when all at once he came to life. He sprang from his crate and, without being prompted, beat my father to the rear of the hearse. Opening the door, he started to tug at the casket as if he'd done this sort of thing before, as if he'd read in my papa's lingering apprehensiveness (he was looking both ways up and down the avenue) a signal to make haste and unload this shipment of possibly dubious goods. After all, in a book, wouldn't this be the part where somebody pulls a switcheroo and the body turns out to be replaced by contraband? But just as Papa was cautioning Oboy to be gentle, the box slipped out of the puller's grip.

49

It fell to the curb, jarring loose the hingeless lid, which slid open, exposing my grandma to any interested party along the street. Thanks to Mr. Gruber's handiwork, the old lady, who'd never looked too awfully alive, now appeared to be entirely artificial, like a furiously puckered toy papoose. Only the single glaucous eye, which the mortician, for all his craft, had been unable to batten down, identified her as the real thing.

I tried to tell myself that she looked very nice considering, but I was skewered by her open eye. As militantly disapproving in death as it had been in life, it seemed to demand to know why all of this was being done to her. Why could she not have been left to carry on sitting in her unscented stiffness by the apartment window, where she had never really been in anyone's way? This was the point where I had to renew my efforts to believe that, for a change, my father knew what he was doing.

"That's my mamele in there," explained Papa, completing his admonition to Oboy despite the fait accompli. The puller grunted like he was pleased to meet her, though his place was seemingly not to question why; scruples, so far as I could tell, were not a part of his makeup. Then, closing the lid quickly lest she create a public nuisance, Oboy resumed tugging at the casket. This was how he always moved on those occasions when he was disposed to move: like he was in a hurry. As if he were one of those golems out of my grandfather's antiquated books who must take swift advantage of their quickened bones before they were turned back into inanimate clay.

Mr. Gruber came padding forward to lend his tacit assistance. He was joined by a couple of loiterers with jaws like blue charcoal, with vests displaying old war medals and torn hobnail shoes showing the toes of union suits. I'd seen this before, how these down-on-their-luck characters would appear as if from the steam vents at the least chance of earning a handout. I was left, as usual, with nothing to do.

After unlocking the lattice, my father turned around and began, somewhat uncertainly, to orchestrate the entrance of Grandma Zippe into Kaplan's Loans. As you could tell by the way he was beckoning the pallbearers, with his left hand contradicting his right, the role of director did not come to him naturally. But once he'd backed through the shop door, sweeping aside the show racks that had yet to be hauled outside, my papa was another man. He was competent, even cheerful, a regular impresario leaving no question as to who was in charge. Behind him the pallbearers — who had veered drunkenly at first, grumbling under their burden as they stooped to compensate for Oboy's dwarfish size — followed faithfully where he led. Gingerly Papa steered them down the aisle between the narrow straits of the display cases. Having thus conducted their safe passage, he left them a moment to fend for themselves. He unlatched the little gate that led through his tiny office to the storage area, then strode on ahead to the chicken-wire cage where he kept his so-called valuables.

This was my papa's holy of holies, the cache in which the really vintage rubbish had been culled from the garden-variety — a fine distinction that required a more discerning eye than my own. A little too fastidiously, under the circumstances, Papa cleared a space among the lady-shaped mood lamps and the fractured Victrolas, the model locomotives and the dumbbells endorsed by Eugene Sandow, the alleged papyrus scrolls. He posed a dressmaker's manikin, outfitted like a headless Marie Antoinette, as a sentry beside the open door of his bauble- and gadget-filled vault. He dumped a brace of dueling pistols and some rubber Walt Disney rodents into a nest of fancy crinoline gowns. He shoved aside the colonnaded ant plantation, the plaster of Paris saints, the clutch of prosthetic limbs, and the taxidermed beaver with a windup mechanism that caused it to spank a bare-bottomed baby doll with the flat of its tail — arranging them all like witnesses at a nativity. He dragged in a couple of sticker-covered steamer trunks to use as a makeshift catafalque; then "Chop-chop," Papa clapped his hands and summoned the pallbearers to lumber in with the casket.

The two volunteers especially seemed to be overstating the effort of carrying what was, after all, just an old lady. This was obviously for the sake of sweetening their gratuity, or else it was further evidence of the way that my grandma commanded a gravity beyond her nominal size. In any case, amid universal groaning, they lowered her box too fast. They dropped it onto the steamer trunks in an agitation of dust, which left you expecting them to vanish behind it like magician's assistants. When the dust cleared and all were accounted for, Papa shooed everybody out of the cage. He tipped the pair of vagrants to get rid of them, though not before shaking their hands, then turned to settle with Mr. Gruber. Meanwhile Oboy had begun to yank at my father's sleeve.

"This here yo mama's ticket," the puller flatly submitted, offering Papa the stub of a receipt stamped with the name of the shop. It was the kind of liberty I'd seen the little whosits take once or twice before, like it needed his involvement to make things official. Like he thought he had to cover for his boss's oversights. But this time it was the puller who had the wrong idea. An expired bubbe in temporary cold storage shouldn't be confused with the other superannuated property of Kaplan's Loans; and I waited for my papa, with his fresh new assertiveness, to notify his employee of said fact.

But instead, Papa took the ticket without hesitation, smiling like he and Oboy were thick as thieves. He even went so far as to give a playful tug at the bill of the puller's cap, pulling it over his eyes, which Oboy never bothered to correct as he groped away. That's when I began to worry that my papa's pack-rat instincts had finally gotten out of control, knowing as I did how an item in Kaplan's pawn might molder away forever without being redeemed.

When the shop was cleared of vagrants and morticians, and Oboy had reassumed his post outside, Papa went whistling back into his cage and began to reorganize the displaced merchandise. In moments the entire top of the casket was covered with assorted junk, its knotty pine hardly apparent to the uninformed eye. Then, brushing his palms and snatching an eyeshade from a hook, adjusting his necktie by the reflection in a silver serving spoon, my father stepped forth to greet the customers who had started to trickle in.

He began formally, with an unusual reserve — as if, instead of bringing in their worthless goods to pawn, they had come by to pay their last respects. But soon Papa dropped any pretense of formality, succumbing to the infectious high spirits of his clientele. There was one old shvartzer, for instance, a rake-thin, bow-backed regular known as Cousin Jabo, who leaned on his whittled cane to click his heels. "The river she up, and the cotton she down!" he sang out like a password — he might have mistaken our shop for a speakeasy. At the same time his partner, another old scarecrow in a motley of calico patches, shook his bristled head contemplatively. "Unh unh unh," he opined, "them foty days and nights sho do go fast when you havin fun." Then both of them started cackling in a way that made you feel like ripe fruit was dropping on your head.

A little later a trio of stout, tight-skirted ladies stationed along the length of an oriental rug, their bottoms graduated according to width, congaed into the shop like a darktown version of a Chinese New Year dragon. After them some joker, whose open dustcoat revealed an old-fashioned bathing costume, came in looking to make, of all things, a purchase. He went away happy after Papa had outfitted him in a full-length diving suit complete with helmet.

The rain had driven everybody out of their minds. In the face of things, the wisest course would naturally have been to crawl into the front window with book in hand, but in the confusion surrounding Zippe's postponed funeral I'd come unprepared. I was a captive audience. But every so often, on the flimsy excuse of dusting off the show, of passing the time with Oboy, for whom time always seemed to stand still, I ducked out the door. I checked to make sure that the Beale Street bayou had not disappeared before I had the chance to get a proper eyeful.

All that afternoon we heard the sirens. We saw the press gangs of police rounding up errant Negroes for the purpose, as we learned, of sandbagging the levees. A number of refugees from forced labor, undiscouraged by my father, found their way into the shop, and always they brought with them some late-breaking rumor: The water was still rising; there were plans afoot for evacuating the city. The mayor's council had moved its offices on board the *Island Queen,* which had slipped its moorings and drifted away. Memphis was without any government. But Beale Street never surrendered to the general alarm. Pawnbrokers and merchants alike stood in their doorways with folded arms, showing themselves prepared to sink or swim. No disaster was so great that it could disrupt their appointed hours of business, nor deter them from an opportunity of turning a profit. And my father no doubt prided himself on being a member of this fraternity.

But around dusk Papa got one of those phone calls from my mother, which usually spelled trouble. From where I stood I could hear her voice over the line, sounding a little like a muted kazoo. Whatever she was demanding, Papa was resisting, trying for all he was worth to pass the buck.

"Listen Mildred, we're awful busy here," he protested, his cheeks coloring slightly with shame. "Can't Morris . . . ? Can't Dr. Seligman . . . ?"

By now I'd assumed the nature of her summons: Grandpa Isador must have been inconsolable again, his pacification requiring all available hands. That's why I had to sigh aloud when

Papa volunteered, "Okay, I'll send Harry right over," as if that settled everything. To my relief the proposal, which had overtones of sacrifice, apparently did not meet my mother's terms.

While his lips continued to mouth a few more silent *but but buts,* in the end Papa sulkily conceded to her wishes. With such tender consideration did he remove his sleeve garters and visor that I thought he was going to kiss them, like sacred vestments, before returning them to their respective hooks.

"C'mon Harry." His voice was approaching a whine. "We got to go home." It was a pathetic echo of this morning's rousing call to the funeral. Of course the family ought to be together at the end of such a day, just as we'd been together at the beginning, but the idea of going home now seemed like a kind of defeat. It meant returning to where we'd started, as if everything were the same as before the flood. But if nothing had changed, why was I seized with the impulse to say what I said?

"You go ahead. I'll stay and mind the shop for a while."

Papa looked at me like, Whose little boy are you? "Look, it's Shabbos already," he pointed out, as if this were supposed to mean something, coming as it did from one who'd told his own father that the Sabbath was a luxury a man of business couldn't afford. For this I figured "Nu?" was enough of an answer. Then he tried another angle, telling me that my presence would be required to help make a minyan. I asked him since when did the ritual mourning come before the burial, and besides, Jews didn't sit shivah on Shabbos.

"A k'nocker I got here," Papa said to the bossed tin ceiling. "Awright, Mr. K'nocker, I ain't got time to argue." He gave me a look that I guess was intended to probe my murky depths, then hunched his shoulders to signify that I'd won. But this was too easy. Defiant sons aren't supposed to overthrow their father's mandates so handily, are they? And the realization that I'd done just that resulted in my immediate loss of nerve.

My sinking heart, on its way down, passed my papa's on the rise. With a proud hand on my shoulder, he shrugged again, plucked a wayward thread from my lapel, and tossed me his keys. "Okeydoke, Mr. Big Shot, today you're a man," he informed me. "Don't stay open too late." And he was out the door in an arpeggio of chimes.

His parting words, however intended, resonated odiously in my ears. They sounded to me like the kind of command you gave some flunky accomplice, that he should stand lookout while you returned to the scene of the crime.

"This is just ducky," I said to the ceiling, catching myself in an impersonation of my father. Was it fair to say that Sol Kaplan was finally certifiably meshugge? Not happy with having turned his pawnshop into a museum of derelict rubbish, he'd gone himself one better: he'd made it a mausoleum as well.

I resolved to try and make the best of it, though I could have done with a little more in the way of a commencement exercise. What happened to the part where I recited the Moneylender's Creed? Still, I supposed I was glad Papa hadn't made a big thing of it. Better that he should treat my taking over as a matter of routine. Because, if I'd thought of it otherwise, at the appearance of my first customer — a sartorial darkie in a bug-back coat, with powder-gray temples and serious, blood-rimmed eyes, carrying what looked to be a grainy black doctor's bag — I would have panicked.

As it was, I was able to perform before the tired eyes of my audience a quick study of my father's bluff spirits, screwing my face into what I thought would pass for the spitting image of his benevolent smile.

"Howdy doody," I greeted, excusing myself to snatch down Papa's eyeshade. "Now what can I do you for, uncle? Heh heh heh."

So far so good. This is what's known as an aptitude for meeting the public. But judging from the suspicious frown on my client's face, I might have been trying too hard. He was hugging his bag to his chest as if to protect its contents, which I imagined as smoky vials, polished instruments, possibly cunning devices for cracking safes: augers and drills, small explosives, a stethoscope that could sense a mechanical pulse through lead.

"Where Mr. Solly at?"

"He's out. I'm his son, Mr. Harry," I informed him, tugging at my lapels to simulate an expansion of my chest. But the old sawbones, or safecracker, still seemed unconvinced. He further confirmed this when, giving a disappointed tilt to his head, he turned and left the shop.

It was a scene that repeated itself, during the next couple of hours, with only slight variations. As you might guess, this took its toll on my readiness to serve. So much was one customer's reaction the carbon copy of another's that you'd have thought they'd attended the same school of disappointment. Each one clutched his moth-eaten skunk boa, his cracked hourglass, his still humming beehive, grisly fishing lure, last year's Dionne quintuplets calendar, or José Carioca cookie jar, as if such sought-after items were much too valuable to place in the hands of a novice. Nobody even bothered to tell me a story.

I tried to flatter myself that they could see I wasn't such a patsy as my papa. I could recognize their offerings for what they really were, "trash" being, to my mind, too dignified a label; and as for the charade of making them loans, that was charity, if you called it by its right name. But knowing this was small consolation in the face of their wholesale distrust. What was the matter with them, that they didn't identify me as Sol Kaplan's son and heir, a more or less permanent fixture around these premises? It was also beginning to irk me that Oboy was being so conspicuously out-of-pocket. He was, after all, more suited than I was, by body type and disposition, to caretaking this chamber of curiosities, this shmutzerama. If you asked me, he was born for the job.

Naturally I appreciated the unsolicited corned beef and soda he brought me from Segal's deli, but what I needed was moral support. Okay, so that wasn't a service that typically figured among the puller's duties, but tonight I had the feeling he was leaving me alone on principle. Was this supposed to be some kind of test? If so, I resented it. Here I was, doing my papa this favor, looking out for his interests and all, and what sort of thanks did I get? You couldn't blame me for feeling a little put upon, confined as I was to this white-elephant graveyard. No wonder I decided to take the first opportunity to close up the shop.

By about eight o'clock (though the reckoning of time in Kaplan's was always only an educated guess) such traffic as there was had anyway ground to a halt. I supposed that my father's customers must have put the word out that an imposter was at large in his shop. So I locked the register, closed the account books, and rehung the accessories of the pawnbroker's trade. Then I switched off the lights and felt my resolution falter.

Though my heart was hinting vigorously that I ought to hurry up, something else made me want to linger. The drowsy glow from my father's scarlet neon sign was falling over me the way the poppy dust settles over Oz. It was powdering the padded shoulders of the suit coats, enflaming the glass eyes of stuffed animals, highlighting the brass of the instruments, which smoldered as if they were playing red-hot music beyond a pitch that mortals could hear. There was also the quiet, the type that suspicious heroes in cloak-and-daggers call "too quiet." I felt like an uninvited guest, though I still couldn't leave. I knew that the instant I stepped out the door, I would have missed my chance to see how the typewriters and pruning hooks, the fretless banjos, the scored china dishes and the birthday spoons, began their secret lives.

I tried to tell myself there was nothing special about this particular brand of quiet; it was just that I'd never been alone in the shop before. Then I remembered that, in a sense, I wasn't alone.

"Good Shabbos, Grandma Zippe," I called out half in jest, though of their own accord the words turned reverent in the air. "Aleha ha-sholem," I thought I'd better add, and by way of further assurance: "You're in good company. Nothing but the choicest merchandise here at Kaplan's." Hoping that Kaplan's was satisfied at having reduced me to talking to myself, I judged it was time to make tracks.

Outside I unfolded the lattice and locked it, then looked east where the street was a mirage come to life. The lagoon was still bobbing with shadowy skiffs, some of them hung with lanterns on the end of cane poles like fishing rods baited with light. There were reflections that the boat hulls scattered into running schools of electric minnows, and now and again a lanternless boat would scoot by like a dark blade in the air. Despite the persistence of the sirens and the faint, tinny music off in the distance, you could still hear the splashing of oars. Maybe it was because I'd been stuck inside the shop for so long, or maybe I just hadn't counted on the kind of changes that night would bring, but the scene took me by surprise all over again. You could lose yourself in it if you weren't careful.

The awning had to be cranked up for the night, a chore I performed so distractedly that I never noticed Oboy sitting beneath it. Consequently, some residual rainwater that had collected in the canvas spilled over, drenching his cap and streaming down both sides of his face. This likened him, in my mind, to a sculpted rainspout on a cathedral.

"Uh-oh," I think I said as I produced a handkerchief to make a clumsy pass at drying him off. But when he lifted his face, offering me the insoluble riddle of his hatch-marked features, I thought it best to let him tend to himself. I tucked the hankie into his fist, thrust my hands into my pockets, and tried to look casual. "So sorry," I told him, hoping he'd assure me that these things happen. When he stayed silent, I threw in an apology for the early closing. "Business isn't so terrific tonight, eh Oboy?" Once spoken, his name seemed to contradict the regret I meant to express. "Oh well, good Shab — I mean, g'night."

I'd intended to walk away, leaving him to think what he might. That's why it startled me when, before I'd taken a step, I heard him croak, "You the boss," as he slid from his perch with a smart salute. Since it was my understanding that only the proprietor had the authority to make the puller budge, it gave me a jolt to see him lurch off like that, as if my wish were his command.

I watched him scurrying down the sidewalk toward the water's edge and wondered where he went. With a bandy-legged gait that his limp arms did nothing to assist, he looked like something you might throw a net over, then demand he show you his pot of gold. It wouldn't have surprised me to see him duck down a manhole or nip under a fat lady's skirts. Or was there a room waiting somewhere, furnished only with a single three-legged stool? Then, jostled by a couple of evening strollers ("Watch yosef, young ge'man!"), I realized that I was following Oboy.

Among the things of this night that I couldn't previously have pictured was the sight of so remote a character as the puller rubbing shoulders with his own kind. Nevertheless, when he reached the part of the pavement that might now be called the shore, Oboy began saluting here and there, chummily waiting his turn in the boats. In front of him was a sporty fellow in an acey-deucey fedora and a suit with shoulders at least three feet across. He had the arm of an elegant lady, slender as a licorice whip, hair coiled in the shape of an inverted tornado. She was daintily lifting her gown to steady a rocking skiff, pinning its hull under a heel the length of a carpenter's awl. A burr-headed kid in rolled-up bib overalls, waving the white flag of an unraveled diaper, chased a naked, squealing infant into the shallows. Nearby stood a rag-headed mama shouting threats in the name of the Lord, shaking her muslin parasol like she had a nagging hold of the Lord's own leg.

All around, the colored people played ducks and drakes with slab bottles and chicken wings. They flirted, swapped insults and shadowboxed, gigged a bullfrog with a brace and bit. In general they behaved as if, rather than a recently materialized wonder of the Western world, this choppy pool of standing water had been there all along.

I had stationed myself behind a lamppost to spy on Oboy and prayed that my jackhammering chest wouldn't give me away. He was negotiating with a couple of boys, one sitting and one standing in a grounded skiff. Tossing a coin to the standing boy, who snatched it out of the air with a practiced motion, the puller stepped gingerly into the weather-beaten skiff and took a seat. That should have been my cue to turn around and quickly lose myself among the strollers. But in the instant that I hesitated, leading with my receding chin from behind the post, I met Oboy's eyes through a gap in the gathered ranks.

It was too late. I had no choice but to step out into the circle of light. I stood there foolishly, a bashful debut during which I tried to remember my lines, but all I could manage was "Um, what it was, I mean, the thing I forgot to mention . . . ," before falling speechless over the nothing I'd forgotten.

Meanwhile the kid who'd taken the coin leaped over the bow onto the pavement, the wind scissoring the tails of his hopsacking coat. Issuing strict orders, apparently to himself ("Heave ho, ya'll bad man rousterbout! Suck a egg, ol River George!"), he began to shove the boat back into the lagoon. He paused, however, when Oboy, who hadn't seemed the least bit perplexed by my presence, asked me, "Is you want to ride?"

I looked around like he must have been talking to somebody

61

else, and even pressed an inquiring forefinger to my shirt button. "Oh no," I assured him, shaking my head emphatically. I couldn't possibly, had to get back, they were waiting for me on North Main Street, don't you know. But it was clear that no one was going to go out of his way to persuade me; no one was interested in talking me out of playing coy. In fact, if I hadn't decided on the spot to hold my breath and hoist my already too short trousers to take the high step over the gunnel, I guess I would have missed the boat.

Before I could sit down, the boy who was still delaying the business of launching put his face uncomfortably close to mine. "Ain't no free ride on the earth," he apprised me, turning his head to spit. "Now, take this here ferry, that it a cost you for yo information a nickel."

"Pardon?" My giddiness combined with his faintly whiskey breath left me slow on the uptake.

"Cost you what we calls the bumper, in yo Negro language, which it are five cent all round the world. What you thank, we in this fo our health?"

I didn't see why he should have to take a such a high-handed tone with me. This was disrespectful, wasn't it? Of course it didn't help to look to Oboy for guidance. You'd have thought it enough that I had stepped into this leaky tub in the first place, never mind I should have to pay for the privilege. Indignant, I saw myself splashing out of the boat and back up the street, then turning to wave goodbye to myself still in the boat, dredging my pocket to grudgingly hand over the whole of my carfare.

"Bon voyage," I said to the greasy nickel, which nobody thought was funny. Attempting to take the passenger seat next to Oboy, I stumbled on a bamboo pole that snapped in two. I plunked myself down and scowled to cover my embarrassment.

Putting his back to the task again, the wisenheimer kid gave us a shove and leaped on board. Directly we scraped clear of the asphalt and slid out into the shimmering lagoon, a progress so smooth it stole my breath as if we'd taken flight. I squeezed the paint-peeling edge of the boat, feeling it give under my fingers like cork, and watched the winking hill of pawnshops recede.

Having handed over the paddle to his silent partner, the wise guy plopped down in what had now become the after end of the boat. Producing a wallet-thin bottle from the inside of his coat, he gravely explained, "Doctor order," as he took a swig. He passed the bottle to Oboy, who chugalugged in a show of good fellowship, then offered what was left of the kerosene-looking liquid to me. I told him no thank you, since the fumes were revolting enough, but he pressed it, saying, "Take jus a lil sweet corn to settle yo nerve."

I couldn't tell whether he was taunting me or expressing honest concern, but I supposed it wouldn't do for the crew to think I was afraid to drink after shvartzers. On the other hand, here we had only just left the shore and already they were trying to corrupt me — and why should my nerves need settling? Come to think of it, I *was* scared to drink after shvartzers! But God forbid they should discover this and throw me overboard. So, to oblige them, l'chayim, I took a sip.

The breath that I'd only just recovered immediately escaped me. The boiling in my middle released a steam, or so it felt, that threatened to float my head from my shoulders if I didn't hold on. When I could see again, I checked the back of my hands for excessive hair or any change in pigmentation. Then I held out the bottle to the wise guy, who was nestled against the stern as if for a nap. His tweed cap was pulled down over his brow, jugging his ears, which made you wonder how his arm knew when to shoot out and snatch the shnaps.

"Steady as she go, Mistah Michael." He continued uttering pointless orders, maybe piloting a ship in his dreams. "Hump that bale, y'ol bullneck Stacker Lee." Not wanting to rock the boat, I turned around only once, which was when I got my first real look at the other boy. He was facing west, his eyes hooded by the wide brim of a raggedy panama, manning his oar with the single-mindedness of a galley slave.

I told myself that everything was fine. I was anyway only a block, then a block and a half, from my father's place of business. I was in a soggy boat on a warm spring night with three darkies, sailing east on Beale past the swamped but still illuminated New Orleans Café. In order to get to its neon front entrance, the people were having to straddle a bottleneck of rowboats and dinghies, which made them look like they were wearing enormous water-walking shoes. Then we were abreast of a wholesale meat market called Nello's Tenderloin, its windows, fogged in condensation, displaying headless animals like a warning on a hostile coast. Next came the Snow White Laundry, strung with year-round Christmas lights, bundles tumbling over its fire escape as if dropped from the beak of a stork, caught by children in inner tubes. At the tributary where Hernando Street met Beale, a lady in a window above the Pantaze Drugstore was tossing her garter, drawing such cheers from the boats you'd have thought she'd inaugurated a fleet.

When we'd sailed past those islanded storefronts, out beyond the quicksilver reach of their reflections, I noticed a change in the air. The mild breeze, brackish with the stench of the renegade river, was laced now with the keener odor of barbecued treyf. This, I assumed, is the way that dry land announces itself when you cross a channel at night.

There was a bump and I turned around to bright pandemonium, the skiff having butted against the pavement on the other side. Sprung from his repose, the cheeky kid piped up, "All out for the *famous* Beale Street" — as if the other end of the street were *un*famous, or maybe not Beale Street at all. "The famous Pee Wee," he continued like an elevator operator, "the One

Minute, the Palace The-ay-tah, where the home folk plays the fool and the blues have done first come uptown, the fabulous Gray Mule, the famous Mambo's Tonsoral Parlor . . ."

All over the sidewalk and out across the avenue, people were milling and knocking about. They were clapping in time to the unholy racket of a street band playing on washboard basses and gallon jugs, shoving to make room for the gyrations of a pair of young jitterbuggers with rubber knees. The boy in loose trousers, his baseball cap on backwards, was twirling a girl in cardinal red, her glossy legs kicking her dress above frilly cream drawers. One moment they were cheek to cheek, two halves of one snaky sashay; the next she was riding him, a female devil that he tried with mighty shudders to shake off his back. Shvartzers stumbled in grubby shmattes, strutted in glad rags fit to kill: dead foxes with their tails in their teeth, watch chains that dragged the ground, ostrich feathers, boutonnieres, jewels as arresting as stoplights. They rattled tin cups, gnawed neckbones, and flung melon rinds, which hung in the air for an instant like green crescent moons. They smashed jars over the curb and squared off. They hooked arms, squeezed bottoms, slipped hands into each other's pockets, stabbed ice picks between fingers that were spread over the hood of a sedan. They carried ragged-combed roosters with plumage like an aurora borealis and wicked spurs.

Above the fracas you could hear the odd voice hawking catfish, "Ain't it yo sweetmeat," and something called the dreambook, "I'm stone-guarantee will change yo luck." Somebody offered a cure for heartbreak while another promised the end of days. A caramel-skinned woman in an Alice-blue nightgown, out of her head with pain or delight, drifted past singing a plaintive air about cutting a throat.

Beside me, Oboy nodded like this must be his stop. He stood and delicately hitched up his pant legs before stepping out of the boat, then turned to present the puzzle of himself for me to decipher. One solution was that here was my papa's employee offering to show me the sights; another was that the wizened little mieskeit was bent on treachery. Having already introduced me to strong drink, he would lead me into more unspeakable types of temptation. He would slip me a mickey and sell me to scoundrels who trafficked in Jewish boys, and I would wake up on a slow boat in chains.

My ears were ringing and my stomach felt like someone was braiding my kishkes into holiday bread. Still, I wanted to get up and show myself ready to take my adventures as I found them, but I couldn't find my feet. Whatever bravado I'd imbibed from the wise guy's tonic had evaporated during the passage.

With a sharp jerk or two of his flinty features, Oboy appeared to be taking the measure of me. Then he shrugged as if to show that what I did or didn't do was a matter of indifference to him, and scuttled off into the thick of things. I watched him sidestep a little street band in clanging competition with the rolling piano in an open door of one of the clubs. Pausing to tip his cap, he actually hoofed it a few sprightly steps; he dropped a coin in a jug and moved on into the crowd, where he ducked under a theater marquee and vanished from view.

I wished I was back in my alcove already, at a safe remove from all of this hell broken loose. I had the distinct feeling that I'd seen more than I was meant to, that I'd violated some unwritten law. When I clenched shut my eyes, the street continued to run amok in my brain. So I turned around on my splintery seat and let the boys know that I was ready to be ferried back.

"Cost you a nickel," said the kid with the lip, laconic for a change, his infuriating grin echoing the frayed crescent bill of his cap. "Ten cent the round-trip fare."

I gave him a smirk. Where had I heard this before? It was time to advise him that colored had been lynched for less audacity than his. Their dismembered parts — I had this on my papa's more or less unimpeachable authority — were mounted for trophies beside the wrestlers' photos in the barbershop of the Claridge Hotel. But I was beyond striking attitudes. In fact, I was beginning to wonder if I would ever see North Main Street again.

"Look," I said, turning out my pockets, which were empty but for a key ring and some hamentashen crumbs from a Purim banquet years before. Like a good boy, I'd taken only trolley fare from the till. "I gave you everything I had!" Unimpressed, the boy stepped out of the boat and began to tug at the stem while the other, as if in need of rewinding, sat staring into the lap of his filthy overalls.

I turned over my mind for some straw to clutch at, coming up with only "I'm Harry Kaplan!" Like the lampposts should bow down. "You know, Mr. Solly the pawnbroker's son. My IOU is good!"

Standing practically astride the silent oarsman, the cheeky kid cocked his head. He allowed his grin to contract to a thoughtful pucker, then turned up the bill of his cap to give me the once-over.

"You Mistah Solly boy?" he asked, still apparently unconvinced, though I was nodding for all I was worth. "Do you be Mistah Solly boy, I speck you can say where he keep his lil Natchez boat which it sets in a lightbub."

There was no end to the kid's impertinence. Having failed at extortion, he now wanted to wheedle out of me the whereabouts of my papa's most coveted junk. Of course I didn't believe for a second that Kaplan's held any serious allure for thieves, but if I'd thought it would help get me out of here, I'd have drawn him a blueprint.

"Top shelf on the end nearest the windows," I fired back, "next to his General Lee in a milk-glass bladder."

"Where Mistah Solly keep his traption make gold out a belly lint and such?"

"His alchemistry set? Under the counter in his patentless inventions bin," I answered confidently. I was ready for anything he might throw my way, oral exams having always been my strong suit. But just as I was warming to the quiz, it seemed to be over.

"You ain't say nothin don't every mother son awready know."

So how could you win? "I'm his son all right!" I shouted, turning my head in profile, the better to show off the distinctive Kaplan beak. "Have a look."

The kid made a slow appraisal. "Do kinda favor the man."

"Favor? Are you blind? Like two peas in a pod."

"I wudn a put it izzackly like that," he said, leaving me to imagine just how he might have put it. But then he gave a little chuckle that sounded like assent. "Mis-tah Sol-ly boy. Well, it am sho nuff a small worl. My, my, Michael" — he thumped the crown of the other kid's hat — "don't it jus beat all? What you think, this here be Mistah Solly boy. I got to say it, yo daddy he been good to colored folk. Done give me fitty cent one time for a ol Mason fez, which I tell him it belong to a African kang." He added with a kind of wistful satisfaction, "I drops by his shop after hour now and then just to shamooze."

I gave silent thanks that my father's reputation for a soft touch had preceded me in these parts. The Kaplan name seemed to have some real currency down here, philanthropic associations even. I felt almost like an ambassador.

"I please to make yo quaintance, Mistah Harry did y'all say?" the wise guy went on, doffing his cap which a couple of coins fell out of. He had a large, topheavy head the shape of an eggplant stood on end. His hair was an itchy-looking mat of black fleece like a field tilled by a runaway plow, and his ears, even without the pressure of his cap, looked like handles. "Name Lucifer," he submitted huskily. Before I had time to beg his pardon and make sure that I'd heard him right, he once more unzipped his showy grin. "And this be my goodest one an only sweet brothah Michael."

He removed the other kid's hat the way a waiter uncovers a dish, exposing a head shaped identically to his own, though completely bald. He had deep scooped hollows at his temples, the brother, as if he'd been dragged out at birth with a pair of ice tongs. He had lips like a bagel and a slack and brooding jaw. But his eyes, glancing up at me an instant before turning inward again, were every bit as lustrous as Lucifer's.

Defensively, as if he knew what I must be thinking, the wise guy was quick to inform me, "He ain't no dummy, he jus never speak." Then he restored both hats to their respective heads, giving his brother's a pat for good measure, and proudly folded his arms. It was a pride suggesting that more had been revealed than just their names. And when it was clear to him that I had no idea what he was getting at, he swelled his chest, this Lucifer, announcing in a voice which implied that any ninny could see, "We is twin."

At this point things began to happen fast. A large man in an oilskin coat with a flat mud pie of a face pitched toward us from out of the crowd. He loomed over Lucifer, demanding that we separate our booties "lickry-spit" from his skiff. Without even turning to inspect the menace, Lucifer stepped nimbly over his brother, who, reactivated, wasted no time in digging in with his oar. In seconds we were embarked and Lucifer was lounging with his back against the gunnel, his hands folded comfortably behind his head.

"Dead folk," he remarked with a philosophical detachment, directing my attention to the dwindling hubbub behind us, "they gon be jump around like that on Jedgment Day. Mr. Handy come back and solid blow his horn."

I told him I would have to take his word for it. All of a sudden it seemed important that I shouldn't be thought of as dull company. "So this is a typical Friday night, or what?" I inquired.

Lucifer drew back and let go a sound like surf. "Shhhoot, you ain't seed nothin. Oughta see it round Jubilee time. People dance the dark rapture start-bone-nekkid, lovin and killin in the street, so low-down jookin the Lawd hissef cain't look. They be steady carryin em from the Monarch to the meat wagon all night long." He leaned forward to become more confidential, turning briefly aside to swat a rat trying to crawl on board. "But this what you see ain't the *real* famous Beale Street. The famous Beale done been long gone before our time."

I didn't think it was exactly his place to assume that his time and mine were the same, but given the circumstances, I wasn't complaining. In fact, I felt almost happy to be included. That's when it first occurred to me, as the kid rattled on, offering me another sip from his flask, that Lucifer and I must be about the same age.

"In them day you had the river nigger eight foot tall. You had yo barrelhouse got roof shangle made a silver dollah, got a whooskey spigot shape like a golden catfish. You had them gambler would carry a hoodoo walkin stick an fight a duel with a blindfold on. When they done the dirty dozen drag-style, they be known to spit pison. You had them fancy womens wearin unders made a orange blossom, wear a snake hold they stockin up. Wear kiss-my-kitty perfume — one whiff, it a turn a chile to a man in a minute flat. You had yo conjure mens that would swallah a live lamparee . . ."

Absorbed in his litany, Lucifer didn't seem to notice — when we'd sailed past the smoldering beacons of Handy Park, figures moving among them who looked several parts smoke themselves — that we'd bumped against the mercantile end of the street. But as anxious as I'd been to get back across the lagoon, all of a sudden I wasn't in any hurry to leave the skiff.

". . . You had a bush preacher would Injun-rassle the debil," droned Lucifer, "had a green-eye root woman turn the preacher to a pissant . . ."

Finally I snapped out of it and asked myself what I thought I was doing. Clambering to my feet, I told them, "Excuse me, but this is where I get off."

I wobbled a bit in an effort to get clear of the boat, my sea legs slow in readapting to dry land. Then I straightened up and tried to inject into my voice a note of dauntless chutzpah, the kind that this Lucifer (such a name!) was so proficient at. Jerking my thumb over my shoulder to distinguish between the honorable edifices behind me and that bedlam across the lagoon, I declared, "This Beale Street is famous enough for me!"

Lucifer was now standing in the bow of the skiff, arms folded admiral-wise. His saucy grin, nearly eclipsing his face, did a fair impersonation of the sickle moon and hinted that the joke was somehow on me. At that moment, as there were no waiting passengers, the close-mouthed brother started to shove them off again.

"Wait a minute!" Having had such an earful of this so-called twin, I might have a thing or two to say for myself, though for the life of me I couldn't think what. Still, they shouldn't be in such a hurry. Did I need to remind them of the oilskin man, who was probably waiting for them now on the other shore?

But Lucifer had already dropped his grin (which I half expected to see subsiding beneath the dirty water) and put on a strictly business face.

"Y'all can bring us yo nickel tomorrah," he called as they drifted out among the other boats. They had merged with a shadow fleet, outlined by ripples like a storm of phosphorescent butterflies that left only a boat-shaped silhouette where the skiff had been. "This here a moonlightin operation." Lucifer's voice, grown thinner among a chorus of others, still carried across the glimmering soup. "Daytime come, find us at Mambo Tonsoral. I'se a shine . . ."

This is where a terrible sinking feeling overtook me. Turned around is what I was, discombobulated — a Moishe Kapoyr, as my grandpa might have said. I was a stranger at my papa's own end of the street, while at the same time, by some topsy-turvy logic, belonging where I had no business to be. "Man overboard," I exhaled in a whisper that aspired to a shout. I felt that the twins had as good as left me marooned. Years would pass: my hair and beard would grow rank and twined in garbage. I would grub for roots and vermin, and light vain signal fires with the shreds of my bar mitzvah suit.

Then I looked around toward the pawnshops and slapped my own cheeks. I took several deep breaths, counting hup-two, alef-bais-gimmel, placing one foot in front of the other until I began to get my bearings again.

Five

Naturally I had no intention of taking a nickel to the twins or, for that matter, ever returning to the *famous* end of Beale Street again. It was no place for anybody who valued his peace and quiet, not to mention his mortal gizzard. Besides, didn't I know where I was better off? These days I was content just to hang around the pawnshop. Customers aside, it was entertainment enough just to watch my papa performing his monkeyshines.

The more moping, taciturn, and altogether scarce he was around the apartment, the more versatile it seemed that he became in his shop. On any given day you might see him become a ringmaster, a rug merchant, a connoisseur of antiquities, the keeper of a shrine. There was no expertise that he didn't pretend to possess. And on the fat chance that I should ever be bored, I still had what I persisted in calling my studies, though books had lately lost a little of their old appeal. All those voyages and caravans and flights by balloon to the perilous ends of the earth now hardly seemed worth the effort. Sometimes I asked myself why all those so-called heroes didn't just stay home where they belonged.

But at night when I shut my eyes to try and sleep, the black boys snuck into my alcove. They dragged me through the window and up a gangplank, tied me to the mainmast of a mutinied slave ship. A crew of hog-wild Negroes jitterbugged in the rigging and all along the rails, and Lucifer, with his fluorescent grin, manned the helm.

Meanwhile the floodwaters showed no signs of going down. The Harahan Bridge groaned and sagged under the constant procession of bedraggled refugees. They slouched across it like soldiers returning from lost battles, sometimes clogging to save the soles of their bare feet from the burning boards. They rattled in overladen buckboards hauled by teams of children, the elderly lashed to bedsprings and rocking chairs. They washed ashore on chicken crates and stiff beasts of burden, riding painted pianolas and fugitive rooftops, outmoded but still-puttering jalopies upright on pontoons. In this way they swelled the already unmanageable ranks of those dispossessed by hard times.

In the Pinch they made a Hooverville out of Market Square Park. They strung their patched tarpaulins from the limbs of the chestnut and the joints of the jungle gym, until some began to refer to the park as the Casbah; the less resourceful merely squatted in the pavilion or under the beds of their trucks in the wagon yard. Along North Main Street they began to displace the corps of resident luftmenshen, the bearded loons in their ratty caftans among whose number my grandpa had lately been spied. For all their celebrated beggarliness, these crazy old men now seemed hale in comparison to the pitifully uprooted "rivergees."

At the fairgrounds, according to the local papers, the lucky ones were provided sanitary barracks with flush-toileted latrines. They were given their first taste of oranges, after which their gums stopped bleeding, their spines uncurled, and the clouds passed from their eyes. But the ones who you saw in our neighborhood were still crooked and oyster-eyed, their skin like porridge. With offspring wearing Red Cross flour sacks, scratching heads teeming with beggar lice, they wandered penniless into the shops. They overwhelmed the smells of shoe leather and bug poison, of fresh pumpernickel and pickled meat, with their high bouquet of Delta mud.

For a few nights my papa kept up his show of observing the ritual mourning. Rather than endure the scorn I was assured of if I stayed behind in the shop, I joined him, though it made me feel like a party to a hoax. Admittedly it didn't require a great change in attitude to behave as if Grandma Zippe were already buried; nevertheless, it seemed kind of indecent that the family should conspire, for the sake of convenience, to forget that she had yet to be interred.

Of course it made sense not to recall such details in front of Grandpa Isador, who was already addled enough with grief. Witness how he rounded up flood refugees to complete the minyans. While there were any number of volunteer mourners around the Market Street shul, my grandpa had to go and impress the shiftless with the promise of a bowl of soup. He'd shepherd them into the apartment in a docile single file, line them up like a rogues' gallery in front of the sideboard, and lead them in a perfectly incoherent responsive recital of Kaddish. My horrified mama complained that their muddy footprints would be stamped into the carpet in perpetuity. She keened aloud what could have gone without saying: that they weren't even Jewish.

To this Grandpa Isador, wearing an expression quite reasonable for him, explained that their homelessness gave them a de facto status. "Tahkeh," he'd add with an admiration reserved for the utterly destitute, "they're even holier."

After those token nights of mourning my father began to keep even longer hours in his shop. Nor was there any recurrence, at least around the apartment, of the galloping lightheartedness he'd shown on the morning of the aborted funeral.

Sometimes leaving before the family had woken up, often returning after everyone was long asleep, my papa was as lost to the life of North Main Street as his departed mama. Uncle Morris, however, was much in evidence. Wreathed in cigar smoke and reeking of after-shave, combing the fine hairs forward from the back of his head over an otherwise bald scalp, he was forever reassuring his sister-in-law that she could lean on him. Then, purring and tittering, my mother would tell him that, widowed as she was by the pawnshop, it was nice to have a man around for a change.

Some of the prosperity that Uncle Morris had promised, always saying it was just around the corner, was actually starting to appear. Even as the mirrors remained covered to keep us mindful of the recent passing, newfangled appliances began making their way into our apartment. Electrical modernism had dawned in Mama's bread-line kitchen. Her work was revolutionized now by a three-speed Mixmaster and an oven with a window, through which you could observe her chickens in flames. A humming monitor-top Frigidaire replaced the old icebox, whose runoff had warped the floorboards, leaking through the Ridblatts' ceiling downstairs. Armstrong linoleum concealed the rotting floor. There was a chrome-plated hand iron that spat steam like a dragon, a clothes wringer that also rolled dough, a shining fan-shaped toaster that discharged the bread in a breathtaking twin trajectory.

To think that my father was responsible for the dramatic changes in our standard of living was just too farfetched. On the other hand, it was equally hard to believe that Uncle Morris was playing Lord Bountiful purely out of his generosity of heart. For his own reasons my grandfather seemed to share my skepticism. The more he played the broken record of his resolution that he would soon follow his wife's lead, the less he was inclined to accept the things of this world. Progress was vanity, and all labor-saving devices the fruits of Mammon. His censure, however, did not extend so far as to include the new free-standing Zenith radio, for which he had reserved the right to be fascinated. With an ear to the cloth-muffled speaker in its mahogany cabinet, atop which he'd placed a faded tintype of himself and Zippe (at Coney Island, their heads superimposed above cardboard surf bathers), the old man was oblivious of everything else.

He spun dials that alternated from a whirring wind to a sizzling static like rain. When he finally found voices, he listened so intently that you'd have thought they were revealing prophecies, issuing instructions for his ears only. He seemed to take everything personally, from the news of bloody labor strikes to "The Town-Crier" persiflage to the Lone Ranger's endangered anonymity. The crackling artillery and wholesale homicide on "Gangbusters," the failure of aspiring talent on "Major Bowes," the diaspora from the dust bowl, the scandal of Kate Smith's flatulence, the lament for humanity upon the wreck of the *Hindenburg* — everything apparently served to confirm his worst fears. An earful of Father Coughlin's tub-thumping, for instance, elicited from Grandpa Isador the same fearful "oy!" as the trials of Fibber McGee, especially when the radio shnook, like a latter-day Pandora, released the cataclysm from behind his closet door.

When he'd heard enough, my overwrought grandfather would take to the streets. "Zol gornisht helfen!" That was the watchword with which he regaled the bench in front of Jake Plott's: Nothing will help. Not that this was news to the worn-out alter kockers and the walking wounded of North Main.

The week arrived when the already dense population of the Pinch was even further increased by relations come to visit for Passover. Whether for the convenience of being within an easy stroll of the synagogue or out of the necessity of escaping their floodbound homes, mishpocheh flocked to North Main Street from all points. They crammed themselves into the stuffy little apartments above the shops until the walls began visibly to bulge. With their faces pressed against the windows, they leered at the street strewn with human flotsam, as if the neighborhood was under siege. On the lips of all the neighbors was the complaint that they were being eaten out of house and home: Elijah himself would have to be turned away.

Except when my grandfather brought back the occasional shnorrer for dinner, we were thankfully spared the overcrowding. What we weren't spared was the disoriented presence of Sol Kaplan, obliged to close his shop early in deference to the first night of Pesach. For hours he wandered around the apartment as if under a curse that wouldn't let him sit down. Kaplan's Loans, which was the center of his operations, must also have been my father's center of gravity, because away from the shop he seemed unsteady on his feet. He alternately complained of headache, nosebleed, a dull griping pain that would not locate itself. At dusk he posed the illogical proposition that it might be a real fling for the family to make a holiday retreat to the pawnshop. Halfheartedly chopping liver with a gadget like a dynamite plunger, Mama let him know that he was getting on everyone's nerves.

"Go back to Beale Street already if you don't like it here," she snapped. It was the tone I'd heard taken with local greenhorns who dared to express nostalgia for the old country.

Then Uncle Morris arrived with an offer we couldn't refuse: he insisted that Mama drop the preparations for her Passover meal and invited us to a Seder at his stately home out on the Parkway. "The maid's an old-timey Shabbos nigger, makes a real pesadig feast. All right, all right, you can bring your Jell-O mold." Suspicious as always of my uncle's motives, even I had to admit that the rescue was timely.

A shady, genteel street at the northern boundary of the Pinch, whence it embarked on a loop of the city, the Parkway was the seat of all that North Main Street yearned for. Its median, arcaded in pink and white dogwoods, was one long bridle path. There it was not unusual to see the equestrian Jewish daughters of doctors and department store owners, wearing jodhpurs and brandishing leather crops, looking indistinguishable from the shiksas who rode alongside. The street was flanked by Mediterranean-style houses with screened-in sleeping porches, roofs of emerald-green tile, verandas furnished with wicker chaise longues, and stone lions recumbent on manicured lawns. Everyone in the Pinch, to hear them tell it, was going to be neighbors on the Parkway by and by. "Next year on the Parkway," the popular saying went, the street being about as accessible to most as Jerusalem itself.

We piled into Uncle Morris's Studebaker touring car and were driven in style to his opulent abode. The shamrock-shuttered windows in walls of eggshell stucco, the wrought-iron balconies, the classical frieze over the vaulted front door — all rose like a palace conjured out of the flames of its flowering azalea bed. It was all Grandpa Isador needed to see. On the short trip over, bemoaning some injustice he'd overheard on "Death Valley Days," the old man had already begun to get out of hand. Now, as the enemy of conspicuous wealth, he positioned himself on the porch beside an urn spewing geraniums.

"I pish on this temple of Baal," he declared, actually reaching for the buttons of his fly when my mama slapped his liver-spotted hand. She hustled him briskly through the marble vestibule, where the mirrors on adjacent walls contained receding infinities of chastised Isador Kaplans.

In her dudgeon, Mama complained to anyone who might be listening that something would have to be done about the old man. And the sooner the better. "Insti-*too*-shnalize," pronounced so that you wanted to say gesundheit, was becoming her favorite word. Roughly she seated Grandpa Isador in the heraldic dining room, which had walnut wainscoting and halberds crossed above a retouched studio portrait of my anemic Aunt Nettie, whom I'd never met. She tucked a napkin into his collar, muttered something about its being handy in case she needed to gag him, and continued to kvetch to Uncle Morris.

Forgotten but not gone, my father felt called upon to put in a word in his own father's defense. "He'll come around as soon as all this mishegoss in Europe blows over." Grandpa Isador, interpreting the news broadcasts according to his whim, had seized on a master focus for his forebodings: projecting from his own personal woe a worldwide epidemic, he'd concluded that the chancellor of Germany was about to murder all the Jews.

At the mention of Europe the old man folded at the chest, emitting a sound like he'd swallowed a harmonica. Papa leaned over to comfort him, suggesting that he might come down to the pawnshop tomorrow. There my papa would see to it that he was kept safe from the doings of the momzer Hitler, may his name be blotted out. At the head of the table Uncle Morris exchanged a meaningful roll of the eyes with my mama at the foot. With their eyes, they seemed to be making a pact to wash their hands of the pair of them, Solly and Isador. Wondering if their pact included me, I wanted to tell them: You're too late, I beat you to it. I've washed my own hands already.

I'd had it up to here with the family Kaplan. What had happened to everyone since Zippe's passing that they behaved so ludicrously? Like the bubbe had been an anchor or something, and now they were all set adrift. Not that Papa was really any screwier than usual. But more and more I was coming to see the ways my father took after his own, making me resolve that whatever loose screws had been passed down from father to son should stop with him. This is not to say that I joined with my mother and uncle in their holier-than-thou alliance; as far as I was concerned they deserved each other.

Neither did I exempt my cousin Naomi, seated across the table from me, whose mere presence was enough to remind me that things could be better. All dolled up for the occasion, she drooped nevertheless, the shoulders of her dress enfolding her like the limp wings of a taffeta bat. Her stringy black hair, pulled into a listing topknot over her bangs, bristled with stray strands. Whenever I happened to glance in her direction — which was as seldom as possible — she instantly lowered her perennially moist eyes. But when I wasn't looking, I sensed that she stole occasional glances, the way you sneakily pick food from somebody else's plate. It made me feel that she might want to steal a peek into my mind, which I forthwith tried to make a perfect blank.

On a lordly cue from Uncle Morris, all casual table talk came to an end. We donned the silk skullcaps, opened the food-soiled Haggadahs, and began an uninspired reading of the Passover service. As the male child, it fell to me to recite the Four Questions, but I had trouble mustering the proper enthusiasm. Rusty with the Hebrew, I garbled it under my breath, and was almost as incoherent with the English translation.

"Whyzissnighdiffren . . ." I mumbled until they asked me to speak up, after which I vociferated like a quiz show emcee, "Why is this night different from all other nights?" Then, to my amazement, I made a sound like a buzzer and said, "Sorry, your time is up." The silence that followed shamed me into asking the remaining questions in an appropriate tone of voice.

Next, treading heedlessly on each other's words, the family read a collective explanation of the holiday's significance. They told the part about how the slaves stuffed their cheeks with cracker crumbs and escaped through a God-made hiatus where the sea used to be. At least a couple of miles away, I was thinking of a miniature sea where before there had been only dry land.

With Uncle Morris holding up every item like an endorsement, we repeated the stories behind the symbols of salt water, shank bone, and bitter herb. Then, following a custom that called for sympathetic bleeding, with all eyes on old Isador lest he open a vein, we dipped fingers in our goblets and dripped wine across our plates. (Licking my pinkie, I was pleasantly surprised, the tepid grape juice of my childhood having been replaced by the authentic fruit of the vine.) Throughout, my grandpa, that his wellsprings shouldn't run dry, gnawed sticks of horseradish with his rattling dentures to summon more tears.

Just when you thought it was safe to put down your Haggadah, Grandpa Isador cried out, "Dayenu!" This was the signal to begin a recitation of the blessings heaped on the heads of the Israelites. At the end of each blessing in an endless list, you were supposed to shout "Dayenu," which meant, "It would have been enough." But Uncle Morris nipped this in the bud.

"Enough is enough is enough," he broke in. "Let's nosh!" Then he wadded up his yarmelke and tossed it over his shoulder. "Shinola!" he bellowed toward the kitchen, turning to tell us confidentially, "I call her Shinola, get it? Come to think of it, what *is* her name?" Now that all the mumbo-jumbo was out of the way, my uncle was our genial host again. In fact he was hamming it up. Taking a large carving knife and a sharpening steel, he proceeded to fight a duel with himself, then plucked a hair from his forward-combed locks to demonstrate the sharpness of the blade.

A door swung open and a colored maid padded in, her crisp, white-aproned uniform strained fore and aft by her generous dimensions. On her broad face was an expression of tolerance under pressure, an expression that made you wonder if there might be something funny about the gefilte fish she was placing before us. That's what comes of taking too much note of the hired help. When she returned a second time, with a hen on a platter, I avoided studying her face.

As Uncle Morris set about slicing the bird, he faked ecstasies over its texture and the aroma released from its stuffing. Then he fell into his habitual doting on Mama. He congratulated her on her patient fortitude in putting up with him and all of the pesky Kaplan clan.

"If only my Nettie, may she rest in peace," he sighed, dabbing an eye with the corner of his napkin, "if only she'd had your strength."

He cast a mournful glance over his shoulder at the portrait of his expired spouse, sere-faced and wilted despite a photographer's best efforts to add color and prop her up. She'd died shortly after giving birth to Naomi, as if in bringing my cousin into the world she'd fulfilled her purpose. Some purpose. I would have liked to credit my uncle with having bored her into an early grave, but you could see from her portrait that being dead must have come naturally to my nebbish Aunt Nettie.

"Now Morris," Mama chided him gently, toying with the bangle of her earring, "we mustn't speak ill of the departed." But you could tell that she was kvelling fit to burst. One indication was the way she gazed so fawningly at me, which was not her style. Groaning over what a burden I was to bear — that was more like her. But here she was all agloat, her strapping male offspring a testimony to her strength.

Meanwhile Papa was absorbed by his hard-boiled egg in its bed of charoses, prodding it with his fork as if to coax it into motion. Maybe he expected the tiny bald noggin to lift its hidden face and tell him a story. When he began to speak, it was difficult to tell whether he was talking to the egg or to us. "Your attentions, my brother, have made our Mildred a regular Samson," he said, peering sheepishly over his spectacles.

"Another country heard from," grumbled Uncle Morris, and let it rest. But Mama, for all her ardent blushing, scolded, "Solly, have a heart! You could learn a thing or two from your brother's example." Daintily removing a sliver of chicken from her horsey, carmine-stained teeth, she added mysteriously, "Morris has had his disappointments too."

I supposed she meant he was disappointed that she'd married Solly instead of him, and from his expression Papa must have guessed it too. He went back to studying his egg like a crystal ball. What he saw — I would have bet on it — was himself snug in his pawnshop, safe from the insults of history and his surviving family. He looked as far away as I felt.

The maid reappeared to inform Uncle Morris that someone was in the kitchen to see him. His sense of humor reserved now for business hours only, Papa didn't say it, so I had to say it myself: "It must be Elijah." This captured the momentary interest of Grandpa Isador, who interrupted his lugubrious chewing on the off chance it might be true. Grousing that this someone had better have a good reason for disturbing his peace on this night of nights, Uncle Morris threw down his napkin and waddled out of the dining room. When the door swung inward, I saw what might have been a burnt gingerbread man, popped from the industrial-size oven in front of which he stood. Not until the door swung to again did I realize that I'd seen my papa's puller with cap in hand.

Papa had mentioned that Uncle Morris sometimes "borrowed" Oboy to perform certain odd jobs, and knowing my uncle, I'd figured that they had to be dirty work. This was no concern of mine, but it still came as a shock to see the puller turn up this far from Beale Street. I was aware by now that Oboy's sphere of activities extended beyond the pavement in front of the shop. Nevertheless, I couldn't kick the notion that, if I jumped up and sprinted all the way, I would still find him there on his perch outside Kaplan's Loans.

Uncle Morris returned huffing in his sour apple face, which meant things of moment were on his mind. Oboy might have brought him the message that his tenants were in revolt; they had torched their slum dwellings and stormed the office of his downtown operations. That was the sort of problem I supposed my uncle would have, though as to the actual nature of his business (real estate, wasn't it?), I hadn't a clue.

"Solly," he began offhandedly, stabbing his fork at a slippery lima bean, "if a couple of boys, you know what I mean, should drop by your shop, and if these boys should be looking to un-load —" All of a sudden he lit up in a phony grin. He swiveled his head dummy-style back and forth from his daughter to me and began to chirp, "Hey kids, don't you think it's time to go and look for the afikomen?"

Ordinarily I would have been offended. I hadn't hunted for hidden matzohs in years, not since the times when Papa had made a wild-goose chase out of it, complete with hand-drawn maps full of obstacles and false leads. Nor did I care for the idea of teaming up with my cousin, whom I was practically allergic to. On the other hand, it beat having to sit here and listen to my blowhard uncle angling to involve my father in some shady scheme. It beat having to watch my mother chafe in her stays and declare that she was about to plotz. Besides, after repeatedly toasting the clean getaway of the children of Israel, I'd begun to feel a little woozy. A stroll around the rambling house might be just what I needed.

I rose a bit shakily and followed my cousin from the dining room. Behind us my father was grumbling vaguely, my uncle charging that somebody had to take care of business. It was, after all, "the boys" who made possible what amounted to a charitable foundation.

Naomi and I crossed the vestibule and mounted the carpeted staircase beneath a glorified jack-o'-lantern of a chandelier. Feeling no pain, I was at the same time in need of a focus, some point of reference to help steady the tendency of the stairs to tilt. So I fixed on Naomi's oily topknot, which looked about to tumble, like an unraveling ball of twine. Then I lowered my sights to the hem of my cousin's dress. The material, typically coordinated to match the floral wallpaper, swished to and fro above her scrawny calves. It was a rhythmic swish, a kind of fabric metronome, accompanied by the whisper of her stockings and a jungle drumbeat in my head. It was the sort of thing that could induce hypnosis. So I asked her, if only to break the spell, "Where do you think he hid it?"

She turned at the head of the stairs without replying and gave me a look that seemed to ask what I meant by following her. "The matzoh," I persisted in hopes of refreshing her memory. "Where . . . ?" But, fanning my lips with my fingers *b-b-b-b,* I gave it up in mid-question, suddenly unsure whether Naomi and I were playing the same game.

She tottered in her wobbly pumps down the long hallway, dimly lit by electric candles in brass sconces. Their flickering reflections made altars out of a row of mullioned windows facing the street. A ghostly woman bearing a candelabra, her I could have seen myself pursuing down such a hallway; my flesh-and-mostly-bone cousin was something else. But since my forward momentum seemed anyway irreversible, I thought I might just as well see where she went.

It turned out to be a bedroom so intensely pink it could shrivel your petsel. The precious furnishings looked almost edible, spun-sugar ornaments on a cake. There was a canopied four-poster with a hand-painted headboard, the mattress heaped with satin pillows to protect the princess from the pea. A ruffled curtain in the shape of a valentine framed a cushioned window seat cradling a stuffed-animal zoo. A wide mantelpiece supported a row of delicate porcelain and china dolls in gingham and lace. Their pantaletted gowns formed an awning over a fancy arched fireplace, tucked inside of which was a modest bookcase. With its bowed and slanted shelves, the volumes in disarray, the case looked as if it had been dumped down the chimney. In the midst of all that cloying prettiness, the books seemed out of place.

They were her poor relations, Naomi's books — ghetto urchins who have crashed a fancy-dress ball to hide beneath the unwitting skirts of the ladies. So tell me why I thought that, for all its prevailing frivolity, my cousin's boudoir revolved around those books. Was it because, without their ballast, that airy confection of a room was in danger of floating away? Or was it just that everything else looked untouched? Whereas the books, with their broad creased spines and torn dust jackets showing stitches like undressed wounds, had obviously been the objects of constant handling. Though I couldn't read their titles from where I stood, I suspected that Naomi's books might be pretty heavy going by my standards. They might even belong to the same exclusive brother hood of tedious stuff I'd lugged home from the Front Street library.

My cousin was poised on the edge of a chair in front of her skirted dressing table, gazing intently into a circular mirror as if she couldn't quite place the face. Then she reached up, dislodging a shoulder pad in the process, and removed a pin from her hair. The untidy bun collapsed like a burst bubble of ink, trickling in a twist down her neck. Taking up a silver brush, she proceeded with luxurious strokes to rake her meager tresses into a mild electrical storm. She persisted until her split ends were in full levitation.

She was behaving as if she were in her element, as if she belonged to all that fluffy pink sissification. But I wasn't fooled for a second. Nobody knew better than I the type she was — a slave to books. She could pretend all she wanted, but the books told the story. She would be shackled to them her entire life, dragging ever thicker volumes behind her. They would weigh her down if she tried to grow up. They would see to it that she ended the long solitude of her days as a pixilated old maid, her calendar full of other people's birthdays and yahrzeits.

Standing in the door of her bedroom, I felt stupid. Also a little nauseous, like I'd eaten too much cotton candy. But just as I started to turn away, I could have sworn I heard her speak.

"Maybe it's in here?"

For a moment I thought she'd posed the question to the mirror. "Beg your pardon?"

"The matzoh, silly. Maybe it's in here." She turned to me, aiming one of those pointedly significant looks I'd been dodging throughout dinner.

I might have suggested that we forget the whole business, but instead, a good sport, I shrugged and stepped into her room. In making a show of hunting the afikomen, however, it's possible I went a little overboard in my thoroughness. Suddenly I was the scourge of hidden matzohs. I scattered the throw cushions in the window seat, playing havoc with the quilted unicorns. I manhandled her gallery of dolls, interfering with the cobwebs that moored them to the mantel, coughing over their odor of stale potpourri. With the bookcase I was no more respectful, rifling fat volumes and lean alike, fanning their pages without any temptation to stop and browse.

I was at some pains to conceal my enjoyment from Naomi, nor did I want to see how appalled she must be by my disdain for her things. So I dropped to all fours and stuck my head underneath her bed. What I saw there among the dust kittens was a maverick cache of books with luridly colorful jackets.

"Nothing here," I quickly assured her, bumping my head on the bed frame as I started to rise. This was at least partly due to a sudden movement of my cousin's, which kept me on my knees.

Pivoting away from her vanity as she hummed a lively air ("Ma, He's Makin' Eyes at Me," I think it was), Naomi had hoisted one spindly leg high over the other. Studying me all the while like I was the object of a laboratory experiment, she raised the hem of her dress to her thigh. She did this with a painfully slow deliberation, allowing her humming to dwindle into silence, all the better to savor the *shush* of the dress against silk. Then she hitched up a baggy stocking. She pulled it taut, indolently stroking the long blue vein of the underseam.

As if to punctuate the whole affair, she snapped a garter — the sound penetrating my chest like a gunshot — and inquired with point-blank sincerity, "Harry, do you ever have fun?"

From my half-crouch I tried hard to pretend that here was nothing out of the ordinary. She was fixing a stocking, for God's sake; with legs as skinny as hers, it was no wonder they wouldn't stay up. But my eyes betrayed me. While I made an earnest effort to lift them far enough to meet my cousin's, my eyes found a level of their own, falling irresistibly on Naomi's legs. I was interested, despite myself, in the way the wine-dark sheen of her stocking top met the milk-pallid flesh of her thigh. It looked warm, her naked thigh, a desert island beach where the sea, redolent of roses, washes onto a sandy shore. Then there was the wispy hint — forgive me — of a grotto that beckoned just out of view.

I wanted to ask if this was her way of inviting me to leave no stone unturned in my search for the matzoh. But that was the Passover wine speaking, and something told me that joking would only make things worse. After a first failed attempt during which I felt a little faint, I got up with the intention of giving Naomi an honest reply.

"Do I ever have fun?" I repeated thoughtfully, then tried to turn it into a bold-faced statement: "Do I ever have fun!" But it still came out sounding like a question under consideration.

I suppose you could say that I'd been having a good time in the pawnshop, but ever since I'd crossed over the water on Beale, things had been different. I was different, like a traveler who'd come back from distant lands disguised as a pawnbroker's son. Meanwhile familiar places had begun to seem new to me. For instance, I had become addicted to the rival aromas of North Main Street — boiling cabbage versus baking strudel, rust versus rising sap — as they wafted through my alcove window at night. I liked listening to the neighbors, picking up snatches of their gossip. I liked when their gossip was drowned out by scratchy Galli-Curci or a breeze that carried some phrase of a swing clarinet. I liked trolley bells and sirens and the foghorns from the river barges, baleful as shofars blown by giant Chassidim. And so help me if I didn't take pleasure in looking up my puny cousin's wallflower dress.

Did I ever have fun? I'd had a little, I guessed, but the *real* fun, the *famous* fun — that, I felt, had yet to begin. So to Naomi's question I had only this to reply, my voice skipping up the register till I cleared my throat: "Not much." Then I turned my head from left to right and asked her where else the thingie, the afikomen, might be hidden.

Peevishly, Naomi dropped her hem over her knees and went all shmulky on me again. With a weary impatience she told me to go and look in the dumbwaiter where her father hid the matzoh every year.

$\mathcal{S}$ix

In bed that night I had shpilkes something awful, if you know what I mean. The whole town was cockeyed in the aftermath of the disaster, and I guessed I was no exception to the rule. I'd had my glimpse of the world beyond Third Street, and had finally to admit that all it gave me was an appetite for more. This is not to say that my alcove wasn't cozy, and the pawnshop always had its moments, provided you could find the space to watch them from. But outside, the overrun city was more interesting than any book I knew. There were local attractions as rare as anything that Richard Halliburton, Memphis's home-grown Marco Polo, had crossed oceans to observe. Or so I'd heard.

There was Happy Hollow, for instance, the shantytown at the bottom of the bluff, below the Pinch. That's where the victims of murders, their flesh peeling off like wet paper, were said to wash up under the pilings of houses on stilts, houses constructed out of packing cases and Moxie signs. Towheaded and whey-faced, with eyes like Orphan Annie and shriveled limbs, the citizens of Happy Hollow were popularly bruited to be the issue of fathers and daughters, cousins and cousins, and so forth. There was Mud Island, low-lying as a whale's back in the middle of the river, formed from silt accumulated around a steamboat sunk before the Civil War. That's where the fisherfolk lived in their patchwork tents and converted automobiles, who drank sacramental moonshine on Sundays and danced before the Lord with rattlesnakes in both hands. Also, according to the Chamber of Commerce literature, there was a museum in a pink marble mansion that once belonged to a bankrupt millionaire. There was an aerodrome housing a dirigible as big as Goliath's lung, and a view of three states from a café on top of the Cotton Exchange.

But when I closed my eyes that night after my uncle's Seder, I was voyaging with shvartzers again. This time, for reasons that would not come clear, we had abducted a young white girl bearing an unfortunate resemblance to Naomi, though the girl in question was more amply endowed. We were sailing through fog toward a cannibal-infested coast in search of a legendary lost mine of unleavened bread.

The next afternoon I went back to the famous end of Beale Street. I'd been hanging around the pawnshop, which now bulged so at the seams that Papa talked of annexing the colored dentist's office upstairs. While he was at it, he would take up Joshua's trumpet — which must have been somewhere in stock — and blow down the walls between us and Uncle Sam's Loans on one side, Pinsky's Custom Tailor on the other. Kaplan's would occupy an entire city block, become a Kaplan's World of Loans.

To his regular clientele, Papa had recently added the flood refugees, who straggled in with items that were questionable even by his standards. Nevertheless my papa, with his unquenchable passion for novelty, took in their crocheted samplers and whittled ax helves, their impermeable ascension shrouds, their divining rods like outsize slingshots, and their foul-smelling panacea herbs. But not before he'd heard their sad stories, jotting down the occasional note.

The inventory ledgers took up as many volumes as a Talmud. Their columns of lengthy descriptions and bewildering numerical entries were limned with glosses that overwhelmed the margins, thus giving the pages the actual look of commentary and responsa. This was a recent feature of my father's behavior, how he labored over his ledgers like a scribe, refining and expanding the texts. It wasn't enough, for example, that a wooden crutch belonged to a man who had lost his foot to a snapping turtle; but a cane pole, no apparent relation to the crutch, might once have caught a turtle that slipped from the hook to leave a human foot dangling in its place. In this way my papa endeavored to connect various items along family lines.

It was a method that drove at least one auditor to smoke two packs of Luckys and leave the shop in disgust. It caused the detectives from the pawnshop detail, McCorkle and Priest, to curse the day they'd attempted to make heads or tails of Kaplan's books. I'd watched them flipping the pages in frustration, unable to distinguish the fishy from the legitimate. It was a sight that put me in mind of overgrown cheder boys struggling with a haftorah portion.

So filled to capacity was the pawnshop that Grandma Zippe, were she ever to be properly buried, would first have to be disinterred. Nor had it escaped my attention that the curios surrounding her casket — the ram's horn deaf aids and the painted bisque Betty Boops — had recently been joined by an empty copper samovar.

So how did my dotty papa manage to keep from going belly up? Because, for all of his foolhardy squandering of capital, the cash drawer still seemed bottomless, and the level of our family's newfound affluence had not been reduced. We still enjoyed the freshest whitefish and the choicest cuts of brisket from the butcher, not to mention the most up-to-date in household conveniences, the latest being an electric Hoover, which my mama maneuvered as if she were wrestling the tail of a cyclone. If you subscribed to the theory that my uncle was behind our prosperity, then you had to suppose also that the time would come when he would seek to collect what he was owed.

But on that afternoon following the Seder, the future of my family was hardly even in the running with my major concerns. Besides, with only a minimum of floor space left to accommodate the customers, wasn't it clear that my own services, marginal at best, were no longer required? What choice did I have but to take up a post out on the sidewalk next to Oboy? From there I could at least keep vigil with the puller until my papa had finished walling himself up alive. And after that we could signal prospective customers to pass on.

Of course I had been a little uneasy around Oboy since the night of our rowboat ride. I was grateful on the one hand that he hadn't brought it up, which was as good as saying that my secret was safe. But on the other hand I resented that, for him, the event apparently wasn't worth mentioning. The problem, I suppose, was that I just didn't know how to read such a character — though I decided the best policy was to settle on distrust. Hadn't I seen with my own eyes that he was the servant of at least two masters? What functions he performed for Uncle Morris, I didn't even want to guess. If this so-called puller was making it clear that he didn't need my company, I could assure him the feeling was mutual. That's why, when Papa came out in his apron to hand me a fifty-cent piece, asking me to nip around to Segal's for some seltzer and heart-attack buns, I was glad of an excuse to get away from Kaplan's Loans.

As I walked down toward the bayou overflow, the afternoon sunshine felt intimate, as if it were getting under not only my clothes but my skin. Dutifully I rounded the corner into the dry side of Third Street, heading straight for the delicatessen, but the clamor from across the lagoon kept distracting me. The Negro flood refugees, having been forbidden from the barracks at the fairgrounds, had made their encampment on the little rise of Handy Park. I could see them, just over the road from where I'd paused to look, beating time on their number 9 washtubs, strumming cigar-box banjos, and presiding over the mounted halves of smoking oil drums. I could see the whole show, or all that I needed to anyway, from my own side of the street, though it was hard to distinguish one voice from another. But then why would anyone want to do that? And besides, my papa was waiting for his pastries; I would be missed if I was away too long. Moreover, after the ferry, it wouldn't be nearly as exciting just to walk across Third Street here, above the waterline. Though you had to admit that it involved a good deal less fuss.

Jumping over a gutter full of swimming tadpoles that turned out to be wider than it looked, I had a sensation of leaping on board a departing raft. Then I was in the park and surrounded by voices vying for dominion; snatches of howled and rasping lyrics assailed me from all sides. Someone had a mule as hard-headed as a woman, and vice versa, while someone else had nasty habits that high water couldn't wash clean. One had a boll weevil in his jelly roll, and another was fixing to swap his pillow for the railroad track. There was a preacher on a stump with his thumbs stuck in his armpits like a flapping crow, spouting Pentecost and citing sinners by name: "They's ol Tyrome don't think Jesus know he talkin that talk, and Do Funny Weeums, he jus waitin on Mistah Zero, gon give him a thousand-dollah bill." Behind the preacher a circle of hunkering men, lassoed by smoke, were passing a jar and saying prayers to a pair of yellow dice. They were aped by a bunch of ragged boys gathered around an ashcan lid, tossing knucklebones snatched by a dog half hairless with mange. Broad-beamed mamas balanced clouds of dirty laundry on their heads, cackling evil rumors as they sauntered past: "The gal cain't have no back-do man ef she ain't have no back do." A young girl hollered in her barefoot hokey-pokey as if the patchy grass were on fire; an old man cooed to a catfish in a hubcap full of sputtering oil.

I moved cautiously among them beneath branches through which the sunlight dropped like doubloons, and told myself I was a bold explorer. I was the first white man to have penetrated these remote parts as far as this settlement. It wouldn't have surprised me if they'd welcomed my arrival with gifts: a hog maw in redeye gravy, say, which I would sample with gusto, and to hell with the rabbi's dispensation. So I was disappointed to remark how, wherever I passed, I seemed to put a crimp in everyone's good time. There was the woman nursing her child, for instance, who quickly buttoned her bodice over the head of the suckling infant. There was the character with the striped cane and dark glasses, bottle caps on the soles of his shoes, who left off his tap dancing on a bench when I came near. A hefty kid with rolling shoulders, holding a watermelon over his head, continued to keep his audience in suspense — as if whatever might spill out of the melon after he'd smashed it on a rock were not for my eyes.

Though it hurt my feelings, I was beginning to take the hint. So maybe it wasn't in the best interests of white people to know too much about how the other half lived east of Third. Maybe the natives weren't as friendly as I'd been led to believe, and the color of my skin wouldn't necessarily keep me safe. Maybe it was time to turn tochis and run. But the thought of retracing my steps in front of all those inhospitable eyes gave me a sickly feeling in the gut. Besides, now that I'd almost crossed to the far end of the park, the fastest way out was simply to push on.

I picked my way gingerly over the perimeter of the camp, detouring around the lagoon, which was frankly not so picturesque by day. For one thing, the skiffs, a practical enough mode of conveyance, now had to compete with any number of jerry-rigged contraptions. Wallowing rafts made from uprooted hoardings and unpilotable outriggers rammed everything in sight. I saw a delivery boy on a mired bicycle watching the loaves and tomatoes float out of his basket. I saw mounted cops on skittish horses kicking up a spray that left everyone drenched in what looked like minestrone soup. They splashed the washerwomen sprinkling the water with Oxydol and the man in the hip boots who forged on ahead, indifferent to the curses of the old lady clinging to his back.

Then I was out of that jangling park, if not yet the woods. I had reached by an overland route the northeast corner of Hernando and Beale Street, the famous and fabled and so forth, without even the excuse of having followed Oboy. This time I had only my own bulbous nose to blame.

The street was just about as populous as it had been on the night of my boat ride, though the skylarkers were mostly supplanted now by a more commercial element. Here also was the smorgasbord of voices. Where the farmers had set up shop along the curbs, behind their ramparts of vegetables, the smousers were operating out of raincoats and the tailgates of trucks. Someone was hawking "Greasy greens, don't y'all love em!" and "Yams is what it am!," someone displaying a tree of red felt mojo bags. There was honeycomb, known as the righteous Tupelo sugar tit, "made by the bee have done fed on the blossom a the gospel bush." A woman stood on a chair to introduce a product whose results would give the user a bust as generous as her own, which resembled a pair of water wings. A man placed over his head a metal device called the Kink-No-More.

It was like North Main Street, wasn't it, only with the screws a little looser and the volume turned up — North Main as seen through a funhouse mirror, darkly. And if I knew what was good for me, I should beat it back to my own side of the looking glass. So tell that to my feet, which seemed to have no reverse gear this afternoon. In a minute, however, I would be clear of all the tummel; I would cut over to Gayoso Street and make my way up to Third, having taken a scenic loop back to my father's shop. But the farther I walked along Beale, the farther I felt I had to walk, as if in order to get out of this mess, I had first to pass all the way through.

I was lurking along steadily enough, keeping close to the fronts of buildings, never turning my head for fear of seeing the heads I might have turned. Having edged around a tamale vendor, I scooted behind some grills displaying ribs like fire-damaged xylophones. Then I proceeded at a fair clip past the theater, a greasy spoon café, a saloon or two, a recreation hall loud with the reports of knocking billiard balls. That's when my forward progress snagged temporarily on what I saw in a show window trimmed in faded black bunting.

Sitting there ramrod stiff in a thronelike armchair was a colored gent of untold years. He was wearing a high starched collar gone arsenic yellow with age, a wilted string bow tie, a formal getup ventilated in moth holes that looked like grimy Swiss cheese. Under his flattened chimney-pot hat, behind lopsided spectacles, his eyes were reduced to slots like in a vending machine. His weathered face, which was lightly whiskered and as fierce as a fisted glove, never flinched from its halo of flies. I took account of the awful blue length of his fingernails and the dust that coated his ancient evening clothes; I noted the sign above the window, crudely painted on tin, which declared the place a funeral parlor, and the sign at the foot of the throne: YOUR LOVE ONE PRESERVE FOR ALL ETERNITY. Then it finally sunk in that the old man was a corpse.

At that moment it helped to remind myself that I was still on earth, in Memphis, just the other side of Fourth Street. But at that moment "the other side" had uncomfortable connotations. It put me in mind of what my grandpa called sitra achra, the place where the soul goes after death. It was also the place from which — if certain things went unsettled (such as the burial of mortal remains) — the soul might return to rattle your dishes.

I stumbled away from the mortuary window and got as far as the middle of the block, where I stopped again beside a corkscrewing blue-and-white-striped pole. Adjacent to the pole was a shopfront with a Coca-Cola sign reading MAMBO'S TONSORAL PARLOR. There was a string of red lights around a plate-glass window across which prices had been scrawled in soap:

Harcut & Shav	20¢
Conk & Lektrik Massaj	20¢
Hot Towl & Bay Rum	10¢

Inside, the barbers, in white smocks with military creases, wielded their clippers as if they were conducting a symphony of flying black fleece. Behind them was a long shelf of tonics and pomades in bottles like an oriental skyline. There was a row of basins with blue-tinted mirrors in which you could see the whole shop reversed; you could see my own pale puss off in the distance, looking out at myself looking in. High on a wall was a flag-draped portrait of President Roosevelt, and next to it a stenciled sign warning *No Dozen Playin Aloud*. There was a blacking stand in the corner where an elegantly turned-out character sat in a raised tubular chair. Kneeling at his feet, a kid in a floppy cap was giving his two-tones the once-over with a chammy cloth. Even from where I stood, you could see that, as he worked, the kid was jabbering away.

With the benefit of hindsight I understood that this had been my destination all along. I took a breath and opened the door to the barbershop, stepping in before my better judgment could intercede.

Everybody froze. Scissors stopped in mid-snip, razors stalled in nicked chins from which blood refused to flow. Patrons lowered their newspapers and raised their brows. Like resurrecting mummies, they unwound steaming towels from their faces. Everyone was staring in bafflement, including the shoeshine boy, who'd swiveled about to reveal himself as none other than Lucifer, the moonlighting navigator. But even that was small comfort to me now. So what was it made me think that white boys didn't stroll into colored barbershops every day?

I wanted to tell them to relax, Harry Kaplan ain't exactly John Dillinger, but the best I could muster was a feeble grin. So confusing was their reception that I found myself waiting for someone to tell me why I was there. Seconds passed before I remembered that the explanation was mine to give. Odors of hair oil and rose water stung my nostrils till I almost reeled; I closed my eyes and saw a missionary trying to offer a reason why he shouldn't be made into soup. Then it came to me, albeit slowly, that my journey had in fact had a purpose from the outset. I had come all this way, hadn't I, just to settle accounts, to fork over the return passage that I still owed the twins. In lieu of finding my tongue, I shoved my hand in my pocket and produced my papa's ink-stained fifty-cent piece.

I stood idiotically in the middle of the shop, holding up the coin as if I thought it could deliver me from any tight spot. Only its spell-breaking properties seemed to be defunct. But just as I was wondering if this general paralysis might endure until the coming of the Messiah — kaynehoreh! — Lucifer turned back toward his client long enough to crack his cloth in a final flourish, then stood up and recollected me out loud.

"Mistah Harry from the pawnshops!" he declared to my limitless relief, doffing his cap to fan his bright face as he shambled forward. "Well now, as I live and breave, this indeed a most pleasant suh-prise."

His eyes goggled as he snatched the half-dollar, proving its authenticity with a chomp before dropping it into a yawning pant pocket. There was a breathless second, then a clink as the coin hit bottom. This was apparently the signal for the barbershop, satisfied that I wasn't quite a stranger, to resume its suspended activity.

The spotlight was off me, and Lucifer and I were almost as good as alone. At least that's what I felt, or how else would I have found the gumption to remind him, "That's um, let's see," strewing hair around the tiles with the toe of my sneaker, "forty-five cents change I still got coming." But Lucifer was already a step ahead of me, chattering as if he hadn't heard a word I'd said.

"Ordinary, this here four bits get you a mess a ferryboat rides," he assured me, selling the point with his keyboard's worth of teeth. "Onliest thang bein we done retire from that partikler enterprise." In the barely perceptible shift of his eyes, I could imagine the hasty abandonment of the skiff, the hotfooted exit pursued by the oilskin man. "Now, do you woosh to make a sportin investment, they's this popular game a chance what am the current fashion." He paused for a between-you-and-me sort of look. "An I just might could see my way clear to advise yo venable self all about it."

I kept wagging my head like I knew what he was talking about, though I hadn't a clue — something to do with a game called policy and the way that it was related to your dreams.

"Dream you flyin, put yo smart money on numbah five. Now say you dream you done lost yo left leg, numbah two is yo man, tha's the numbah to remumbah. Lose yo right leg an play the combo, one two three. Wet yo bed, tha's a lucky seven." By this time my jaw had begun to hang. "Wake up with a worry mind, put yo wage on numbah nine. Tell ol Swami Lucifer yo dream an I tells you what to play. I got some power . . ."

While I was still trying to grasp the concept, Lucifer promised me beginner's luck and the sure-fire benefits of his proven expertise. Then he remembered that he had first to collect his book of tickets. They were over at a place called the Baby Doll Hotel, where he had anyhow some pressing business to conduct. I was about to tell him thanks all the same but I'd never been much of a gambler, when he turned to the gent who'd stepped down off the blacking stand. As he helped the man into a box-back sport coat, taking a whisk broom to the shoulders, Lucifer tossed an offhand remark in my direction: "Come on along do you like."

Here the spiffy customer made a fussy inspection of his pocketwatch. "Yassuh," chimed Lucifer, "it gone time on-the-money fo to carry you to yo pointment in the lap a glory." Then, ceremoniously presenting his client's straw hat, he began to back toward the rear of the shop, beckoning the man the way you'd encourage an infant to take its first steps.

When they'd disappeared through the curtained doorway, I waited for conversation to stop again, but Lucifer's recognizing me seemed to have done the trick. The place was still humming, though not necessarily about yours truly. And while I didn't want to push my luck by outwearing my welcome, neither was I anxious to return to the conspicuous anonymity that awaited me back on Beale. Not to mention the reception I could expect at Kaplan's when I turned up without the pastries or the fifty cents.

Hurrying past the garrulous barber chairs, I ducked through the curtain into a storeroom lit only by its open back door. Immediately I was face to face with the boy whose aggressive silence announced him as Lucifer's unidentical twin. With his head wrapped in a bandanna that pinned back his ears and practically hid his eyes, he was pushing sawdust around the floor with a long-handled broom. He pushed with the same deliberateness that he'd applied to his boat oar, like somebody swabbing the deck of a ship that's been otherwise abandoned by all hands. A little flustered, I raced out the door and across an alley, stepping over a trampled wire fence to catch up with Lucifer. Though his client turned, the wise guy was much too busy with his come-on to acknowledge my tagging along. He was promising the man (whose stiffness suggested he'd already had an earful) that it was soon to be Christmas in April. It was coming up get-down time. I coughed once or twice to let him know I was there.

We were kicking through a rubbish-filled back yard where a rusty clothes wringer, half sunk in mud, did a poor impression of a wishing well. There was a foul-smelling wooden privy on top of which sat a featherless rooster, like a weather vane come partially alive. A clothesline, strung from the outhouse to the porch of a narrow three-story building, sported an array of ladies' bright waving scanties. They bussed your cheek as you stooped to pass underneath. With Lucifer still arm-in-arm with his client, we mounted the tilting back steps. Through a screen door we entered a passage that was dense with a stew of odors. Dry rot, boiled meat, and cat spray were what I recognized, but what I didn't recognize, I somehow associated with sin. All along the dim passage Lucifer kept insisting that his man was about to think he was dead or dreaming. "Gon think you the Lawd High Muckamuck a Fanny Land." Then we rounded a staircase at whose foot was a bamboo curtain, which the wise guy flung dramatically apart.

What I'd been prepared to see, I saw: a cavern of topaz light inhabited by languid mermaids. Then I blinked and a tawdry room appeared. It was a room that hadn't decided whether to be an exotic harem or a more or less respectable parlor, and so made halfhearted pretensions toward each. There were cheesy chintz draperies through which the sunlight was sifted into a fine brown dust, brass cuspidors anchoring the corners of a woven carpet, floor lamps covered in veils of red gauze. On top of a cast-iron mantelpiece, framing a gas stove, was a collection of guttering aromatic candles. (They had been poured into the shapes of bearded heads, these candles, their features melted to monstrous stalactites.) There was a neon clock, an enamel Dixie Peach calendar on a water-stained wall, and a portrait of a gimlet-eyed Jesus with a rich golden tan. A footstool supported a phonograph playing a record of what sounded like a tomcat in the rain. Around the phonograph, relaxing in moss-grown armchairs and sunk in a deep-cushioned divan, were several women of dusky hue.

They were wearing kimonos in orchid prints and pastel dressing gowns. Some of the gowns were left carelessly open, revealing silk shimmies and stockings rolled to the knee. One of them, with her crossed leg kicking, her full lips in a pout like a lilac bow, was sniffing powder from a pillbox with a straw. Another, whose buttery bosom was barely contained by a torn lace border, rolled the condensation from a jar of chartreuse liquid round her brow. A yellow girl in a short white slip was kneeling beside the draperies, her wavy ocher hair spread across the wing of a table. Standing over her, a turbaned woman in a skin-tight housedress licked a pinkie to test the heat of the flatiron in her hand. She made a similar gesture with sizzling sound effects as she touched the finger to the curve of her backside. When she put down the iron on the girl's lush hair, the room was suffused with an odor of burnt oranges.

Meanwhile on the divan, a pair of ladies sharing a single cushion, their arms about each other's shoulders, made turtledove noises as they passed a pipe back and forth. From its shallow clay bowl rose arabesques of azure smoke, out of which you might imagine that the room had just materialized.

"Frail sustahs, may I have yo undivide tention if you please!" This was Lucifer demanding to be heard, flagging the women with his cap, though not one of them so much as bothered to look his way. "I have the distink pleasure," he went on undaunted, "of introduce to you Mistah . . ." He turned toward the dapper client, who only grunted. "Mistah Rather-Not-Say," christened Lucifer, "a traveler in notion what tooken a notion to sample y'all wares."

He grinned in appreciation of his own turn of phrase and, his mission apparently accomplished, held his empty cap under the traveling gent's nose. But the gent proved as tight with his pocketbook as with his name. This prompted Lucifer to expand on the special generosity of the colored traveling salesman, who understood the value of a hard-earned dollar, and so forth. When it began to look like the proceedings would not be hastened any other way, the gent dropped some change in the cap; and when the cap never moved, he was forced to cough up some more, each coin increasing the width of Lucifer's grin. It made you wonder what it would take to extend the grin a full three hundred and sixty degrees.

Summoned from dreams, the pair of ladies rose in unison from the divan, moving in a fluid traipse toward the traveling salesman. Stationed in what I took to be relative safety (between the doorpost and a fishbowl on a pedestal), I watched them remove his straw hat and muss his freshly embrocated hair. The hair remained in upstanding spikes like a woodpecker's crest. By the time they'd enticed him into the depths of the divan, they had his coat off, his tie undone, his paisley suspenders pulled down over his shoulders. They'd picked his pockets, relieving him of wallet and watch, never mind his unshakable composure of moments before. Rather than made comfortable, he looked, as he slumped between them, succumbing to their dalliance, like a patient being prepared for surgery.

Clearly amused by his client's broken defenses, Lucifer couldn't resist adding insult to injury. "When they done with you, m'fine feather frien," he taunted, "you ain't remember yo name do you got one."

It was then that the building began to shake. Maybe I was a little distraught, because my first thought was that the city was on a major fault line. Crevices might be rupturing the surface of the earth, broadening the lagoon till the distance between this place and my father's shop was unbridgeable. With every tremor the record skipped, the tomcat hiccuped. Then the bamboo parted beside me with a sound like breaking glass and the seismic disturbance stopped, its source having descended the stairs and entered the parlor.

Keeping my head down at first, I saw her feet stuffed into worn mules, the protruding toes wrapped for bunions like bonneted babies. Gathering courage, I saw the thick maple trunks of her legs. She was wearing a flowery housecoat as large as a landscape, hung on hulking shoulders surmounted by a perspiring, monolithic head. Her hair was a nest of curlers over which she was pulling on a tangerine wig.

"Loosfer boy," she singsonged in a genial, high-pitched voice, "you got some rascal mouf almighty on you. It gon get you strung up one a these day." With a movement that was all of a piece, nimble despite her bulk, she snatched the flat bottle out of the wise guy's coat and cuffed his ear. She uncorked it and took a deep pull before consigning it to a pocket of her housecoat. "Everybody gettin quainted in here?" she continued in her cheerful vein. "Now you gals make the genleman feel to home. Sugar Monkey, don't be mess with his private e-fex, you hear, or I switch ya." She wiped her glazed forehead with the bladderlike back of her hand. "Do one a y'all kindly loan me yo hosanna fan? It a mite sticky this afternoon."

So far, happily forgotten, I'd been enjoying a measure of invisibility. But as the fat lady plodded forward, smiling with a menacing sweetness at the beleaguered salesman, I began to feel pretty vulnerable myself. I hugged the wall, managing, as I edged toward a corner, to sidle into the wooden pedestal supporting the fishbowl. The pedestal toppled with a resounding thud, though not before I was able to get under the bowl. Then, with all eyes upon me, it was the barbershop all over again.

The fat lady pivoted her head on neckless shoulders, giving a malevolent squint that nailed me in place. Trying not to cower, I presented the bowl of flat-headed, mustachioed fish like a peace offering. She pointed a pudgy finger and changed her tune. "What this?" she inquired, frowning. Her voice, having dropped several octaves, was practically a baritone now, a voice that you felt like a growling stomach.

I turned hopefully toward Lucifer, who was looking like he couldn't quite place me either. Was I supposed to come up with another coin? He circled me warily, chewing his lip, yet to decide whether it behooved him to identify me twice in one day. I urged him with a look to be big about this. In the end, please God, he awarded me a conciliatory wink, whispering the word "supper" as he relieved me of the dingy fish. He raised the pedestal and replaced the bowl.

"This here be Mistah Harry from the pawnshops," he volunteered at length, though his usual hubris seemed a little subdued in the presence of the giantess. "He have come down to try his luck at the policy sweepstake. Meantime I be scortin him round the Negro quarter, kinda edumacate him bout the lay a the land." His voice swelled as he tugged at my sleeve, which caused me to stumble forward. "Mistah Harry" — always the soul of diplomacy — "I delight for yo honah to meet my gracious Aunt Honey, the very one have fetch I an my brother out the bullrush. She'm the awful grand propriatricks of this fine stablishment, which it is known far and wide as the Baby Doll Hotel."

I looked up at her avalanche of flesh, the chins rolling in terraces toward her bosom, where the whole prodigious mudslide disappeared into the arbor of her billowing housecoat. My thoughts turned from earthquakes to volcanos.

"Happy to know you," I stammered, a salutation that came out like a question. "I'm sure," I added, hoping to resolve the ambiguity. I even went so far as to extend a hand, which, because of my nervous condition, shook itself. This earned me a sonorous horse laugh from Aunt Honey. The windowpanes rattled, the floorboards buckled like waves.

"Got nice manners, don't he," she nickered, coming closer to drop her heavy hand on my shoulder, further weakening my knees. Then, sharing the wind from her fluttering fan (which might have blown me away but for her leaden grip on my shoulder), she was ominous again, her narrowed eyes nearly lost in the folds of her lacquered face. "Mistah Harry," she inquired, placing her fan-holding hand on my other shoulder to correct the list, "yo people know where you at?"

Detecting a way out, since out of this fix was where I was definitely ready to get, I wanted to tell her no. I wanted to say that as a matter of fact, given the unaccountable length of my absence, my people were probably speculating on my whereabouts even now. That is, if they hadn't already panicked, notifying the authorities, who might be tracking me down as we spoke. But the best I could manage was a tongue-tied shake of the head.

Meanwhile one of the ladies had glided over. It was the chartreuse sipper, rampant tsitskehs nosing curiously out of the torn lace of her camisole, who began to run her fingers through my hair. "Bout nappy as a home boy" was her disappointed conclusion, though it didn't discourage her from continuing to tease. Then another pair of hands, very slender and cloyingly fragrant, began to snake their way around my ribcage from behind. They invaded my shirtfront from which a button popped.

Aunt Honey stepped back to cock her head and fold her ham-size forearms, the flab hanging off them like unfurling sails. "What game it was you say that Mistah Harry come lookin to play?" she insinuated. Lucifer, to whom I silently petitioned for help, favored me with his most patronizing grin so far.

Ticklish as I was ordinarily, I couldn't laugh. In fact, no sound escaped my throat beyond a miserable whimpered squeak. It was the squeak you sometimes heard out of bubbling mashed potatoes. In seconds I would be reduced to the same degraded circumstance as what was left of the traveling sales-man on the divan. The ladies — with their hair of floating seaweed, with their gills and their tailfins shaped like simper-ing lips — would drag me down, and I would drown here in a fleshpot a couple of blocks and an ocean away from Kaplan's Loans.

The problem was that I didn't think I would particularly mind. They could have done whatever they wanted with me, if I hadn't been so scared. If good old fear hadn't rattled my bones, even as they were turning to mush, and given me the strength to break free.

"Thank you for your hospitality!" I cried out like bloody murder. As well as I was able on rubber legs, I bolted through the bamboo curtain and made blindly for the nearest crack of light.

I don't think I'd ever been so happy to see the pawnshop. Hav-ing wheeled around the corner from Third Street, I burst in panting on my papa, who was poring over his books. "I'm back!" I declared, like he should slaughter a fatted calf. Not only did he fail to look up at my entrance, to take note of how recent experience had marked my face for life with a terrible knowledge, not only did he ignore his only son, who elsewhere had brought brothels and barbershops to heel, but he never even missed the pastries I hadn't bought with the money I'd forfeited.

Later that night in my alcove I couldn't sleep. I wrestled with my pillow, which kept turning into a woman the color of twi-light. Then I wrestled with my conscience. After all, there was a point of honor at stake: the matter of forty-five cents change that had yet to be refunded. That Lucifer, he was some kind of sharper all right, and I for one didn't like being taken in. Of course you could argue that the wise guy had bailed me out of a couple of tight situations, never mind how he might have gotten me into them in the first place. And as for having been careless with Kaplan capital, so what? You had to get up awfully early to be more careless than Kaplan himself, who threw away cash like confetti at a parade.

But if it wasn't the money, then what was it that prompted me to put on my glasses, to slip out of my pajamas and into my pants at such an advanced hour of the night? Was it really that I thought I had something to prove to some motor-mouthed colored bunco artist? It's the principle of the thing, I decided, and left it at that, stuffing some dirty clothes under the covers — this in case my father should look in on me, as he sometimes did when he came home from the shop. I pulled on my sneakers and straddled the open window, swinging into the branches of the blossoming mimosa tree.

The spring peepers peeped, the katydids ululated like bicycle bells. The night air, laced with honeysuckle and the high taint of the river, went immediately to my head; I felt, give or take forty-five cents, like a million bucks. I dropped into the alley and picked my way through rank grass, stepping over the corroded pedal cars. Rather than turn toward North Main, which was certainly quiet enough, I preferred to seek out other alleys and back streets. That way, with the stars as my compass, I traveled toward Beale by a kind of underground railroad.

At the corner of Beale and Hernando, there was the usual crush of frantic activity despite the late hour. I walked along briskly, pumping my arms, so that anyone looking would think that the white boy must be on urgent business, let him pass. Intending to head straight for the tonsorial parlor, I glanced to neither the left nor the right. I tried also to disregard their voices, lest some discouraging word tossed my way should spoil my good mood. Still, I couldn't help catching the odd remark: somebody making supernatural claims for an alto saxophone, somebody threatening to send somebody else home directly — "What you mean *home?*" "Mean yo home over Jordan, fool!" — somebody saying, "Whoa now, looka here Michael, the man be smoke up the road!"

It took me the better part of a block to put on the brakes and turn around. I hadn't quite counted on how apprehensive I would be to see him. He was standing next to a fireplug in his undershirt and rug coat, his hands thrust nearly to the elbows in his gaping pockets. It was a posture studiously duplicated by his brother beside him in the ragged straw hat and overalls.

"Mistah Harry," commented Lucifer when I'd come back within greeting distance, "you must be the most runninest white folks in town."

I wanted to explain to him how, when last seen, I wasn't exactly running away. It was just that I'd remembered I had important matters to attend to. There was no end to the responsibilities associated with a pawnshop, he should understand. But instead, still winded from my long dogtrot through the alleys from North Main Street, I leaned casually against the fireplug, like I was accustomed to taking the air at this hour in shvartzer neighborhoods.

There followed an awkward moment when Lucifer, who'd hailed me amiably enough, retreated to a more impersonal "Hidey."

"Hidey," I replied with perhaps a little too much bluster, picturing in my agitation a colored girl picking edelweiss on a mountainside. Then I braced myself and came right out with it. "That forty-five cents you still owe me." At the mention of this Lucifer made a face like he hadn't the foggiest. Like, even if he knew what I was talking about, it didn't erase the fact that certain parties were starting to become a nuisance. So be it, I thought: a nuisance is better than the chicken-livered wonder I was determined he shouldn't see again. "Course, it's all the same to me," I went on, "but now that I think of it, that forty-five cents . . . How much, you know, sightseeing will it get me?"

Lucifer reared back with his hands on his hips to size me up, shaking his head like I just wouldn't do. He tugged at an earlobe to coax the subtle workings of his brain, then looked toward the silent twin for advice. When none was forthcoming, nothing but the other's somber vacancy, Lucifer nodded anyway; the point was well taken. Pulling a toothpick out of his cap, he began to pick at a point of light that gleamed from a prominent incisor.

"I have you to know," he formally announced, "that I an my honable brothah, we bout to commence our shank-a-the-evenin round. Got to visit certain underworld stablishment. Be proud do you woosh to company the bofe of us two."

It was a dare only thinly disguised as an invitation. But before I could puff myself up enough to answer, the wise guy had already started to walk away. "Jus say uncle when you done had enough," he added over the shoulders of himself and his brother, who shambled in lockstep at his heels.

I told myself that this was what I'd come for, wasn't it? — though I wished he'd given me time to study the pros and cons. But never mind. I intended to show him what I was made of, how I had graduated in a single afternoon from a fraidycat to a full-fledged I-don't-know-what. The word "goat" came to mind.

The way the kid behaved, you'd have thought that he owned the street, which I was perfectly content to believe. Dogging Lucifer's coattails, slightly to the rear of his brother's single-strapped overalls, I was happy to be a shadow once removed. Hadn't I been sore thumb enough for one day? I kept close behind them with my profile low, imitating a little (as did his brother Michael) Lucifer's loose-limbed walk — the way his hands scooped the air as in a swimmer's stroke. Once I paused only long enough to do a double take at the spectacle of a one-man band. Then I learned, as I hurried to catch up with them, just how much I didn't want to be left behind.

When I asked what exactly was the nature of these evening rounds, Lucifer turned to say only, "Round mean lak in a circle." But pretty soon it became apparent that what they were doing was running errands. They were couriers, delivering messages to men in Stetsons with snakeskin hatbands. Men with hair like crows' wings and parts like zippered seams, with gold-inlaid stars in their teeth. These were none too friendly characters whom Lucifer didn't seem to mind distracting from intense pursuits. They might be, for instance, involved in drawing a bead down the shaft of a custom pool cue; they might be blowing on a pair of dice or shuffling cards with such dexterity that it looked like they were playing accordion — when Lucifer chose to butt in.

With his mouth running in its fluent patter, he took what looked to me to be dangerous liberties, hailing these rough customers by name. "Hello Hardface. Shithouse, how do, y'all still on the ruination train? Ol Nine Tongue here be drinkin that ugly milk, fo long his head turn to a biscuit. What say Mastah Ajax, which his mama she be teachin me to lawdy-lawd. An they's Race Riot hissef, what I'm hear got him a sissy man . . ."

From the depths of his fathomless pockets, he would draw forth the ribbon-bound envelopes that the men sniffed discerningly. Then they appointed the scholar among them to read aloud, for the edification of all, the sometimes amorous, sometimes petulant (often vengefully poison-pen) billets-doux from the ladies of the Baby Doll Hotel. After that the scholar, turned scribe, would draft a dictated reply, naming rendezvous and such. This was dutifully scrolled and handed back to Lucifer along with his gratuity. Sometimes there were tokens exchanged in the transaction — say, a lady's frilly nothing for a gentleman's solid-gold something — which Lucifer might fetch from and return to an office annex under his brother's headrag.

Occasionally the tidings were not so welcome: subpoenas and court summonses for those who used the Baby Doll as their mailing address. Then I noticed that the wise guy's tip wasn't so readily forthcoming.

Sometimes Lucifer carried their markers. These were items toward which the gamblers, usually seated in front of a depleted stack of chips, would profess a deep sentimental attachment. They were rabbit's feet, cat's-eyes, souvenir bullets dug out of old gunshot wounds — apparently anything would do. One character at a rummy table offered the lesser half of a wishbone; another yanked a dogtooth out of his grimacing head, spitting gobs of blood onto the floor. Then the markers were dutifully carried to fat men eating ribs in airless back rooms. (Rooms even farther back than the back rooms were where the gambling took place.) The fat men would in turn, and according to the reputation of the man who'd sent the token, either grumble, spit, or flick ashes, which meant to get lost. Or else they would hand over a wad of grease-stained bills.

That's how it was that I got to see the Monarch Club of evil repute. "This a bad luck house where the boss man get put on the spot bout oncet a week," Lucifer had informed me, making a revolver out of his forefinger and thumb. "Putty soon ain't nobody be boss less they dead already, livin mens need not apply. See that skillethead over by the do?" He pointed toward an obsidian gorilla in a double-breasted suit. "Tha's Big Six the take-off man, like to mess with folks' bones an he ain't no doctah. So ugly he hurt yo feelins, now don't he?"

If he was trying to scare me, then all right, I was scared. What else was new? But I was also glad that he'd begun to take the time to talk to me. I was glad that he remembered I'd come along, even if it was only to remind me of the terrible, sinister places we were in. Besides, had I decided to break and run — which I confess that I was once or twice inclined to do — I would have been on my own again. And the thought of facing

116

the street all alone, now that I'd gotten used to the cover of their company, made me stick even closer to the twins.

When he realized that I wasn't going anywhere, Lucifer eventually began to drop the scare tactics. Then he was anxious, in his proprietary manner, that I shouldn't overlook the classier features of a nightclub's decor. "Ain't nothin can compare this side a King Keedoozle commode!" he'd boasted as we entered the Club Panama, waving a hand that took in brass rails and leather banquettes, a fairy ring of lights around the dance floor. There was a raised bandstand where the soloist for the Rhythm Hounds, a lady horn player in a gown like an aluminum rain barrel, had been brought to her knees by her own shrill signature. People at the tables jerked and squirmed as if the music were running loose in their clothes. They hallelujahed as the lady unbent her high note and allowed it to dissolve in the air. Then it seemed that the music had vaporized into the lavender smoke that hung over the green gaming tables at the rear of the room.

As the night wore on, Lucifer became ever more expansive, as if he'd made a decision that nothing should be lost on me. The sights that had been previously supposed to inspire fear now seemed to serve only for my enlightenment. In Pee Wee's Saloon, bobbing his head in time, he called my attention to an upright piano: "This what you call the hesitashum beat, an tha's the very bar it own self where Mistah Handy done first writ down the blues" — indicating it the way my grandfather might have pointed toward Sinai.

On top of the bar, in the absence of Mr. Handy, a kiss-curled tootsie was lifting her dress to bang together cymbal-clad knees. A dusty crowd was milling about in the acid yellow light, some dancing a slow drag near the piano, others clustered around the bumpered crap tables. These tables, as Lucifer (like a flea in my ear) divulged confidentially, could be converted to billiards the second that the cops arrived. By the same token, the roulette wheel became a clock on the wall, and the lottery barrel a canary cage. In fact, the whole place was fraught with contrivances that instantly transformed the furniture from its felonious purposes back again to innocence. Which was maybe why Pee Wee's was also known as the Garden of Eden.

There was a portrait on the wall of a giant Negro with a head like a polished plum, straddling an angry ocean in which a ship was going down. Again Lucifer: "Tha's Jack Johnson was worl champeen, which the XX *Titanic* have refuse to carry him on board." Beneath the painting was a bench where a group of old men, several of them amputees, were holding guitars and beat-up cornets like badges of office. These, I was told, were the emeritus musicians whose years on the road had cost them literally an arm and a leg. But as Lucifer assured me: "It don't take but three fanger to play the blues Delta-style."

Here I would have liked to toss in a tidbit of my own, just to show I wasn't so dumbstruck as some. Unlike the tagalong brother Michael, for instance, I had a mouth. I tried to tell the wise guy that in my own neighborhood there was also a bench. There the old kockers sat in front of another tonsorial parlor, missing digits that the Cossacks had relieved them of long years ago. But before I could finish my footnote, Lucifer was in motion again.

Even on the street he made every minute count. Brazenly he collared members of the colored baseball league strutting in their red-socked uniforms, their cleats on the sidewalk like munching teeth. He stopped the roustabouts and country boys stumbling out of juke joints, pie-eyed from too much temptation. He hooked thumbs in the bibs of their overalls and stood on tiptoe to whisper in their ears. Then they would lick their lips, their eyes waxing banjo, and turn over whatever they had in their pockets. Like sheep they would follow Lucifer and Michael (and Harry!) around the corner and through the portals of the Baby Doll Hotel.

As the designated envoys of their redoubtable Aunt Honey, the wards of the Baby Doll had carte blanche everywhere. And Lucifer, he was a regular Pied Piper of Beale Street. Running with him, I began to feel almost indestructible, like when someone touches the Baal Shem's robe in a holy story. So long as you hung on tight, you could go anywhere; you could travel out of time to paradise. Or you could plunge into the thick of some dank and flyblown hole-in-the-wall, where Lucifer would shout "Western Union!" or any of a dozen variations on "Open, Sesame" to clear the way.

Then we would nudge and shove through an overheated press of stump drinkers, of dancers shaking in the throes of the shimmy-she-wobble. (I was beginning to pick up the lingo.) We crossed floors so sticky with tobacco juice, bellywash, and blood, for all I knew, that they squished like a swamp under the soles of your shoes. I heard hysterical laughter and language that could have wilted flowers. I saw cryptic high signs and tempers at the end of short fuses, a man in a corner fingering the outline of the pistol in his pocket, a woman on a table skirt-dancing herself into a stupor. I saw rose-colored lights illuminating the cavern of a crooner's mouth, his uvula vibrating like the devil's own speed bag. I saw the lights playing off sweat-spangled shoulders and cheeks, saw them flash from a drawn knife blade. In short, I kibbitzed to my heart's content a life that was never meant for my eyes. A life that waited until gentlefolk were safely tucked in their beds before coming out to play.

If anybody looked askance at me or aimed some barbed remark my way, I never noticed. In league with Lucifer, I'd begun to take it for granted that I shared his immunity. Not only did I feel unthreatened, but I'd begun to assume that my presence was as naturally accepted (or ignored) as the twins'. That's why I missed my stride when a gambler in one of the dives, his splayed nose spread like a sand dollar over his face, brusquely called me to his table.

"Hey white folks," he'd tipped back his chair to ask me, "y'all mind do I rub yo hade for good luck?" After I'd obliged and he'd frowned his dissatisfaction with my hair, that it lacked the fine texture he'd been led to expect from my race, I froze. I groped for an excuse. But before my backbone could turn entirely to jelly, Lucifer was there beside me to set him straight.

"He ain't white," he was sorry to have to inform the gambler. "He Jewrish."

Seven

fter that first night I began to sneak out of the apartment two, sometimes three nights a week. Sometimes I stayed out till the small hours, coming home even later than my father, whose shop was often the last on Beale Street to close. On such nights I would only have time to catch a couple of winks before getting up for school. My teachers — imposing women in durable tweeds, formidable of bosom and tush, "bout six months in front and nine months behind" as Lucifer might have said — were large on discipline. They were ever vigilant, quick to resort to thumping with thimbles and hacking with rulers, to confining you to the purgatorial depths of the broom closet. Nevertheless, though they caught me catnapping with some regularity in my classes, they tended to let it go. I took this as a measure of just how inconsiderable I was in their eyes. Also, while my years in books had marked me for a social nobody among my classmates, they had given me a knack for making tolerable grades. So if my teachers thought anything about me at all, it was probably that I'd been burning the midnight oil.

As for my family, they had their own affairs to attend to. Out of sight, it was safe to assume, I was out of their minds. That *they* might be out of their minds was another subject, though even the casual observer couldn't help noticing that the Kaplan household seemed to have entered a state of decline.

More cantankerous than ever, Grandpa Isador had stepped up his campaign of waylaying homeless yokels in Market Square Park. To their greater confusion he regaled them about the false messiah of Germany and his latest crimes against the Jews. Recent evidence had revealed that they were being dispatched by the boatload for ports that everywhere denied them entry; the seas were littered with a second diaspora of wandering Jewish ships, condemned to sail for all eternity without hope of landfall. Meanwhile you'd have thought that my papa maybe subscribed to such wild disclosures, that he bought them the way he bought the bogus merchandise filling his shelves, because he dug himself ever deeper into the burrow of his shop.

In her virtual abandonment my mama turned to the rock of Uncle Morris. It was to him she petitioned for help in her efforts to have old Isador put away. Of the various available bughouse institutions, she was leaning, for reasons of convenience and economy, toward the Western State Asylum at Bolivar. This was a place where, according to my father, the inmates were frequently murdered, after first being made to sign over their earthly holdings to the asylum. The dead were then ground into meal and force-fed to the living, chained to their racklike beds — or so it was rumored. My uncle, whose blowsy waistcoat and roving smokestack cigar were now fixtures around the apartment, assured Mama that he was checking out the possibilities. And lately, cruising around in the afternoons in his cucumber-green touring car, my mama and Uncle Morris had begun to check out the possibilities together.

In the midst of all this I was as happily neglected as Grandma Zippe behind the chicken-wire cage. With the habit of making lists that I owed to my apprenticeship at Kaplan's, I took an inventory. Item: my family had certain notable screws loose, which who could deny. Item: the streets were awash with a multitude of ghostly strangers, among whom my grandfather conducted a tireless search for righteous men. Item: on top of which, the city had run riot with growing things — blue morning glories, yellow japonica, pink dogwood, wisteria seeping like purple sap from anything standing still. Was it any wonder that with so much going on in the way of distraction, nobody noticed that Harry Kaplan had begun to lead a double life?

If Papa no longer seemed to remember why he'd invited me to come and work in his shop, then I could forget just as easily. What's more, I'd become impatient with my papa's indifference to what were clearly disreputable goings-on. What else could you conclude when you saw Oboy repeatedly give up his post to confer with questionable characters on the street? Characters with eyes that ticked like windshield wipers and black sandpaper jaws, whom I'd heard him direct to the loading dock in back. While I couldn't quite believe that my papa was in cahoots with the puller, neither could I believe he was entirely innocent of what went on under his nose.

Weaned from any lingering sense of duty to the pawnshop, I nevertheless continued to stick around. Write it down to force of habit, though the shop still remained a good vantage from which to keep your eye on the hijinks in the lagoon. There was also the matter of my weekly salary, which, even if it amounted to little more than carfare, was certainly better than nothing at all. In the meantime, though he didn't ask and I didn't offer my assistance in taking stock anymore, I was there if Papa needed to send me out on errands. I didn't mind going if he didn't mind my sometimes taking roundabout routes to get there; it was a way to kill time in the afternoons. And late at night, two, three, sometimes four nights a week, I escaped out my alcove window.

I liked the secret disgrace of running with shvartzers, of having forbidden friends, if that's what you want to call them. Of course I didn't really include the dummy Michael, who'd been thrown into the bargain, like it or not. Nor did I believe for an instant Lucifer's ridiculous claim that his sullen shadow had a passion for reading books. Tell me another. With his hunched-over shoulders and his slouching gait, the slow shifting of his hooded eyes, Michael might have auditioned for Oboy's understudy. But where the stationary puller was sometimes given to fits of bustling animation, Michael was always the same steady goon. He was his brother's dim creature, good for nothing but following orders and keeping unobtrusively out of the way. And if Lucifer sometimes deferred to him, asking advice that was never given, this was only out of playfulness, the way you'd talk to a pet. Nor was I fooled by a brightness that occasionally invaded the dummy's eye, like a light switched on and off in a deserted house.

But that Lucifer, he was another story. For a while he'd continued to make out that our relationship was purely in the nature of a business arrangement. He'd been quick, for instance, to let me know when my forty-five cents' worth of rubbernecking was all used up. Then it had been time to renegotiate. It was "Gimme a nickel an I takes you backstage at the Midnight Ramble. Nother nickel, it a get you a peek at the Vampin Baby dressin' room. Sniff they hangin-up costume do you like." But even though he persisted in addressing me by the formal "Mistah Harry," somewhere along the line he dropped the pretense of free enterprise.

It could have been that he was simply getting used to having me in tow, since what was one more straggler at his heels to Lucifer? Or it could have been that — somewhere between helping him hide a fugitive from the Parchman Farm and carrying orders from the bootlegger under Pee Wee's Saloon — I'd passed muster. Whatever the case, the last time or two that I'd tried to compensate him for my tour of the underworld, the wise guy had taken offense. He'd swelled up like God forbid there should be a mercenary bone in his body. Then he'd relaxed into one of his sphinxier grins. "Maybe sometime y'all can return I an Michael the favor," he suggested dreamily, as if he hadn't quite decided what it should be.

I'm the first to admit that, outside my acquaintance with the heroes of books, I'd had little enough experience in making friends. But while I had nothing to compare this with, I decided that what could it hurt if I considered myself and the colored kid to be pals.

There came a night when Lucifer said that the famous Beale Street could get along without us for a spell. "What I'm have in mind are a change a scene," he'd asserted, pausing in the middle of Fourth Street to lick his finger and test the wind. This was an interesting prospect. To tell the truth, I'd been feeling that I'd seen what there was to see between the honky-tonks and social clubs and fleabag hotels of the neighborhood. Now I was curious to learn just how far the wise guy's sphere of influence extended.

We "borried" (a word I had lately come to interpret pretty loosely) an unattended skiff and rowed across the lagoon to the mercantile end of the street. It was my first ferry ride with the twins since the night of our original encounter, and I took the occasion to reflect on all that had happened, how far I'd come from the confirmed bookworm of old. I guess you could say I was proud of myself, proud to the point of entertaining delusions: I was this white hunter returning from an exotic port with human trophies. It was a notion that gave me a secret thrill — that is, until we beached the skiff and I was suddenly beset by misgivings.

After all, it was one thing to hobnob with Negroes on their own side of the fence; it was fine to play at being chums beyond the reach of prying eyes and all that. But it was quite another kettle of tsimmes to be caught in their company at my father's end of Beale. You might even call it grounds for scandal. And here I was in full view of the pawnshops whose gossipy brokers knew me well.

"Listen, Lucifer . . ." I was already starting to hedge as I climbed out of the boat, looking for some graceful way to take a powder. But the wise guy was ahead of me, as usual. He'd darted off, trailed by his brother, shagging it around a corner into the alley that ran behind the shops. When I caught up with them, he was lamenting to Michael, "I don't b'lieve Mistah Harry think we knows how to be pre-cautious." I was as grateful as I was ashamed.

Then we were scuffling past the battered tin back door of Kaplan's Loans, stepless above a wooden dock fitted out with tire treads. Somewhere behind the door my papa would be laboring over his books while marauding youths prowled the alleys, and frustrated customers, blockaded by his surplus merchandise, were taking their business elsewhere.

"That's my papa Mr. Solly's place of business," I announced, wondering if I could've gotten away with saying "famous." "As you know, he's got a thing for junk, my papa. Got all kinds of shmutz in there, piled to the ceiling. It's jumbled in the aisles so you can't hardly . . ."

"Got a moon rock," broke in Lucifer with solemn authority. "Got a stack a ol shin-plaster money, which it a turn to dust do you breave on it, an a suit made out a tobacca leaf. Got the Six Book a Moses and a feverroot coction make yo johnson stand up an say howdy. Got a angel skeleton with wangs an I disremember what all else."

I didn't know whether he was taking the words out of my mouth or putting them in. But it excited me to hear him reciting the contents of my father's shop, like it was another of those places on the far side of the water he was always telling whoppers about. It made me feel all of a sudden that I never wanted to set foot in the pawnshop again, lest I find out it was only full of junk.

It wasn't until we'd wound our way down to the swamped foot of Beale Street — scrambling up an embankment onto the Illinois Central trestle and looking out over the immeasurably glutted expanse of the river — that I thought to ask where we were going. It was a question that brought Lucifer to a sudden, thoughtful standstill, as ditto his brother, who could stop on a dime.

"Where we goin?" Lucifer echoed vaguely, as if it had taken my asking to prompt the consideration. He reached under his cap and began to rub his scalp like this would maybe reveal the future. Then he turned toward his brother as he so often did. "Michael, whooch way you feature we be goin?"

Barely lifting his finger, Michael pointed down the tracks in the direction we'd been headed in the first place. But judging from Lucifer's reaction, you'd have thought that the dummy's gesture was somehow fateful. It was a characteristic of Michael's gestures that in their stingy economy they all seemed fateful. Nevertheless, the wise guy nodded slowly as the wisdom began to sink in.

"Izzackly," he confirmed. When I couldn't help rolling my eyes over such a charade, Lucifer told me, like I should have some respect, "That am the direction toward yonder time ago."

We kicked along the bed of the railroad, stepping from tie to tie with Lucifer in the lead, playing the fool. He was pretending to lay track out ahead of us, lifting his knees in what he called his gandy dance, wielding an imaginary sledge. "O de black gal she piss in de coffee," he chanted, shouting "Hunh!" with every stroke of his hammer. "O de black gal she piss in the tea, hunh!" I was so spellbound by his antics that he caught me off guard when he stopped, and I stumbled into the backs of the twins like a heedless caboose.

"There she be," proclaimed Lucifer with his typical gift for obscurity, "the onliest way to travel." Then he stepped off the gravel skirt into the shaggy grass that lapped the top of the bluff.

I still wasn't sure what we were supposed to be looking at. Not until Lucifer had waded into the brush and taken hold of it was I able to make out an antiquated hunk of machinery. It was one of those relics that had so far outworn its usefulness that you took it for just another feature of the landscape. It was only after the wise guy had torn away some of the kudzu and scrub, shedding a little more starlight on the subject, that I could tell what it had been: an old railroad handcar turned over on its side.

With his brother's grim assistance, Lucifer set about freeing the thing from its leafy restraints. They rocked it back and forth, he and Michael, a little farther with every exertion, until the handcar eventually began to topple toward them. There was a sickening sound of deracination as the vehicle wrenched itself clear of the vines, then a thousand grasshoppers scattered along with the twins, making room for the machine to land upright in the shuddering dirt.

I stepped down from the tracks with a sigh and pitched in, though what was the point? The point was that I should show how I was solidly with them even in folly — what else could you call this business of trying to salvage such a heap of corrosion? The planks were splintered and encrusted with the earthworks of dirt daubers and fire ants. Its mechanical parts were caked in grease so ancient it was turning to moss. None of which prevented Lucifer, shouting inappropriate phrases from work songs, from exhorting us to stop at nothing short of busting our backs. So, if only to humor him, we set to. With herculean grunts, we wrestled the ungainly contraption, bullying it by main force up onto the bed of gravel. Then, pausing only long enough to wipe our brows, we heaved it across the tracks, fitting the grooves of its rusty wheels over the rails.

When I could draw a breath, I decided I'd earned the right to say, "It'll never work." Lucifer gave me his ye-of-little-faith expression. "Ain't you never hear of nigger-rig?" he said. Then he crooked a finger at Michael, pronouncing a name that, for all I knew, was supposed to make old things new again: "Earl!"

From somewhere in his overalls, Michael produced a small, hemispherical oil can with a needle spout. (By now I was used to how, between them, the twins carried whole general stores in their pockets.) He tossed the can to Lucifer, who proceeded to swarm over the handcar, lubricating its works with a sound like a clucking tongue. With his free hand he scooped out the gunk, the trilobites and spiders, dusting and squirting until moving parts became distinct. The crankshaft began to look like a crankshaft, the flywheel a flywheel, familiar to me from bits of engines that had found their way into the pawnshop. Removing his cap for a shoeshine flourish, Lucifer spanked away the vestigial crud and stepped back to grin. Then he replaced his cap, mounted the handcar, and grabbed one end of the weather-split wooden handle, winking at Michael, who'd already taken hold at the opposite end.

Still confident that the cumbersome museum piece would never budge, I wasn't too worried about being left behind. But, good sport and all that, I climbed on board anyway. I stationed myself in the middle, at the place that my physics book would have labeled the fulcrum. I was between point A, which was Lucifer, bouncing on his end of the lever like he was prying a tree stump, and point B, which was Michael, hoisting with his rounded back. I tried to remember correctly the principle of virtual work: how the displacement of A, when it's consistent with the steady restraint of B . . . or did I have it backwards? Then I noticed an iron tiller sprouting from the vehicle's innards, and figuring I couldn't do any damage that hadn't already been done, I gave it a tug.

Instantly Lucifer dropped to the planks like a sack of potatoes, while Michael, but for his tenacious grip on the handle, came close to being launched into the air. A hobbled gear groaned and turned over, some skinny rods jogged in place, and the wheels screeched like an aviary. The handcar had lurched into motion. When they recovered themselves, the twins began pumping the handle with a furious zeal, pouring on the elbow grease like competing washboards. After we started to pick up a little speed, the handle began to seesaw practically on its own. The twins bobbed alternately up and down at either end of the planks, themselves become working parts of the machine. This seemed to suit Lucifer, who performed a yipping frog kick with every ascent. Michael remained oddly dignified as he squatted and hopped.

We were rattling along the top of the bluff, catching glimpses — between stands of mimosa — of the river, umpteen miles wide. Where the slope turned steeper, there was a horizontal park of crape myrtles, their red flares not quite extinguished by the dark. The usual armada of debris floated on the water, intermingled tonight with silver islands of gliding ice. They were fragments, I supposed, of some frozen northern state migrating south, on their way to melt in the Gulf of Mexico. Then the tracks swerved abruptly away from the river, and we were shouldered on either side by abandoned warehouses. There were walls of broken windows like open mouths with uneven teeth, dangling block-and-tackles, and jutting iron booms. I held my breath for a space until the sky opened up again and we burst clear of the derelict buildings, sailing across an overpass.

In a moment we were rolling under the eaves of Central Station, with its uncoupled coaches lurking behind plumes of steam on parallel tracks. Along the platform the red-capped porters and waiting families, the stylish ladies sitting cross-legged on baggage dollies, all regarded us like we might be something new in the world. But before they could even make up their minds to wave, we had come and gone. We were headed down the tracks past the red and green beacons into the windy darkness south of the city, our wheels clacking like runaway tap shoes.

I knew that nothing about this excursion was possible. So how was it that I had come to accept what was plainly *im*possible? I tried not to think about it, keeping busy, hanging on to the engine housing with one hand and squirting oil into its works with the other. Then the oil can was empty and, since everyone else was occupied, I threw it away. Or rather, I flung it into the starry firmament like Aladdin returning his lamp whence it came. That left me free to straddle the teeter-tottering handle, which I rode like some kind of wild bucking broomstick.

"Hot-cha!" I shouted, and "Hooee da hooee!" followed by an inspired "Minnie the Moocher, come shake your drawers in my face!" I felt good — knocked out, cross-eyed, birds-in-the-bosom good — and frankly afraid of nothing on earth, except that I might never feel so good again.

"Mistah Harry done gone me-sugar!" shouted Lucifer, holding on to his cap and grinning like he was personally responsible for having engineered the scattering of my wits.

After a mile or so, however, my exhilaration was checked a little by the sound of a train whistle approaching from the opposite direction. So it came as a mixture of disappointment and relief when Lucifer called out a timely "We has arrive!" Although, given the remoteness of our whereabouts, the news didn't exactly announce itself.

The twins left off working the handle, which pumped with diminishing returns for the stretch it took the handcar to slow to a halt. We jumped down and put our shoulders to it again, derailing the handcar with no less difficulty than it had taken us to mount the contraption in the first place. As it happened, we were just in time, because the locomotive had already appeared, bearing down on us in a tumult of clatter and chuff. To the Lord of my Grandpa Isador (if He could hear me from this place) I gave silent thanks, then looked to Lucifer to find out what was next.

He was gazing meditatively at the crawling flood plain, his face flickering amid an intermittent galaxy of fireflies. Then he seemed to have made a decision based on his observations.

"B'lieve I shake some dew off my lily," he declared above the cacophony of the passing train. When he began to unbutton his trousers, Michael beside him followed suit. The excitement of the handcar ride having taken its toll on my bladder, I also felt the call. There we stood, three pishermen angling our water down the brushy slope, our backs to the boxcars from which hoboes (I suspected) were staring quizzically. Satisfied that the arc of my stream was at least the equal of the twins', I stole a sneaky peek, comparing their larger lilies to my own — which I conceded, to the mournful tune of the departing train whistle, had neither toiled nor spun.

"O Lawd, the train done gone," sang Lucifer, who had not a bad singing voice, with a plangency that gave me a lump in the throat. On that note we buttoned up and backtracked along the ridge a bit, stopping at a point from where you could just see the downtown lights around the bend. Here, advising us to take up fallen branches for cudgels, Lucifer called to all crocodiles to keep out from underfoot. Then he dropped into the weeds below and began to beat the bushes. Behind him we stumbled and slid downhill, swatting stalks hung with little boats that exploded into white asterisks, bats that swooped menacingly at our heads. With Lucifer citing items of interest, as on a field trip — the pair of unmentionables caught up in the cockleburs, the severed possum foot in a trap — we staggered to the bottom of the bluff and burst from a canebrake where the terrain began to level out at the water's edge.

And there it was, like some primeval skeleton, drawn to the surface by filaments of starlight from a depth of immemorial years: the ruin of a paddle-wheeled packet boat. Its decks were rolling hills and valleys of warped and rotten slats, some curling at weird angles like cardboard shirtfronts. The twin smoke-stacks would have toppled but for a rigging of ivy that nearly obscured them, and the gangplanks lay broken in the bow. On the shore side of the boat, the blades of the paddle wheel stood exposed like an immense, decaying nautilus shell.

For me it would have been enough (Dayenu!) that the thing merely existed, but Lucifer, as usual, had to add his two cents to what was already stupefying enough. He would have me to know that we were in a cove beyond the levee, where this old wreck had lain aground in shallow water since the time of the Bible.

"Is the *Yazoo Queen* float," he concluded, as if what we beheld was a legend come to pass, "then a nigger be next mayor of Memphis."

I wished that he could sometimes just stand there and be quietly dumbfounded like his brother. Still, you couldn't help but appreciate how, through the offices of the wise guy, the past seemed to be getting a second chance tonight.

Lucifer asked his brother if he wouldn't mind picking a bunch of cattails, preferably of the dead variety. There apparently being no request too strange for the silent Michael, he immediately turned and wandered off. No sooner had he done so than Lucifer took a running jump. He trounced the canebrake, cleared a gully, and launched himself from what looked to me like a turtle. Cycling his legs in a mad trajectory through a cloud of mosquitoes, he landed in a four-point crouch on the deck of the steamboat. When he stood up the boat shifted under him, restless in its cabled moorings, making noises like an agitated sleeper.

I would have been happy to stay where I was, admiring the kid's agility, but Lucifer called out to me, "What you waitin on?"

"On dry land," I replied. I might have added that athletic prowess had never run in our family, with the possible exception of an ancestor who Grandpa Isador claimed could pray in midair. But rather than waste my breath on excuses that no longer seemed to apply, I ran forward and flung myself from the riverbank.

I landed tochis-over-elbows in a sprawl across the slippery deck, the agitated sleeper lurching under me, threatening to perhaps turn over. I crawled a few paces before venturing to get to my feet. Then I sidled over to the wise guy, who, instead of congratulating me, remained deep in the contemplation of a huge ship's bell. Its wooden frame having long since collapsed, the bell, which was bordered in an algae like luminous jasper, was half sunk beneath the splintered deck. To show I wasn't nervous, I tried to make conversation: the bell put me in mind of the skirt on an iron maiden. But Lucifer only looked at me like I should show a little class.

"Spose you the man what can lift it up and rang her clapper?"

It was at times like these that I would have liked to remind him that he was, after all, a Negro, but I didn't like to pull rank. Determined in any case that he shouldn't have the last word, I followed him through what was left of a hatch, clambering up a treacherous companionway of mostly missing steps. We emerged into the steamboat's fulsome and cavernous interior. Here again the pawnshop stood me in good stead, and remembering the nomenclature of ships in bottles, I recognized our location as the grand saloon.

The floor, or the part of it that was still intact, stretched away from us in a long, sweeping curve like a rocker on a rocking chair. A finely milled blue light spilled through the blasted roof and the transom of a bottomless pilothouse. It fell past a gallery overtaken by clematis, onto the pane of broken pier glass — runneled in lead like a branched menorah — that lay at our feet. In our strolling inspection, we nosed about in rubble of recent vintage and vestiges of yore: a hand-carved acorn pendant snared in a swatch of mosquito net; a wadded Chesterfield pack in a bull's-eye lantern; a tooth at the end of some string attached to the porcelain knob of a fallen stateroom door. With his toe Lucifer stirred some ashes littered with Sterno cans and something like a deflated rubber thumb. There were posts scratched with names and dates from this century or that; a stringless harp frame, overlooked for kindling, which resembled in this grainy light the relic of a bleached jawbone.

Appearing to know his way around the place pretty well, Lucifer had begun to make a speech. Using (instead of an oil can) the all-purpose agent of his mouth, he restored the *Yazoo Queen* to her heyday, only with a difference.

"See, Mistah Harry, after them white folk done been made to walk the plank, ol Razmus he be relax, sip his bourbon an branch on the hurricane deck. Down in the hole you got the Ku Kluxers stokin the biler, so's the colored chirrens can ride the paddle like on a Ferris wheel. Mysef, I be up on the cap'm bridge, peepin through a spyglass, talkin that deep water talk . . ."

He went on to liberate stewards and chambermaids, awarding them the linen suits and bustles of the keelhauled planters and their wives. At first I wanted to let him know that I thought this kind of talk was uncalled for; it was insensitive. Then it occurred to me that two could play at this game. After all, hadn't my hard-working North Main Street neighbors also earned their right to a holiday?

"How about we let old Mrs. Ridblatt," I suggested, "break a bottle of Manischewitz over the bow? Then the Chassids from the Litvak shul, they can take up shuffleboard — they need the exercise. And the band can play some of whatsisname, some of Stephen Foster's lesser known klezmer tunes. Whaddaya say?"

Lucifer kicked a can across the floor and opened his mouth

like he might be about to ask me for another nickel. But before he could speak, his attention was diverted by the sound of shuffling footsteps behind us.

It was Michael, the nochshlepper, carrying a bushel's worth of rustling cattails. At such moments as these he really gave me the willies, because just when you'd managed to forget all about him, there he suddenly was. Never mind how he'd been able to get on board with such an armload. Relieving him of all but a handful of his awkward bouquet, Lucifer praised his industriousness. "Very good," I half hoped he would tell him, "now go and pick a peck of pickled peppers." But instead the wise guy passed the burden along to me, saying, "Mistah Harry, y'all mind do you bring in the sheaves?"

Of course I minded. But looking around from behind the dry stalks, I was too curious about what he was up to to object. Having taken the flat bottle out of his pocket, he began to sprinkle the reedy spikes in Michael's hand. Then he dredged up a match, cocked a hip to strike it on, and set fire to his brother's cattails. The sudden blaze eclipsed the ship's saloon, which seemed to retreat back into the dark years.

Sending the dummy on ahead of us, Lucifer guided me in close behind. He crowded my side to have access to the cattails, bunches of which he kept extracting to feed Michael's hungry flame. As the torch tended to flare up and quickly burn out, my load soon became more manageable, not that I was enjoying it any more. Sandwiched between the twins like that, I had the uneasy impression they were conducting me into a dungeon.

We proceeded in silence through the periodic darkness. The only sounds I heard, beyond our footsteps and the crackling flame, were the old tub's slosh and groan as it rocked underfoot. (Maybe I should have enjoyed the vacation from Lucifer's mouth, but it was just like him to keep quiet when you most needed him to remind you that you hadn't stepped off the world.) We were groping amidships, or underneathships — I honestly couldn't tell where we were, though with every renewed flaring of the torch — like when a Viewmaster clicks into place — some aspect of the steamboat's eroded vitals was revealed. Now you saw it: a warren of trashed cabins and riven gangway walls. Now you didn't: and the darkness, which deepened after every dying flame, squelched nauseatingly under our unsure feet. I had the sensation of treading on toadstools and slipping in clumps of mulch, breathing stale air out of the earth's own descending colon.

At one point something heavy lumbered across my foot, and when I yiped, all I got by way of comfort was "Ruvah rat down here be big as a yard dog." After that I went so far as to hook a finger through the hammer loop of the dummy's overalls. The torch had expired again and the air was almost too close and stinky now to inhale. Furthermore, we seemed to have deadended. Striking another match, Lucifer rekindled the reeds, which showed us to be in a blind space the size of a closet. We were facing a boxlike affair covered over in a furry pelt of moss, a kind of inside-out terrarium. In the center of the box was a turfy hole sprouting spores around its rim. This was no ordinary toilet. On this one you could imagine that some fiendish creature, half goat and half man, came to rest his shaggy nates and unload his corruption straight into the pit of Gehinom.

Taking the few remaining stalks from my hand, Lucifer borrowed a light from Michael's failing torch. He removed the slack belt from his trousers, which slipped halfway down his shorts, so that I wondered a moment if he intended to compound the indecency of this place. But instead of sitting, he wrapped his belt around the fistful of cattails, drawing it tightly through the buckle. Then he knelt in front of the box and lowered the flame through a sizzle of cobwebs into the hole. Instantly we were plunged into the most abysmal degree of darkness yet. There was nothing now amid that sulphurous stench

— save the knock and sway of the riding boat — against which to gauge your position in the universe.

Because the torch had such a fleeting life, we got only a momentary glimpse of what lay in the hole. I had just enough time to see a torpor of iridescent ripples, braided rainbows on the surface of oily water, as if invisible fingers were smearing paint in slow motion with glossy, serpentine strokes. Then darkness again, and I bit my trembling lip to try and figure it out. Didn't rushes under water look something like that, all undulating like sinewy hair? But what did I know from rushes? Well, for one thing — rubbing the goose pimples on my arms — I knew that they weren't ordinarily so corpulent. They didn't coil and twine in such radiant loop-the-loops, artfully unknotting themselves.

Lucifer unriddled the mystery. "Mus be a millyum moccasin down there," he reckoned, freezing my blood.

Back on terra firma, I could have kissed the Mississippi mud. It was great, I assured the twins as we scrambled up the slope, to be alive in the twentieth century, which was frankly the only century worth being alive in.

"Ain't no right-in-the-head centry would have you," said the wise guy.

We arrived at the top of the bluff just as another string of boxcars was being shunted slowly back toward town. Never one to pass up a free ride, Lucifer directed us in camouflaging the handcar so that it shouldn't fall into the wrong hands. This we made short work of, covering it with brush until we'd restored it to its status of a nearly invisible eyesore. Then we ran alongside the train and grabbed on at the first available boxcar door; we hauled ourselves into the open car and rolled out of view, hugging the walls. When we'd determined we were the sole occupants of that dark, jolting space, completely tuckered out, we collapsed, sliding down the walls to the hay-strewn floor.

From where I slumped adjacent the twins, I could hardly see

them, except when an occasional slant of light made their eyes (and Lucifer's teeth) dance a duet. But tired as I was, I still had to hand it to him, the way he could keep on talking even while disembodied. I guess it was an acquired taste, this chin music of Lucifer's, but you could get addicted. You could come to depend on the way it made outrageous events — witness Harry Kaplan riding the rails — seem almost commonplace.

He was making the usual medicinal claims for his corn liquor. "Put a hair on yo hiney ef it ain't tear it apart," he cautioned as he handed the bottle to me. I accepted in a spirit of comradeship. But after I'd swallowed, I detected a change in his tone of voice, as if the fighting for breath that accompanied my drinking had put him in a serious mood.

"Our daddy name us after angel," he divulged like someone had asked him, then waited for me to say "Un-hunh" before going ahead. "He was a educated man, know everythang."

He paused again until I'd inquired after his father's whereabouts — though since when had he ever needed any prompting from me? This confessional mode was so unlike Lucifer that you could almost suppose it wasn't. You could imagine, for instance, that it belonged to the dummkopf brother beside him, an idea that caused my scalp to crawl. But once the voice had found its groove, I was reassured that it was none other than the wisenheimer twin's.

"They say he stay somewheres up no'th, my daddy, round Chicago what it is call the sweet home, an I bet you he rich is he ain't in jail. Putty soon us gon after him, gon know him soon as we sees him. He be dress snappy like a G-man, wearin them reptile shoes, talkin Humpty Bogart–style, prolly in rhyme. Be lookin smart as a solid-gold wisdom toof. We meet up, he bound to make I an Michael his partner, say, 'Where y'all been, I be needin boys what am sly but ain't fly.' He gon set us up to manage his juju factry, gon operate his wet-yo-whistle concern out the back of a Hupmobile . . ."

As always, I appreciated Lucifer's confiding in me, though it also made me a little uncomfortable. You never knew where the facts left off and his imagination began. All you could really be sure of about the twins was that they were orphans, though certain parts of the story tended to remain consistent — such as that their mother had died giving birth to them, leaving the brothers to the care and guidance of Aunt Honey. The rest, including the father who'd presided at their christening, Lucifer might have been making up as he went along. It was his orphan's prerogative, I supposed, and the truth was, I kind of envied it. I figured that by now I'd earned the right to be considered an honorary orphan, and was even moved to mutter as much aloud. Taking another swig from the bottle, I added that my own fershluginer family could drive a person to, I dunno, read a book.

While he'd continued his speech straight through my complaining — "We own sit in our daddy congregation, get the spirit mos every night" — Lucifer perked up abruptly on the tail of my last remark. It was apparently all he'd heard.

"We been to school," he bluntly informed me, as if I'd challenged him to the contrary. "Aunt Honey, she up an pull us out, say them high-tone notion turn a po boy brain to puddin. Say it have fill us with dicty idea till we ain't even sweat. Say, 'I lam yo nappy hade do you don't be workin, y'all already in the college a bust-yo-butt.' Now I ax you, man, when do I gots time prepare yo lesson? Course, Michael here, he feature our daddy, be a fool for a book. The nigger got a reglar readin jones."

I didn't know why Lucifer should set such store in their having been to school when what I admired most was that they no longer went. And as for the stuff about the dummy's literary bent, that I'd heard it all before didn't make it any easier to swallow. Maybe guessing as much, the wise guy was quick to assure me that, while Michael had read his Bible cover to cover, along with any stray copies of *Crackajack Funnies* that fell into his hands, what he really preferred was a storybook.

140

"He have a partikler sweet toof fo them itchy-pants littachoor, got a very romantic nature, don't you know." The problem was that — if you excluded the illustrated dreambooks (combining spiritual advice with tips on policy play) and the ubiquitous Mr. G. P. Hamilton's *Beacon Lights of the Race,* a copy of which could even be found among a stack of *Silver Screens* at the Baby Doll — books were a scarce commodity on Beale Street. Nor did it help that the colored people of Memphis were forbidden to hold library cards.

"So they it is, yo honah," said Lucifer, seeming to rest his case. Though just exactly what case that was, I couldn't have said. I supposed that I was expected to offer a word of sympathy. I deplored the drought of reading matter among the Negro citizenry; I shared his helplessness in the face of injustice. But before I could work myself up to it, the wise guy had attached a postscript.

"Now, do you reckon y'all can find it in yo raggedy heart, which you might have to reach fo it in yo britches, an do my brothah Michael a favor?"

So that's what he'd been leading up to. Having gone to such lengths to escape the side effects of my own reading, now I was being asked to procure books for others. Of course it wasn't as if I hadn't been expecting something like this. In fact, I was actually pleased that the time had finally arrived when there was something for which the twins had to come to me. It was turnabout, wasn't it? What's more, I would be a figure of intrigue, a smuggler, running contraband books to Negroes at the risk of giving them ideas above their station. There was more than a little Scarlet Pimpernel in such a project.

So what was eating me? Was it that, having fooled around all I wanted in the twins' own preserve, I still wasn't too cozy with the notion of their encroaching on mine?

Since I could only make out one pair of eyes now, I assumed that Michael's were closed. Lulled by the rhythmic tattoo of the

rails (fershlepta krenk fershlepta krenk, they seemed to be saying after my grandpa: a lost cause a lost cause), he must have
fallen asleep. Except when a light along the tracks flashed an
extra form slumped in the corner, no part of Lucifer's phantom
of a brother was visible. So even as I agreed to the favor, I had
to sigh over its pointlessness, the idea of wasting books on
someone who wasn't there.

Eight

In the beginning I went to the old frame pile of the Neighborhood House, where Mrs. Birnbaum taught the greenhorns how to brush their teeth and do the box step. She also kept a little library of mostly bound *Reader's Digest*s and illustrated Bible stories, with here and there a book based on a movie or an Earl Derr Biggers mystery thrown in for spice. I asked her if I could borrow some kiddie books for a neighbor's sick child; lockjaw was what I said the child had. Maybe I shouldn't have appointed myself the judge of what Michael ought to read, since Lucifer was, after all, the authorized spokesman for his brother's tastes. But who could believe Lucifer's amazing claims for the dummy's aptitude? In any case, I still wasn't too clear about the kinds of books the wise guy suggested, so I decided to proceed with care. Anything too sophisticated might prove an irreversible shock to the dummy's system.

So for his own good I brought Michael *Mrs. Wigg's Cabbage Patch, The Bad Child's Book of Beasts, Uncle Remus,* of course, some Mother Goose, and a Lucky Lindy coloring book. Lucifer promptly returned them, thanking me kindly but reminding me that his brother had been out of didees for some years, or hadn't I noticed. Then he added, getting down to specifics, "Ain't no lovey-dovey in these here book, ain't nobody be drop they drawer."

This was when I began to get suspicious. Could it be that the wise guy was using his brother as an excuse to ask for books he was too ashamed to request for himself, books that were not likely to be found on Mrs. Birnbaum's shelves, or any other shelves within my immediate reach? Though in all my browsing I'd never actually come across these books, I knew well enough that they existed; they had titles like *Confessions of a Stableboy* and *Betty's Petticoat Nights.* And I'm not saying that I wouldn't have liked the chance to examine such properties at first hand. But it was beyond me why anyone who lived in such a sink of depravity as the Baby Doll should care to read about more of the same. Talk about your coals to Newcastle.

I apologized to Lucifer for having insulted his brother's intelligence, and the next day I went to the public library on Front Street. Not without a little meanness, I selected a stack of the fattest volumes I could carry. They were triple-decker novels whose jackets proclaimed them to be great tales of love, though when you flipped through their pages, you could see that nothing happened: ladies had long talks with the vicar, they got the vapors and drank tea in bed. They were the sort of books that gangsters might tie to your legs before throwing you into the harbor. As a bonus, I kicked in a couple of volumes of poetry, the type where every other word is in Greek, and the endpapers have swirling designs like flushing commodes. When Lucifer handed them back to me after a week or so had elapsed, he assured me that these were more like it.

This was confusing. Now I wasn't so sure anymore that the wise guy had wanted the books for his own purposes — unless when he said hanky-panky, what he really meant was dull and turgid goings-on. So maybe he'd merely misrepresented his brother's tastes in favor of his own salty preferences. But then you had to buy the idea that it was Michael who had read the books. One thing certain, however, was that someone had read them, or at least put them through some kind of harrowing paces, because the books came back to me looking like they'd been to war. Their bindings were bowed, the unstitched cloth corners showing cardboard fanned into tassels. The spines were unglued and the pages limp and dog-eared where they weren't actually torn. They were books that gave the impression that someone had looted them for their contents.

The library didn't look with favor on such abuse. They gave me a stiff fine, which I would have to pay in installments, nor would they let me borrow more books until I'd made good on the damaged ones. In the end I was left with no choice but to sacrifice a part of my own private collection. I told myself that, since I'd outgrown any serious interest in such juvenile fare, it was a small price to pay for renewing my passport to the underside of life. So why was it that I couldn't shake the feeling that I was throwing good books after bad?

Among the casualties were E. W. Hornung and Lord Dunsany, *Lost Horizon, When the World Shook, The Land That Time Forgot,* and *Voyage to the Center of the Earth,* the latter in its vintage Big Little Book edition. So roughshod was their treatment on Beale Street that, by the time I got them back, the books were maimed beyond a hope of ever being read again. What's more, they were filled with fishbones and crumbs, watercolored with pot-likker stains; they were smeared with yams as if the reader had literally consumed them with his meals. This wholesale laying to waste of my library might have been easier to take if somebody had shown a little appreciation. But while the books were returned with their pages as wilted as sucked artichoke leaves, nobody so much as belched to prove they'd been digested.

I had not entirely ruled out the possibility that Michael was a closet reader, but where was the evidence? Not that I expected him suddenly to acquire the coolheadedness of a Raffles, the cheek of a Richard Hannay or Harry Faversham's calculated recklessness, but Michael remained always only his own stolid self.

"It look like he be steady rasslin with them storybook," Lucifer had alleged. "Sometime he be trine to get on top of it. Sometime them story, it have thow him on his funky behine." But when I asked if I could see for myself, Lucifer told me most assuredly, "Nosuh!" Michael was very sensitive about being observed at his reading. I said I was sorry, feeling like I'd asked to spy on some act of intimacy.

After another week of seeing my once prized collection so savagely used, I decided that my part of the bargain had been fulfilled. Hoping to preserve the few volumes that remained on my shelves, if only as souvenirs of my youth, I told Lucifer that my library had bottomed out.

He clucked his tongue and doffed his hat, frowning into it, then looked at me and said, "Tha's a sho nuff cryin shame." I shrugged and Lucifer concurred — all of this, incidentally, in the presence of his brother, who showed not a trace of disappointment. But no sooner had I relaxed, assured that the subject was dropped, than the wise guy revived it again. "Now wherebouts y'all reckon you might see can you borry some mo?"

I told him that this was no longer my problem. If it was so all-fired important that his brother should be in the business of mutilating books — which he'd done well enough without before I came along — then Lucifer could just go and find the victims himself. I would be happy to lend him whatever advice I could, though if you asked me, there were probably very sound reasons for keeping shvartzers in the dark. No good could come of this kind of indulgence.

Lucifer stood there grinning like he was proud of me for having gotten it all off my chest. Then, politely inquiring whether I was finished, he repeated his request: "Whereabouts you say you reckon?" Hanging my head, I said that there was in fact someone whom I had yet to put the touch on. It was a long shot but I'd see what I could do.

The following Saturday morning I made the trek out to the Parkway, and was left by my uncle's maid to cool my heels in the marble entrance hall. After some minutes she returned with the stiff information that Miss Naomi would receive me in the garden. I told her thanks and gave her a wink. This was to show that she didn't have to stand on ceremony with Harry Kaplan, who was after all a friend of her race. But as she failed to respond, I supposed that the rumors of my dual existence had not traveled among her people as far as the Parkway.

Naomi was sitting on a bench in the shade of a hexagonal cedar gazebo. Its trellised walls, laced in a webwork of vines, sprouted blossoms that might have been poison orchids. There was a small pond full of pea soup and lily pads like floating paw prints, with a putzless stone boy in the middle holding a leaky jug. Beyond the patio was a border of steamy, wax-leaved foliage — the kind that Amazon travelers, lured by bird calls, wander into and disappear.

As I approached her, Naomi was fussily picking lint from her pleated skirt. Her legs were crossed at the white anklets, and the knobs of her knees peeked from beneath her skirt hem like potato faces. Squirmingly she arranged herself into a stiff-backed approximation of what she must have thought was a fetching pose. Without question, she was the strangest fruit in her father's garden.

"Hello Harry. Take a load off, why don't you," she invited in a tone of voice like the spider to the fly. She was toying with her hair now, which had been braided into a queue like a scorpion's tail. Then she looked up at me for the first time, and regis-

147

tered acute disappointment. It was as if she'd been expecting an entirely different Harry, one who arrives bearing flowers and chocolates. Have a heart, I thought, already beginning to regret that I'd come. But as the morning sun was doing a sultry number on the garden, I ducked under the gazebo roof and plunked myself down.

We sat there for a spell in awkward silence. I rocked on the stationary bench while Naomi blew the bangs from her sweaty forehead. Out of the corner of my eye I watched her, lest she pull some repeat performance of her Seder night funny business. Uncomfortable as I was, however, I took heart in observing how my cousin seemed just as agitated by our proximity. I decided to seize the advantage of her discomposure and come directly to the point.

"I won't beat around the bush," I blurted with a resolution that startled us both. Then I cleared my throat and tried again. "What I come for is to borrow some books, if it's okay with you. See, I kind of outgrew all that stuff I used to read, you know, like adventures and um, well . . . adventures. Used to be I was gaga for a saga, heh heh. Ahem. So now I'm looking for something more, whaddayacallit, mature."

Naomi's drooping eyelids began to flutter. Heaving a sigh that seemed to express a preparedness to do her duty, she gave me a sidelong smile accompanied by an exaggerated wink. I had the crazy thought that this was in some way a delayed response to the wink I'd given the maid; it was a wink bespeaking a knowledge of dark secrets I should understand were safe with her.

"I think we can take care of you," my cousin archly advised me — a discreet clerk to the customer involved in some humiliating purchase. I could feel a pimple on the back of my neck throb and come to a head.

"Now see here, Naomi," I protested, sounding a little like a phony Jack Benny. "I think you're jumping to the wrong conclusion." Somehow it didn't help matters that the garden was practically narcotic with a medley of humid fragrances, musical with a chorus of twittering birds. "Look," I explained through gritted teeth, "I came, like I said, to borrow some books of enduring literary merit, all right? So don't get any funny ideas." And in case she hadn't gotten the point yet, I added, "Besides, don't you know that first cousins have kids with two heads and three tochises?"

Naomi's oval face began to cloud up with confusion as she assured me, "I don't know what you're talking about." Her pooched lower lip started to quiver like a plucked bowstring.

So maybe I had overdone it a bit. It was possible that I shouldn't have assumed that there was more at stake here than the issue of borrowing books. My turtlelike cousin works herself up to stick her neck out, and I throw cold water in her kisser; she beats a hasty retreat back into her shell. I should have been ashamed of myself. Not only had I hurt Naomi's feelings but I'd probably blown my chances of walking away with a new batch of books for Beale Street. Now I'd have to face Lucifer with a report of the failure of my mission. Together we would mourn the absence of fresh titles to be mangled in the terrible wringer of somebody's reading, and that would be that. It made me almost want to cheer.

Then Naomi was speaking again, though not in the sulky way you would have expected. You might have said she sounded downright haughty, with her plum-veined eyelids aflutter again, her impressive Kaplan nostrils flared.

"Anyway" — she picked up where she'd left off — "who do you think you are? You think you're the sheik of North Main Street or something? You think you're the prize in the box of Wheaties, is that it? You open up your breakfast cereal and bingo! Instead of Jack Armstrong's hike-o-meter, there's Harry Kaplan and your morning is made. Well, let me tell you for the record, Harry, you're no prize!"

149

I guess you had to hand it to the little nishtikeit, the way she spat out my name like a piece of rancid treyf. It occurred to me that I might not know Naomi so well as I thought. But in any case, the joke was on her, wasn't it? Because if she'd known the truth about me, she'd have to eat her words. After all, unbeknownst to my cousin, there was a red-blooded sensation of nocturnal derring-do sitting next to her. So what if my physique was a little on the puny side. Granted, my feet tended toward flatness, my hair looked like black excelsior, and my eyes were foggy green bubbles behind their horn-rims. And despite the hours I'd logged in the company of certified ladies of the evening, I'd yet to touch the pinkie of a living girl. I might look outwardly harmless — no more striking a specimen than, say, my moody cousin herself — but what better cover could I have chosen? Harry Kaplan was the perfect disguise.

It would have served her right if I'd spilled the whole story of my dazzling exploits then and there. She would have begged my forgiveness if she didn't just swoon from the shock. Still, I sometimes wished there was someone I could trust with my secret.

We sat stewing in our mutual hostilities while all around us birds sang, boughs dripped, frogs croaked like rusty bedsprings. The dragonflies, which Lucifer called snake doctors, were riding piggyback, which only served to further my aggravation. I was contemplating how I should leave, whether I owed her an excuse or just an abrupt goodbye, when Naomi ventured to mumble, "So you want to borrow some books or what?"

I shrugged and told her, like I was the one who was doing her the favor, that I guessed it would be all right, I'd be willing to take a look at a couple of volumes. But, just in case there was any question about the seriousness of my motives, I was quick to stipulate, "Something weighty, know what I mean? Kind of stuff you can sink your teeth in." Naomi cocked a tweezered brow. "Kind of stuff where the hero gets all farmisht because somebody died, or he lost his girlfriend or his whatsit, his muse." Then her other brow went up, making me wonder if I'd given too much away.

"I think I can . . . ," she started, whirling about, setting her braid in motion so that I had to duck the barrette. Then Naomi was on her feet. With her hands clasped behind her, she began to pace the bricks, which were flushed with purple herbs like spilled wine.

"What you want is, let me see," she was thinking out loud as if jimmying a lock in her brain. When the lock sprung, an entire card catalogue tumbled forth. The air was suddenly thick with authors and titles that Naomi proposed and then discarded as not quite the thing. Some of the books that she mentioned I recognized, though their reputations had always made them seem forbidding, like they shouldn't be attempted by mortal men. One of them, *The Metamorphoses,* which I associated only with a stunt once performed by Houdini, was the cradle of most of the heroes you'd ever heard of, if you could believe my cousin. There was Ulysses, always trying to scheme his way out of hot water, and Hercules, who wore a poison shirt, the lot of them doing battle with your one-eyed, snake-haired, thousand-headed monsters.

"But what you want is the more romantically inclined," she said. Was she gloating or did I imagine it? "Like Pygmalion, who makes a statue of a lady which he falls for, because you know what, she comes alive! And Orpheus, whose precious drops dead so he goes straight to you-know-where to bring her back. Come to think of it, he's not the only hero that goes to blazes for the sake of a loved one . . ."

Having struck this theme, she pursued it a while, using examples from the knights of the Round Table who were forever being driven mad by love. (Knights I was incidentally unfamiliar with from Howard Pyle.) It seemed that they frequently conceived infatuations, which resulted in brain fevers and saints' diseases, and left them wearing grass skirts and gibber-

151

ing in trees. Then there was the knight she was particularly fond of, who was exceptional for having first been driven mad by books before advancing to love. This one liked to wear a shaving basin on his head and to convince scullery maids that they were of noble birth. What a line.

She was having a fine time, my cousin, dropping names from all over the map: Tristan and Werther and Mr. Rochester, Sidney Carton and the Man Who Laughs. Occasionally she might even blow raspberries or cross her eyes to show the extremes to which love could reduce a hero. This was not a Naomi I'd seen before, neither the shrinking nebbish nor the amateur femme fatale. But as she unclasped her hands to wave aside the sunbeams that hung like heavenly flypaper around the garden, you might almost have thought that this was the most authentic Naomi of all. So involved had she become in relating her stories that I was afraid she wasn't paying attention to where she was pacing. Any moment she might stumble headlong into the lily pond and be swallowed by a giant hibiscus. Next spring, when the flower reopened, there would be my cousin, still chattering away.

Listening to her, I felt a twinge or two of my old greediness for books, and for an instant I thought I might like to know what Naomi knew. Then it passed and I became impatient, remembering that the books were intended for a dumb shvartzer who might not even know how to read.

"Naomi, slow down already!" I tried to interrupt. "What, are you gonna recite the whole history of Western literature?"

But she ignored me, still pacing, her steps describing an ever-widening arc around the pond. It was a pendulumlike movement, on the downswing of which she alluded to the tale of some disinherited momzer and his beloved. Then, on the counterstroke, wondering aloud if the book was still on its accustomed shelf, she continued across the patio and vanished through the double doors of the solarium.

With the memory still fresh of what happened the last time I followed Naomi, you couldn't blame me for taking my time. In the glass-roofed solarium the maid, who might have been stationed there for the purpose, shook her duster in the direction of a flight of back stairs. I coughed a thank-you, climbed the stairs, and found my cousin in her bedroom, her arms laden with a daunting stack of books. Some of them looked old enough to be rarities, with hand-tooled leather bindings and marbleized pages. Some fell from her teetering pile and lay open, showing tissue-covered illustrations, pages blemished with thumbprints of people probably long dead.

"Boy, have you come to the right place!" exclaimed Naomi, dumping the whole hefty stack in my unready hands. For some reason this put me in mind of a shikkered rabbi on Simchas Torah, how he might pass the holy scrolls with the same abandon. While I assured her that these were more than enough, she had already stooped to snatch more books from her shelves.

"In this one the star-crossed lovers" — and she paused to savor the phrase — "they don't even know what the other one looks like. See, they can only meet in the dark . . ."

The more volumes she tried to unload on me, accompanying them always with some tempting snatch of narrative, the more embarrassed I became by her generosity. Never mind that the books, most of which had already seen action enough, were destined for such an unkind end. Where they were going, Naomi's treasures would be brutally cracked open, their contents devoured, leaving only their unrefundable shells for me to return. Besides, my arms were so stretched from the mounting heap, which I held clamped in the vise of my chin, that I thought my shoulders would pop from their sockets.

"Uncle already!" I cried, hoping that by accident I hadn't roused the lord of the house. But my plea fell on deaf ears.

Having substantially pruned the bookshelves, Naomi was

now on her knees beside the four-poster, plundering her cache of lurid jackets.

"I think you're gonna like this one," she teased, "and this one, ayayay!" It was her version of hard sell.

I was a little disappointed to see that, among her hidden volumes, there were no such titles as *Betty's Petticoat Nights*. Instead, they were mostly novelized versions of movies of the day, with cover portraits of Jean Harlow and Joan Crawford in dishabille. Nevertheless, after the hidebound standards of her formal library, you'd have thought Naomi might be ashamed to haul out such junk. But what was apparent was that for my cousin, be it high literature or cheap romance, a story was a story. Rather than presenting them like tawdry secrets, Naomi seemed to bring out the books with pride. She looked like someone who'd finally gotten around to spring cleaning, clearing away her stuffy volumes to make room for these bright novelettes.

"You'll die when you read this one," she was impishly promising. "There's this girl with red hair and — you know vilder moid? I mean, this girl is wild . . ."

"Naomi, shah! I already got more than I can carry."

". . . No man can hold her, she gives them all the slip, keeps running off to join the Ziegfeld or the Gold Rush or . . ."

Unable to clap my ears, I shut my eyes, shaking my head so vehemently that I chafed my chin on the grainy top of my stack.

"But it's only light reading," she urged.

"No more!" Peering at her over the books, I gave my cousin a look that was meant to convey my profoundest obstinacy.

That's when she started to shrink again. Before my eyes she was turning back into the old Naomi, the one I could do without. The one with the wounded-doe weepers and the eternally quivering lower lip. She was sitting cross-legged on the fluffy pink carpet in the shadow of a leaning tower of books, which I had half a malicious mind to let topple back into her hands —

idle and quiet as they now were in the lap of her skirt. Then it seemed to me that I had done precisely that. Though I still held the books, I felt that I had somehow dumped my ballast in her lap, then risen into the air. I was watching my cousin grow smaller as I helplessly drifted away in a balloon.

"When you finish those," she was saying, her voice becoming faint and almost out of earshot, "you're welcome to come back for some more."

"Thanks a million," I muttered, resisting the impulse to shout down to her. "Maybe I'll do you a favor sometime."

Maybe one day I would tell her of the humanitarian service she'd rendered, how her books had been placed in the hands of the needy, who tore them asunder in the name of higher literacy. I would explain how, even while she'd endured such exemplary sitzflaysh in her garden, she had been instrumental in helping me pull off a conspiracy. Then she would understand it was not for nothing that she'd parted with her precious cargo. But just now Naomi looked to be completely out of reach, and I'd done all the favors I had it in me to do for one day.

Nine

J ust because I'd had to go to such lengths to keep up my part as librarian didn't mean I still wasn't having fun. Since my father seemed to have forgotten all about grooming me for his successor, my association with the pawnshop was no more than nominal. Nowadays I considered myself an apprentice confidence artist or an aspiring "sweet man," which is a kind of outlaw shadchen who makes matches at hourly rates. I had begun to take a studious interest in Lucifer's so-called errands, though it was often difficult to distinguish between the official ones and the ones he'd trumped up for a lark. Business and pleasure were such near relations, by his lights, that you could almost have called them twins. In any case, these errands involved such a variety of destinations that we were never at a loss for excitement or for excuses to make expeditions beyond the immediate vicinity of the Baby Doll Hotel.

On the strength of a whispered complaint from one of the ladies, for instance, we might be sent after graveyard dirt, popularly known as goofer dust. This, along with certain bodily discharges and the bones of black cats — not to mention the gris-gris made from the devil's dandruff and imported from

New Orleans — was an essential ingredient in recipes for casting spells. To get it we would make a moonlit trek to the potter's field behind the bayou, where Lucifer maintained that the twins' mama was buried. This was a pretty safe bet, since the weathered wooden markers bore only numbers instead of names. (Not that it would have mattered, since Aunt Honey — the only available source of information concerning their birth — never managed to recollect the same surname for the brothers twice. As for their mother's given name, it was sometimes Junipurr, occasionally Beulah Love or Nectarine. Their father was always John.) Also, I noticed that Lucifer seldom led us to the same grave site, that it varied according to his disposition like odds in a policy game. Nevertheless, he took every least occasion to steer us through the lot, never failing to place some dandelions or a sprig of chicory on a grave.

Another place where it was said you could find the really vintage dirt was across the river at the old slave burial ground on President's Island. One night in a "borried" johnboat, with both brothers paddling furiously while I bailed with a coffee tin, we actually attempted the rough passage. Before the current turned us back, we saw how the cemetery had been desecrated by the flood. How the high water had performed a kind of postmortem emancipation, robbing the graves of their rotting cypress caskets, setting them free in a bobbing skeleton fleet.

Sometimes we might be sent to the root doctor after the cure for a lady's ailment, such as the bedevilment or the piss-out-of-a-dozen-holes disease. We might be sent after the remedy for having swallowed (as they say) a watermelon seed. Frequently we were endowed for these journeys with some article sacred to the lady in question: an unlaundered intimate garment or the flap of a boyfriend's union suit, materials that would be useful in the manufacture of an effective medicine mojo. Then we would set out through the quarter east of Mambo's, past Wellington, into what Lucifer called the rat cellar of Beale

Street. That's where you saw the dogtrot shacks in their barren garden plots, the fallen chimneys and tilted pump handles like buried saber hilts. You saw neolithic chassis stranded on cinder blocks, eroded vertical landscapes of crazy quilts, children peeping out from under barrel lids. You saw children wearing croker sacks like cocoons they couldn't shed.

The root doctor, Washington Legba A-men by name, lived alone in a rattling antebellum mansion at the farthest reach of Beale. The house, along with several others still standing, had been abandoned, according to Lucifer, during the plague of the yellowjack: "Which it ain't actual oughta be call yallah, cause what I'm hear, you will tend to ejackalate black." As the wise guy had it, these ancestral residences, after the flight of their wealthy owners, had been taken over by colored who were naturally immune to your buckra infirmities. For a time, in fact, the shvartzers had actually run the city. They'd taken over the ghost hotels and worked miracles in the madhouses and hospitals. They'd worn opera hats and suede gloves, occupied box seats at the dogfights and the Piscoble church. In the evenings they'd roasted pheasants over the pyres that burned the cracker victims of the plague. Then the epidemic had ended and the quality folk returned to find the Negroes whistling somewhat smugly in their rags.

But some of the richest never came back to reclaim their estates. Their once palatial houses fell into disrepair, and those at the far end of Beale Street in particular became the frequent subject for tales of weird goings-on.

Dr. A-men could usually be found tending his herb patch or manipulating the colored glass bottles on his bottle tree. These he arranged the better to catch, as I understood, the energy of the spheres. (It was an activity that bore a certain resemblance to one of my grandfather's pastimes, rearranging the branches on mystical diagrams of the Tree of Life.) At other times Dr. A-men might be out under the stars, digging in the earthworks surrounding his tumbledown house. Using a coiled coat hanger with a rag tip dipped in magnetic sand, a device he called a treasure witch, he'd divined that the original occupants had buried a fortune somewhere on the grounds. So far, however, his bewildering complex of ditches had turned up nothing but more bottles and animal bones. These latter he'd put to good use, grotesquely reconstructing them, turning the interior of his trash-appointed mansion into a museum of monsters.

Whenever the doctor saw us coming, he perfunctorily tipped his beaver hat, revealing a head like a scorched kettle. There were cracks in the kettle that became eyes and a mouth when he spoke, then reverted back to cracks when he was silent. After he'd heard our request, he would ask us to kindly excuse him while he repaired to his "elabbatoy." We would follow him anyway as far as a vine-tangled porch, then look through a window into a room that had seen better days, where ladies had probably entertained suitors, and fathers informed errant sons they were being disowned. There we'd see Dr. A-men poking around among his bones and the jugs that sprouted tubes like curling copper smoke.

We would be back waiting in the yard when he returned with some inky decoction or a root shaped like a pair of frog's legs. Making great claims for the medicinal properties of the article to hand, he might declare: "This one give me by the bad news Right Reverend Razzpeeyutin, who done had it off his longtime ladyfrien Joan a Arc, who done got it direckly from the man a the hour, that am to say his ramblin majesty High John de Conqueroo."

Once, at the behest of Ringworm the gambler, who tipped us papershell nuts with dimes inside, we carried a message to a hoochie-kooch dancer in Professor Miller's All-Mahogany Revue. From a catwalk in the wings of the Palace Theater, we watched their glittering precision; we counted aloud the propeller revolutions of the tassels on their tushies, and applauded the way they dispatched with uniform high kicks the customers who tried to climb on stage. We stuck around for the amateur segment and heard one of a series of comics called Kokomo claim that his wife was so fat he had to hug her on the installment plan, so ugly that when she went to the zoo the monkeys paid to see her. But the audience shouted his punch lines before he could get them out, and the tummler, known as the Lord High Executioner, wearing a leopard-skin toga and waving a revolver, chased him off the stage. Then came a sister act announced as everybody's favorite pair of canaries, Mercy and Circe the Café au Ladies, who proceeded to argue over the order of their songs. They were followed by a hypnotist who caused an apparently prim volunteer from the audience to hike her skirt and grind her hips to a rolling drum. There was an infant billed as a tap-dancing prodigy, who turned into an evangelist once he'd mounted the boards, and had to be carried off by the seat of his pants. There was a magician so unpopular that his mere appearance provoked a hail of rotten vegetables.

Several times we'd been sent out to hunt some missing novice who'd run away in a cold-footed funk from the Baby Doll. On those occasions Lucifer had judged that the likeliest place to look for the girls was at the picture show. Duck-walking past the box office of the Orpheum Theater on Main Street, we would steal up into the "nigger heaven" gallery. In the lofty darkness just under a ceiling hung with gilded fruit, we'd plop down in half a dozen laps before finding vacant seats. That's how, during a period of late-night detective work, we saw the tail end of *The Invisible Man, Captain Blood,* and *Snow White.* We'd seen a midnight double bill in its entirety *(Gunga Din* and *Lives of a Bengal Lancer),* and a vaudeville troupe that featured Eddie Cantor, before Lucifer had admitted that we might be barking up the wrong tree.

We saw Bessie Smith, to whom Lucifer allowed a degree of famousness beyond his ordinary use of the word. He said she had a voice whose pitch could break your glasses or cut diamonds; it could set your rinktum free. She was coming out of the Club Panama, wearing a peacock plume headdress and a gown made of mirrors. Surrounded by gaping admirers, who were reflected in the gown, she looked like she was decked out for the evening in the myriad faces of Beale.

Carrying unpaid hotel tabs into the rooms behind the Chop Suey House, we saw men lolling like tent caterpillars in a network of crisscrossed hammocks. We got silly breathing smoke that smelled of burnt rubber and sour cream. At the forge on Vance Street we saw the blacksmith playing his bottleneck guitar for a white man, who kept mopping his brow and boasting, "I told them I'd go as far as Hades for the genuine goods." Then he would tap the microphone to make sure that the song — about the failure of a key to fit a certain keyhole — would not be lost. We saw a local undertaker sitting defiantly astride a man lying face-down on the sidewalk, his shirt slashed to red spaghetti.

"Ol Hylo," the undertaker had offered to explain to one and all, "he been kilt now three, fo time, but it look like this one here done took. I ain't be cheat outta his funeral airy again."

One night we came across a moonlight baptism in progress. It was being performed, said Lucifer, by the congregation of the First Beale Street Church of the Everloving Shepherd Who Dwells on High. Having traditionally used the snake-ridden Gayoso Bayou for such functions, they had shifted their site to the new lagoon, which was considered, as a relatively fresh act of God, to have greater qualities of sanctification.

Backed up by somberly clad parishioners, the procession of prospective saints — or "haints," as the wise guy liked to say — gathered at the water's eastern edge. They were clapping their hands and singing a hymn: "What it say in the ten chapter ten / Is you die you bound to live again." One by one the candidates for the sacrament of immersion would wade out into the muck, their white gowns parachuting about their hips. After their dunking at the hands of owl-faced deacons, dressed impractically in slickers, the newly baptized were given to inspired acrobatics in the street. They writhed and tumbled in full view of the fleshpots of Babylon, outflanking Satan with cunning maneuvers. Giving voice to spine-tingling hallelujahs, they called for a witness, which I supposed was where we came in.

"Do Jesus!" they shouted. "I'm testify to the blood and the recollection!" Then the angels seemed to have gotten hold of their tongues, making them sound like tuneful daveners, like a Torah portion might sound if read by warbling birds. It was an observation that prompted my suggesting to Lucifer, "Could be that there's a little Yid in 'em." Upon which the wise guy, who as always had to have the last word, replied, "What you reckon, Mistah Harry, think they was one or two in the woodpile?"

Another time we saw a fight in a juke joint that was still going on when we went back the next night, though the men were bloodied to featurelessness, moving in a sluggish slow motion, and nobody was paying attention anymore. Then, sent by one of the Baby Doll's high-rolling regulars for ribs to cater a private affair, we went round to Johnny Mills's. In that ramshackle, screen-door institution, smoke feathering out every knothole, I — who'd been more or less kosher from birth — had my first taste of barbecued pork. I chewed meat the consistency of charred embers marinated in axle grease, topped with a pebbly yellow matter indistinguishable from my loosened fillings. Though I put aside the sandwich unfinished, noting how the absorbent white bread held the impression of my fingerprints, I told the twins it was the best I'd ever had. Later on I spat up discreetly in a rubbish pail.

Whenever she saw me hanging around the hotel, Aunt Honey would always ask me whether I was lost. Considering the tumultuous cackling that generally followed this question, I suppose she thought she was being funny. But as much as she seemed to be enjoying herself, moving furniture with her earthshaking hilarity, I can't say I was able to enter into the joke. Aunt Honey excepted, however, the ladies of the Baby Doll had pretty much grown accustomed to having me around. Careless in their attire at the best of times, they seldom took the trouble to cover themselves up for my sake. Quite often I received the heart-swelling mazel, if the heart can sometimes slip below the belt, of a glimpse of magenta nipple peeping out of a flimsy halter. Or, conditions permitting, the fubsy half-moon of a mole-flecked derriere, revealed for the instant it took to scratch a spider bite. Or a long exposure of coffee flank like a shapely greased beanstalk that only the most nimble could shinny up to paradise.

If ever the women caught me looking, they would gently rebuke me: "I ain't hear'd you say thank y'all, Mistah Harry." Then they would laugh over the way my ears became inflamed and I tried to cross my legs while standing up. Some of the things I liked most to watch them doing were sighing contentedly at what they saw in a hand-held mirror, tapping their slender fingers on a saucily cocked hip, raking their hair until it stood up like a nest of serpents, dropping an ice cube into the hollow at the base of their neck. Then I liked to watch the slow snail's progress of the ice and the trail of moisture it left as it slid into the dark valley between their bazooms.

In time I came to know them all by name. There was Dido ("cause I likes to cut me one, ef you takes my meanin"), who enjoyed a drop or two of belladonna in her lemonade. And Casauba, who embraced her customers like poured molasses, but kept her face unavailable for kissing behind the veil of her cardinal cloche. There was the back-sassing Sally Sweetmeat, always with a ready remark, with the silvery laughter of a glockenspiel. Her boast was that she'd served time in prison for matricide: "See, we have done quoil bout which side the mattress I spose to be." And the lazy Sugar Monkey, whose splay-legged bones had turned to rubber under the conflagration of her auburn hair. Concerning her great rolling bosom, the popular theory was that it was subject to tides. Snowpea, the freckle-faced, biscuit-skinned albino, liked to show off her various keepsakes: the whistle made from the ring finger of a dead lover, the ashtray made from the patella of one still alive. She told me, "It were the loup garou what scare me white. Now what done scare you, home boy?" There was the practical-minded Oraldine, who pinned a rose behind her ear during business hours, keeping tally through a system of plucked petals like a botanical abacus. And the devout Sister Pacify, who was a charter member of Brother Scissors' Do Right Church. There it had been revealed that, in the descending chronology of her former lives, she'd been a bride of John Henry, the Shulamite from the Bible, and an Ethiopian priestess turned into a bird and exiled to an island that had sunk off the Florida coast.

The ladies, in turn, had their string of pet names for me: Humpy Moses, Breath'n Britches, Young Massa Calamine, "cause you pank like the lotion and we gon have to spread you where we's itch." Sometimes they could be relentless in their teasing, always fingering my hair into kiss curls and playing at telling my fortune. Tracing the lines on my palm or the configuration of virgin whiskers on my chin, they would solemnly prophesy the number of hearts I was fated to break. Then, though I didn't understand why this should pass for humor, they would howl themselves into tears. At other times, however, they might suddenly seem not to be playing at all, such as the night that I'd eaten a surfeit of sardines with the twins, and Snowpea tickled me till I let go a resounding fortz. Sniffing the noxious air around me, the ladies had reached the consensus that here was the harbinger of an authentic ill wind. I thought they were kidding, of course, until Sister Pacify sanctimoniously proclaimed, "Fartomancy ain't never lie."

Frequently the ladies would follow me back to my alcove, or visions of them anyway, which spilled from my mind to crowd around my bed. They stepped up their campaign of teasing me, not giggling anymore but growling low in their throats, their bodies swaying with a feline urgency. That's when they'd swear me to secrecy, then proceed to teach me tricks of love forgotten since the time of the Pharaohs. They taught me tricks named after long-extinct animals and ancient machines, tricks that the Lord Himself was ignorant of — because if He learned of such shameful goings-on under His sun, His out-of-countenance blush would incinerate the world. On such nights I lost the few hours of sleep that were still left to me.

During my trips back to the Parkway to borrow more books, I started to relax a little in the company of my cousin. It was a situation that seemed to be mutual. A certain chumminess, if you will, had begun to evolve between us — so sue me. This is not to say that she entirely dropped her theatrical posturing, or that she didn't occasionally revert to her poor-in-spirit routine. But on the whole she greeted me with what I took to be a healthy enthusiasm. What's more, she even looked to be putting on a little weight. Her gaunt cheeks had acquired what might almost be described as a tawny hue, this from the tan she'd gotten while pacing in her garden. The sun had also tinged her blue-black hair with threads of scarlet, which set off to some advantage the slightly bloodshot cast to her eyes. I don't think it's an exaggeration to say that Naomi had acquired a kind of gypsy air.

It was clear that my visits were doing her good. This was not a role that anyone could have accused me of seeking, but I confess to having been a little curious about the extent to which Naomi might yet be transformed.

Sometimes I hung around even after she'd loaned me the books, which she'd taken to bringing down to the garden before I could ask. The maid would serve us iced tea with a sprig of mint and sticky macaroons. I munched and sipped while Naomi paced the herringbone bricks, relating the pleasures awaiting me in what she thought I was about to read. I listened attentively, thinking that this might come in handy should she want to quiz me later on. But she never bothered. She was much too busy getting the stories off her chest to inquire how I might have enjoyed them. She was too delighted by the evidently liberating act of giving her library away to worry about whether or not it was put to good use. Not once did she pry or ask for the return of her unsalvageable volumes, nor did she pull a long face when I carried them away, now that she knew she could trust me to come back for more.

Often I felt that, even if the books weren't for me, I still owed my cousin something in exchange. Once I even went so far as to reciprocate after a fashion, telling her snatches of what I'd seen with the twins. I told her about hickory-striped gamblers and double-brained witch doctors, frail sisters with rabbit fever who flounced their dresses to stir the breeze. But, catching myself, I pretended that these were references to characters in books I'd read on my own. I would have been happy to loan them to Naomi, but they didn't belong to me.

In the meantime, having theoretically fed Michael a whole curriculum's worth of reading, I was ready to call it quits. I was wasting my energy, not to mention Naomi's books, on an am horetz, a nincompoop. Of course Lucifer continued to make ridiculous claims for his little brother's progress. (It was "l'il brothah" because, according to the wise guy's apocryphal version of their nativity, only he had been delivered from his mama in time. "Michael, he gots to be prize out after she have already pass on, which it is how he ain't been all the way born.") But while I didn't say it outright, I made up my mind that I'd contributed enough to the dummy's fruitless education. Besides, it was Cotton Carnival time, and with so much going on, who would notice if I turned up empty-handed?

166

Festivities were afoot, and having ignored the whole affair during the previous spring, I was determined this year to make up for lost time. There had been some debate in the local papers over whether the Carnival should be held at all, given the terrible aftermath of the flood. To stage a celebration in the face of so much misfortune would constitute an indecency, said some. But the more common feeling was that a carnival might be just the pick-me-up the city needed. The citizens of Memphis had grown weary of being a population under siege by the river. They moved leadenly among the clutter of flood refugees, like people surrounded by ghosts they refuse to believe in. What they needed, these citizens, was a little relief, and not the kind, as one editorial quipped, that the government distributes along with sanitary napkins and fruit.

Anyway, the Cotton Carnival was one of Memphis's most time-honored traditions, and hadn't the city taken pride all along in its policy of business as usual? The stores had stayed open and the banks had continued to foreclose. The alphabet agencies never slept. While their tracks were hoisted on trestles over the washed-out thoroughfares — except on Beale, which was judged unnegotiable — the trolleys ran relatively on time. And it was safe to assume that the graveyards, give or take a few postponed funerals, remained in use. Bodies were not gathering dust in back rooms, and everyone else's grandmothers were laid to rest with appropriate honors. Not that I worried much about Grandma Zippe these days, or any other members of my family, living or dead.

Like the twins, who were on call for any odd commission twenty-four hours a day, I was learning to do without sleep. As a matter of form, I would put in my appearance at the pawnshop every weekday afternoon, then walk away from it in the early evening. I seldom bothered now with going back to North Main Street for supper; instead, I preferred to scrounge some fried catfish and vinegar pie along with the twins after they got off work at Mambo's. Since my mother thought I was with my father and vice versa — if my father thought about me at all — my freedom was practically complete.

Naturally I still had to return to the apartment at some point each night. If my mama was alone, I would ask her politely — though not too politely, lest she get suspicious — how her day had gone. I would nod with what patience I could muster as she recounted "your grandfather's" latest enormity. I made a diligent show of doing my homework, maybe listened to "The Firestone Hour" with Mama, provided she wasn't on the phone to her brother-in-law. I listened to "The Green Hornet" with Grandpa Isador if he happened to be around and sitting still. At about nine I yawned ostentatiously and remarked what a long day it had been, hoping that anyone hearing me would take the hint. Shutting myself up in my alcove, I waited for the apartment to grow quiet, then I unfolded the bed, plumped the bedclothes, and slipped out the window.

Only once did I feel that my family's influence might have extended farther than I liked to give them credit for. That was when I saw my father's puller in the faded front parlor of the Baby Doll Hotel. I was about to climb the stairs behind Lucifer and Michael when I caught sight of him through the bamboo curtain. He was wearing the mohair sport coat that hung to his knees, making his nautical salute to Aunt Honey and a couple of her girls. Frozen in my tracks, I listened to him croak, "Y'all pardon my hand say gimme do my mouf say much oblige." It was about the longest speech I'd ever heard him make.

Backing up in a panic, I ducked under the staircase and wondered how I'd been found out. My delinquency discovered, Papa had sent Oboy, citizen of both sides of the water, to bring me back. Well, he wouldn't take me without a struggle. I'd kick his knees, I'd rub out his wrinkles like the writing on the golem's forehead, and he'd sleep for a thousand years. The bamboo jangled and I peeped out to see him scuttling toward the front door, lugging a stuffed leather satchel. When the door shut, I crept from my hiding place and went to a parlor window to look out. I saw him under a lamp on Gayoso Street, handing the satchel to a cigar-puffing fat man in the back of a Studebaker touring car.

"That they landlord, I swan." It was Aunt Honey grumbling at my shoulder. "Man so evil-greedy he ain't have a shaddah."

If I hadn't been so shaken, I might have argued that not only did he have a shadow, but it was longer than you would have guessed. This is not to say that I wasted much time in contemplating the reach of my uncle's dominion, or the way that it compromised Aunt Honey's much vaunted proprietorship. On the contrary, by the time the twins had come back downstairs — their pockets full of whatever the night might require — and we hit the street, I'd put the entire episode out of my mind.

Once or twice Lucifer had mentioned the arrival of the royal river barge, "which it a come down like a floatin fizgig, like the glory boat." But beyond looking forward to the barge, he seemed to have no particular interest in the other Carnival events. This disappointed me, since I didn't regard the merry-making on Beale Street as an authentic part of the Cotton Carnival. Then Lucifer was obliged to set me straight about the "real" Carnival, which was, as he explained, a sort of by-invitation-only affair. It consisted mostly of "yo private funkshum," a phrase that on his tongue sounded obscene. These functions were held behind the closed doors of mansions and hotel ballrooms. They were sponsored by your "hinkty" elite: "Kinda folk will play golf on a horse so cain't nobody caddy. Eat fish turd look like buckshot, be alla time talkin" — and here he held his nose — "faw faw faw."

So I had no choice but to agree with him: who needed the snobs. There was, anyway, plenty of action (when was there not?) right here in the neighborhood. The Cotton Maker's Jubilee, which was the colored answer to the restricted Carnival, was now in full swing. The shvartzers had set up their own impromptu fairgrounds in the wagon yard behind the Daisy Theater. They had booths selling ribs and fried pies made by the ladies of rival churches, and try-your-luck concessions run by a shadier element whose proceeds went to fly-by-night charities. They had their own royalty, who put in an appearance in their own unofficial parade, a complement to the authorized parade down Main Street in which traditionally unshod Negroes in stylized antebellum rags were harnessed for the purpose of pulling the flower-decked floats. It was not a sight, as Lucifer spelled it out, that inspired the colored people to abandon themselves to good times.

So we were there among the crowd in front of Mambo's on that early evening in May, bobbing for a glimpse — over fedoras and children on shoulders — of a procession two miles long. In the vanguard were the high-stepping school bands, playing blue notes in a dazzle of sequins and polished brass. Precision marching, they headed for the bayou runoff as if they expected the waters to part, then splashed in up to their hips without breaking stride. The drum major augered the air with his baton, kicking his chin with his knees, and the crowd went delirious. Some broke ranks to join the parade themselves, becoming second-line marchers with mops and brooms that they twirled artistically. They fell in beside the columns of fraternal and benevolent societies — the Knights of Pythias and the Lost Tribe of Canaan, resplendent in their lionskin tunics and admiral's hats, some carrying crosiers. Not to be outdone by the flashy brass bands, they also waded into the water to uproarious applause.

Next came a lumbering caravan of crepe-paper floats, shoved along by gangs of self-congratulating boys in rubber boots. These floats turned out to be as good as their name. Mounted with historical tableaux depicting darkies of distinction, draped with banners advertising local boilermakers and chiropodists, they were fitted out also with amphibious modifications — oil drums and netted bundles of cork. When they were launched across the lagoon, the spectators were beside themselves again.

Because I was frankly bewildered by some of the scenes that the floats portrayed — the gingham-clad granny holding a branch hung with tinsel stars, the codger with the cardboard test tube frothing cotton wool — Lucifer had offered to fill the gaps in my education: "Tha's the Moses lady have lead the slave to yo promise land Chicago Soufside, an tha's the man what have invent the peanut." Then, "lastest but not leastest," appeared the reigning mayor of Beale Street, standing among a bevy of young ladies in the back of a shining black La Salle.

His election, according to the wise guy, was annually uncontested. This was due to his inherent stateliness, and the gold-braided livery that belonged to him by virtue of his head-waiter's job at the Hotel Peabody. The girls alongside him were mostly content to throw chocolate kisses and Monopoly money, but a couple of them (none other than the Baby Doll's own Sugar Monkey and Oraldine, who'd insinuated themselves to the scandal and delight of the crowd) seemed bent on ruffling the man of the hour's composure. Looking somewhat martyred by their fawning attentions, the mayor, however, managed to retain his poise. He flung fake money and repeated the benediction "Every man a kang!" until the car had entered the lagoon and promptly stalled.

Meanwhile the parade proper had been convoyed over the water, where it broke apart and dispersed into the side streets of the pawnshop district. The crowd around us had also thinned, as families remembered their whereabouts and began to return the tenderloin to its regular denizens. It was here that I surprised myself by making a proposal. This wasn't like me, but in the wake of the hoopla I was left feeling restless and ready for more. I was thinking there were places other than Beale Street to be.

"Why don't we go to the midway?" I suggested, then right away wanted to take it back. What I'd meant was the regulation Carnival midway, erected in Confederate Park by the river — featuring, as the billboards blazoned, miles of sideshows and games, and rides such as the Slide of Death. But the shvartzers, as I'd suddenly recalled, were only allowed to attend on specified "colored nights," and I didn't think this was one of them.

I waited for Lucifer to bristle a bit and remind me of this fact, thus letting me off the hook, but since when had I known him to shy away from the prohibited? Instead, he'd put on his thoughtful face, pretending to consult with his brother. Then he turned back to me with his yard-wide grin. "Copacetic, Mistah Harry," he said. "Do y'all lead us the way."

I'd never before led the way. It had always been Lucifer's show, naturally, since we'd always been more or less on his stamping grounds. By the same token, when invading the territory of the white man (before sundown, I might add), it was just as natural that I should be the one to chart the course. So why was it I felt like my bluff had been called?

Once we were on our way, though, I started to get into the swing of things. I kept several paces ahead of them so that no one would realize we were together, and began to enjoy a sense of cloak-and-dagger. I was a double agent, smuggling books one way and Negroes the other, up and down the treacherous pipeline of Beale. I was the Moses man. By the time we'd angled our way through the downtown streets, arriving at the park, now surrounded by bill-plastered hoardings, I felt I was completely in charge, confident of certain skills I'd developed thanks to the crafty company I kept.

Such as breaking and entering. Witness how I steered the twins away from the crowds that were streaming toward the gate. I told them to follow me as we circled the fence to the eroded river side of the park. Employing the sixth sense I'd recently acquired, I located a loose slat in the hoardings; I pulled the board from its nail until there was room for us to slip through.

In the dusty compound behind the sideshow tents — the loudspeakers broadcasting yowzahs and step-right-ups — we kept our noses low and began to snoop around. I was of course aware of a certain pointlessness in this. If I'd wanted, I could have walked abroad at perfect liberty according to the birthright of my race. I could have ridden the bumper cars, to say nothing of the Slide of Death, and thrown baseballs at a target that, if hit, would dump a mugging shvartzer into a tub of water. But these days I was happier skulking about the underside of things.

Dropping to all fours, I stuck my head under the taut canvas skirt of the nearest tent, heartened that the twins still followed my lead. Then I had to look back at Lucifer to ask silently if he saw what I saw. Was I mistaken or wasn't the interior of this tent out of joint with the world in which our uplifted rumps remained? I yanked my head out to make sure that we were still under the same pink twilight of moments ago, then took a breath and ducked beneath the flap again. It was there as before, what might have been the "One Man's Family" living room, complete with carpet and standing lamp, sofa and armchair, an end table with a bakelite radio and a hanging bird cage — in short, a comfy domestic oasis amid a waste of sawdust. But seated around it, instead of Mom and Dad, were an assortment of jokes played by nature, not necessarily in good taste.

There was a man like a zeppelin in a sleeveless undershirt that could have swaddled Aunt Honey, with enough material left over to sail a boat. Wedged somehow into the armchair, he spilled over like tons of dough allowed to rise unattended. Here and there you might have identified a telling detail: a tonsured fringe of hair, a lit cigarette, a ring on an upraised pinkie above

173

a teacup; but these were only clues to the character who was lost under that deluge of flesh. Sitting across from him on an arm of the sofa was something that even the wise guy referred to in reverent whispers — something he called a morphodite. This one had on an appliquéd dressing gown, fallen open to reveal a leg much smoother and shapelier than the hairy one over which it was crossed. It had a pair of what could have been boobies or impressive pectorals beneath its gown, and a face divided into two distinct halves. One side was conventionally pretty, the other handsome in a courtly sort of way. On the handsome side it sported one half of a salt-and-pepper beard, into which it was vainly braiding colored ribbons.

There were others: a limbless boy with sausage lips and a broken nose, wearing a knitted vest and lying like a belly-up turtle on an embroidered pouf. There was a sharp-chinned creature in a silk shawl with the face of a maiden aunt, though her sticklike anatomy had more in common with a praying mantis. She was spoon-feeding a ropy gruel to the turtle boy with one hand, tuning the radio with the other, chattering all the while: "It's almost time for 'Mary Noble' which is one program I never miss you know her husband left the hospital with amnesia and yesterday he sits down at the Horn and Hardart with his poor blind mother now you take another bite for your own poor mama in heaven . . ."

There were a couple of teenage kids on the sofa with interchangeable, dark-eyed vinegar pusses. They had on matching pairs of lederhosen which revealed the fact that, between them, they had only three legs. They had their arms around each other's shoulders in what might have passed for geniality, but their words betrayed a heated argument. The quarrel, which seemed to involve mutual accusations as to the other's complete lack of rhythm, looked like it was about to turn physical.

You couldn't blame me for feeling proud of myself. My first

time out as trailblazer, and look at the spectacle I'd led us to. But when I looked toward the twins for some confirmation of this, they were already gone. I slid out from under the tent and there was Lucifer with an arm around his brother, walking him through what appeared to be a rehearsal for a three-legged race.

"Lessee can us nigger twin make like the Si-maneez," he was saying. Sometimes these shvartzers had a rude way of reminding you how short their attention spans were.

"What's the matter," I snapped at both of them, trying hard to keep my voice down, "my freaks aren't entertaining enough for you?"

Lucifer left off the monkeyshines, though he kept his arm around the dummy's shoulder. "Powerful sorry, Mistah Harry," he told me with mock sincerity, "we ain't knowed they was yourn an tha's a fack."

I didn't think he needed to be so cheeky over a mere turn of phrase, even if he had a point. He didn't have to make such a palsie production of conferring with his idiot brother, asking him, "Michael, my man, where the fanny show at?"

Michael aimed his ineffable gaze at a nearby tent full of raucous shouting. It was lit from within, a large and shapeless shadow rippling on the canvas. Lucifer nodded and the two of them hit the dirt and slithered under the tent flap. My term as ringleader had expired for the night.

Resentful, I crawled under the flap behind them and chinned myself, as they had, on the back of a plywood stage. What I saw made me forget to keep moping. Beside a portable phonograph playing a slow drag of crackling trombones, a chunky woman with chrome-yellow hair that looked scorched at the roots, wearing nothing but a pair of high heels, reclined in the puddle of a cast-off lamé robe. She was resting on her elbows, her thick back toward the rear of the tent, the seahorse tattoo at her shoulder riding a spume of powder-blue moles. Toward a rowdy audience of unshaven yokels in red kerchiefs and washed-out overalls she had spread her lumpish thighs. She'd lifted her hips as if to make a table of her loins, a lazy Susan perhaps, as her undulant rotations implied.

The men in the audience were of the type that Lucifer might have labeled "peckerwood," as opposed to buckra, cracker, ofay, and pure white trash — distinctions generally too fine for me to grasp. But something about this crowd's off-color cat-calls and the way they beat each other with their hats seemed to identify them positively as peckerwood. Then a cry went up from the back of the house, a regular wild-animal howl, which brought all the other noise in the tent to a head. A boy was being lifted above the heads of the assembly — a lanky, flax-haired kid not much older than I, his face tallow white from what at first I took to be pain. He'd been injured or had a fit, and the men were trying to get him clear of the fray. But when I saw that he looked perfectly undamaged, with no hint of lunatic foam about his wide-open mouth, I concluded that it wasn't pain but fear that made him so pale.

They passed him horizontally from hand to hand toward the stage, then slid him, careless of splinters, along a brief runway. Like a bubble-eyed log at a blade, they aimed him toward the junction of the woman's splayed limbs. There was clapping and stomping in unison, a ruckus building toward a pitch that made you worry for the precariousness of the river bluff. There were "Great Godamighty!"s and a couple of "Thank you Jesus!"es as the woman grabbed the gaping kid by the hair. She snatched up the spangled robe from beneath her and spread it daintily, as if for a picnic, over the head of the boy in her lap.

A few of the men threw their hats but most of them fell silent, a silence more complete for the tumult of moments before. It put me in mind of that part of the moonlight baptism where a person is dunked under water and everyone else holds their breath.

"Oolala!" squealed the naked lady, her accent most decidedly un-French. "The kid never known it was such good eatin' at the Y."

This was when I got the nod from Lucifer. He had spotted a straw-skimmered sideshow sharper who, having apparently spotted us first, was advancing from around the corner of the stage. We dropped to the ground running but were forced to turn back for Michael, who'd remained glued to the scene. By the time we'd dislodged his grip on the stage, the carnival man was upon us, backing us into the canvas, which we needed no invitation to scram underneath.

Out in the compound, however, it was my turn to pause and look back toward the tent. Shoving his brother ahead, Lucifer stopped long enough to tug my sleeve and give a word to the wise. "Bes absquatulate, Mistah Harry, else they circle-size you all over again."

This helped me to remember that I'd been seen in the company of Negroes tom-peeping on a buck-naked white lady. If for such crimes the shvartzers had their eyes gouged out and made into buttons to sew shut their mouths, then what of me? What of the youth of Hebrew extraction who'd helped them to see what they should never have seen?

Then I was hightailing it through the lot behind the twins, keeping pace with my pounding heart, its din driving the stray thoughts from between my ears. Lucifer found the loose hoarding and the three of us scrambled through as one frantic multilimbed klutz. Fleeing the park, we stuck to the dry side of Front Street, putting half a dozen blocks between ourselves and the amusements before we dared to draw up in an alley to catch our breath.

Mine, though, stayed elusive. We were safe enough here in this cul-de-sac behind the classing houses, so what was the trouble? The question seemed also to be on the wise guy's mind as he passed me his medicine bottle. He was giving me the once-over, with special attention to the area below my waist, which I attempted to cover too late with my shirttail. Then he puckered his face to make the diagnosis, this doctor from Chelm. "Mistah Harry," said Lucifer, "we has to fine you some poon fo yo britches split an ol Hambone done join the party."

He made it sound like my inexperience was everybody's burden to bear. It was enough to make you want to take issue with all of his own windbag claims — the boasts that, if intended to make me eat my heart out, had been pretty successful. All that stuff about how he'd been initiated by this one or that one at some impossibly precocious age. How he'd done it under dogtrots or in the branches of persimmons, in the dressing room at Schwab's Emporium while the clerk outside the curtain asked how was the fit. He'd done it in the deep leather back seat of Colonel George Lee's double-parked DeSoto in the time it took the colonel to run into the Pantaze Drugstore for cigars. He'd done it, to hear him kiss and tell it, with all kinds — from the ones who'd been around the block to the daughter of the pastor of the Jesus Wept Tabernacle. He'd done it with the big ones, which felt like you were squeezing a cloud, and the skinny ones who clung like marsupials when you tried to leave; the ones who bit plugs out of you and the ones who spoke languages they swore they'd never heard; the seasoned ladies who gave you instructions that, if followed to the letter, caused their skin to ripple like it was made of rolling pins; the young things who hollered like they'd been gutted of their slippery souls.

To all these conquests the wise guy laid claim to, I would have liked to pronounce a hearty Bronx cheer. Not that it would have mattered to Lucifer, always his own most gullible audience. For him, the mere saying was believing.

"Why pick on me?" I demanded in any case, about to point out that his brother was having the same difficulty with his breathing as I was.

But Lucifer was busy again. He was examining an imaginary wristwatch, checking its precision against a fading smudge of sunset over the river. "I makes it bout a hair past my chegro bite," he said. "Time fo the barge be comin in."

Because of the unretreating floodwaters, there'd been some controversy over whether it was safe to sail the royal barge this year. The problem, as the papers saw it, was not actually sailing so much as docking the barge while the levee was still submerged. But as in the case of the Carnival itself, tradition won out over cautious opinion and a temporary landing stage was constructed at the foot of Beale.

When we arrived at the scene, the crowd was already at high tide; a solid mass of spectators was backed up almost to Main Street. There were people riding one another's shoulders, in some cases double piggyback. They were standing on rooftops, hanging out of windows and fire escapes, clinging to the bannered lampposts. The sight of such a mighty crush of spectators dampened what hopes I'd had of getting an unobstructed view of the river. But Lucifer, as usual, didn't know enough to be discouraged.

Darting eel-like, tapping on shoulders and pinching when necessary, he sidled through the multitude so neatly that you'd have thought he was following a predetermined route. Behind him his brother fitted himself snugly into the spaces that Lucifer left in his wake, leaving me to suffer the scorn of the onlookers as they tried to close ranks again. In this way we negotiated an acre of perspiring humanity, coming to a full stop only when we'd reached the rope that divided the crowd from the floating dock.

I guess you could say that this was my official debut in white society among colored boys. None of the smattering of Negroes I'd seen on the fringes of the crowd seemed to have penetrated it to this depth. So if this wasn't tempting fate, I didn't know what was. But as Lucifer had made it quite clear that I wasn't in charge anymore, I was happy to let him worry about things — that is, if he even knew how to worry. Of course, given the boisterous density of the spectators, nobody seemed especially concerned about the company I'd come in. Besides, it was dark out now, and the swordplay of spotlights along the levee was trained on the river and the sky.

From where we stood on the cobbles, just below the trestle and not ten feet from the water, we could already see the barge passing beneath the Harahan Bridge. From this distance it looked like a multilayered seagoing wedding cake, riding the platter of its own reflection. It was a storybook vessel, or so it appeared, making a preliminary stop before it continued upstream toward its real destination, which was probably the moon. Immediately I understood why Lucifer had suspended his disapproval of the Carnival for this single event.

There was a band on board, which you could now make out in their toy soldier outfits, posed up and down a staircase of footlighted cotton bales. They were playing what sounded at first like a variation on the general drone of the crowd, this until the barge came closer. Then melodies began to detach themselves from the surrounding murmurousness. They played "Waitin' for the Robert E. Lee" and "Mr. Crump Don't 'Low," a local favorite that listed the activities that the political boss had proscribed for the welfare of all. As the barge drew near the landing, the band went into a spirited rendition of "Dixie," and there was scarcely a dry eye in the crowd. In fact, some of the yokels — hatchet-faced river refugees by the look of them — placed their hands over their hearts.

Meanwhile the sky above Arkansas had begun to crackle and thunder with salvos of fireworks, causing some to cover their heads. Explosions rained over us: fantastic blossoms that grew in an instant to the size of the firmament, then dripped bright nectar as they swiftly faded away. There were nets of silver and green incandescence, spilling cargoes of luminous fruit, jeweled spiders spinning gas-blue filaments by which they dropped from the upstaged stars. People pointed as if they were about to attach a name to the lastest array, but "ooh" and "ahh" were all that anyone, including Lucifer, could think to say.

Under cover of all this, a couple of Carnival pages began to unfurl a tongue of red carpet, rolling it across the gangplank and up the cobbles toward a suite of waiting limousines. There was a flourish of lights and pompous music and a voice over the public address bidding unctuous welcome. Then, from their thrones atop the highest tier of the pyramid of cotton bales, the sovereigns of the Carnival rose. Followed by the slow train of their glittering retinue, they began their triumphal disembarkation from the barge.

Surging forward for a better view, the crowd shoved us up against the braided rope. Thus were we within spitting distance of the passing royalty. For all of his finery — the crimson cape trimmed in spotted ermine, the gold frogs and epaulets on a snow-white tunic, the medallion like a gilded pie crust — I thought the king looked a little uncomfortable under his heavy crown. With gravy eyes, the clef sign of an oily forelock setting off his dissipated features, he looked like the victim of a practical joke. Like he'd passed out after too many toddies, only to wake up on a showboat in monarchical robes. Still, he seemed committed to making the best of it, swatting the air with a scepter that he wielded like a tennis racket. This was in contrast to his pretty consort, who waved her own scepter as blithely as a magic wand.

She was a doozy all right. You name it, she had it: the vapory coif arranged in a heart-shaped setting around her serenely smiling face; the buttermilk skin highlighted by the port-wine nevus on her shoulder, like a fleur-de-lis. She had the plump boozalums crushing a corsage that had tried to come between them, plunging dolphinlike into the deep bodice of her emerald gown. All of which I appreciated, even if she wasn't my type.

Her rose-petal lips were too simpering for my taste, her

181

eyes, which the lights showed a transparent china blue, too dreamy and far apart. They lacked the candid come-hither quality that I liked in the ladies of the Baby Doll; give me their saucy temptations any day. This one was for yawning behind her dance card, or waving her hankie at a departing troop train. At best she might tear a strip from her petticoat to bind your mortal wound as you expired with her name on your lips. But she was altogether too much the universal shiksa for me.

Still, you had to hand it to her. She carried herself with a pleasingly self-possessed grace, what you might almost call majesty. To say nothing of how her sparkling diadem looked like a tiny castle in the cloud of her corn-silk hair.

But if I wasn't impressed enough, others certainly were. All around us the spectators kept up a jubilant ovation, some of them (albeit the more primitive and confused) actually falling to their knees. Here and there some frail onlooker, overcome by an excess of pageantry, might crumple into a swoon; they might be revived by furious fanning and spirits of ammonia, only to crumple again. Who would have thought that his shikkered highness and a milk-fed tootsie could have created such a holy stir? Even Michael, as I noticed, wasn't above being moved by it all. With a spasmodic though somehow prayerful rhythm, completely out of sync with the processional march of the band, he'd begun to sway from side to side. At one point he uncovered the burnished knob of his head and began to gnaw at his hat brim, taking a healthy bite out of the straw and chewing earnestly. On top of all this, if my ears didn't deceive me, he seemed to have started to moan.

It was an irritating sound whose source I couldn't locate at first, until it began to rise above the general commotion. Even then it took a minute to convince me that this unjoyful noise did in fact belong to the dummy. It was the first peep that, to my knowledge, had ever come out of him, a thick, gurgling whine from somewhere deep in his diaphragm, like a noise bubbling up out of an antediluvian well. By the time it had my complete attention, as well as Lucifer's (with whom I exchanged a puzzled look), by the time it had the attention of every bystander within earshot, the noise had graduated to a sharp but still throaty keen. It was a wrenching ejaculation, which had contorted the dummy's face into the shape of a horn.

Then suddenly Michael's newfound voice had lost its rust. It was a voice that had swapped its gills for wings, bursting forth in an exultation of virgin words.

"Lawd ha mercy!" he cried, sailing what was left of his hat into the pyrotechnical sky. "I wusht I be blind! I wusht I be struck blind di-reckly! She'm the las thing I see, everything else be disrumumbumf . . ."

The rest was muffled in the hand that Lucifer had clapped over his brother's mouth. Like a thief caught in the act by an alarm, the wise guy frantically whipped his head from left to right. He looked as if he wanted anything, a sack or a handy hole, to stuff the dummy into, a blunt instrument to clunk over his skull. He crooked an arm around Michael's straining neck for the purpose of strangling him, or so it looked, though I suppose the hold could have passed for a lifesaver's embrace.

At no time during our acquaintance had I ever seen the cocky kid so farshvitzed with panic, and the truth was that I could have done without seeing it now. As Lucifer manhandled the bug-eyed ex-mute through the crowd, dragging him toward higher ground, I was satisfied to trot along faithfully after. I was content to keep a discreet distance behind them, wondering if miracles would never cease.

Ten

O nce he'd been wrestled away from the levee, and the royal entourage was finally out of view, Michael ceased to put up a fight. All his energy, it seemed, had been enlisted in the making of language, and toward that end he continued to struggle while his brother continued to shut him up.

Thus, mumbling and sputtering against the gag of his brother's hand, the dummy was brought to Gayoso Street. He was hauled up three flights and hustled down a stuffy passage into what Lucifer called their crib. He always pronounced the word with a fondness that put you in mind of freshly scrubbed children, tucked in by a fawning watchdog who sat vigil at the foot of their bed. It was an unlikely association, given the airless oppression of their little closet, its water-stained ceiling with the peeled paper streamers glinting with crystals of sap, its solitary window more cardboard than frame.

"Now go ahead on and squawk all you wants, devilment!" said Lucifer upon releasing his brother, thrusting him onto the cheeping springs of a hobbled bedstead.

Although he lay there quite passively, words tore out of Michael's mouth like bats from a cave. There was a sensation of words crashing into the walls and ruffling the funny papers that covered the cracks in the plaster where the laths showed through. They spilled a drawerful of policy stubs and fluttered a pile of already ruined books under the bed. They spun on its thumbtack the photograph that Lucifer claimed was of their father (though the taped-together jigsaw, which included such features as a cleft chin and hair like Cab Calloway's, could have been a composite of several men). While nothing really stirred in that stifling space, least of all the delirious twin himself, still, you had the impression that their flyblown wreck of a room was a casualty of Michael's ferociously broken silence.

"She got to be mine!" he wailed, his limbs spread in limp surrender to the eruption of his mouth. "I'm be struck the diasticus side a dumb! I'm be snakebit. Cut a hex in my heart with yo razor, suck the pison, taste like sweet muscatel! O get back y'all railhead and heap-a-meat and split-foots ain't got a nose, I be studyin beauty here! Her am the one and only puredee supreme, the realest gospel dove. Done made up by a opostle on a bootleg still, then sprankle her on a cypress knee which it is whittle into a honey gal by sweet Jesus hisself. How we meet up is I strum ol Prospero's starvation box, or do I bust me a jack bottle fresh off a bottle bush, and out she pop. She give me a wish and I wusht I'se a sportin man. I wusht I have win her in a wile craps shoot: thow them bone down Pappy Haddon horn what he got it from a ol-timey knight, and she roll out the other end. Her ain't no bigger'n a minute, bone shakers sayin thow it back, but she fit nice longside the piece in my bull-fiddle case. Ain't two step down the road though, when she start in a ruction: 'Lemme out this here coffin, I ain't begin!' I open her up in my sankshum round back a Mambo's cause she still ain't have a stitch on. I drown them nits in her wig and rinse her feets, then feeds her on a mess a magnolia in whiskey sauce till she get her growth. I give her a housedress done belong to Hester Prine, rake her hair like you drag a river with serpent toof tine, get back. She light up like a punkin. Be radiatin like a buckshot bucket a moonlight, which I kotch it up in a abalone cistern fo her bath. And she say, 'Mistah Mighty Fine, y'all have done tickle my mind.' Ain't nobody harm her. Is she conjure by a wootch, be a ivory figgerhead on a glory packet makin downstream fo No Return, I kotch her up on my flyin fish name Bad Lazrus. Is she abduck by the debil, I flag a ride on the damnation train nonstop fo perdition, ride free cause I knows the conductor name a Shine. Get to blazes, I fetch her off a coolin board, raise her up with my juice harp rangement a 'Ramrod Daddy' and a cordial a 'Easy Life Numbah Nine.' She sit up and pitch a boogie, hair comin down like the sorghum been tump off the table, say, 'Mus be Michael, my hot chocolate man.' Do some white folks giant look at her sideways, I'm a mash his ding-dong, poke his eye out with a ugly stick, which it a get me sent up Siberya fo life and the dark day. See me tote round my shaddah like a towsack bout a hundred year. It like to bust my back till Daddy Mention, he have learn me to swang the diamond. I have learn from ol Doc Fustus how to signify a man, make his bowel turn aloose to the tune a 'No Ways Tired.' He have learn me also to frail a medicine tree, flap them leaves up a chokecherry sermon till I scapes the workhouse in a whirly wind. Be crazeh now, wear a horsetail didee, run with them lawless nigger in the piney wood, till the day come she be waitin on me in the shade. She ain't wear nothin but skivvy, got a halo a candlefly look like Lorna Doom, say, 'I'm a want you is you ain't already spoke for.' She say, 'Michael, my jelly boy, come squeeze my soul. Squeeze ri-cheer,' she say, 'through my peekaboo shift,' which I done it till it have get me back on my balance mind. But the nex thing you know I be kotched again, put on a guilloteem, do a chitlin strut when the ax have fall. She colleck my hade in her apron, wear it round her goosy neck tween her dinners like a asafetida bag. Plant it in her yard till it come up a chinkapin, branch be hang with a pair a travelin shoes. Meantime death, it don't take but jes a touch, see, so bimeby I come back from hereafter. I follows a road map give me by the Holy Ghost, wear a suit a flame tuck up in the seat by Herkules. Whoa boy, be magic now, who need a hade? Have a owl wang, a rooster spur, a monkey tail I have win playin coon can with Natty Bumpo in pa'dise. Got High Johnny's sangin lodestone and lightnin in a jar. Y'all have hear them song bout how the rascal Michael, he done rassle a walkin windmill. He have bushwack a posse a Ku Kluxers, make em pull off they sheet say uncle, he say don't call me uncle. Make em pull off they sheet, they turn out to be angel, say, 'That honey gal done belong to you.' Then I swear, can I find her, she sho nuff gon have my chile. Cept it ain't be no yard chile, got Jane Airs fo a midwive and Jesus' mama too, so the chile a be golden . . ."

He raved this way without a pause into the evening, swallowing air with every sentence like a preacher. Watching over him, Lucifer had begun to show conspicuous signs of gloating. He kept tugging at his suspenders and grinning his grin, apparently bursting with pride that the dummy had finally shot off his mouth. Here at last was proof of what the wise guy had always contended, that his brother had been able to speak all along. Feast or famine, that's how it seemed to go with these people: one minute you're as dumb as a post, and the next you couldn't shut up to save your life.

Of course, I hadn't been deaf to the occasional scraps of familiar stories, albeit in mongrel disguise, that kept turning up in Michael's rant. Could it be that there was some connection between this delirious narrishkeit and the glut of books on which he had supposedly stuffed himself? If so, if he had indeed been reading the books, then perhaps their provocative contents had been quietly seething away in his system, taking their time to build to a boil. And now he was letting off steam!

If this was the case, then I was as responsible as anyone for Michael's verbal coming out. The queen of the Cotton Carnival had only been a sort of coincidental catalyst. I was the engineer. So now when Lucifer grinned, I grinned hugely back at him. We were exchanging smiles like scientists congratulating each other on the successful conclusion of a bold experiment.

But just when I'd begun to enjoy taking credit for my part in Michael's relentless shpiel, Lucifer started to look a little troubled. In fact, I thought I detected more than a trace of the panic that I'd seen on his face for the first time down at the levee. It made me wish that he would for God's sake make up his mind how he felt about his brother's talkiness.

"Hesh now, fool," he cautioned gently at first, repeating the phrase until the pitch of his voice began to rival his brother's. He'd begun to rub Michael's hands so vigorously between his own that you'd have thought he was trying to start a fire. When this had no effect, he took to issuing stern warnings of grave consequences; he promised lammings upside the head at the hands of Aunt Honey if he didn't pipe down. All else having failed, Lucifer sank to his knees and proceeded to bang his forehead against the bedframe.

I didn't see why he should get so excited. All of a sudden he was acting like Michael was in some kind of danger. He was behaving as if the reformed dummy's incessant nattering was as good as a wound that wouldn't be stanched. It was true that Michael could have looked a little rosier. It was disturbing, for instance, that the cords of his neck seemed to tug at his jaw like taut reins, that his eyes showed only their whites as if he'd been clobbered. His body, bathed in sweat, looked completely bereft of bones, tossed willy-nilly into the sack of his overalls, and his voice in its maiden rant had already begun to grow hoarse. Granted, he didn't make a pretty picture, but was this any reason for Lucifer to get so upset?

"My love ain't never go to glory!" declared the dummy in one of his more fervent outbursts, training his nostrils left and right like a loose double-barrel. "Do she die, I be haint by her still! She my bride!"

"You crazeh!" Lucifer attempted, a little feebly, to shout him down. Then, making a face like he was forced to swallow a bitter pill, he stated the obvious, "She a white woman," wearily adding that the pale-faced lady in question already had a king.

Seeing the wise guy this downhearted, I thought I should maybe try and make an effort to take up where he had left off. "Shah!" I said once or twice to Michael, and "Allaloo," which was what my mother used to croon when I had tantrums. When these failed to quiet him, I took off the gloves. "Hold your tongue, blackguard!" I shouted, thinking that a literary approach might be the thing. "Belay that! Enough already! Shoyn genug!" But Michael apparently meant to persist in his folly until he'd done himself an injury. And my considered opinion was that we might as well let him.

Besides, I had become kind of interested in his monologue. I kept trying to identify bits and pieces of old stories as they were tossed up in the stream of Michael's babel. Here you might recognize Crusoe's blunderbuss, there Ayesha's veil, before they were muddled and modified to the dummy's own ends. It was a dizzying exercise, a bit like trying to rescue articles from a raging torrent: you could drown in the attempt.

But I was intrigued by the screwball turns of the defective twin's fantasies. Take, for example, the many incarnations of the Carnival queen. Sometimes she might be an unspoiled bird-girl, treed by high water in branches otherwise reserved for carrion crows. Another time she might be an orphan held captive by a usurer, held as collateral on a loan. She escapes with a troupe of minstrels in a traveling medicine show, only to be apprehended by authorities for possession of a talking goat. Taking asylum in one of the unidentical twin steeples of the Beale Street Baptist Church, she has to be rescued — rescue figuring throughout the shpiel as a cardinal motif. First she's rescued from the charity ward of the colored infirmary, where she's been stricken while nursing the blue balls of untouchables. Then she's rescued from a gibbet at a Delta crossroads, where she's been hauled up for the crime of wearing a dress too red. She's provided safe passage in a hollowed-out watermelon with a periscope. Disguised in burnt cork and Jemima calicoes, she performs a hucklebuck for the swamp-dwelling fugitives from the road gang, among whom Michael has placed himself. When her makeup runs, revealing her as her lily-white majesty, Michael bends a knee to thank her for the manumission of his tongue. He pledges that he and his men will fetch her an apple from the mouth of Boss Crump's prize spitted hog.

Somewhere in the midst of all this I had to return to North Main Street to put in my nightly appearance. I told Lucifer that I'd be back a little later, though he never bothered to lift his head from his hands. I went home, opened my schoolbooks, and made educated noises, invoking such watchwords as Teapot Dome Scandal and Manifest Destiny. I recited aloud the internal organs of the crayfish. Confident that I'd been largely ignored, I looked around the living room and had the giddy sensation that I'd entered the wrong apartment. When it passed, I yawned and waived my usual practice of waiting for my grandfather to come back from his public prophesying and for my mother to get off the telephone. I went into my alcove, lay down for the couple of minutes I could stand it, and was back at the Baby Doll before ten p.m.

Michael's marathon gibbering had not petered out during my absence. Drawn by his ballyhoo (apparently much to Lucifer's acute dismay), several of the ladies had drifted into the cramped little room. If they'd been shocked upon learning that the silent twin could talk, they didn't show it any longer, which isn't to say that they weren't expressing genuine interest. In fact, the ladies of the Baby Doll appeared to be all ears. Draped over the bars at the head of the decrepit bedstead, reclining at the foot of the mattress, they'd composed themselves as if attending a serenade. Now and again you might hear them utter some whispered comment: "The boy be ride by a talkin blues wootch," or "He be sho nuff cookin with natchl gas," but for the most part they kept a respectful silence.

In the end, however, they weren't so spellbound that they couldn't recognize cause for concern. They took turns holding the dummy's limp hands and coaxing him to sip sassafras tea, which they spiked with alum and grain alcohol. They sponged his face and massaged his potholed noggin with fingers that seemed to search for irregularities beneath the skull. They applied hot compresses to his forehead and passed hankies sprinkled with sneeze powder under his nose. Sometimes during these processes they grazed one another with inadvertently tender touches, with a solicitude that seemed more than sisterly.

What this put me in mind of was one of Naomi's stories, the one about the sailor who has himself strapped to the mast so he can listen to the mermaids sing without jumping overboard. But Michael had turned the tables on the mermaids; he'd lured them out of their grotto so they could listen to *his* cockamamy song. That's when it hit me what he'd done. The blithering eight ball had gone and found his muse, and his knocked-out word slinging had woken up a terrible longing in me, never mind the effect he was having on the ladies. As they swabbed his flickering eyelids, Michael looked, in his exquisite agony, almost what you might have to call handsome.

The close little room was generating a terrific heat. My T-shirt was pasted to my chest with perspiration and my shorts kept riding up between my cheeks. To make matters worse, Aunt Honey appeared in the doorway, sealing the exit with her girth. Huffing like a boiler about to blow from the effort of her ascent, she demanded to know what the ruction was about. Why weren't the ladies taking care of their clients below? But her first sight of Michael in the grip of his misguided infatuation brought her up short. She cocked her head to one side, causing her hairpiece to slide dangerously, and peered with interest through the slits of her flesh-sunken eyes. She cupped an ear, though the kid was still railing at the top of his ragged voice.

"Lawd hep us," she exhaled with a thoughtful regard devoid of her typical bemusement. "Debil done got aholt a that boy's tongue." She leaned back for a better appraisal, hands on her prodigious hips, her expression a struggle between consternation and disgust. Then up went her eyebrows, signaling a draw, as she asked ingenuously, "What it all is that he yappin about?"

Here Lucifer forced himself out of his slump and stepped forward to represent his brother. Hangdog though he was, he still managed to work up a little pantomime. First he aped Aunt Honey's hard-of-hearing, then flapped his arms one time in a show of befuddlement. It was his turn, it seemed, to play dumb.

"Sound to me like some kinda gal misry" was what he finally said. This struck me as a sort of tribute to Michael's new fluency: under its spell his fast-talking brother couldn't even manufacture the whole of a lie.

Despite the stuffiness of the room, I could hardly stand to tear myself away just before dawn. Still dopey with fascination, I wondered where was the harm if I stayed a little longer. Such unbridled diarrhea of the mouth couldn't be kept up indefinitely, and I thought I should see the thing through to its bitter end. Certainly nobody at the Baby Doll would mind my lingering. Wasn't I almost one of the family, so to speak? Chances were, my absence from the breakfast table on North Main Street would never even be noticed, and the same went for my attendance at the Market Square School.

A shudder passed through me, as if invisible fingers had given my shoulders a jerk, and I wondered what on earth I was thinking. I was thinking of breaking the ties to my old life for once and all, but it suddenly seemed a crime that it should be such an easy thing to do.

*   *   *

195

Late the next afternoon, before returning to the hotel, I stopped off at Mambo's Tonsoral just in case. Last night's mishegoss had probably passed with a little sleep — Michael would have had finally to sleep — and I would find the twins at work as usual. That's what I told myself, if only for the sake of my conscience, because the right thing was of course to wish for the dummy's speedy recovery. A speaking disorder like his could have debilitating results, and was nothing to fool around with. But when the chief barber told me I would most likely find Lucifer over at the Baby Doll, where his brother had taken ill, I practically rejoiced. I tore through the back yards to save the few seconds that the street route would have cost.

Michael still lay sprawled in his unchanged overalls, his back against the bars of the swayback bed, his arms and legs disposed like a discarded rag doll. His face was the color of charcoal and his voice, born yesterday, had already aged to a reedy bray. But his raving now seemed somehow less hysterical, more confined to the palpable particulars of his obsession. Having cast and recast his queen in such a variety of improbable roles, with himself alternating between savior and saved, he'd begun today to sharpen the focus. When I came in, he was extolling the various parcels of his beloved's anatomy like an auctioneer.

". . . See them eyes she got, mo bluer than Silk the Sport sapphire cufflank such as he steal from out the belly button a Delilah. See that hair — hunnerd proof straight evenin sun pour through lace britches. She got them titty like sand dune, and I'se a teenintsy A-rab ringmassah, lead my flea circus ca'van through the valley a they shaddah, cross her middle while she giggle the conniption, make fo the waysis fo winter set in . . ."

Crowded into the corner by the ministrations of the ladies, some of whom had spelled the nurses of the previous night, Lucifer hunkered disconsolately. His turned-around cap gave the impression that he was wearing his long face on the wrong side of his head. How else account for such an unheard-of show of grief? In some respects, you could have said that the wise guy looked as much the worse for wear as his blabbering brother. When I squatted beside him, I had to strain to hear him mutter what may or may not have been intended for my ears.

"Brothah Michael, he ain't eat nothin, don't know nobody. Just woofin — tongue be steady flap like I don't know what. Like a whip done whale his trouble mind to jelly. Go to sleep runnin his mouf, talk in his sleep, wake up his mouf still run . . ." Here, while I still wasn't sure that he knew I was next to him, he surprised me by speaking my name. "Mistah Harry," he said in that tone he reserved for asking the dummy's advice, "what we gon do?"

I was stunned that his desperation had reduced him to the point of deferring to me. "But I thought you wanted him to talk" was all I could think to reply.

"This ain't talk," he explained with a patience that I was clearly trying. "This woofin."

"So why'd you have me bring him all those books?" I wanted to know. Just what had he expected would come of putting literature in the hands of such a feeb?

The wise guy was looking at me like what did my question have to do with the price of eggs. "Cause he like to read," he said simply. That's when I saw in his eyes that I understood something he didn't. With his street wisdom of a ragged-trousers Daniel, Lucifer had yet to get it. He still hadn't made the connection between Michael's insatiable reading and his current unhinged state.

He hung his head, crumpling in his corner as if somebody had wadded him up and tossed him there. "Jus seem like my lil brothah have done splode," I heard him say.

I was disappointed that the ordinarily unsinkable Lucifer should give in to such shameless sulking, and I suspected that he was feeling as sorry for himself as for his brother. He was mourning the loss of his shadow, who'd taken the spotlight away from him. He even looked physically smaller to me, as if he were shrinking in direct proportion to the unchecked swell of his brother's delirium. Never before had I been inclined to take Lucifer to task, but I thought he was fair game for it now.

"Shape up, why dontcha," I exhorted him, the way Dr. Watson might cajole Sherlock Holmes out of a cocaine funk. "Get hold of yourself, man! You're Lucifer, named after angels and all that."

He gave a snort like a nasal full stop. "Name after evil angel," he brooded. "Name ain't nothin but my daddy's joke, do I even got a daddy."

This was the limit. "Ye gods," I sighed in exasperation, "sometimes I think I just don't know you at all."

At that, Lucifer cut his eyes back toward me again, though only for the instant it took him to declare, "Mistah Harry, you ain't never know me."

The ladies, meanwhile, continued their doting on Michael. They dabbed his parched lips with cheesecloth soaked in Essence of Van Van and Royal Crown soda, then circled him with sheets to hoist him over an enamel thunder mug. They hummed to him as they massaged his neck — though if you didn't know better, you might have mistaken their humming for encouragement instead of an effort to calm him down. They administered the odd home remedy, trying in vain to get into him a little crow's meat in sardine oil, or a julep of mashed snakewort and tuckahoe mold, renowned for its sedative properties. They placed a knife under the bed to cut the cord between the boy and whatever jimjams had taken over his tongue.

Under Sister Pacify's direction, they poured his specimens into a bowl of egg whites and topsoil. They brushed the mixture in weird ideographs on the wall over his head, then covered the bowl with a page of Scripture, which they put at his feet. But mostly they debated the virtues of this or that, of jimweed paste and saltpeter poultices versus horse leeches or cupping glasses or mustard and Jack of War enemas. (I seconded enemas as having been good enough for Harry Kaplan in his grandmother's day, though nobody took much note.) They argued so much among themselves that you might reasonably have accused them of trying to stall Michael's recovery.

It was a suspicion I'd had ever since the gentlemen callers had started checking up on the twin. The word was out on the prodigy of the Baby Doll, and the word was that Michael's babbling had certain benefits. As I'd heard more than one of the ladies mention, it helped prime their clients for the act of love.

Not that you could have read much in the way of amorousness in their expressions, the same poker faces they'd worn straight from the clubs. Spitting out their plugs of Red Man, they let it be known that they were skeptical about whether the kid's condition was naturally induced. They placed bets: Was it reefer, dreamstick, witch hazel, or Lady Snow that had rattled Michael's cage? They put money in a kitty that would go to the one who came closest to estimating just how long the boy's jaw would keep flapping. Some bet on which would expire first, the speaker or the speech.

Around the third day of his raving, there having been no perceptible improvement, a couple of the ladies invited their sorcerer of choice to have a look. It happened that Macedonia, a lynx-eyed octaroon, and the esteemed Dr. Washington Legba A-men arrived at approximately the same time. Briefly listening to Michael's palaver, they made pious judgments, beginning what amounted to a competition, each attempting to outdo the other in the fancifulness of his analysis. One attributed the twin's febrile condition to an alignment of planets nobody ever heard of, while the other named a specific demon loa and the organ it occupied. They were engaged in a full-blown contest of dueling methodologies — the one exhibiting symptoms of a divinely inspired palsy, the other chanting hermetic syllables sounding vaguely like pig Latin; the one flinging moondust, the other rattling painted bones — when Aunt Honey turned up to shoo them both away with a broom.

Still reluctant to admit that Michael's infirmity might be serious, Aunt Honey was nevertheless fed up with the superstitious carryings-on of her girls. So in the end she called in a respectable physician. A frosty-faced little man with a genteel cough, he complained that this was not the sort of house that his idea of a house call brought to mind. He implied that the distinction would tell in his fee. Turning the dummy's eyelids inside out, he squeezed his wrist and inquired discreetly about his bodily functions or the lack thereof. He nodded and hemmed professionally but preferred to reserve his judgment until a more thorough examination could be made. When the proprietress ventured to ask when that would be, the doctor suggested that, frankly, it might behoove her to consult a specialist.

"Speshlist in what!" boomed Aunt Honey, upon which the doctor stiffened, as if it were beneath him to have to labor a technicality, and bade her good evening.

Another doctor, this one in fact a specialist in the area of internal disorders, was brought in for a second opinion. Taking one quick baffled look at the patient, he recommended that Michael be transferred to a hospital for observation. Whether she'd lost faith in the medical profession or was balking at the expense, Aunt Honey failed to see the urgency. For one thing, the colored infirmary, built by Mr. Crump to the greater glory of his name, was reputed to be a pest-ridden hole. It was said that there were dozens of patients to each grubby ward and sometimes more than one to a bed, that they languished with undiagnosed diseases beneath pipes from which the tails of rats flicked indolently. The sick, regardless of their extremity, were generally acknowledged to be better off at home.

Anyway, since no negative prognosis had actually been pronounced, it was just as easy to assume the danger would pass. Whatever had gotten into the dummy would surely have to get out again. And that — despite the gathered momentum of his mouth and the evidence of his physical decline — was the attitude that prevailed.

When the rumors of her ward's strange affliction had begun to attract the curious, Aunt Honey threatened to close her doors, until she realized what this would mean. So while she still reserved the right to grumble at the men who visited Michael's bedside, she never made noises so loud as to discourage their patronage. Ultimately her practical turn of mind won the day. First she had her girls record the time their clients spent in the dummy's aphrodisiac presence. They were instructed to add the time to the customer's tab at the rate of a nickel a minute.

Enthused by the windfall profits, the utilitarian proprietress began to see the virtue in enhancing her ward's notoriety. Sometimes she spoke of removing Michael to the parlor, where the air was more breathable and he could be more properly cared for. But in the end she decided against it, judging that the sight of him downstairs during business hours would disrupt the normal trade. Besides, it would be easier to regulate attendance if the twin was kept confined to the tiny room.

With whetted ambitions, Aunt Honey took to her front stoop. Posting herself spraddle-legged in a wicker lawn chair, she barked at the passers-by, "Lady an gemmun, step up see a dumbo got the gift a gab!" As her pitch only served to promote general bewilderment, she then got hold of a sandwich board, intending to paint a slogan that would describe for the potential customer exactly what awaited him inside. Unfortunately, she hadn't the knack of inventing a neat turn of phrase, and as Lucifer was still sunk in his torpor, she began to pick the brains of hotel guests. This was when I came forward. Wanting to demonstrate my usefulness, I'd come up with an advertisement that I thought was both catchy and to the point.

"It's Alive! It's Alive!" I submitted. "The Love-Struck Loquacious Wonder of the Negro Underworld!" But Aunt Honey only asked me whether I was lost or what.

Nevertheless the gawkers got wind of the phenomenon, and in the days that followed they filed endlessly in and out of the fetid little room. Amid the Jubilee crowds, which were dense to the point of congealing with flood refugees, Michael became another sideshow attraction. Purely on the basis of hearsay, people forked over the price of admission, expecting I don't know what — maybe a nickel's worth (then a dime's, the price increasing along with the dummy's popularity) of some shady thrill. Once admitted, it took them a moment or two to adjust to the frenzied outpouring of language, which was sometimes garbled or inaudible, sometimes stupefyingly eldritch. Then they would wonder what kind of thing it was they'd paid their good money to see. But before they could demand a refund, some wild declaration of careless love would draw them in, and they were hooked.

Viewing the prodigy was now limited to one minute per ticket holder, though more than one ticket (or poker chip) could be purchased at a time. To institute this policy, Aunt Honey had stationed Oraldine at Michael's bedside with a stopwatch. Still, the spectators lingered past their turn. Often the proprietress would be called upon to remove them forcibly, to make room for the next in line.

Not just the Baby Doll regulars but all kinds trooped in to bear witness — field, house, and freshwater shvartzers, cotton-patch types who swayed and bore up as if they were at a camp meeting. Upstanding citizens, who publicly decried Aunt Honey's establishment, were told that until they'd seen Michael their education remained incomplete. Thoroughly edified, they would go away and return with their wives, women who wore hats like setting hens. As they listened, these ladies no longer remembered to feel compromised by their surroundings; they sighed over rampant bosoms and fluttered their fans with the speed of hummingbird wings. Then there were the young girls sidling close to their escorts, who in turn tried to make light of it all. They would waver between pugnacity and embarrassment while their girlfriends squirmed, looking in their disheveled garments — blouses come off the shoulder, buttons sprung — like they'd been roughhoused by unholy ghosts. There were the elderly who acknowledged "Tha's right" in pensive surprise, as if reminded of something they'd forgotten long ago.

Occasionally some vagabond musician would stand in the doorway and strum a whole convulsive spectrum of chords. It was anyone's guess whether he thought he was backing up the lunatic twin or egging him on.

Eventually the local churchpeople, convinced that events at the Baby Doll needed their special stewardship, sent around a delegation of elders to save the day. They brushed past Aunt Honey in her lawn chair without a by-your-leave and disdainfully ignored the file of spectators that stretched to the foot of the stairs. Marching up to the topmost floor, they demanded to see the saint — as one legend of recent vintage had it — who dwelled in the house of iniquity. They were met in the narrow passage by Oraldine and some of the others, barricading the door.

"Get back, y'all fallen daughter a easy vir-choo!" admonished one of the elders. "Us here on a solemn crusade." As none of this helped endear them to the ladies, they made room for their spokesman, a deacon whose hair was processed to the sleekness of sealskin. Mincing forward to clarify their position, he explained with humility, "We has come prepare to deliver up the boy to a mo sanctify enviromen."

At this point, half in and half out of the room, I saw Lucifer begin to stir. He rose from his baseboard slump and slid slowly up the wall from the corner where his dejection had kept him in silence these several days. While everyone was well aware that Michael's bushwa had placed his health in jeopardy, nobody but me seemed to have noticed the toll it took on his brother, though the wise guy had already proved himself impervious to any amount of wheedling from Mistah Harry. So I'd backed off but couldn't help noticing how, banished from the sickbed that the twins ordinarily shared, Lucifer looked like he could use a rest.

With an animal groan, he stormed out of the room and broke through the cordon of ladies, on his way to assaulting the churchmen. It took all the women, plus a couple of gawkers and myself — closing my eyes against his flailing fists — to restrain him. Otherwise, I don't know, he might have torn the deacon's Adam's apple from his throat and munched it with relish before the reverend gent's expiring eyes. It was yet another side of Lucifer I thought I could do without.

At length the fracas was squelched by the appearance of Aunt Honey, who'd clunked up the stairs, broom in hand. "What all this is?" she bellowed.

There was a hush before everybody started to talk at once. Again room was made for the oily deacon to pad forward and state his case. Making multiple chins, Aunt Honey looked as if she might be about to second Lucifer's notion of having the deacon for lunch. "Now lemme get this here straight," she began, rising to her full alpine stature. She puffed herself up even more imposingly before the accusation that her house might be less than a haven of godliness. Reinvigorated by her show of resistance, Lucifer was again at the point of breaking free, so that Aunt Honey had to turn and wallop him with the business end of her broom.

Then she calmed down a bit herself. She allowed that she

was sometimes too hasty in jumping to conclusions, though she had never been one to rule out the possibility of negotiation. Now if the churchmen could offer her some tangible guarantee of their good intentions . . .

The deacon put a finger to his lips, listening with an attentiveness that caused everyone else in that crowded hallway to listen as well. Michael was still at it, of course. He was describing a trip through what he billed as tunnels of love measureless to man. If you'd heard enough of this stuff, you understood that the voyage was his vision of his true love's internal geography. Returned from one of his numerous deaths as a hookworm, the dummy was aswim in her juices; he was looped in the loops of her vitals and lights. En route he admired the architecture of her dream-secreting organs, her toilet-water gland, her lungs like a pair of Mercury's new shoes. He called the roll of her tender innards like a conductor calling stops on the *City of New Orleans.*

When the deacon had gotten an earful, he swapped his humble demeanor for indignation. "The chile ain't no saint," he called upon his brethren to witness. "He done belong to the debil!" Which consensus was pretty much old hat by now. Prevailed upon by their spokesman to clap their hands over their ears, the church elders retreated the premises forthwith.

When the scene was dispersed, I discovered that Lucifer, whose arm I'd been holding, now had a deathly grip on my own. I had to pry loose his fingers, which left a row of red welts, before he came to himself a bit. Talking to me, he kept his head lowered, so that he could just as well have been speaking to the wavy floorboards.

"My sweet Michael, he be alla time upchuck his sorry soul," he said in a voice as distinctive for its flatness as his brother's was for its mad expression. "Putty soon he have been heave dry. Be choke an pass over in front the whole popeye street lookin on."

I'd been thinking that Michael might never run out of words. The wasted ground of his fleshless body would somehow indefinitely sustain the babbling fountain of his mouth. He would remain forever the Baby Doll's own continuous novelty act, a bigger draw than the amateur nights at the Palace. He was a fixture now, permanent and abiding, the perpetual main attraction of Beale Street. So why did Lucifer have to be such a killjoy? Why did he have to spoil a pleasant picture by speaking the simple truth: that in pining aloud for his impossible love, his brother was talking himself to death.

Of course this wasn't my problem. You couldn't say that Michael and I had ever been close. Who could blame me for having had no fellow feeling for a dummy who, until recently, seemed to have no feelings at all? Besides, with all of these obliging chocolate ladies around — who would surely be willing, despite his defects, to give one of their own a tumble — why did he have to go and fall for a marshmallow frail? Then there was the matter of Michael's talkiness itself, which I was not alone in having developed a taste for. So you had to wonder was it worth it to save the kid's life if it meant that his farcockte lovesong would come to an end.

But if I wanted to stay in the wise guy's good graces, I would have to agree that something must be done. Suddenly Beale Street wasn't fun and games anymore.

"Okay," I said for the sake of keeping up the conversation, as Lucifer's silence was even scarier than his brother's terminal logorrhea, "what have you got in mind?"

Eleven

Soon Lucifer was back to his old tricks. He began to look a little less chapfallen, actually going so far as to change his socks and rake the lint out of his rough-dried hair. He readjusted the tilt of his cap, smoothed the crease at its bill, and put some hip-slung strut back into his walk. I even saw him pick at a plate of head cheese to keep up his strength. But his face remained sere, the skin stretched too tight over a skull too large. Startlingly haggard, he looked, oddly enough, more unlike his twin brother than ever, whose cadaverousness was somehow becoming. What's more, the wise guy's schemes for retrieving his brother from the brink of a Gadarene rapture lacked something of his trademark pizazz. They were measures that seemed more suited to curing the kid of hiccups than saving him from a fever that threatened to burn him alive.

Still, I went along with his shenanigans, while the ticket holders mistook us for a part of the act. Rather than discourage this, we found it more convenient to play a little to the crowd. Holding fast Michael's jaws, for instance, I would ham it up a bit, like a man wrestling an alligator. Lucifer, meanwhile, would probe his brother's throat with a number of devices, not the least implausible of which was a feather. This he withdrew and examined with a clinical intensity, as if he expected words to cling to it the way doodlebugs cling to spit on a weed. He filled a syringe with a vinegar and chili powder solution, and squirted it up the dummy's nose, then pinched his nostrils till he sputtered like a backfiring engine. But this only resulted in momentarily redirecting Michael's verbal discharge, sharpening the taint in the already noxious air.

Abandoning the idea of physical insult as a remedy, Lucifer turned to psychological terror. We rolled newspapers into dunce caps and draped ourselves in sheets with eye holes. Then we made a cross out of the broomstick that Aunt Honey had broken over the head of a defaulting customer, and set fire to it at the foot of the dummy's bed. While this created quite a stir among the spectators, it made no particular impression on Michael at all. Nor did the noose that we hung from the light cord, though its sinister shadow alerted Lucifer to the possibilities of shadow play. So we turned the sheets into a screen, behind which we projected — with the help of gnarled fingers and a predatory-looking phonograph arm — what we hoped would appear to be monsters. The monsters turned up in Michael's driven soliloquy, where they were vanquished one by one. Instead of shocking him out of his obsession, we seemed only to be giving him more food for thought.

We then embarked on a course of comic distraction, Lucifer having scrounged a pair of Aunt Honey's pajamas. Helping me into one leg, he climbed into the other. Unable to coordinate our effort, however, we couldn't even manage to stumble bilaterally, and splitting our mutual crotch, we fell apart. While the audience was nonetheless amused, our performance was entirely lost on Michael, who had never been known for his sense of humor.

But Lucifer was still sold on the idea of a theatrical solution. The problem was that the entertainments he suggested involved absurdly elaborate staging. They required effects —

cloud-borne galleons, the interiors of twisters, blind leaps from casement windows — as impossible as the dummy's own sick fancies. In fact, they *were* the dummy's own sick fancies. Where Michael was taking some of his cues from our antics, Lucifer had now begun to borrow inspiration from Michael's flights. A kind of brotherly cross-pollination was at work, the theory being that, by performing the figments of his mind before the dummy's eyes, you could exorcise his festering brain. You could turn out its contents like pockets, and afterwards, with Michael's head empty again, peace would be restored.

I couldn't help wondering where the wise guy got off thinking amateur theatrics would work when his brother had already swallowed such gruesome home remedies with scarcely a burp. Still, it wasn't for me to sound the note of discouragement, though in the end I didn't have to. In the middle of concocting one of his unstageable charades ("Mistah Harry, y'all can play like you done catch a mighty fish, splits him open an it's Snowpea up inside, play like a queen") Lucifer seemed to hear himself talking. He came down with a clunk and was dismal once more.

I was confused when I returned the next evening to find him all fired up again, and with a vengeance. Intercepting me on the stairs, he was rattling on about something he'd read in the papers. Since when did the wise guy read the papers? His professed expertise in most areas notwithstanding, I was no longer so sure that Lucifer could read at all. But here he was, citing a certain item that made urgent claims on his attention, something to do with a high-society banquet.

"Now am the time we done quit pussy-putz around."

With his arm locked in mine, he steered me down to the kitchen, assuring me that it had come to him what steps must be taken, and along with this revelation had come a plan that was virtually foolproof. Shoving aside some skillets and a coffeepot, he sat me atop an uncomfortably warm coal-burning stove. I slid down, protesting, "What am I, dinner?" only to be hoisted back up again. From his pocket Lucifer produced a compact can of black boot polish, waving it in front of my nose like I was supposed to know what it was for.

All this was making me very nervous. Nor did it help that his grin chose this moment to make its spectacular comeback. Beaming, Lucifer related a scheme so preposterous that I was at a loss for words.

Not that I didn't know what I was supposed to say. "I've got a hunch it just might be crazy enough to work!" or some such shtus was what your faithful sidekick would have exclaimed. But given that Lucifer had just removed my glasses and begun to daub my forehead and cheeks with the polish, smearing dollops of it in thick waxy circles with his fingers, the best I could offer was "Wait just a cotton-picking minute!" Ignoring my complaints and brushing away the hands I held up to fend him off, he warned me not to move, then brought out his chammy cloth and gave it a snap. He proceeded to buff my face like a shoe. After a few strokes he registered a nod and clucked, "Mistah Harry, I is proud a the way you done took a shine."

Black as a old crow belly is how he assessed me, guiding my fingers into a pair of black gardening gloves. Then he stepped back and told me to look sharp. "Hop down, else you sweat an spile my handy work."

"Listen," I said, to buy time, "my grandpa's got these old books he used to read me to sleep from. They got all kinds of recipes how to get rid of evil spirits and such." I was thinking specifically of the stuff about the demon Lilith, Adam's first wife. In the books there were prescriptions, fairly simple incantations with a minimum of burnt offerings, that kept you safe from her interference in the night. They protected you from wetting the bed, an emission that Lilith was held directly responsible for — and, who knew, they might also retard incontinence of the mouth.

"So what do you say? It might just be crazy enough . . ."

Lucifer only snorted and replaced my spectacles like he was pinning a tail on a donkey. "Them book," he said contemptuously, and snorted again. "Now looka here. What you think have got the boy in this suckumstance cep them book."

"Where've you been? You never heard of fighting fire with fire?" I asked him, conviction fizzling from my voice as I spoke. It was useless to try and turn him around when he had such a head of steam. Up to some risky business, he was back in his element again, but this time I told him in no uncertain terms that he could count me out.

Who would have thought that the wise guy could be so sensitive? His features caved in, and all of a sudden he was pitiful. "Mistah Harry," he confessed, "I dasn't do no sich a thing less you come along."

That's how I happened to be trotting beside Lucifer through a twilit concatenation of alleys on our way to the Peabody Hotel. Or the Hotel Peabody, as it was called, on account of its distinction and class, its history of visiting potentates and notorious gangsters. On Beale Street it was often referred to as the Big House, since almost everyone had worked there in some capacity, including Lucifer, who'd served the odd stint as a bellhop. There'd been this notice in the *Commercial Appeal:* it seemed that one of your grand Pooh-Bah secret societies (somebody tell me what's secret about a society that announces its doings in the papers) was hosting a banquet for the Carnival royalty on the hotel's Plantation Roof.

Lucifer had made up his mind that we would attend the banquet and seek an audience with the Carnival queen. There ought not to be any problem getting in, since during the Carnival season there was always such a rabble of extra help. "You got yo house nigger run every whoochaway, look like a rumpus race, allus in a fine confunkshun. Who goin to know we ain't on the ficial payroll?" Once we'd successfully infiltrated the affair, the wise guy would take the first opportunity to approach her highness and plead his brother's case. An understanding and benevolent monarch, she would tap his head and shoulders with her scepter, saying, "Rise up, Sir Lucifer." She would graciously accompany him back to the Baby Doll, gliding through a gauntlet of curtsies into the sickroom. At the sight of her hovering there at his bedside, summoned into flesh from the words of his love-crazed shpiel, Michael would be jolted out of his fever. He would at last be restored to good health and his ordinary dumbfoundedness.

I had given up trying to point out the many ways that this scheme was full of holes. That it lacked the twin's typical shrewdness went without saying, never mind that it wasn't quite logical. Also, I didn't like the sound of this secret society business, which made me think of blood-stained altars, people wielding curved knives like moels. But what troubled me most was what the plan said about Lucifer's state of mind. Ever since Michael had been struck undumb, the wise guy had been, in his own way, as out of control as his love-bludgeoned brother. When he wasn't too wretched to move from his corner, he was walking around half cocked, in need of someone with sense to look out for his welfare. And who else was there but Harry Kaplan to fill that bill?

Through a revolving door we entered the lobby, which no other place in the city could touch for its swank. The place seemed to give the lie to the rumor of hard times. If, as was popularly touted, the lobby of the Peabody was where the Delta began, it was also where the Depression ended.

Its rich jade carpets were ankle-deep and echo-absorbent, its chandeliers like meteors. A pink marble fountain tossed a silver plume of water over a gaggle of paddling ducks, and a grand piano played itself. The cigarette vendor had legs like a thoroughbred, her face a dead ringer for Carole Lombard; bellhops on roller skates paged guests with expensive names. The sofas and satin loveseats, shaped like soft orange squeezers, were lousy with cotton barons in spotless white suits. There were film stars in the company of mobsters, courtesans like jaguars escorted by financiers conspiring over pastel drinks with paper parasols. There were espionage agents on the mezzanine, peering from behind false goatees, or at least that's what I took them for. And they all reminded me just how far we'd strayed from Beale Street.

No doubt sensing my reluctance, Lucifer kept a tight grip on my arm, leading me where we had no earthly business going. Shifted into his furtive mode, he hurried me past a bell captain leaning across the check-in desk. He jerked me while I looked over my shoulder for house detectives behind a humid wall of caladiums and banana plants. We bungled up some stairs where the opulent lobby abruptly gave way to an unadorned passage, its ceiling low with exposed steam pipes. At the far end of the passage was an open service elevator, toward whose scuffed recesses Lucifer had begun to shove me. He had to shove because I was starting to dig in my heels.

Under different circumstances I might have appreciated how well the kid knew his way around. But tonight I feared the worst. It was becoming increasingly clear to me that this enterprise was beyond foolhardy: it was suicidal. The greasy minstrel makeup that was clogging my pores wasn't going to fool anybody, and I didn't mind telling the twin.

"Say what, Brothah Sambo?" chirped Lucifer, tugging a cord inside the elevator, which in turn closed a gate from above and below like jaws. For a moment he looked at me as if he actually expected an answer, then broke into a fit of chortling laughter, slapping his thigh.

"Go ahead and knock yourself out," I told him stiffly. "I'll worry enough for the both of us."

He yanked a lever, and my knees buckled suddenly from the risen floor. As the column of numbers on the wall winked on

and off in their ascent, I gritted my teeth. I held my nose to pop
my ears, thinking I wouldn't put it past him to launch this contraption crashing through the roof. Then a bell sounded, a *P* at
the top of the column winked red, and my stomach rose from
my shoes to my throat.

When the gate yawned open, we were presented with a
scene that made me wonder: had we been hurtling somehow in
the wrong direction? Cauldrons steamed and braziers flared.
Black men with broad, lustrous faces and aprons stained in
gore, with tall hats like ossified smoke, labored with dripping
brushes over turning racks of meat. They presided over boiling
pots and flaming grills, stirring and basting with a grim-visaged
intent. Stoically they endured the antics of waiters who looked
like they'd lately been tumbled from a barrel of monkeys. A
swarm in white jackets, they balanced their trays with a breathtaking precariousness on the fingers of a single hand, or with
no hands at all on the tops of their heads. Dodging one another
in a deftly executed series of near pratfalls, they came that
close to taking what appeared to be choreographed spills.

I wasn't in any hurry to leave the elevator, but Lucifer had
me by the wrist again, hauling me out into the thick of that infernal activity. Waiters swerved and skidded all around us,
avoiding us so narrowly that I had to cover my eyes. When I
peeked through my fingers, I discovered that the traffic had
begun to give us a wider berth in deference to the stately emi-
nence, his chest decorated in a bonanza of gold buttons and
braids, who'd planted himself in our path.

By his finery I recognized him as none other than the honorary mayor of Beale Street himself, and was a little relieved. But
his unbending military demeanor kept me at attention. Arms
folded, he was demanding in a mellow baritone, "What you
burr-heads think you doin out a uniform?"

Instantly I was plunged into unreasonable guilt, while Lucifer was quick to offer, "Weeuns have a illness in the fambly."

I lowered my tray to the crown of my head, crushing my chin against my collarbone. Uncomfortable as this was, it gave me a chance to take in the rest of the hotel roof. Under paper lanterns orbited by moths, the guests were seated about a U-shaped arrangement of banquet tables facing the fake plantation and the dance floor. Wearing silk sashes over tuxedos and night-blooming corsages on ball gowns, festive in cardboard fezzes, laurel wreaths, and pirate hats, they were raising their glasses, toasting the middle table, from which hung a banner bordered in hieroglyphics, embossed with this glittering proclamation:

The Bluff City Chapter
of
The Mighty Sphinx Order
of
MYSTIC MEMPHI
Honors
The Court of King Lamar IV
and
Queen Marva June

As secret societies went, this one didn't look so diabolical, but I still felt that, of all the strange places Lucifer had taken me to, this was the most alien. Couples might be gearing up for a lindy hop on the polished dance floor, while the band went into the ever popular "Bei Mir Bist Du Schön." Ladies might be worrying their escort's bow tie, or wetting fingers to batten down a wayward cowlick. But I wasn't fooled. This was a perilous place, and we would never get away with it. We would never pass for the servants of the food of the gods — which was, incidentally, pork ribs, baked beans, coleslaw, and corn on the cob, with a choice of fruit cup or pie à la mode for dessert.

I spotted Lucifer making straight for the table where the crowned heads were seated. There was the stinko King Lamar

217

IV and, beside him, the silky blond queen. She was smiling with incurious eyes, her tiara close to capsizing in the permanent wave of her hair. Having picked up a slab of ribs, she held it as delicately as a panpipe, then proceeded to tear flesh from bone with flashing teeth and a winsome toss of the head. Okay, I thought, so she's your grade-A shayne maidel. Even smeared with sauce like a daub of warpaint, her skin has the sheen of what? freshly minted shekels? And her coloring bespeaks generations of having kept mongrel impurities clear of the blood. She was a doll, I wouldn't dispute it, but prettiness aside, was this a face to make the dumb speak? What did this ambrosia-stuffed Queen Marva June have to do with the lady whose praises were being sung in that squalid closet off Beale?

Oh, she could flirt all right, patting her lips with a napkin to hide a yawn. She could blow a kiss with deadly accuracy, perfectly at her ease at this celestial altitude. But it still took a knocked-out shvartzer back on terra firma to make her divine.

A poke in the kidneys from the head waiter/mayor roused me. Once again I was forced to assume a variety of unnatural postures to keep from spilling the contents of my tray. By the time I recovered myself, the mayor had moved on, though not before warning me to get the lead out of my tail.

I approached the tables with the intention of filling empty place settings with plates. This was easier said than done, especially given the amount of wobbling I was prone to. Nor did it make things more manageable when I tried to brace the tray against my hip, since my arm wasn't long enough to hold it — though even if it had been, I still would have been short by at least another arm to perform effectively. I was further unsteadied by constantly having to swivel my head back and forth to keep track of Lucifer. Calamity came quickly enough, when I upset a glass of wine into the lap of one of the guests I was trying to serve.

"Watch it, boy!" snapped this horse-faced character, hair

combed into a pompadour like the neck of a violin. I don't know why this should have especially hurt my feelings. He hadn't used strong language, only called me boy, which after all was what I was. But something in his tone of voice made me feel misused, bent under my serving tray like an ancestor under a pyramid stone.

Wanting somehow to erase the whole incident, I set down my tray and began to tug at the edge of the tablecloth. I meant to use it as a towel, to assist the guest in wiping the spill from his trousers. But my efforts succeeded only in dragging his dinner to the brink of the table, where it teetered just shy of following the lead of his drink. In the end all I got for my trouble was roughly shoved aside.

The band struck up a polka with a beat like a leaky faucet. Close to tears now, I was nearly at the point of letting them go, but for the prospect of spoiling my makeup. Without thinking, I stooped to lift my miserable tray again, then wondered what I was doing. Why should I stand here struggling with this ungainly burden when Lucifer had already rid himself of his?

Maybe he thought it was better to be empty-handed, gesticulating like an idiot, when you pleaded your case before a royal court. The sight was astonishing enough in itself, but even more remarkable, if the pert tilt of her head was any indication, was that the queen seemed actually amused. This went for Lamar IV as well, who'd arranged his squiffy features to approximate concentration, leaning forward lest he miss a word. Several other members of the court within hearing did likewise, all of them beaming with rapt indulgence at the nervy kid.

Had I been guilty of having too little faith? Come to think of it, why shouldn't Lucifer's patter, which worked so well on the street, be even more persuasive up here in the thinner air? Who said Michael's situation couldn't have a happy conclusion? Once convinced of the philanthropic import, what was to prevent this shining entourage from rising en masse and making an impromptu royal progress down Third Street from the Peabody to the Baby Doll Hotel? Surely stranger things had happened.

Maybe I'd sold her short, this mistress of Michael's dreams. Maybe she was a lady of charity and social concern who was personally not above slumming. She was the ultimate good sport. Or was it just that she was easily amused? Because, in the midst of the cheeky kid's song and dance, she seemed, just as easily, to have become bored. Whatever interest she'd taken in Lucifer's performance had evidently run its course. Unburdening herself of a sigh, she looked suddenly testy, her expression degenerating into an impatience bordering on outrage. Turning sharply to the left and right, she signaled that the joke had gone far enough: it was time for someone to remove the offense. This was when Lucifer chose to fall to his knees.

Almost simultaneously I heard a piercing shriek from the table beside me. I went so far as to utter an audible "Nu?" but still couldn't bring myself to look. Then I looked. A small enamel bowl, slid from my tray, had plopped upended onto the pale, strapless shoulder of a garlanded debutante.

"What's that!" she cried (a little irrationally, I thought), twisting her neck to watch rills of mayonnaise plunging down the close-pored slope of her décolletage. Because it was all I could do to be literal under the circumstances, and meaning no disrespect, I politely informed her, "It looks like slaw."

A vein pulsed in her velvet-chokered neck, and she flushed a color that, even in the failing light, rivaled the red of the overhead lanterns. She plucked the bowl from her shoulder like some gross sucking insect and slammed it down on the table in disgust. With his napkin her escort assaulted the little mound of coleslaw that remained perched on her bare shoulder blade. As if he'd knocked off a chip that she'd placed there in defiance, this only served to rekindle her wrath. Looking around for some further means of expressing her vexation, she raised herself to give me a stinging slap across the cheek. She shrieked again to see how my complexion had come off on the palm of her hand.

Her escort got to his feet to take charge, then looked like he wasn't sure what he was taking charge of. Inclining his head, which was the pink of strawberry ice cream in the inverted cone of his party hat, he frowned as he examined my cheek. I could feel how the young lady's fingers must have left their half-chevron of parallel markings, which the gent seemed to find familiar but couldn't quite place. He leaned back for a better appraisal, giving my nostrils a rest from his essence of Wildroot and Sen-Sen. Then he folded his arms across his belly, cradled snugly in the sling of a watered silk cummerbund.

"We wheel get to the bottom a thee-us, son," he said, drawling so mellifluously that I couldn't tell whether he meant to threaten or console. Nevertheless he seemed pleased with himself, as if he'd spoken for all honorable men. He was building toward such a fine indignation that it was almost a shame to see him so upstaged, but at that moment the debacle behind the royal table had captured the attention of the entire banquet.

Lucifer had finally gone too far. He'd grabbed Queen Marva June by the arm — intending what? To topple her from her throne and drag her out by the hair? With the kind of hold usually associated with victims of drowning, one of the waiters had locked his hands around Lucifer's chest. He was lifting the kid from his knees in an effort to detach him from the white woman. It was an action repeated from his side by King Lamar himself, who, without leaving his chair, had taken advantage of her predicament to embrace his beleaguered queen about the bust. He was himself clasped from behind by a concerned peer of the realm, a spruce young man who looked as if he in turn wanted assistance — someone to help him hang on to the king, or at least to correct the cant of his bow tie. It was a full-fledged tug-of-war, in the middle of which stood the moonlighting mayor of Beale Street, his comportment, as ever, unimpeachable. Trying to pry loose the colored kid's fingers from the lady's alabaster wrist, he might have been presiding at a ribbon-cutting ceremony. His attitude suggested it was all in a night's work.

Meanwhile the harried young queen was no longer making a pretense of self-control. Her eyes were utterly given over to horror. Her immoderate whoops and yelps had stopped the band.

So this was it, the absurd and pathetic end of the wisenheimer's once illustrious career. Oh Lucifer, that it should have come to this! The banquet guests would no doubt agree that lynching was too good for him. They would probably pull him to pieces, like the popular musician in one of my cousin's stories, with their bare hands. They would afterwards wear his dried parts, the party favors from this red-letter occasion, as lucky charms on their bracelets and key chains. Thus resigned to the worst that might befall him, I watched helplessly as the twin was made to let go of the object of his brother's desire. I saw, though it didn't sink in, how he wrenched himself out of the clutches of his would-be captors, leaving his empty jacket in their hands. It wasn't until he'd hotfooted it past me, chiding, "Mistah Harry, you slow as mule blood!" on the way, that I understood Lucifer had broken free.

Taking heart, I said so long to my serving tray, which I let fall with a resounding clatter to the patio tiles. Before I had managed to jar myself into motion, however, I was overtaken by a pack of puffing gentleman guests. Galloping after the wise guy, they were throwing off any impediments to speed, shedding tuxedo jackets and sashes, letting paper hats fly where they might. Several of the waiters, dispatched by their captain, had also sprinted forward. They kicked out their legs in suspiciously stylized strides, after a fashion that looked more suited to a cakewalk than to giving chase. But even they had a head start on me in pursuing the twin.

This is not to say that anyone was close to catching him. Making a beeline across the footlighted dance floor, he swerved only to avoid one of the escorts (who, in his attempt to tackle the elusive twin, had skidded on his boiled shirtfront across the floor). He hurtled a railing and cut across a corner of the mock-up piazza while band members snatched their instruments out of his way. Shagging it over the gravel that bordered the formal terrace, he lifted his knees like he might be about to take flight — and did. He bounded into the air, landing kerplunk on the tin-plated parapet that surrounded the hotel roof.

Backlit now by the huge neon sign straddling the hotel's opposing wings, Lucifer struck his stance so purposefully — jerking his cap out of a back pocket to pull it on — that the host of pursuers were brought to a sudden halt.

I figured that this was a calculated effect. What was also calculated was the way that he looked behind him toward oblivion, then back toward the hostile mob, as if weighing alternatives. The kid sometimes pushed make-believe to such lengths, though, that you couldn't tell it from the real thing. My kishkes having tied themselves in knots, I cried out, "Don't you dare!"

But mine was not so dissimilar from all the other angrily raised voices. Apparently set on preventing him from cheating them out of his retribution, the banquet guests were bellowing in varying degrees of rancor. Much as I wanted to reach the kid, like everyone else I was glued to the spot. Still, I was a little encouraged that, while I couldn't see his face too clearly, I thought I could make out a trace of his devilish grin. Then he turned his back on the whole affair and was gone.

My ribs slammed shut like a trap sprung over my heart. Surging forward along with the gentleman guests, who cautioned their dates to stay put, I stumbled over the gravel to the parapet. Leaning against the bird-fouled tin for support, I hid my face in my hand. I was in no hurry to look down the long stories toward the crumpled body at the bottom of the shaft. Flanked as I was on either side by irate tuxedos, I still thought I could hear him calling: "Mistah Harry, you bout to miss the boat!"

I uncovered my eyes, though my brain took its time in corroborating what they saw. He was waving his cap at me from a fire escape catty-corner to the Plantation Roof, across a chasm some ten feet below.

"You birdbrain!" I started to yell at him. "You pinhead stovelid jungle-bunny momzer coon!" I was that glad to see him. Removing my glasses to wipe my eyes, I delivered myself of a gut-wrenching sob. I clutched the wall again, braced against the event of some joker's congratulating me on a fine choice of epithets. But everyone else was too busy spitting curses of their own.

That's when I began to think — as the wise guy still waited, urging me to take the leap — that I wasn't so glad to see Lucifer after all. He had some nerve inviting me to risk my neck, especially when I could just as easily stay where I was, under cover of the general acrimony. Across my cheek I could still feel the debutante's smarting handprint, exposing me as neither one thing nor another. If I wanted, I'd have bet I could back up crabwise into the kitchen; I could wipe off the blackface, put on a funny hat, and come out to join the party. Having passed for a darkie, I could certainly impersonate my own kind, more or less.

Lucifer shrugged a mighty shrug and started down the fire escape alone. Myself, I began to slink backwards, meaning to take advantage of the foofooraw and disappear. But what I was doing, I was coming to my senses, I was losing my mind — take your pick. I was backing up to give myself room to take a run at the wall.

While you couldn't exactly say I bounded onto it, I got a leg up just the same. I raised myself slowly until I was standing erect on the tin, which shuddered like distant thunder from my trembling. I was leaning out over dizzy nothing, shouting at Lucifer to hold his horses, wishing that someone would for God's sake stop me before I did something rash. They should try and stop me if they dared.

Then my legs were churning in midair for a purchase. My waiter's jacket billowed about me, providing resistance (I could have sworn it) against the velocity of my descent. How else could you explain the way that drop seemed to last some considerable fraction of forever? Long enough for people gazing out of hotel windows to remark in passing the nearly aerodynamic boy.

I hit the steel slats of the fire escape with a brain-shuddering *ping-ing-ng,* my legs collapsing under me, knees striking the platform studs, which tore my pants. Frantically I set about taking stock of my broken bones, of which there seemed so far to be none, though my knees could have used a little first aid. "Mistah Harry," came the voice of patience under pressure, and I looked up to find Lucifer standing a couple of steps below me, offering me his hand. Still somewhat addled from my landing, I thought he wanted to give me an amiable shake, mazel tov on the occasion of having made such a valiant leap. But no sooner had I extended my own hand than he latched on to my arm, and for the umpteenth time that evening — indifferent to my abrasions and before I could even get properly to my feet — the wise guy began to drag me in a blind rush behind him.

Only this time there was a difference: instead of pushing deeper into trouble, we were making good our escape. Realizing this left me silly. It tickled me further that the guests were continuing to hurl abuse, which rained over us as harmlessly as ticker tape. As I banged down the steps behind Lucifer, sliding along the railing on my belly whenever I could, I was seized with uncontrollable laughter.

At the bottom of fifteen ringing flights, a horizontal staircase tipped us gently into the street, where we were discharged like a pair of wobbling dreidels. Even from that far below the hotel roof, you could hear the band cranking up another tune — the old standard "Bye-Bye Blackbird," if I wasn't mistaken. Then we were beating it down Third Street, the music growing ever fainter, diffusing into the surfy sounds of traffic like an orchestra on a sinking ship.

We didn't slow down until we'd reached an alley off of Gayoso Street, where we practically fell out, winded from our dash. Leaning against a wall, I kept on cackling — between healthy gulps of air — over the amazing handiness of our escape. Now that we were clear of it, the whole episode seemed to have been one colossal hoot. Shvitzing buckets, I tore off my waiter's jacket and began to wipe my face, then cracked up again at the sight of the jacket smeared with black stains.

Bent over, panting, hands braced on his knees, Lucifer resisted joining me in my hilarity. Full of fellow feeling, however, I stepped over and gave him a friendly slap on the back. Instantly he began to whoop it up with an abandon that put my own wheezing laughter to shame. He heaved and quaked, hugging himself to keep from splitting his sides. It took me a minute to understand that this was not a happy noise he was making, that the wise guy was bawling desolately.

"I have done fail!" he cried out at length. "It a judgment on me, I done rurnt what ain't never be fix!" He began to curse himself, striking his forehead with the heel of his hand, increasing the cadence with every name he called. "I'se a mosshead . . . gator bait . . . suck-hind-tit . . . eight rock . . . momzer . . . coon!" Then he turned and banged his head against the brick wall. Here, as if he'd decided that this was the ticket, he backed up a couple of paces, about to repeat the process with a running start.

I grabbed him by the belt loop and reeled him in. Flinging my arms around him from behind, I locked my fingers over his chest as I'd seen them do at the banquet. Quite honestly, I was embarrassed for all his carrying-on, not to say revolted by the combination of tears and snot dripping onto my sleeve. Beyond spoiling the fun, he was blubbering so woefully I was afraid I might break down and blubber too.

But I hung on just the same, squeezing with all my might until he stopped trying to pull away. I squeezed the last squeak of caterwauling out of his system, until he'd subsided into hiccupping sobs, then silence. It was almost too easy, Lucifer's surrender, and I wondered why, back before it was finally too late, we hadn't tried the same maneuver on his brother.

Not without a feeling of getting even for all the shoving I'd endured that night, I pushed the docile wise guy in the direction of the Baby Doll Hotel, then made tracks back to North Main Street in record time. I collected my schoolbooks from under a box hedge in Market Square Park and entered the apartment reading aloud from a biology text. I turned my head neither left nor right to see who might be home. Walking straight to my alcove, I made my voice — ad-libbing now about lipids, which I may have confused with limpets — manifestly drowsy. Then I nipped out the window into the nodding mimosa tree.

Back at the Baby Doll, Lucifer had retired to his miserable corner again, and as for Michael, he didn't look quite so beatific anymore. Now, when you looked at him, you might think to yourself: If this is love, kaynehoreh, keep it away from me. His fluttering eyelids were ragged as chewed thumbnails, and his cheekbones, above their deep hollows, had the bleached appearance of old rubber. His body in its dirty nightshirt was an empty hand puppet. For all the tender attentions of the ladies, never mind the adoration of the gawkers, the dummy showed no signs of pulling out of his decline.

His voice, after more than a week's worth of uninterrupted prattle, was reduced to the drone of a tiny faltering motor. Sometimes his visitors had to put their ears so close to him that you'd have thought they were listening for a heartbeat instead of words. But usually he was audible enough, and extravagant as ever in eulogizing his beloved. He stalked her through his relentless imaginings, conceiving whole Baedekers of peoples and places along the way — describing territories that, while they'd certainly never figured in his experience, could neither be accounted for by the breadth of his reading. Such an alphabet soup poured out of him that I sometimes pictured Michael's mouth as a shofar from which tumbled something like the contents of Kaplan's Loans.

He showered his sweetheart with gifts, cloaked her in fabrics and anointed her with scents gathered from the place where Beale Street intersected (let's say) farthest Bong Tree Land. He tracked her into terra incognita, where standard-hung castle walls beetled over sharecroppers' shacks and jungle escarpments were terraced in cotton rows, where the Mississippi Delta flowed into the Sea of Tranquillity. He called upon a legendary lost tribe of hoofers and the devil's brother-in-law to come to his aid, and saints from outside any recognized canon, with names like Ribeye and Mandrake Willie. But necromantic intervention notwithstanding, the erstwhile dummy was often heard to complain that he was losing sight of his queen. These days she seemed to give him the slip at every turn.

It made you want to shake him, especially when you knew what she was made of, and say, "Michael, shmuck, get wise to yourself!" But the more I listened to the kid's sick fancies, the more I believed he was only half mad. The other half was making some kind of a deathbed confession that it would have been a sin to muffle up.

Now that the entire neighborhood had shelled out their hard-earned wages to view him, the spectator business had finally begun to fall off. Moreover, since the kid's voice had lost much of its volume, the gawkers were growing impatient, if not bored, with the trouble it took to hear him. There was also the matter of his physical deterioration, the way his delirium no longer seemed to transfigure his mumbling bones. This everyone found plainly depressing. As a consequence, though never really resigned to the fact that his value as a meal ticket had come and gone, Aunt Honey gave up her promotional activities. She'd settled, along with her ladies, into going through the motions of restoring his health, or at least making him comfortable.

Still, you had the steadfast few who kept coming back. Paying the recently devalued admission fee of a nickel, they bent their heads low as they entered the room. Sometimes they came bearing little offerings — personal photographs, jars of preserves, which lay strewn around the bed alongside the broken books. They brought snacks in grease-stained bags and, since nobody bothered with the time limit anymore, folding chairs. Numbered among these diehards was a blade-thin church sexton, always with a lady's stocking on his head. He sat and dribbled his knee like a bouncing ball, horselaughing and exclaiming, "Tha's a good'n," as if the dummy were reciting some comical shtick. A stout woman with berries in her hat, who never came without her knitting, would steady her needles from time to time to cup an ear, then proceed at a vigorous clip like she was stitching dictation.

I wanted to ask them what they thought they were doing now that Michael's lovesong was failing, its words little more than a rattle. Were they waiting for the final extinguishment of the fever that still lit his blasted features? Or did they think that, after it had consumed his body for kindling, Michael's fever might burn on with an enduring life of its own? It might, once it was no longer confined to the bones of a solitary sick kid, torch the Baby Doll in a bonfire that would spread to the rest of Beale. It would ignite the oily surface of the new lagoon, devour the hill of pawnshops, and advance over those parts of the earth that remained unflooded.

A couple of nights after our Hotel Peabody caper, there was a new wrinkle on the scene — or, rather, a whole sack of wrinkles in the shape of a very old man. In his antiquated getup (celluloid collar and Edwardian serge, beribboned pince-nez) he was seated before a panel of machinery that flickered with tiny bulbs, their orange filaments possibly lit by something predating electricity. He was jotting notes, fiddling with wires, spinning reels that apparently needed cranking by hand. Meanwhile Aunt Honey loomed in the hallway, showing him off.

He was, as she would have us know, an esteemed professor of an unpronounceable discipline from the local Negro college. For a modest sum, which she wasn't too modest to broadcast to her girls, she'd allowed him to install his equipment to the exclusion of any further visitors.

"The fessor here," she boasted, laying a hand on his brittle shoulder, which appeared to dislocate, "he own put the Baby Doll on the map. Gon prove siren-tific that a nigger have got a soul."

I squatted beside Lucifer, who had himself been evicted from the sickroom and was slumped on the floor of the hall. He didn't have to say anything, I knew what he was thinking. So why didn't he rouse himself and put his foot through the infernal contraption? But weary, hanging his head like his brain was some ponderous stone, Lucifer didn't seem to be Lucifer anymore. He was so gray about the gills now that, outside the Baby Doll, he would have been hard to recognize. When at last he spoke, you'd have thought he was repeating a hypnotist's suggestion, his voice — even less audible than his brother's — carrying no conviction at all.

"This am the finalest straw," he said to his feet. He removed his cap and began to massage his patchy scalp, muttering like someone trying to read a barely legible sign. It was high time, was what he haltingly said, for a seat-of-your-britches strategy.

"Just what would you call the Peabody?" I wanted to know.

Beyond taking in any sensible remarks, Lucifer muttered on. He was still stuck on the idea that the queen of the Cotton Carnival's fleshly presence was the only antidote to his brother's ills. Since appeals hadn't worked and kidnap was out of the question, involving as it did such overwhelming technical concerns, there was only one course left open to us: "See, we gots to carry him round where she stay . . ."

I could imagine what he intended — how we would transport the gibbering Michael on a litter to her ancestral mansion, then abandon him on her colonnaded doorstep for her to find. Or maybe she should come upon him more haphazardly — say, floating in her lily pond. A note would be pinned to his swaddling clothes assuring one and all that despite his damaged appearance he was a gift fit for a queen. The joke had gone far enough. It was time to call a spade, excuse me, a spade.

"Lucifer," I interrupted him, "what do you think? I mean, what do you really think would happen if Michael ever met his — what was her name? Marvy June?"

But Lucifer only looked at me like any shnook would know. "Why, Mistah Harry," he said patiently. "Do them meet up, Mistah Harry, she own be b'wootch jus like him. She lie down an die if she ain't be the mystifyin Michael's solid good thang."

For a split second I was almost taken in. Then I couldn't contain my aggravation anymore. If I'd ever humored the kid, I was sorry, and resolved to make amends.

"You don't believe that!" I accused him, loud enough (I hoped) to penetrate his thick skull. "If you believe that" — I pointed toward the sickroom — "then you're as crazy as he is! If they met up, I'll tell you what she'd do. She'd call the cops is what!"

The first to drop were his tired eyes, followed instantly by the collapse of his puckered chin. Then his shoulders sagged, and had I bothered to blow in his direction, I could probably have crumbled the rest of him like a house of cards. So I guessed that I'd reached him. Of course this was nothing I hadn't seen before; in fact, it was getting to be almost a matter of routine. It was another of his ploys, I suspected, meant to sucker me into feeling sorry for him.

"And don't think I feel sorry for you either," I was suddenly moved to add, though he was evidently too absorbed in self-pity to hear me.

To look at him, you might have thought that he and his brother were suffering from two unidentical halves of the same disease. It was a case of the draykopf following the dummkopf into hopeless insensibility, unless somebody hurried up and turned him around. Somebody who was wise to the wise guy, cagey enough to pull the leg puller's leg. And just who would you suppose that somebody might be?

Over the whir and click of the professor's machinery, you could still occasionally make out some babbled phrase of Michael's: the lady was trapped in a topaz stickpin on a take-out man's lapel; she was spinning the smoke from Pee Wee's back room into her bridal veil. Inwardly I petitioned the Lord of Grandpa Isador to help me help His servant Lucifer, who, come to think of it, had saved yours truly from dying a bookworm. Then it came to me, a brainstorm, an idea so implausible as to bear the authentic stamp of Lucifer's own peculiar brand of folly.

"Listen," I said, "this is what we'll do. We'll get hold of my cousin Naomi. She's not so hard to look at, my cousin, and we can dress her up all farputz — you know, like a regular queen. Then we'll introduce her to Michael. Don't all white girls look the same to you people? He'll think she's the genuine goods and it'll bring him around. It'll work, you'll see. Don't ask me how I know, but I know."

Having said as much, I found myself wondering, Why not? After all, Michael was already so far gone, what was the differ-

ence? One thing was as likely to snap him out of it as another
— not that I really believed that anything would snap him out
of it. Still, you couldn't overlook a certain sympathy between
the dummy and my cousin. Though they might not know it,
they were actually two of a kind, both of them addled in their
respective ways by their sick yen for stories. There was something almost star-crossed in my idea of bringing them together,
something that brought out the matchmaker in me. Anyway,
what could it hurt? It was certainly no more harebrained a
scheme than Lucifer's, and not nearly so hazardous. At the
worst, Michael would only ignore Naomi the way he did everyone else; on the other hand, you never knew but I might be
doing them both a favor. Not to mention the mitzvah I'd be
doing the wise guy into the bargain. It was worth a try.

Lucifer's response was slow in coming. Having raised his
raw pink eyes to mine, he gazed at me swimmingly like a drunk,
like he was seeing double and the images refused to resolve
themselves. In the end, however, the two Harry Kaplans must
have merged into one, because Lucifer relaxed, and, like a
wedge of moon dredged out of dark water, his old reliable grin
began to reappear. Then he pinched my cheek and gave me a
convivial cuff on the ear with his cap. He jumped up and
slapped the cap against his hip, dancing a few steps of an impromptu buck-and-wing.

"Mistah Harry," he declared with a jubilation that my gut
greeted with righteous fear, "sometime I gin to thank you ain't
so dumb."

233

Twelve

Because I hadn't been back to the Parkway for a while now, I found myself looking forward to the visit despite my somewhat irregular reason for going. Once she'd finished showing off her several personalities — the pendulum swinging dizzily from lost lamb to fledgling vamp — Naomi had settled down to being not such a bad companion. Of course she was sometimes still a little too eager to please, which made me nervous. She still insisted on breathlessly imparting the contents of her books. Nevertheless, I missed my weekly retreats to her tropical succah of a garden. Giving me a break from my taxing exploits on Beale Street, those trips must have done me more good than I knew. Besides, what with the progress she'd made toward becoming a person in my company, I was anxious to see if my cousin had continued to mature on her own.

I hoped that she hadn't matured too much, or else she might dismiss my proposition as idiotic — which was how, in the hard light of day, I was inclined to see it myself. I realized I must be crazy to have contemplated such a thing in the first place. If Lucifer hadn't pinned his outrageous hopes on me, I'd have been happy to call the whole business off. I even considered lying to the wise guy, though I knew he'd see through me in an instant. At any rate, I owed it to him at least to go through the ordeal of asking. After that I could report back with a clear conscience that our project had fallen through.

Meanwhile there was Naomi herself to consider. When I imagined how she might react to such a proposal, I thought I had better sugarcoat it a bit. So I did the unthinkable. I spent my carfare on a cellophane-wrapped box of chocolate turtles from Old Man Levy's pharmacy. Later, as I headed out to the Parkway, dodging riders in polo attire, I picked a spray of pink and yellow flowers. I felt ridiculous. The nearer I got to my uncle's palace, the more I realized what my duty entailed. I would have to make a clean breast of things to my cousin. There was no way to get around telling her that I'd been leading her on from the start. And since I'd already muddied the water by dropping so many hints, I knew that it wouldn't do to tell her anything short of everything.

So why was it, I wondered, that despite a stomach full of dogfighting butterflies, I could hardly wait to see her again?

Up the walk through a gauntlet of trade winds I approached my uncle's house and was met at the front door, as usual, by the uniformed maid. While she regarded the flowers and candy with suspicion, I beat her to the punch. "I know," I said. "I should wait in the hall."

Pacing the marble vestibule, I was trying my best to ignore a certain mush-mouthed voice coming from behind the study door, which was slightly ajar. ". . . Now your cathouse revenue, that's skim, that's small potatoes. But the hot properties fence, I can tell you, he's the boy that brings in the bucks. Take a shop like Cohen's on North Main Street, or Kaplan's on Beale . . ."

Uncle Morris was up to no good — so what else was new? The words "crooked" and "uncle" were as inseparably paired in my mind as "prune" and "Danish." Then why did it give me such palpitations to catch him in the act of perpetrating his dirty deeds? After all, I wasn't exactly a stranger to the dealings of underworld types, many of whom could have had my flabby uncle for lunch. So maybe it was the casual mention of my papa's shop that gave me a start, and drew me irresistibly toward the study door.

I heard a couple of voices grunt in agreement, then Uncle Morris again, apparently getting down to brass tacks. "I'm counting on you boys to move the stuff before Shavuos. Certain antsy-pantsy parties have already expressed an interest that the goods get delivered on time. And I think you'll find their gratitude will more than make up for any inconvenience, farshteyn?"

One of the "boys" remarked, while the other sniggered, that he'd heard the hockshop was already filled to capacity. Uncle Morris cut him short with the brusque assurance that room would be made. "It ain't your business to worry, the shucha will take over at that end."

I had some vague notion of bursting in on them. In the name of my father I would demand an explanation. Did they think they could get away with such treachery behind Sol Kaplan's back? Though what couldn't you get away with under his very nose? The truth be told, I was never really sure about what my father did and didn't notice. In fact, I wondered if, in his readiness to look the other way, my papa might be a willing accomplice, a silent partner, so to speak.

I was brooding on this when the maid, who seemed to take my eavesdropping in stride, poked my shoulder to inform me that Miss Naomi was waiting, and everything I'd just overheard slipped to the back of my mind.

She was sitting on her bench without the usual stack of books, wearing the wrinkled tartan pinafore of her private school uniform. (She attended the snooty Saint Somebody's Parochial Academy run by nuns, a secret kept from Grandpa Isador lest he rupture himself over the shame.) This was a switch from the dressier duds she'd put on for my previous visits. Gone too were her tan, faded back into her trademark pallor, and her essence of Sweet Gardenia, which could outcloy the garden. Missing from her hair were the glowworm barrettes worn, I assumed, for my benefit, which had arrested the fall of stringy bangs over her shiny forehead. Also missing was her serenity. Instead she was fidgeting, her head bent over the tangle of fingers in her lap, as if she were more interested in the outcome of their skirmish than in my arrival.

Who could blame me for being disappointed? Only a couple of weeks had elapsed since my last visit, and already she'd retreated into her old nebechel self. So we were back to scratch, me and my cousin, and this one didn't look like the type who'd be receptive to what I had to say.

I noticed that she was peeking expectantly at my hands. "Oh yeah," I blurted, having followed her gaze to an awareness that my hands, for a change, were not empty. "These are for you."

She accepted the flowers and candy with an expression which said that, no matter how sunk, she still knew enough to beware of Harry Kaplan bearing gifts. The flowers were already wilted on their strangled stalks, and the candy, when she'd unwrapped the heart-shaped box, was melted into the semblance of a single cowpat. I thanked her all the same when she offered me some.

I waited for this presentation of damaged goods to make a bad situation worse, but Naomi was, as ever, full of surprises. Heaving a sigh like she would take what she could get, she straightened herself up on her bench. All of a sudden she was a girl of modest dignity, accustomed to receiving gifts from her suitors; she was aware that gifts were often a prelude to some proposal, which she showed herself ready to hear out.

I wanted to tell her not to jump to any conclusions, that whatever she might have in mind, she shouldn't. On the other hand, this seemed as good a moment as I was likely to get for speaking my piece.

"Naomi," I said, reciting lines that should have been better rehearsed, "I am here to enlist your aid in a matter of life and death. If there was any other way, I would bite my tongue before asking, but you gotta come with me down to Beale Street tonight."

When I paused for effect, I saw that Naomi had pooched out her lower lip. Bracing myself against what was coming, I lost the thread of my speech. I realized I was doing it again, tramping into her garden, demanding favors I would never return. It served me right if she should cloud up and sulk.

On closer inspection, I observed that my cousin wasn't pouting so much as considering thoughtfully. She assisted the process with a sniff of the flowers drooping from her hand. With the forefinger of the other she probed the box of candy — the several turtles fused into one sizable snapper. Raising the candy-coated finger to the tip of her tongue, she licked it inquisitively, as if the taste of the chocolate was the issue in question. Then she gave a pert nod and said, "Why not?"

"Why not what?" I was confused.

"Why not go with you to Beale Street," said Naomi, starting up there and then from her shady gazebo.

With a firmness that shocked us both, I grabbed her by the shoulders and sat her back down. "Not so fast!"

Having opened her mouth to speak, she promptly shut it again. Here Naomi had shown herself willing to comply, with no questions asked, so what do I do? But the problem was, I still had a tale to tell. Besides, it didn't seem right that my cousin should be in such a hurry to leave her fragrant bower. Even I had hesitated before daring to enter the haunts of the shvartzers, and I never had any garden to kiss goodbye.

"Don't you even want to know why?" I asked her, trying to soften my bullying tone.

There followed a revival of Naomi's contemplative moue. She shrugged another "Why not?" and made a little fuss of arranging herself in a listening attitude.

I blew out my cheeks and dropped onto the bench beside her, accidentally dragging my fingers through the candy box. When I pulled them out of the goo, I saw on my cousin's face a look of predatory tenderness; she might have snatched my fingers and licked them clean if I hadn't hurried to wipe them on the mossy bricks. After that I sat up and proceeded to dump the entire improbable megillah in her lap.

"You won't believe it," I assured her, exhilarated to be finally spilling the beans, "but it happened like this . . ." Once I'd launched into the telling, however, I found that I kept needing to back up. The more outlandish parts lacked authenticity unless corroborated with further details. Naomi insisted that this wasn't necessary; I should get on with my story without so many interruptions. She was happy, it seemed, to accept as gospel what would have sounded to any intelligent person like pure cock-and-bull.

She didn't even get angry when I described the false pretenses under which I'd made away with her library. If anything, she tended to view the duplicity as an interesting twist. It was as if all that I related, though stranger than fiction, was just another story cribbed from a book.

"It's the truth, for crying out loud!" I insisted, and my cousin assured me that she had no cause to doubt it.

This was infuriating; it took all the fun out of confessing. Where she should have been astonished and scandalized, Naomi was only amused. It made me want to see how far I could push at the bounds of her complaisance. If the facts didn't move me, I could do better than facts. I began to touch up my descriptions, adding lush harem trappings to the decor of the Baby Doll, suggesting more than friendly relations with its resident females. Talk about gilding the lily, I even went so far as to exaggerate the effects of the dummy's shpiel: how it could

239

modulate in pitch to cause internal bleeding and set off alarms in your cavities; how, during his more ardent outbursts, he levitated above the bed.

I know I should have been ashamed of myself, but I was too busy adding refinements to my narrative to care. Blame it on Naomi, whose gullibility kept egging me on. Myself, all I wanted was to make her understand that, give or take the odd embellishment, this story was based on actual fact. She should appreciate that, beyond the neat fuchsia border of her pungent preserve, Harry Kaplan was consorting with Negroes. He was fraternizing with undesirables in places dangerous to his health, and had himself become quite a rascally piece of work.

"It happened, so help me!" I threw in whenever I thought the story needed further guarantees. Then I crossed my heart and went on inventing lies.

By the time I got to the part where I had to tell Naomi just how she figured into all this, I was worn out. Though I tried to inject some excitement into my voice — "See, we'll dress you up all farputz" and so on — it wasn't any use. By now my mind was practically a blank. I felt so out of touch with the actual Beale Street that it was almost as if I'd never really been there. I'd replaced my own honest adventures with something like "Jack Armstrong Goes to Tan Town." Not that it mattered to Naomi, whose mind had been made up all along. One trumped-up reason was just as good as another when you were as anxious as she was to leave your father's garden for the world.

"So what do you say?" I asked her for the sake of form at the weary conclusion of my tale. Then I mouthed along with my cousin a silent "Why not?"

"Sounds like a lot of laughs," she tossed in for good measure, Miss Been-Around-the-Block-a-Time-or-Two, and was on her feet again.

"Will you hold your horses!" I pleaded without bothering to get up myself, since it was obvious that no one could hold her horses for her. "You think we're talking about snooping after matzohs here? This kind of thing takes planning, split-second timing. In the first place, we'll have to wait until it's late at night . . ."

Naomi was pacing the patio, thinking aloud. "We'll have to do it late at night."

"Right," I concurred. Now we were getting somewhere. "So after my papa comes home, what I'll do is, I'll swipe his keys. Then we can get into his shop, where he keeps these costumes . . ."

"You can carry me down from my bedroom like Helen of Troy," she went on, her anticipation having taken a dreamy turn. Catching sight of me, however, she sobered a bit. "Well, maybe you better just whistle — that is, if you know how to whistle. Or do you think you can throw some rocks without breaking the window?" She turned toward me for confirmation, and saw that my jaw hung open, inviting flies. Then Naomi smiled and waxed dreamy again.

"You'll be standing in the shadows under the sycamore tree, and I'll slide down the trunk into your arms."

I watched her shiver at the thought, and understood that I was definitely in over my head.

"Now what'll I wear?" she wondered, coiling a lock of hair about a finger as she considered. "Basic black, of course, though I've got this cashmere thing with a hood, only it's jade — excuse me?" She was challenging me to interrupt. "Let's see, there's my sailor pants which are navy, but that's close enough, and my turtleneck jersey, y'know, like a safecracker's. Espadrilles will have to do, but what do you think is more suitable for the head? A scarf — Cathy Earnshaw wore scarves — or maybe a beret?"

She sounded like a girl who was planning her elopement, and far be it from me to suggest that Kaplan's Loans was less than the perfect setting for a honeymoon.

$$* \qquad * \qquad *$$

That night I lay in my alcove far past the time when I usually snuck back out to join the twins. Because I'd made such a habit of coming and going, catching my winks on the run, I felt like an interloper in my own bed. I was some night-prowling orphan who'd crawled in through the open window of a strange apartment, who was curled up and listening to the lullaby of North Main Street as he took refuge in the dark. It was a notion so cozy that it soothed my jumpy nerves, and despite myself I dozed off for a spell.

I had a dream that I was living comfortably in a tree house, which turned out instead to be a one-man ark on the crest of a mile-high wave. The wave was about to come crashing down on the nappy black heads of the children of Israel. But they were too busy praising the Lord and kicking up their heels to hear me when I called to them to get out of the way.

Look out who? Who look out?

I opened my eyes to find myself sitting bolt upright in bed with a hammering heart. In the glow of a lamp just beyond the open French doors to my alcove stood my father, looking as shaken as I felt. His bushy brows had inched themselves halfway up his long forehead, and he was clutching his hat over his chest like a shield. Presumably he had just returned home from work.

"Who did you want should look out?" he was asking in a sweat. "You shouted 'Look out.' "

"I guess I must of been dreaming, huh Papa," I told him, though wasn't it his place to reassure me? He also seemed to come to this realization once he was convinced that he shouldn't take my dream warning personally.

"You were dreaming, kiddo, that's all," he affirmed, showing me the inside of his hat, as if its empty crown somehow meant I had nothing to fear. "Go back to sleep. Everything's shipshape in the land of Nod."

He switched off the lamp, but when my eyes readjusted, I could see that he still hadn't moved. Then he was gone.

242

I listened for the flush of the toilet and the opening and closing of doors, then got out of bed. Stuffing the covers — though
I doubted there would be any more visits tonight — I dressed
and tiptoed into the hall. I waited until I heard my father's ster-
torous snoring begin to mingle with my mother's whimpered
burbles. From the adjacent bedroom I could also hear my
grandpa's tortured crepitations, as if his beard were crackling
flames that he was trying to blow out.

I snuck into my parents' bedroom. From a doily on top of
their dresser, beside a photograph of Mama feeding Papa a
piece of wedding cake, I lifted my father's key ring. The theft
went off without a hitch, naturally, since stealth had become my
middle name. In fact, I'd become so adept at it that I sometimes
wondered if I could call attention to myself now if I tried.

Minutes later I was in the alley behind Petrofsky's market,
where I took the liberty of borrowing his delivery boy's bike.
Along the bridle path of the Parkway, lurking branches threatened to unseat me, the bushes lashing out at my arms and
shins. By the time I reached my uncle's, I had scars to show for
my journey. I aimed the pebbles at my cousin's window with
the precision of one whose skills have been perfected through
adversity.

Naomi was as good as her word. She appeared at her window in the outfit of a cat gonif, done up in black from head to
toe. With her face half concealed by her upturned turtleneck
and her hair hidden beneath a babushka tied turban-style, she
was a shadow wearing the mask of my cousin's eyes. With the
attitude of a creature accustomed to walking on air, she
stepped from her window ledge. She caught hold of a limb of
the sycamore and, while I chewed my nails to the quick, traveled the length of it hand over hand. She shinnied down the
trunk with a nimbleness that suggested a dress rehearsal or
two in her dreams.

When I held my arms wide to catch her, I was disappointed
that she didn't seem to need my help. Once she'd reached the

ground, she moved with an authority (further affirmed by the finger she held to her lips) that discouraged me from even opening my mouth. Without prompting she padded over to the bicycle, which I'd left leaning against a stone lion, and motioned me to come and sit astride it. Then, rather than flop into the basket behind the seat, she mounted the handlebars with the poise of a hood ornament on a limousine.

Strenuously pedaling through the soft and sticky brink-of-summer night, I honored Naomi in silence. She held my admiration all the way to the corner of Second Street and Beale, where I turned east into the pawnshop district.

I had already begun to scour the shopfronts, making sure that the street was closed up tight. I was satisfying myself that the moneylenders and — especially in the case of Kaplan's — their pullers had all gone wherever they go, when Naomi let out a gasp: "What's that!" She nearly lost her balance, having turned loose one of the handlebars to point at the lagoon, which was as spangled as ever with barn lanterns on bumping skiffs. All of a sudden my cousin wasn't so at home in the night anymore.

"Oh, that," I replied coolly over the croak of the bicycle seat. After all, wasn't it time she recognized how her cousin was a party to things she'd never dreamt of in her storybooks? "Where you been, you never heard of the flood?" I said.

Naomi kept quiet until I'd wobbled the bike to a halt in front of my papa's shop. Then she slid from the handlebars, rubbing her tochis, and in a chastened undertone admitted that she'd never been to Beale Street before. "My father always forbid me," she apologized. "He always calls it a 'nigger sink.' He says 'shlecht,' then spits out the side of his mouth."

She looked toward the lagoon as if to say, A sink isn't bad enough, but this one has to be clogged. She seemed suddenly so much the babe in the woods that I wondered if I might have made a terrible mistake. For the first time since I'd hatched this ridiculous scheme, I considered the consequences. What if, for instance, my hot-headed uncle should discover how I'd led his only daughter into the precincts of depravity?

"Well, it's too late to turn back now," I declared for the inspirational sake of us both — only to have the words turn into a question before leaving my lips. Naomi, who looked no less fearful for refusing to let us both off the hook, retorted, "Who said anything about turning back?"

Grumbling something about how we'd already been out on the sidewalk too long, I began to move fast. I leaned the bike against a window, stuck the key in the padlock, and worked at folding the lattice. Going *pssst* a couple of times to no effect, as Naomi was gawping at the standing water again, I stepped up behind her and took her by the hand. Gently, then not so gently, I tugged her across the rubber mat at the threshold of Kaplan's Loans.

To avoid exciting the suspicions of some strolling cop on the beat, I thought better of turning on the lights. This presented a problem, since the aisle between the display cases was bottlenecked with junk and, having scarcely set foot inside for almost a month, I no longer knew my way around. No sooner had I cautioned Naomi — who kept a sweaty hold of my hand — to watch her step than I barked my shin on something that clanged like a gong. Starting at the noise, I knocked over something else that sounded like clattering bones. Then I stepped on God only knew what, which was soft and doughy and exhaled a nasal sigh. After that I paused to thank my own foresight for having remembered to bring along some matches.

When I'd managed to disengage myself from my cousin's clutch, I struck one. Shadows scattered as if we'd caught them doing something they shouldn't, and Naomi grabbed my hand again. On either side of us the shelves above the cases were bowed from the weight of gizmos defying description. You had model cars whittled from salt licks, animal mugs and assorted whirligigs, clocks like a gallery of clucking tongues. There were Prohibition radios that converted into bars, a nickelodeon shaped like the Heinz red-tomato man. A whole new generation of outré merchandise had found its way into the shop in my absence, much of it overlaying the stuff I'd been familiar with.

"Hock shop, shlock shop," I blustered, hoping to dispel a little the freakish atmosphere. But to judge from my cousin's moon-eyed condition, it didn't work. She was looking around like she couldn't believe that we'd entered such a place without a password, without rolling aside a boulder and making some scaly beast retract its claws. As she tightened her grip till my fingers went numb, I felt a twinge of pride in the sheer magnitude of my papa's peculiarity.

Again I freed myself to strike another match and moved forward past the cash register counter to unlock the wire cage. The door opened with its spooky mewling on the cache of items that my papa considered to be specialties.

Slowly Naomi entered the cage behind me as I yanked on the overhead bulb. While she blinked in stunned silence from the sudden glare, I shielded my eyes to look over the recent acquisitions. There were some new additions to the taxidermed orchestra, for example, more varmints with mechanisms that let them play cymbals and drums. There was a life-size stand-up poster of the Philip Morris midget, hung with primitive box cameras, Torah amulets, and rosary beads. Some of the artificial limbs had been attached to one another with leg irons, and an oxbow posing as a pair of giant handcuffs leaned against the open safe. The rack of fancy-dress shmattes now included a few butternut tunics and a lost boy's squirrel costume from a production of *Peter Pan*. There were a couple of pairs of overalls shaggy with feathered fishing lures.

Naomi was still looking on in open-mouthed astonishment, the reluctant guest at a surprise party in her honor. Worried that she might be about to go into shock, I decided to get to work without further ado. From a hanger I tore off a frilly ball gown, then another, dancing them in front of my cousin's unfocusing eyes. The effort of having to choose, I reasoned, would soon bring her into the spirit of the masquerade. But Naomi stood blinking like she'd come to a morgue to identify a body and couldn't find anyone she recognized.

As patiently as I was able, I told her, "These are costumes. Pick one. Let's get the show on the road." Still, nothing.

Flinging aside the dresses in my hands, I made yet another selection. A hill of taffeta and shot silk, velvet, crepe, muslin, and bombazine had begun to grow between myself and my cousin, who'd ceased paying attention to the dresses at all. Instead, with a gesture that threatened to become a habit, she was pointing at a knotty pine box that was all but hidden under miscellaneous junk. She must have assumed, from its oblong shape, that what it contained was out of the ordinary even by the standards of the surrounding company.

"What?" she demanded apprehensively.

I came that close to saying, "Three guesses," since I figured that she already had a pretty good idea. But this didn't seem like the moment to remind her of our family's unfinished business and of how we were standing in what passed for our grandmother's crypt.

"That? Oh, nothing." I tried to sound offhand. "That's just, um, you know . . ." I chuckled unconvincingly. "Just an old crate full of more rags and bones." If ever there was a cue for the dead to contradict the living, to sit up in an eruption of curios and call me a liar, it was now. But Grandma Zippe thankfully remained as immobile in death as in life.

Apparently pacified, Naomi seemed to breathe easier, as if aware of having escaped a brush with an uncomfortable fact. Maybe now she'd be ready to get on with the business at hand. She still hadn't rolled down her turtleneck, which must have been smothering her in that sweltering shop, but since all that was identifiable of Naomi were her eyes, she seemed to me ripe for changing into somebody else.

"Now how about this?" I coaxed her, crinkling the gathered furbelows at the hem of the antebellum creation in my hands. "And these?" I teased the tiny rosettes at the neckline, the flounced leg-of-mutton sleeves. "Or maybe you'd prefer something a little more what we like to call in the trade ali mode?" I was beginning to think I'd found a missed calling. "Take this chichi little number, which they'll be wearing on the cover of *Hotsy-Tchatchky* this season."

I was hamming it up, dangling a slinky confection like the skin of a rainbow trout. When she failed to take the hint, I moved right along, though the pickings were getting slim, trying again with a flapper affair in gossamer and beads. But Naomi was hardly even showing any vital signs. That's when I came to the end of my patience.

"What do you think, this is my lady's chamber? You think we got all night?" Then right away, seeing how she'd been pushed close to tears, I relented. I gave her the go-ahead with my hand and told her, "Listen, I'm sorry, take your time. Take all the time you need — two, three minutes? I don't care."

I had it in mind to back off and leave her to try on the costumes in privacy, which was anyway the gentlemanly thing to do. But before I could get clear of the cage, I stumbled over her voice in its plangent appeal: "Harry, don't leave me."

By the time I turned around, her head had already vanished in the black web of her turtleneck. Then she peeled off the jersey, leaving her knotted scarf in place but revealing a pale pink garment to the waist. With no more ceremony than if she'd been alone, she kicked off her sandals, unlaced her slacks, and stripped down to a pair of fine-spun tap pants. After that she reached for a strap of her cotton camisole and was beginning to pull it over her shoulder. "Stop!" I shouted.

"That, uh, won't be necessary," I hastened to add, swallowing hard.

Naomi shrugged, leaving the strap to droop down her scrawny arm. Her eyes remained skittery, but in her voice, just beneath what was still mostly an appeal, I thought I detected the suggestion of a dare.

"You dress me, Harry," she said.

My throat went dry, my tongue like something washed up on a beach. When I managed to speak, I think that I actually muttered some caution against her taking a chill, though the heat in the rear of Kaplan's couldn't have been more dense. Turning in a full circle before I was able to locate the rack, I snatched up one of the remaining frocks. It was some lavender period piece, as it happened, with an upstanding bodice scalloped in lace-trimmed brocade: Guinevere meets Little Bo-Peep.

Without inquiring whether the gown was at all to her taste, I flung it over Naomi's head the way you might throw water to douse a flame — but not before I'd taken a sneaking account of her spindle-shanked anatomy, which included, item: the furuncular knobs of her shoulders; the bumps like mosquito bites under her bow-tied camisole, which was short enough to show a navel so convex that it seemed to be coming unbuttoned; the frosting of down on her coltish legs, knock-kneed below the edges of her baggy drawers. None of it was lost on me: how she looked, my near relation, like she'd just been hatched from an egg. Only nominally human, she nevertheless gave the impression that she was on her way toward becoming something else. A word I didn't know I knew — *sylph* — popped into my head, and I wondered if I was about to come into a knowledge beyond my years.

Turning away from her again, I started to rummage through the squat iron vault. "Accessories," I muttered; that's what I was looking for, or was it my scattered wits? In a tray containing — alongside the costume jewelry — fake eyeballs and prosthetic hooks, snake rattles and hollow fangs, wishbones, a devil doll, and a sulphur-yellow rock labeled "Philosopher's Stone," I found a conservative strand of tiny seed pearls. I faced my cousin a little stiffly, like I was bestowing them by virtue of the power vested in me as . . . what?, and fastened the pearls around her meager stem of a neck.

While I was asking myself what ought to come next, Naomi read my mind. Stooping, she retrieved a drawstring leather bag from the pocket of her shucked sailor pants. This she pressed into my hands before returning to her passivity of a moment ago, only now she didn't appear to be so floored into confusion by it all. Give her a gown and some jewelry, and all of a sudden she's posing, the pitsvinik; she's above having to wait on herself. Who did she think she was, putting on airs like a princess? Who, for that matter, did *I* think she was?

Inside the leather bag I discovered a variety of cosmetics: Tangee compact cases and aromatic puffs, lipstick tubes, eyebrow pencils, swabs. These were the sort of things that required an exacting touch, the sure hand that delivers the coup de grace. "Oh no." I was shaking my head, pleading inexperience. "What do I know from glamour?"

But in my mind I was giving testimony: I knew the show ladies at the Palace, their dressing tables crowded with toiletries like an Emerald City; I knew the ladies of the Baby Doll with their henna and hare's-foot unguents, their bezoar powder, their bleaching compounds for cutting coffee complexions with cream. What, come to think of it, didn't I know from glamour?

Besides, it didn't take a genius to apply a little lipstick. I'll admit I was worried at first that I might be hurting her, the way her mouth got so inflamed and her lips tightened to a slit. But when she released them in a slow impression of scarlet petals unfolding, I relaxed. Next came the eyes, which I caught on to pretty quick. If you stirred the little brush in the palette of shadow, then gently etched her quivering eyelids in soft greens and blues, you could create all kinds of effects. You could give her startled eyes a deep sadness or, with a deft stroke at the corners, a touch of boldness or even ferocity. You could turn them from the eyes of a girl to those of a tigress, then soften them with your fingertips until the frightened doe peeped through. You could make them fathomless and full of mystery.

Next it seemed that a little face powder might be in order. So I took up a puff and proceeded to raise a storm of fine white dust, from which Naomi emerged with an unearthly pallor. In a hurry to restore her vitality, I dipped my fingers in a tiny paint pot and daubed her with an excess of rouge. By rubbing circles over her cheeks, however, I was able to reduce the garish clown splotches to the merest phantoms of a blush. After that I closed an eye to peer at my cousin over the top of my upraised thumb, and judged that the results were perfection.

I even liked the way the tight black babushka, which still hid her hair, brought out the dramatic features of her face. I liked the way it contrasted with her lavish gown. Still, I knew what was missing. Beginning to shuffle among the bonnets and rug-like toupees on top of the costume rack, I brought down a couple of faceless wooden heads wearing wigs. The wig I chose was a high-piled, blond-ringleted concoction, more of a tawdry Madame du Barry than a Queen Marva June, but it was close enough and so roomy that you could pull it conveniently over Naomi's scarf.

When I looked, however, I saw that my cousin had already whipped off the scarf and was in the process of shaking out her hair. And now that the secret was out, it looked to me like it might be a job to cover it up again. For one thing, she seemed to have more hair than I remembered, or was it just that she'd washed it for a change? In any case, taking a silver-spined brush out of her bag, she began to stroke the shock of it into a

dark and static-crackling tawniness. With every brush stroke
her hair seemed more abundant, acquiring a kind of corona
from the overhead light, which gave me another idea. I tossed
aside the dusty wig and went casting about in the vault again,
this time coming up with a delicate rhinestone coronet. Using it
as a comb to sweep back her veil of bangs, I positioned it in
Naomi's hair. Then I stepped away to watch its blue-black
sheen catch the fire of those winking and shooting stones.

I gave a nod, turned again, and began rooting around under
the costumes, searching for a suitable pair of shoes. I didn't
look over my shoulder when I heard her in motion again; I
didn't need to. The whispered susurrus alone was enough to
carry me back to that sidetracked afikomen hunt on a distant
Passover evening, so I knew that Naomi was pulling on a pair
of silk stockings (in dark indigo, I imagined, or smoke), hoisting
them over her azure-veined thighs.

Taking a deep breath, letting it out, I kept my mind on the
matter at hand. From among a mismatched assortment of ga-
loshes and clogs, elevators and carpet slippers with upcurling
toes, brogans caked in the mud of Verdun, I selected a pair of
blue satin dancing pumps. Hoping they would fit, I swiveled
around on my knees to help Naomi try them on. She obliged me
by steadying herself, placing a hand benediction-style on the
top of my head. With her other she lifted the rustling organdy
of her gown, raising it as far as her ankle. This was a perfectly
functional action on her part, nothing you would call especially
Cinderella. So why did a certain organ in my chest choose that
moment to do its impersonation of a landed fish?

When I stood up to get the full effect of my labors, I found I
didn't quite know how to look at her anymore. I averted my
eyes and said I supposed that she wanted to get a load of herself. "Don't go away," I told her, which struck me as funny, as
if I'd said it to a manikin instead of a living girl.

I flung about outside the cage for another minute or two.

Eventually I turned up what I was looking for, wrapped in a bullet-riddled flag: a cloudy oval mirror in its burnished frame. I went back and held it in front of my cousin's face. I stood just behind her, holding up the mirror, kibbitzing her reflection over her shoulder — so that together we seemed to be gazing at the portrait of one shayne fair lady. In this way I was able to make an objective assessment of my handiwork.

She was a dream, the one in the mirror. She had a comeliness that could have presided over pageants, be they in the city of Memphis or the palace of Belshazzar. She was the type that could tease a dozen suitors, playing each against the other, while behind her fan she exposed the wickedness of his most trusted adviser to the king. She was a corker, all right; she could have fooled anybody. She could have fooled her own father. She could have fooled blithering Michael, shimmering into his field of vision like a lavender-blue flame — a flame composed of all the careless sparks that had flown from his mouth in the course of his long delirium. In fact, she could have fooled me.

As I craned my neck to peer into the mirror, I could no longer see past her radiance to the original shrimp underneath. The difficulty was possibly due to the murkiness of the glass, which I promptly put aside. But when I took her by the arm to turn her around, gingerly, as if she might break, it was even worse. She was beautiful. The thought came to me then that I was seeing my cousin for the first time as she truly was — which was ridiculous. After all, wasn't I the author of her transformation? I was the one responsible for having just made her up, and I knew what was real. Still the thought persisted like an itch that you're embarrassed to scratch in public. So who was in public?

"Naomi?" I said, the way you'd ask, Is anybody home? I resisted an impulse to tap on her forehead. Then she had to give me this smile. It was a close-mouthed smile, gentle and self-

possessed but nonetheless cruel. A smile by way of inform-
ing her cousin that she refused to be so kind as to disillusion
him.

That was all it took. Suddenly I had a dilemma on my hands.
Which was the greater crime, I asked myself: to run out on the
twins in their hour of dreadful need or to come to their aid by
handing over my cousin for them to do with as they pleased?
Because that's what it boiled down to, didn't it? I could either
forsake my colored acquaintances — since to turn up empty-
handed now would be as good as forsaking them — or give
them the tender, night-blooming Naomi at the risk of her health
and well-being, not to mention her honor. There was nothing in
between.

Of course I couldn't leave my old pal Lucifer in the lurch.
Weren't we practically blood brothers under the skin and all
that? Didn't I owe him for all the adventure I'd ever known? To
abandon him at such a time would make me the lowliest kind of
traitor, a rat and a worm. It was unthinkable. On the other hand,
how could I place my defenseless cousin, this knockout darling
in her party attire, in such uncertain peril? How could I lead her
into all that shvartzer chaos on the notorious side of an unnatural body of water that stunk enough to stain the very air?

Then it was funny that the scheme didn't seem so farfetched
anymore; clearly it had been a brilliant strategy all along. She
was perfect for the part, Naomi, just what the doctor ordered to
bring this whole cockamamy situation to a head. Like a living
poultice, she could have drawn out the infection of moonstruck
yearning from the sick kid's system. The septic boil that his
heart had become (which he might have done better to wear on
his dusky behind) would have burst in a spray of fleeing de-
mons at the sight of her; it would have survived, Michael's
heart, exquisitely seared but knitted whole again by the cautery
of her touch. She could have done that — what couldn't she do,
the angel? But she was mine.

So I told her it was all a joke.

"Naomi," I said, "I got a confession to make. You know all that stuff about the colored twins? Well, it was all just a load of bunk." It was, I told her, just a line to get her to come down to the pawnshop after hours. "And why, you might ask, would I want to do that?" This was a very good question indeed, and one for which I had no ready answer.

Stumped, I looked to Naomi, hoping unreasonably that she might provide an answer herself. *You wanted to see how far I would go for your sake,* she might have suggested, and I'd have wagged my head idiotically and said, "Bingo." But as no help was forthcoming from her quarter, I blundered on.

"I was curious to find out how, I dunno, gullible you were. It was kind of an experiment," I submitted, which didn't even make good sense. Aware that I was probably hanging myself with every word, I nevertheless seemed unable to curb my tongue. "I guess you're pretty gullible, aren't you? I mean, just imagine trying to pass you off as the queen of the Cotton Carnival." Here I filled the air with bogus laughter.

Throughout my foot-in-mouth performance, Naomi had yet to give anything away. A little pity or even righteous anger would have been a relief, but no such luck. If her limpid eyes betrayed anything, it was, Look at what you've done to me, Harry. I hope you're satisfied.

"You're really taking it like a champ, kiddo," I assured her, leaning forward to pat her vertebra at the place where her underwear protruded from the back of her gown. Then I told her I supposed the joke had gone far enough, and I was ready if she was (Mr. Big-Hearted) to let the matter drop here and now. I asked her if she didn't think it was time we started for home.

Still not a peep from Naomi, not a tummy rumble. All right, I thought, if she won't cooperate of her own free will, I'll just have to give her a shove. What choice did she leave me except to undo the wondrous thing I'd done?

I began cautiously with the coronet and, meeting no resistance, unhooked the string of pearls. I paused for a moment's regret, then reached around her bodice to unfasten the clasps at her spine. (It might have been less awkward to stand behind her for this operation, but Naomi was slight and my encircling arms were long for my size.) Then I gave a tug at her ruffled shoulders, and in an instant she stood defrocked.

I hadn't anticipated such abrupt results. I'd assumed that Naomi would intervene, having been provoked into taking over herself. But as it turned out, the costume collapsed of its own accord, settling in a sibilant heap about her ankles. Along with it a loose strap of her camisole had been dragged off a shoulder, so that a budding right booby sprang into view. This I pretended not to notice, quickly turning my back to gather her cast-off clothes. As I was picking up the sailor pants and the jersey, everything that was needed to restore Naomi to her former self, I heard a noise behind me. With a sound like a cough giving birth to a whimper, she'd broken her silence for what seemed like the first time in centuries.

When I looked, her tranquil composure had come apart, leaving her racked with shuddering all up and down her bony frame. She was given over to a fit of sobbing, so careless in its transports that she neglected her modesty. I marveled slack-jawed at the way her upstanding pink nipple clung to her joggling breast like a blood tick or a jumping bean. God knows I hadn't meant to disrobe her so violently as to reduce her to such a state — though you couldn't help feeling that, in some respects, this was more like it. Human again, Naomi might now be persuaded to get out of here.

I took a step forward to offer her clothes and maybe some sympathy, then took a step backward to dodge the arm that she was suddenly pointing at me.

"Harry!" she hooted, making it immediately apparent that she hadn't been sobbing at all but laughing hysterically.

Moreover, I myself seemed to be the butt of her joke. This might have upset me more if I hadn't been secretly pleased that the first word she uttered after finding her voice was my name.

"Oh Harry." There it was again. "I never saw anybody look so," — she practically choked, the words swelling her cheeks till they burst forth in a guffaw — "so scaaared!" Doubled over with laughter, she allowed the cotton vest to slip from her other shoulder and fall to her waist, thus lending her mirth more symmetry.

I supposed it was good that she was able to see the humor in our situation, saw it evidently much better than I. I tried to force a grin myself, hoping to show I could enjoy a good yuck as well as the next, even if it was at my own expense. This was turnabout, after all: having more or less played her for a patsy, it was only fair she should pay me back in kind. Tit (so to speak) for tat.

"Ain't we got fun," I said, and repeated it was time to go home. I even suggested that some witching hour might be at hand. Hadn't it just today been confirmed in my hearing that Kaplan's sometimes played host to thieves? At any moment they might burst in on us; she should hurry up and take her belongings, which I tried again to dump in her arms. But it was clear that I was wasting my breath.

She did, however, do me the favor of attempting to suppress her hilarity, subduing it to the level of sniffling and the odd adenoidal snort. She even went so far as to affect a fleeting frown, studying her clothes in my hands as if I'd brought her the evidence of a shed chrysalis. Then she gave herself up to a stormier fit of giggling than before.

I couldn't stand it any longer. Dropping her rejected garments into the sawdust on the floor, I told myself that what I was doing was for her own good. She would understand that, no stranger to hysterics, I was administering a kind of first aid.

257

I threw my arms around her bare shoulders and squeezed for all I was worth to calm her down. In a minute she'd be as limp and unresisting as her discarded gown, ready to see reason again.

With my chin clamped tight against her hair, I inhaled her closeness, her talcum and stale gardenia fragrance. I felt her sticky warmth glued to my shirtfront, through which I was tickled by her jiggling thingamabubs. It frightened me so much, this dazzled proximity, that I couldn't tell where her spasms of laughter left off and my shaking began. Again I tried to assure myself that I was doing nothing wrong — or if it was a sin to hug your half-naked first cousin, then it was the kind that even my grandfather's Scriptures must have made allowances for. Especially in the case of emergencies such as this.

When she pulled her face clear of the hollow of my neck, freeing her gleeful mouth, I saw a worried set of myselves reflected in the wet depths of her eyes. One worried Harry being all I could handle, and as the glare from the overhead bulb was anyway too harsh, I reached up and pulled the cord. In the dark I told Naomi to hush and, though I doubted that she heard me, suggested she might like to lie down for a spell. "Just until the craziness passes," I said. With one arm still hooked about her fitful waist, I guided her in the direction of Zippe's casket. I groped in front of us until my free hand made contact with the knotty pine, then swept wildly from left to right, clearing the coffin lid of bric-a-brac and, judging from the way that it bonged across the floor, an empty samovar.

Apparently amused by all the noise, Naomi renewed her cackling, stumbling a bit as I urged her forward. What she'd tripped over, as I discovered with my foot, was the clump of her party gown, which had yet to be unraveled from her ankles. Crushing the material with my heel, I took Naomi under the arms and lifted her — helplessly giddy featherweight that she was — out of the gown. Think of separating a mermaid from her vestigial fishtail. After that I encouraged her to lie back on the coarse-grained lid of the box, then climbed on board myself to keep her company.

To coax her into stillness, I eased myself down alongside her; I leaned my weight against her ticklish ribs, suffering her bones, blunted only where her underwear was gathered into a sort of breechcloth. Carefully, I took hold of her wrists.

"Naomi, shhhah!" I pleaded, my face so close to hers that I felt an eyelash brush the tip of my nose. "You're making enough racket to wake the —" I waited for the thunderclap, but heard only the continued peal of my cousin's laughter. "Naomi!" I was about to despair of ever getting through to her, when her voice tumbled forth again. It came this time as an assurance that she found our mutual recumbency funnier than anything yet.

"You're a devil, Harry Kaplan!" she squealed between paroxysms of giggling. "You're a terrible person!" But no sooner had I relaxed my grip on her — for such was the heady effect of her voice — than she jackknifed her hips and bucked me off the box.

I picked myself up out of the wreckage of what I think was an ant farm, pulling a splinter or two from the seat of my pants. Thoroughly ashamed of myself, I realized that I *had* been terrible, and I was grateful to Naomi for jolting me back to my senses. What had I been thinking, that I should swarm all over my cousin like a drowning man? Come the first lull in her antic behavior and I would beg her forgiveness. Then she did manage to modulate her merriment a little, so that I now heard only the sound of mild snuffling. But just as I'd begun to frame my apology, Naomi told me to shut up and come here.

"C'mere," she said in her old phony femme fatale voice, which even she didn't seem to be taking seriously. Not that it had ever worked on me when she had — not in her sultry garden or her spun-sugar boudoir. So what was it about the darkness at the back of Kaplan's that made her summons sound not so phony anymore?

Because I hesitated, not knowing whether I ought to step forward or turn tail, she reached out and pulled me down beside her again.

What happened after that is not so easy to say. Is it possible to try and hold on to someone even as you're trying frantically to break away? Because that's what was going on with me as Naomi and I started tussling on top of Zippe's box. Meanwhile, for her part, my kittenish cousin seemed equally confused. So frisky was she that, having just invited me to her side, she now seemed to be trying to throw me off again. Was this the famous fickleness of women? She wriggled, she squirmed, she nudged me with her drumlike tummy, so that I felt her giddiness in the pit of my own. It was a free-for-all, I can tell you, and I was ready to call it a draw. I was ready to call it a night and go home to lick my wounds — while at the same time I ached to cuddle Naomi. Of course I couldn't have it both ways. At least one of us needed to make up his mind for good and all.

Not that I could have disentangled myself from the snarl of our limbs if I'd wanted to. Already I'd lost a shoe in the struggle, and I was in danger of losing my pants, my suspenders having been yanked from their buttons. In a desperate attempt to master the situation, I scissored my legs about my cousin's, but thanks to the sliding ruck of her stockings, she was able to slip neatly out of the hold. I wouldn't have put it past her to slip out of her skin to elude me, a notion that made me redouble my efforts. For my trouble I got my glasses pried from my face and a finger poked in the eye before I had managed to recapture her hands.

I nestled hard against her, her tossing hips bruising my middle, causing my breath to come in tremolos like my papa being pummeled by masseurs at the Russian baths. But in the end, with a mighty grunt, I had her; she was pinned. I hugged her in a mortal vise, hanging on as if I thought she might change into something else, a porcelain doll or a daughter of Lilith or a distant icy queen. She might change into an annoying relation or a stranger unless I kept her nailed to the coffin lid, unless I gathered the gang of Naomis in my arms and confined them to a solitary girl, one I might never dare to let go of again.

But the little minx was still hemorrhaging laughter. It poured out of her in a rising tide that threatened to carry me away along with her if I didn't act quick. This was serious. There was no telling what might happen if, for the sake of us both, I didn't take it upon myself to seal her parted lips with mine.

IV

Thirteen

About the time that the Carnival ended and school let out for the summer, the water began to go down. Looking no more or less bedraggled than they had when they'd arrived, the displaced families started making their exodus. They left as they'd come, like a defeated army, in a wobble-wheeled convoy of buckboards full of featherless poultry, in backfiring two-cylinder jalopies and on hobbled shank's mare. They trailed away toward their various points of the compass with the dust devils bringing up their rear, erasing the dried mud of their tracks from the sun-baked streets. In a few days their numberless ranks were reduced to a handful of stragglers; then they were gone.

I guess the city heaved something like a universal sigh at their departure: think of my mama loosening her stays at the end of a trying day. But otherwise there was nothing especially noteworthy about the event, no big send-offs that anyone heard of, no fond farewells. In fact, if you hadn't known that they'd been there in the first place, you wouldn't have missed them at all, their absence being no more remarkable than the evaporation of dew. On the downtown sidewalks the judges and the cotton brokers in their paisley waistcoats, the shop ladies with their swollen ankles, and the Court Square pensioners in wheelchairs feeding doves went about their business as if nothing had happened. The only difference I noticed was that they all looked slightly distracted, wearing expressions like you see on the faces of people trying hard to remember a dream.

Surfaced again, the levee was strewn with rubbish — as though it might have been raining one-eyed rag dolls and waterlogged mattresses, captain's chairs and tea chests spilling crawdads, bloated family Bibles like risen black loaves, long johns stuffed with straw. Canvas baby strollers, grandfather clocks, and a bleating Angora goat were found stranded in the branches of the scrub oaks along the banks. For every few feet the river receded, another terrace of debris was left behind, the cobbles resembling steps down the unearthed stages of an archaeological dig. Had my father chosen to venture the couple of blocks from his shop to the bluff, he might have viewed the sight of so much diverse trash with wonder. He might have thought that heaven had been scattering his own brand of manna.

During those days North Main Street seemed to have grown a little quieter, at least in our apartment, where there was seldom anyone at home. You'd have thought I might see more of Mama now that she and Uncle Morris had finally succeeded in getting rid of Grandpa Isador. On the pretext of airing him out, they'd taken him one afternoon for a drive in the country, where they had turned him over to the state asylum at Bolivar. I could imagine how he must have battled with the myrmidons as they tried to stuff him into a straitjacket; I heard him howling Yiddish oaths, which the other meshugayim echoed in their respective lost tongues. Not that I believed for a minute that he would find any peace, my grandpa, even in a community of like minds.

The popular scuttlebutt about Bolivar had it that its inmates were often the subjects of unspeakable experiments. They were housed in kennels, kept naked in all weather, made to operate the hospital generator by running a treadmill. But my mama insisted that the place was a regular country club, situated among the pines like Grossinger's. And who should know better than she, since Mama and Uncle Morris were finding such frequent excuses to visit. They were checking up on the old man's progress, so they said; they were taking him his things — though you tell me how an armload of grimy incunabula, some phylacteries, and a couple of moth-eaten suits could require so many day trips, some of which extended far into the evening.

I thought it a shame that old Isador hadn't been allowed to take along the console radio, which in his absence I'd begun to conceive a fascination for. It seemed doubly a shame that my grandfather should have been put away when more than ever the radio was bearing out his prophecies.

If you listened to the postscripts of what was going on in Europe, you heard news that out-Isadored my grandpa's worst fears. Having been denied their God-given license to wander, the Jews were being corralled into cages. The few that escaped were forced to live underground; the overseas relations of our neighbors in the Pinch were disappearing from the face of the planet. They were performing a vanishing act on a scale compared to which the disappearance of the flood refugees was small change. And if rabid voices in certain quarters had anything to do with it, the rivergees were only a dress rehearsal for an epidemic of vanishing that might be spreading our way.

Beyond what was confirmed by the radio, there were rumors afoot, tales carried by a handful of greenhorns who'd fallen through cracks to land in our neighborhood. Remove one Isador and half a dozen others spring up to take his place. But these mournful shnorrers were passing on stories that even my grandpa might have hesitated to repeat, which isn't to say they were heeded any more seriously. Still, it was not so uncommon these days to see the ordinarily sociable merchants of North Main Street making like ostriches.

Having gotten the jump on whatever evil happened to be in the air, my papa had made himself a virtual missing person. So scarce had he become that his wife, in keeping with time-honored tradition, had turned to his surviving brother for support. And if Sol Kaplan had uttered any squeak of protest — if, for instance, from his own asylum he'd objected to old Isador's institutionalization — he made sure that nobody heard him. Nor did anyone hear him if he offered me congratulations on the occasion of my sixteenth birthday.

Of course, I wouldn't have been in any mood to celebrate. After you've betrayed your only friends, who felt like celebrating? Who cared anything for birthdays when you no longer dared to show your face at the famous end of Beale Street? Miserable wretches such as I didn't deserve to have birthdays. I was no better than a leper, a candidate for the colony that some said still existed on the far side of Mud Island.

I knew what I was, all right. I was a despicable blue-gum Jew, harmless enough in appearance but liable to turn at any moment, his bite more poisonous than a cottonmouth's. Or was I only flattering myself? If I'd had a hair on my tochis, I'd have jumped off the Harahan Bridge. Weeks later a fisherman snags his hook and up I float, flesh flaking like soggy piecrust, eyes nibbled away by gars. But none of the names that I called myself nor the mortifications I imagined could make me feel any worse than I already did.

I felt awful not so much because I missed the twins as because I didn't seem to miss them enough. Of course I would have given a lot to know how they were getting along, but wasn't that only curiosity? The truth was that ever since the night I'd denied them to Naomi, Lucifer and Michael had faded to dim apparitions in my mind. If I missed them at all, it was in the way that you miss a story someone once told you, a story you're still very fond of though the details have become kind of vague.

I reasoned with myself that they were probably okay. The floodwaters had gone down, restoring everything to the way it was before. Having weathered the crisis of a mostly imaginary malady — I mean, who besides comedians on "Major Bowes" ever died from talking too much? — Michael was once again pushing his broom. He was shadowing his brother, who, freed from the nuisance of ofay apprentices, was at this moment making his prompt underworld rounds. Whatever the case, there was certainly no future in fretting about the twins. No news of their circumstances would ever reach me, not here in my exile on North Main Street, a place that had nothing much to offer a guy who'd been where I'd been.

In fact, the old neighborhood wasn't quite the same after the flood. It had changed, if possible, for the worse, become even shabbier in the wake of the departed river refugees. The shopkeepers and their wives looked worried, their troubles increased, as if the uninvited guests had left behind more in their care. The buildings themselves seemed untended and forlorn, more than ever overwhelmed by invading creepers, which snaked through the broken windows and wrenched loose the strangled fire escapes. The whole street looked as if it had been trussed in leafy cargo nets, ready to be hauled away. Storks might snatch it up and set it down again in some far-off valley of milchik and flayshik, a land more rich and plentiful than the Parkway. People would stumble out of their shops and tenements to the realization that their season in Memphis had been a bad dream. A clammy, unventilated dream of a stagnant atmosphere that was not very conducive to carrying a torch for your cousin.

The more I tried not to think about that night in the pawnshop, the more my thoughts returned to it, the way your tongue will seek a cavity. I kept remembering how — after we'd toppled off the casket and I pulled the cord to see if she was all right — it was suddenly over. The damage was done. We were both self-conscious again. Oh why had I needed to turn on the light? I offered to switch it off again but the mood was already spoilt; Naomi was peevishly scrambling for her clothes. And I, beyond embarrassment, had assumed an awkward pose to conceal a chafing dampness at the fly of my pants.

I began to pick up some of the scattered costumes, making a sullen effort toward restoring a little of its original order to the cage. I was anxious now, and feeling that Naomi might be deliberately trying to get my goat, because once she'd made herself more or less decent, she'd started to dawdle.

"Did you hear that?" I whispered, hoping to frighten her into hurrying, succeeding only in heightening my own nervousness. Every item in the dark recesses of the shop began to resemble a hunkering Oboy watching over us. "Let's beat it already!" I hissed, practically prepared to remove her, if necessary, by force, while at the same time afraid of touching her again. Then, as I wondered what she might for God's sake be waiting for, I took a stab in the dark. "Look," I told her with no less aggravation, "I love you — okay?"

It's possible that I'd said this before, back when we'd been so inseparable on the lid of Zippe's casket. It's possible that I'd said it in such a way as to alter the course of our grappling, puncturing the humor, pitching us both into a tender loss of equilibrium. But that was then, a time that already seemed like long ago. And now, at this raw early hour of dawn, the words had blundered out as if a toad had plopped from my mouth, a rude little monster that I regarded with horror and Naomi with a certain sly amusement, like she thought it might make an interesting pet.

It seemed that we were in love, my cousin and I — so what was the trouble? The trouble was love. It was enough already for me to try to accommodate my guilty conscience toward the shvartzers without having to share the same space with an overcooked passion for my cousin. It was just too much to fit inside one skin. Other things, such as memory and common sense, would have to be tossed out to make room. After all, we're talking about the teary-eyed, lackluster nishtikeit who used to so royally gripe my can. That's all she was, barring the occasional botched audition as tenderfoot temptress, excluding her headlong excursions into storytelling, night prowling, and masquerading as the queen of heartbreak. But that was it, the complete inventory on Naomi, except for maybe a shtikl of something else.

Something that made me feel as if my heart wore a crown of candles that the ill wind of my conscience kept blowing out, though not before I had the chance to make a wish. So what did I wish? I wished that I could rid Naomi of the something extra. I wished I could shrink her — my darling, my dove, the sweet angel changeling muse — back into a pest again. I wished I could forget all about her.

Whenever I was overcome by the urge to go and give my cousin a squeeze, I remembered the deceit that made me unworthy. I remembered that she was taking up the space in my mind that should have been exclusively reserved for my remorse over the wards of the Baby Doll Hotel. Then I would begin to miss her so much, my Naomi — as if I were marooned on some desert galaxy with a bad case of homesickness. I would feel that my love for my cousin was a punishment inflicted on me for having double-crossed the twins.

So I didn't try to see her, and except for those rare occasions when my mama was around (which meant that the line was generally engaged anyway), I took the phone off the hook. Eventually, in case she should attempt to contact me in person, I stayed away from home. After a week spent lying around the apartment doing nothing, spinning dials on the radio, I'd taken to the streets. I knocked about along the levee for a while, but in the end I went where you went when there was nowhere else to go.

I hung around Kaplan's Loans, which like myself was stuffed full of more junk than it could reasonably contain. Having no pride left to swallow, I thought it might now be fitting if I buried myself in the shlock alongside my papa. Then it seemed cruelly inconsiderate of my father to have surrounded himself with worthless merchandise to the exclusion of the living members of his family.

So I hung around out on the sidewalk next to Oboy and his three-legged stool. If the bullet-headed little golem appeared to have no use for me, I could assure him that he was likewise no friend of mine. It was bad enough knowing as I did that his loyalties were divided between my father and Uncle Morris, but what irked me the most was the perfect impunity with which he moved between the shop and the Parkway and the famous end of Beale. Anyone who lived his life in more than one place — which was as good as aspiring to more than one life — this person was highly suspect in my book.

Even worse than loitering with Oboy, however, was loitering on the spittle-flecked pavement in front of Kaplan's all alone. Which was how I found myself on a morning when the puller, beyond aloof, was entirely absent. It was an event so unheard of that I was tempted to take it personally.

Like the perilous chair in one of Naomi's stories, Oboy's abandoned perch defied anyone to try and usurp it. While I had no special designs on it myself, I couldn't see what harm it would do if I decided to take a little break from killing time. "How do, cap'm, hello doc," I might say, sitting spraddle-legged astride the stool, hailing customers with the sleight of tongue I'd picked up on my midnight jaunts. "What you know, boss, brother, sportin life, my man? Look like that ol suit a yours is canine surplus, cause it sho nuff got the mange. Now Kaplan's here'll fix you right up . . ." Though what customer in

his right mind would want to enter these impenetrable premises anymore? Besides, Oboy's absence had left me feeling
kind of uneasy and adrift. With the stool vacant the shop
seemed somehow vulnerable, and so did I, insofar as I was attached to the place. But I wasn't so attached that, given a hint
of foreboding, I couldn't just walk away.

I followed my nose, which led me, as reliably as a needle on a
compass, down the hill toward the residue from the dried-up
bayou overflow.

From Third to Hernando the street was shmutz, like the
regurgitations of some omniverous fish. The gutters were
choked with corncobs, slab bottles, hairpieces, and turtle
shells. There were tin cans full of swimming tadpoles and
drowned rats, a stove-in bass fiddle plastered in funny papers, a
sausage-fingered gardener's glove wrapped around a knife, a
boot sunk in a spectral scum of oil. By the curb at a corner of
Handy Park was a foundered skiff, occupied by a candle-thin
character in the process of baiting a bamboo pole. Nearby, face-
down in a pool of carnelian broth, lay a man either sleeping or
deceased, a couple of children poking him with sticks to deter-
mine which.

Whereas the department in charge of such things had chosen, throughout the flood, to ignore the standing water on
Beale — they'd put their pumps to better use in other neighborhoods, leaving the lagoon to dry up on its own steam, so to
speak — that same department was taking its time about col-
lecting the dregs. This meant that the street would remain im-
passable for yet a while longer. And since it had also ceased to
serve as a ferry crossing anymore, the block had no function at
all beyond its current status as an open privy.

That was how everybody seemed to regard it, holding their
noses to give the fouled pavement a wide berth. So intense was
the odor of garbage rotting in the sun that for the plain old fishy
stink of the place you might have waxed nostalgic. With their

ranks thinned considerably since the refugees had decamped, their heads lowered against the offending stench, the strollers toiled along the sidewalk. On the south side of the street they kept close to the fronts of buildings whose bases were blanched from the vanished water. The very stones appeared to be turning into vapor from the bottom up.

Oppressed as I felt, I didn't need any encouragement to follow the example of the strollers, shoving my hands deeper into my pockets and watching my feet. Once or twice, looking up lest I walk into a lamppost, I greeted somebody I thought I knew. I said hello to Typhus the ice man, whose mule the twins had "borried" for a kiddy concession during Jubilee: they'd cinched a crutch under the old swayback's belly to keep it from dragging the ground. I greeted R. C. Prettyman, the singing pest catcher, who according to legend had rid the Baby Doll of rats with three pesticidal verses of "If You See My Savior." Then there was Grim Missus Trim the card sharp, into whose beer Lucifer had once poured laxative aloes after she'd stiffed him on a tip. But maybe I was wrong, because none of them had bothered to return my salutation. Anyway it was easy to mistake one shvartzer for another.

Of course it was possible that it was they who had failed to recognize me. But that didn't seem likely, given the enduring impression I was certain I'd made on the street. Who wouldn't remember the renegade Harry Kaplan, who'd been for such a time in and out of everybody's hair? True, I didn't feel much like the kid I'd once been, mascot of a colored bordello and all that, so it was conceivable that in my depressed condition I didn't look like him either. Or maybe I was simply forgotten. Oddly enough, rather than hurt by the idea, I found myself heartened and relieved. If they'd forgotten me already, then so much the better; I was anonymous again, just as I'd been when I first came down to Beale. And being anonymous, nobody would know me for the double-crosser I knew myself to be.

I wasn't so confident about this idea that I was ready to face Mambo's, where a stranger couldn't always count on a welcome reception, but I did suddenly find the gumption to creep around the corner for a furtive glimpse of Gayoso Street.

The shoebox frame of the Baby Doll stood in its perpetual need of upkeep and repair. The whole termite-riddled structure — fake brick shingles frilly with a barnaclelike fungus — was stranded in a dry dock of bitterweed, of bald dandelions and wilted sunflowers like shower heads. The broken windows were stuffed with rags, the Coca-Cola sign hanging crooked, its legend faded to mystery. The red bulb dangled over the door like some raffish version of the everlasting light in shul.

Beneath the light on the broad front stoop, her bottom sagging through the seat of her wicker lawn chair, sat Aunt Honey. She was wearing her three-tiered tangerine wig, a housecoat the size of a gospel tent, and her pair of old mules with the toes out to air her bunions. In one hand she fluttered a church fan with a cloud-walking Jesus, his heart showing through his chest, and in the other hand she brandished a flyswatter. This gave her the look of some formidable dual-sceptered pharaoh. Her legs, constricted by the tourniquets of her rolled-down stockings, were planted far apart: the pillars of a gate at which, before entering, you would have to abandon all hope. Her moon-wide face, satiny with sweat, was frowning in general irritation. But as I stepped from behind a phone pole, palpitatingly edging closer to the foot of her steps, I saw her irritation become more localized.

I planted myself dead in front of her on the dusty walk, having made myself an easy target for whatever she might have to say. Why else was I there but to face the music and place myself in the way of bad news? "So come on already," I beseeched her under my breath, "make with the pogrom."

But Aunt Honey stubbornly refused to do me that favor. She stirred in her chair, and for an instant I had the wild hope that she was about to call up to the twins that Mistah Harry was here. But instead she rolled her slitted eyes slowly in the direction of one of her scepters, then back again toward me, as if she thought I wasn't worth swatting. Then she asked me what had once passed for a breezy byword between us, though you needed better ears than mine to catch the humor in it today.

"Is you lost?"

In an open window behind her a couple of the ladies, their names on the tip of my tongue, were lazily sunning themselves. They were eyeing me with the cool distance that was usually reserved for characters too poor or damaged to be considered as prospective customers.

I could have told Aunt Honey that lost wasn't the half of it, but I didn't want to push my luck. After all, hadn't I just been let off the hook? Hadn't she proved to my satisfaction that, due to the short span of attention for which darkies were famous, I was as good as forgotten down here? It was as if I had never before set foot in these squalid parts. And since they'd dropped me from their memories so readily, then the least I could do was to return the kindness. Twins, what twins? Did I know any twins? Except of course the Gold Dust Twins, those hula-skirted jungle bunnies wiping dishes on the side of the soap flakes box.

Any connections I thought I might still have among the shvartzers were hereby dissolved. I stood exonerated in my mind, released from all outstanding debts. I could go back to Naomi now with a clear conscience. I could go and adore my precious cousin like gangbusters, with no checkered past to interfere. Yellowjackets flew out from under the eaves as if to show me the door, but I needed no help to find my way out of there. I flapped my arms once in a sign of futility, twice to shoo the wasps, then turned away.

The empty bootblack's stand shoved far into its corner told me all I needed to know, though I still had the goading temptation to put my reborn anonymity to the final test. (Or was it that I was more a glutton for punishment than for love?) So I opened the screen door to Mambo's Tonsoral. Clippers and lips ceased to buzz; everyone froze. This, I thought, is where I came in.

"My mistake," I excused myself with a little wave. But before I could back out the door, one of the younger barbers, the part in his processed hair like a bullet crease, piped up, "Where you been, you look so poorly? It look like you done been whup with a ugly club."

"Whup with it nothin," one of his colleagues threw in. "Why that chile are a charter member." He mimicked his own snickering laughter with his scissors.

"Boy so ugly his own mama ain't claim him," said a customer seated against the plate-glass window. "And his mama, she ugleee! man, I talkin mud fence. Talkin stop yo watch whooch it ain't even a stopwatch."

"Talkin gag yo sink."

"Talkin sour yo dough, hear what I'm say?" offered a man bearded in shaving cream, sitting abruptly upright in his reclining chair. "So ugly it a sour the whole a yo marry life, turn yo testimonials to a peach pit."

"So ugly it a make Kang Kong look lak Jean Hollo."

"Make Fly Face look lak Mothah Mary from the Bobble."

"Whoa now," called out a senior barber in an attempt to restore a little order, only to succumb to the general frivolity himself. "Thow Mistah Harry in the bayou, heh heh, skim ugly off the top fo a week."

Until then I'd supposed they were giving the white folks the business; they were letting me know I should take a hike. But when I heard my name, I understood what they were really up to. They were putting me in the dozens, me, my own self, heaping on the insults with a generous familiarity. A recognized citizen of Beale Street, I had been singled out for friendly abuse.

The whole barber shop had gotten into the act. Having exhausted so many variations of "ugly," they moved on to

277

"tainted," "flicted," "rurnt," and "low." "So low he can walk under a snake belly with a top hat on." I was this, that, I put one of them in mind of a dream he'd had one time . . . Everyone was slapping his knees with rolled-up newspapers, yawping over such an abundance of mother wit. I was getting the full treatment, luxuriating in their needling just this side of a steam towel and scalp massage.

The door swung open and in walked a party with the unmistakable severity of a deacon. Frowning, he took a seat and directed his gaze high above the barber chairs, reading the writing on the wall — the sign forbidding the playing of dozens. Such was the effect of his censure that the subject was immediately dropped, joviality subsiding into sighs, and I was left standing with an outmoded grin on the spot where the floor tiles sloped toward a hair-clogged drain.

I wanted to implore them not to stop, I liked it. Call me an unleavened cracker, anything you please. When I saw the senior barber abandon his basin and come around his chair to take my arm, I was hopeful he might still have a lick or two to get in. He tilted his head toward me, a polished caramel dome wreathed in a horseshoe of white wool, but instead of a gibe, all I got was his earnest inquiry: "Where you been, Mistah Harry? Aunt Honey and her stablishment, they be's mad wicha cause you ain't attend the funeral."

I stepped back a pace from the drain, which suddenly seemed a dangerous place to stand.

"The whole syndicatin street have turn out," the barber went on. "Man, it were the biggest plantin party since I disrecollect when." He paused to gather historical perspective. "Yeah Lawdy, if it weren't a reglar grievin jamboree, tha's what I calls it. Shoulda seed all them bobtail lady in they fripry attire, look lak flowers in a hailstorm the way they carry on. And Aunt Honey, she done take the cake; they ain't never a soul could outshine her fo blubberation. Cain't nobody stop her but she

Park. At Third Street I put the dreck of the lagoon behind me for once and all. I was making like blazes up the hill toward my father's shop, almost home free, when I was halted in my skidding tracks yet again.

A little knot of onlookers had gathered outside the pawnshop, a mud-spattered Black Maria parked at the curb.

I dove into the first of the show racks, falling back among the smelly suits, clinging to a basted twill pant leg as I gulped for air. Warily I peeked out to spy on the baggy-faced shamuses McCorkle and Priest in their level straw skimmers, their open jackets revealing shoulder holsters like harnesses for their barrel chests. Solemn in the performance of their duty, each had a firm grip on one of my father's arms, escorting him between them out the door of his shop.

His bow tie was in its crooked, stalled-propeller position, his cuff-linked hands folded modestly in front of his vitals. His fine eagle beak was twitching as if a fly had landed on its tip, or was he about to sneeze? Then I recognized the problem: with his manacled arms pinioned to his sides by the detectives, my papa was trying to work his spectacles back up over the hump of his nose. His weak gray eyes were blinking so much from the sun that, even as he was being hauled off to jail, you'd have thought he'd just emerged from a long incarceration.

He looked around like someone who dimly recollected having once been sovereign of all he surveyed. I burrowed deeper into the rack, though apparently not deep enough: for all his shortsightedness, my papa seemed to have no trouble picking me out from the rest of his irregular merchandise, staring straight at me and shrugging from the eyebrows up.

"The bride and groom here," he remarked with a melancholy good humor, nodding benignly toward the cop on either sleeve, "they asked me to stand up for them under the canopy. So who refuses such an invitation?"

The good son, if only to distinguish himself from the other

spectators, would have fallen to his knees, pleading that they not tear his father from the bosom of his shop — I mean family. That failing, he would have leapt upon the shoulders of the law, shoving their hat brims down around their ears. He would have begged them to take him instead, none being guiltier. But all I could muster under the circumstances was a little more shame on behalf of the Kaplans, though there was already more than enough to go around.

In the end I rallied, able to offer a token something short of standing there like a yolt. "Papa," I managed as the plain-clothes dicks were handing him over to a uniformed officer, who in turn helped him into the rear of the paddy wagon. "Papa," I said, stepping forward now that it was too late, "what should I do?"

With one foot already in the bed of the van, he turned to me with such surprise that I wondered if he'd recognized me in the first place. Biting his lip in a torment of consternation, my papa was either chewing over my question (which was not a particular brainteaser) or trying to place my face. Then he ended the suspense, speaking in a voice that fell somewhere between an afterthought and the gravity of a deathbed request.

"Be a good boy, Harry," he bade me, lifting his hands, which, joined as they were at the wrists, seemed to confuse supplication with prayer. "Mind the shop while I'm away."

As the cop boosted my father into the van by the seat of his pants, I lurched forward; but grabbed by McCorkle or Priest — I never knew which was which — I missed my chance to push his glasses back onto his nose. The door slammed, reducing my papa to four eyes in a window no bigger than a mail slot. Then the slot itself shrunk to the size of a tiny hyphen as the van, with its siren blaring, pulled away. It wasn't until the vehicle had taken a jouncing corner on two wheels that the detective set me free to wave goodbye.

Released, I shrugged my shoulders like I was shaking off the

rumpled evidence of an authentic scuffle. The shamuses were already admonishing the onlookers to break it up, the show was over. I seemed to have existed for them only as a momentary extension of my father's predicament, and now that he was out of the picture, so was I. Of course I could simply leave the scene if I wanted, in spite of my father's final injunction, bestowing a responsibility that I hadn't sought nor wished now to assume. But I wasn't so remiss in my filial duties, not to say uninquisitive, that I couldn't stick around another minute or two. And since it appeared they were indifferent about whether I did or I didn't, I straggled behind the detectives into the shop.

Privy to the logic behind the apparent disorder of my papa's merchandise, I could see how the place had been done over by the police. Though the aisle was no more blockaded than usual, items had been roughly dislodged from their shelves; whereas it had once seemed a stronghold against it, Kaplan Loans was now officially susceptible to disaster.

At the rear of the shop, the open valuables cage was crammed with people climbing over each other, assuming awkward poses in their efforts to move about. There was a man with a toothbrush mustache and a "Press" tag in his hatband, his foot through a drum. Having rested his camera on the headless neck of the dressmaker's dummy, he was attempting to unwedge himself from a tight corner. His companion, a sharp-chinned lady in a smart tweed suit, was straddling the animal orchestra in her tottering heels. Even as she struggled to retain her balance, she kept asking questions and jotting down notes. Stripped to his shirtsleeves, the officer from the street was brushing everything in sight — flintlock muzzles, gramophone speakers, a tumbled copper samovar — with a powder like fine black pollen, an activity I associated with spreading goofer dust over headstones to discover the imprint of spirit hands.

The pawnshop detail detectives, their thick backs pressed into quilting against the wire mesh, edged around the storage

area for a better vantage. I watched as one of them lit his cigarette with the butt of another, while his partner, cocking a hat brim, wiped his brow with what might have been the warrant for my father's arrest. Both of them grinned obligingly when the camera flashed.

McCorkle or Priest, anyway the one with the cigarette and the codfish jowls, was sounding off about how they had been on top of this one from the word go. "We likely come that close to apprehendin yer alleged felon red-handed, which it ain't to say we don't have a pret-ty good lead" — his partner ahemmed — "which we are natcherly not at liberty to tell y'all what it is at this time."

"Yes ma'am," concurred his colleague, Priest or McCorkle, the one with the brow like an éclair and the five o'clock shadow at noon, "we had our eye on this place all along. Fact is, we known they was somethin, shall we say, unkosher about Kaplan's." He rolled his eyes meaningfully. "Jes been waitin on the big heist to prove it. Course, this is strictly off the record, understand."

"Course, tween us'n you," his partner took over, "we'd a probably tore up the premises from here to Sunday, cept" — another ahem, which the speaker ignored — "cept somebody left this ol casket half open like they mighta almost wanted us to find the goods. Don't know as how we ever come acrosst the dang thing on our routine inspections, did we Earl?"

"Oh, I seen her all right, Leslie. The thing looked suspicious from day one, but I figured to wait for the choicetest chance to check her out."

"The hell you say, Earl."

"You would question my word?"

"I would question yer Burma Shave."

But they both managed to exchange collaborative grins as the camera flashed again.

Wanting to protest the violation of my father's holy of holies,

I stepped out into the open like this was the limit. But as no one paid the slightest attention to my huffing and puffing, I quickly lost interest in being outraged. To tell the truth, none of these odd goings-on seemed to have much to do with me. If I hadn't been hovering so close to the outside of the cage, I might have let the whole business go. I might not even have bothered with poking my nose through the wire to see what sort of tsimmes had finally brought down the law.

Just then, announced by their stumbling over obstructions in the aisle, another couple of cops arrived on the scene. Mutt and Jeff in their respective statures, they were trying to be cute, whistling as if they might have ulterior motives. The detectives reminded them that precinct headquarters was expecting the evidence, "So don't get no idears about takin no detours via Honolula, Howareya."

Everyone was resorting to all manner of contortions to make room for the newcomers to enter the cage. That's when — as the new cops rolled up their sleeves and maneuvered to lift it — I got my first unobscured eyeful of the oblong box on its steamer trunk bier.

What the open lid revealed in place of my grandmother's remains was a scintillating hill of plunder. Light from the naked bulb winked and ricocheted off lockets and brooches like fired reports. Whole crisscrossed grids of light, echoing the facets of red and green gems, coruscated from rings, torques, tiaras, and charms. To examine such a lode through my father's jeweler's loupe would have been to ensure your own blindness. As it was, too much of that skirmishing light got trapped inside my specs, which I had to take off in order to rub my eyes.

When I replaced my glasses, I saw things more clearly. The ropes of gold necklaces, for instance, no longer seemed to resemble the braided hair of Midas's daughter; the polished baubles were just that, not the eyes of beasts turned by magic to bijouterie in Aladdin's cave. This was, after all, no dead man's chest found on an uncharted island at the farthest corner of the

seventh sea. It was only my old bubbe's vacated casket full of stolen property, a treasure not so much for voluptuously plunging your arms into as for impounding.

Once they'd hoisted the goods to their uneven shoulders, the cops were so unsteady under their burden that McCorkle and Priest were forced to pitch in and help. Grumbling, the gumshoes first removed their jackets and threw them over the jewels as if to put out their fire.

"Okay, folks," they barked, "the party's over. Everybody out!"

Everybody but me, I assumed, since what could it matter to them whether I stayed or went? As the reporters, still jotting and flashing, fell into the single file that the passage demanded, I hung back. Feeling no special need to conceal my presence, I stood at a corner of the cage, waiting to be locked up inside the shop. It was my fate, I decided, to remain in Kaplan's Loans until I rotted, taking up where my grandma'd left off.

Snapping the lid on his dusting kit as he exited the cage, the black-powder policeman paused to poke me in the ribs. When I sluggishly refused to budge, I thought he might mistake me for another curio and cover me with powder as well. This would have left me virtually indistinguishable from the bunch of plaster lawn jockeys I was standing beside. Unfooled, however, the officer only seconded the detectives' decree, saying, "You too, buckaroo. Amscray!"

Shoved toward the door, I took my place at the back of the weaving column, trying to tell myself it wasn't a total loss: I was representing the family in what amounted to my grandmother's absentee funeral procession. Moreover, during its safe deposit in Kaplan's, Zippe's box had increased incalculably in value, to say nothing of how much interest had accrued . . .

Back outside things were wound up with dispatch. The lidless casket with its dazzling contents was slid into the bed of a second police wagon. McCorkle and Priest themselves dragged in the show racks, though they neglected to remove

the puller's stool. Then, while one of them pulled shut the lattice, the other wove through it a thick length of chain, clasping the chain with a padlock as big as a handbag. Before starting away they dispersed a few persistent bystanders, former customers of Kaplan's who'd ignored their previous warnings but now departed readily enough. In seconds I was left alone on the sidewalk to study the sign taped to the inside of the pawnshop window:

These Premises Closed
Until Further Notice
By Order Of
The Shelby County Sheriff's Office

Not for all its authority could you have called it a striking sign. It needed a little something more than its understated black-and-white lettering to catch the attention of the ordinary passer-by. What it needed was my papa standing in front of his shop as on the night when he'd inaugurated his (now extinguished) name in scarlet neon. It needed him calling on one and all to "Give a look!"

On the trolley ride back to North Main Street, dog-weary, I took the only available seat. I'd traveled all the way to Market Square Park before the hostile stares of other passengers alerted me to the fact that I'd been riding Jim Crow. A total misfit, I got off before my stop and began the short walk to our apartment. I walked slowly, dragging my feet as if my heavy heart were fastened to them by an ankle chain.

Wherever I passed, heads shook and tongues clucked, which I took to mean that they considered me a sorry sight. Then I recalled how our neighbors seemed to practice a sort of telegraphy in their arthritic bones, and thought otherwise. I guessed that the news of my father's downfall must have already

reached them. How else could you account for such acts of unsolicited philanthropy?

First came Mrs. Rosen waddling out of her delicatessen, tugging at a strap of her overburdened brassiere as she consoled me with a jelly-filled blintz. Old Man Petrofsky offered me a cantaloupe, thumping it once or twice in a show of good faith. As I trudged past the garlic-hung door of their shop, Mr. and Mrs. Krivetcher — who appeared to be rearing up on hind legs — waved the shoes they were wearing on their hands by way of telling me I should take my pick. The bewhiskered Mrs. Sacharin leaned over her window box to toss me a geranium. The alter kockers on their bench in front of Jake Plott's awarded me a unanimous "Och un vey!" But even as they competed to endow me like a prodigal returned, I stayed wretched. I thought that this kind of charity, it was what they might have extended to some vagabond shnorrer they suspected of being Elijah. For one of their own they wouldn't have made such a fuss.

I don't know why I should have been thankful to find the apartment unlocked, as who ever locked doors in the Pinch? I don't know why it should have disappointed me that no one was home. Slogging through the front room to my alcove, I unfolded the hide-a-bed and fell over it, then lay there trying to make my mind a blank. But tired as I was, my thoughts insisted on sorting through the events that had led me to this sad state of affairs. I got no further in my efforts, however, than recalling the torrential rains that brought the flood. I recalled them so vividly that my brain began to feel like a sponge — a sponge trying desperately to absorb the rising water, some of which had started to leak out my eyes. Then the telephone rang.

"Ha-a-ar-ry!" greeted my mother, her voice bloodcurdlingly shrill. Never quite trusting the wires to carry sound, she'd always felt obliged to shout.

"Mama, where are you?" I cried, as if she might have spoken

from a cloud, the pompadoured coif of a dark thunderhead. I was amazed at how much I suddenly wished she was here.

"Harry, listen, I'm over at your Uncle Morris's. Too many tongue-wagging yentes on North Main Street, if you know what I mean. So Morris says I should come and stay on the Parkway till this business gets settled. He says tell Harry he's welcome too. Of course I tell him Harry's a big boy, he takes care of himself. The original Mister Does-As-He-Pleases. But you know your uncle, such a worrier — God forbid anybody ain't accounted for. So he insists I should give you a call. Harry?"

I was that close to telling her I was on my way, when I thought to ask exactly which business it was that she was referring to.

"You mean you ain't heard the news about your father?"

"Oh," I said, glad to at least get that much straight. But still I was troubled, because this Uncle Morris she mentioned — she should correct me if I was wrong, but wasn't this the same Uncle Morris who I knew for a fact had been instrumental in effecting his own brother's ruin? Wasn't he the one who was as good as holding his ruined brother's wife (whom I forthwith absolved of any collusion) a hostage?

All this I had it in mind to tell her, plus the assurance that this same momzer uncle would never get his clammy mitts on his nephew, who was wise to his tricks.

"Mama," I began assertively enough, only to feel my voice break, my high horse gone lame in mid-stride. After a moment's snuffling I tried again, this time not so much telling as asking: "Mama, can I please talk to" — pronouncing her name like a quiet abracadabra — "Naomi?"

"Wait a minute, Harry," said my mother. I could tell that she had briefly muffled the receiver at the other end, after which she formally announced, "Your uncle would like a word with you."

keep whatever company she chose. And if you could take her perpetual wink at face value, maybe she was hinting that this colored stiff was at least better company than an empty samovar.

So who was to say that old Zippe wasn't just as well off here as in her box back at Kaplan's Loans? Still, I couldn't help wondering just how my grandma had wound up in such society in the first place. I don't know how much longer I might have stood there trying to puzzle it out, if the door to the mortuary hadn't suddenly opened and out walked Oboy. He was wearing a furniture pad draped like a tallis about his shoulders, pushing a steel dolly as tall as himself with one hand. With the other he was stuffing a wad of bills into his pocket.

Behind him must have been the undertaker himself, a portly man with his thumbs tucked into his suspenders, a gob of snuff distending his upper lip. When he saw me, he spat once and proudly declared, "Young white ge'man, be so kind as inform yo kinfolk, this here Pine the Sky am a ambidexter stablishment. Cater all color clinetele."

To Oboy, who was walking away, I shouted, "Wait just a cockeyed minute!" But he never even looked over his shoulder. He picked up his bandy pace, beginning to steer the two-wheeler at a reckless zigzag down the sidewalk. Coaxing my tush into motion, I started to give chase, though I didn't know quite what I'd do if I overtook him. Would I shake an accusing finger in his leathery kisser, its fixed whammy as immutable as those on the pair that he'd joined in the mortuary window?

He was veering at a dangerous tilt behind a group of street corner vagrants when I blinked and lost sight of him, but rather than pause to investigate his vanishing, I just kept running. Having worked up the head of steam I needed to see me clear of the underworld block, I galloped on at a breakneck clip. I streaked under the Palace Theater marquee and out across Hernando, charging through the litter on the fringe of Handy

281

gots to ride that casket to glory if tha's what it take, which it don't seem to once she got the witness out a her system.

"I declare, you had yo Knights a Pythias band. Got the preacher Reverend Hightower, he be sayin how the devil done unbutton the po boy's lip but it were the angel have fasten her shet again, which what you reckon he mean by that?"

Then the barber let me know that I wasn't the only one who'd been conspicuous by his absence from the ceremony: "Course, he ain't never say a mumblin word one to nobody, that ol rapscallion Lucifer. Boy sho am a study — if he ain't jus up an tooken off!"

It was funny how I seemed to know what the barber would say before he said it. I even knew the part he neglected to tell me: where the surviving brother, the one who's been struck dumb by the death of his twin, sets off to follow the North Star in search of his lost voice, or maybe his lost father. In stories like these something always has to be lost. I knew also that, at the close of the story, the kid would be pumping a railroad handcar over bridges; he'd be rattling across deserts and glacial chasms into rain forests dense with a poison fog. When last seen, he'd be rolling swiftly down the tracks across the plain, toward a vanishing point in a city whose towers cast their shadows a hundred miles.

I seemed to have it all by heart already, but then I knew a lot of stories — only judging from the barber's persistence, he actually meant that I should believe this one. A mute twin dies of a chatterbox disease and his brother clams up and disappears. Have a heart. These people, they were always trying to hand you some line.

"Look," I said to the barber, gently, the way you talk to a crazy person, "I've got to be going." I reclaimed my arm with such a jerk that I practically fell backwards out the door.

Stay calm, I told myself out on the sidewalk, wanting only to put as much distance as I could between me and Mambo's. But within seconds I had broken into a full sprinting flight, bolting past the Pie in the Sky Funeral Parlor, past the cosmetology institute and the Independent Pole Bearers lodge hall and the grease-filmed windows of the One Minute Café, before my brain would admit what I'd glimpsed in the corner of an eye. Still, it took another half a block before I could slow down. I turned and retraced my steps back to the storefront mortuary.

Behind the dirty window the formally attired dead man sat in his timeless rigidity on a bald velvet throne. No longer alone, however, he had acquired an equally shopworn companion, the salt shaker to his pepper, seated a little lower beside him in a Windsor chair. She was wearing a heavily starched serge shirtwaist with a linen apron, the kind suitable for throwing over your head against approaching Cossacks. Her fingers lay twined in her lap like a lump of fossilized challah; from beneath her leaden skirts, looking pugnacious, poked a thick pair of lace-up brogans. A hand-painted babushka, souvenir of Coney Island, was tied toothache-fashion about her wispy jaw, framing a face the texture of a cured tobacco leaf. In that face a single dry eye (the one Mr. Gruber had presumably been unable to keep shut) remained open, so that the other appeared to wink.

This is your bubbe, I whispered to myself. This is your Grandma Zippe, who's been given to a second husband on the other side.

I imagined the indignities she must have suffered during her journey to this window, how her joints must have splintered when she was folded into her chair — though sitting was the thing she always did best. I saw myself kicking through the glass to repossess her, buttonholing passers-by to join me in appropriate prayer. At the same time I tried to assure myself that things could be worse. Wasn't she already forgotten by the family? Even her widower husband had long since graduated from a personal mourning to a more universal despair. Assuming that death constituted a legal separation, she was free to

"Hello, Harry." It was the voice of the enemy, brisk as usual, a voice that slaps your back as it sticks the knife in. He was full of his in-the-bag confidence, his crumpled cellophane breathing. "Look, don't worry — who's worried, right? Your uncle here has got everything under control. Solly's bond? No problem, it's good as taken care of. He'll be back on the street by tomorrow A.M. A little patshed in the dignity department maybe, but knock on wood, that ain't never killed nobody yet. Anyhow, he could use a little vacation, see how the other half lives, probably even make some new friends if I know my brother. And as for the shop — make a phone call here, scratch a back over there, if you take my meaning . . ."

I don't think I ever truly hated my uncle before. But as I listened I got chilled, my spine supplanted by a tree of ice whose branches reached as far as my fingers and toes. My tongue. I should kick myself if I'd ever thought of him as nothing but a harmless old blowhard. Now I knew him for what he was, your authentic arch-villain, your regulation nemesis. While he continued laying it on about how he proposed to fix this, fix that, I conceived an overriding desire to fix my Uncle Morris. I saw myself, a slingshot clenched in my teeth, scaling a mountain of moneybags that he squatted on top of, big as the *Hindenburg.* I would lay him low, mortally wounded in his Achilles potbelly, nothing left of him but flapping jowls and leaking gas. Then I'd make off with the prize of his daughter. Mama, I suddenly decided, he could keep.

But who was I kidding? Just the effort of trying to despise my uncle as much as he deserved had tuckered me out. Nor could you stay chilled for very long in our stuffy apartment. My spine become liquid, I drooped onto the edge of the kitchen table and asked myself where I got off apportioning blame. Especially as, in this case, the recipient was a man whom it behooved me to regard as my prospective father-in-law. Mishpocheh, I should remember, was thicker than water. After all, Uncle Morris wasn't the only culprit in this affair; there was my papa's own tacit complicity to take into account. There was the fact that lies and deceit seemed to run in the family, myself a chip off the block in that respect.

In the end, who could say which of us was really the more culpable — Uncle Morris for his double-dealing, mother-stealing, Judas-kissing treachery, or me, his miserable nephew, who'd forsaken his only friends for the sake of a small-time gonif's daughter, for my princess first cousin, whose nasal intonation I would have given what was left of my soul to hear again.

". . . So you'll come over here, you'll have a nice nosh in the peace and quiet of my humble abode, away from all that yehtehtehteh in the Pinch," Uncle Morris still prattled. "Come on, palsie, whaddaya say — yes Uncle, no Uncle, nu?"

"Uncle!" It came out like "enough already," though I tried to suppress my impatience. "Can I talk to Naomi?" Then my mind wouldn't wait to begin the conversation: "Naomi, it's me!" "Oh Harry, sweetie, kepeleh, it's always been you! I missed you like crazy! Mmm mmm kiss kiss kiss . . ."

"Naomi?" Uncle Morris seemed to be considering, and for an anxious second I thought he was going to deny that he had a daughter. "Why, she's up in St. Louie with my sister-in-law, her Tante Frieda Green. I thought you knew. Course, you never met Frieda, did you? Such a pisk on that girl, I'm telling you, a born matchmaker if ever there was. Always she's shushkening, 'Naomi, meet this one, a Rothschild! And that one's papa made a killing in BVDs.' But you know something, Harry, I'm glad you finally hit it off, you two. It's naches when cousins get along . . ."

Again I smelled a rat. Here was more of his mischief: he'd sent Naomi away to spite me. He'd deliberately put her beyond my reach and in the way of more acceptable suitors. In fact, hadn't he killed two birds for the price of packing one Naomi off to her aunt? While protecting his daughter from unwelcome advances, he had also cleared the coast to bring home his locked-up brother's zaftig wife. It was all very neat. On the other hand, I was vaguely aware that Naomi went to St. Louis every summer, and even if she'd wanted to, she couldn't have reached me to say goodbye.

Then I remembered something else, that I had behaved in a fashion that was practically a tradition among Kaplan males, who often lost their women through being preoccupied. Left unattended, their chosen ones frequently died or went away. I remembered also how it was with my cousin, who was sometimes so excitable, such a spitfire; sometimes, unless you had some talent for noticing, you would hardly even know she was there.

My desolation complete, I said thanks all the same to my uncle and hung up the phone.

It occurred to me that I ought to be hungry, since I couldn't have told you the last time I sat down with my family to a proper meal. As there was no one around to remind me, I had to remind myself that I should keep up my strength. So I opened the refrigerator, which was badly in need of defrosting. But when I got a load of its neglected contents — the potato pancakes like powder puffs, the gelatin ring like an inner tube, the coral-green brisket, an overripe melon, a squished jelly blintz, a geranium, a pair of shoes — I lost what little appetite I had.

I went to my alcove and sprawled face-down on the hide-a-bed. With a motion that used to be second nature, I reached for one of the books on my nightstand, a frayed cloth edition of a G. A. Henty saga, as it happened. Leafing through it, however, I quickly concluded that the book had too many words. I tossed it aside on my mattress and took up another from a small pile of survivors on the floor. This one turned out to be the good old reliable Sir Arthur Conan Doyle, profusely illustrated and morocco-bound. Here was the stuff I'd been missing: dangerous exploits pressed tidily between hard covers, which kept them from spilling over into the reader's real life.

But this book was also giving me trouble. For all its colorful drawings of Arabian stallions and rainbow-plumaged birds of paradise, not to mention thugee assassins held captive in clouds of Baker Street pipe smoke, the book might as well have been written in a foreign tongue. That's how little patience I had left for stories. So I dropped the book beside the other, disturbed by the way their splayed-open bindings resembled the double pitches of rooftops in a flood.

Fourteen

I don't remember falling asleep, though I did notice how the evening stepped especially hard on the heels of the afternoon. Then it must have been late, because the commercial bustle of North Main Street had given way to other noises: the moaning of a barge below the levee, the rattling of a freight train over the bridge, the skirling of crickets, a tinkling toilet, a scratching mouse. Lying in the dark, I isolated every sound in the hope of discerning something particular. Just what it was I was listening for I couldn't at first have said; then it came to me. I was listening for the sound of a turning knob, an opening door, the signal that my father had come home from his pawnshop for the night. Funny how you could miss a noise you never even remembered having heard.

Once I'd closed my eyes, I had a hard time prying them open again. By the time I did, sawing with my fingers at the gluey lids, it was morning; streamers of sunlight were making a Maypole of the mimosa outside my window. I yawned luxuriously as I raised myself on my elbows, creating an avalanche of tumbling books. Thus surrounded by the rubble of a day that had yet to begin, I recalled how unhappy I was.

I got out of bed and began to wander the apartment without

pausing to change the clothes I'd slept in. To stand still was to invite unkind thoughts; add any more to what I was already shlepping around and I wouldn't be able to budge. Keep moving, that was the ticket. Stay busy — though I was hard pressed to think of what to do next. Maybe I should make some coffee; people made coffee in the morning. And while I didn't really care for the taste of it, I liked the musical trickle that the percolator made. It was a pleasant distraction from the silence of the apartment, which the hubbub outside called too much attention to.

Things picked up a little more when, cracking some eggs into a bowl, I turned on the electric mixer. I went into the closet, hauled out the Hoover, and plugged it in. Soon I was conducting a regular symphony of whir, gurgle, and drone, pleased at the way that they simulated the sounds of a lived-in apartment. But now that I'd turned on every appliance in the house, I began to have the uneasy feeling that the appliances were about to turn on me.

This, of course, was nonsense. Nevertheless, in a sweat I switched everything off. In the ensuing silence I realized that I was only being sensible. Beyond the obvious impracticality of running household appliances to no purpose in an empty apartment, the noise might have drowned out the news — which was surely at hand — of my papa's release on bail. Any minute now the door would open, the telephone ring, so I sank into an understuffed armchair to wait. But for all his promised pulling of strings, I suspected that Uncle Morris was taking his own sweet time.

I turned on the console Zenith, consecrated by their portrait to the memory of my grandparents, and listened half expecting to hear some word of my father's difficulties, that he had become an international episode. But while there was no mention of any Kaplan scandal, there was certainly plenty of tsuris to go around. The nation's waters having proven unruly, other elements were getting into the act. The heartland was dust, its silos like desert relics inundated by time. Kindled by the friction of feet that the marathon dancers had fallen asleep on, a dance hall on Long Island was in flames. A lady flier known as the sweetheart of the jet stream had been taken for its own by thin air, and somewhere in the country where misfortune never struck, a baby had slipped down a hole.

You think you got problems? After the expense of son Clifford's wedding (which had to be annulled when it was discovered that the bride had a past), "One Man's Family" were having to tighten their belts. In "Portia Faces Life," Portia was patently refusing to do so, having lost her third fiancé to a freak accident. There was trouble at the lodge hall, the Kingfish bilked out of the treasury by a designing female. Jimmy Durante was mortified, Mortimer Snerd afraid, and the Answer Man stumped by a question concerning the nature of truth.

Spies were in the unions, union defectors among the factory scabs, the criminal element in every walk of life. There were swing fanatics at Roseland, driven certifiably mad by Benny Goodman's horn. There were homegrown loudmouths complaining that Benny's style of music could be blamed for the current hekdish in Europe, where, according to H. V. Kaltenborn's pea-shooter delivery, the murder tallies were announced like the scores of sporting events.

Where had I been that nobody told me how God's Depression-green earth was going straight to hell? Not that you could pin that one on me. If anybody had contributed to the sorry shape the world was in, it was my screwball family. Myself, all I'd done was go about my own business, abandoning everybody I knew.

As the morning wore on and the apartment filled with suffocating heat, I gave up on my father's return. I raised myself with a groan from the armchair and plodded downstairs into the blistering street, where there was still not much to be found in the way of fresh air. A sitting duck for my own dark thoughts and the relentless largess of North Main, I decided that my first impulse was best: I should just keep moving.

Putting the Pinch behind me at Poplar Avenue, I crossed over into Main Street proper and trudged along in the hothouse sunshine. The air was dense with yellow vapor, smelling a mix of roasted peanuts and carbon monoxide, with a tinge of fresh poop from the horses of the mounted police. Clerks in sweaty seersucker dispatched couriers in a tocsin of bicycle bells. Ladies flashed their legs as they got out of taxis, drawing wolf whistles from the ranks of loafing bankers' sons. Negro porters sniffed for some hint of a breeze, leaning at impossible angles to pull their laden handcarts rickshaw-style. Nobody seemed to be actively ignoring me, nor did they regard me with any special fondness or disdain.

When I turned left into Beale, entering the hurly-burly of the pawnshop district, I actually felt a kind of smartness insinuate itself into my step. I began to breathe a little easier as I drew nearer my father's shop, to feel despite myself a little more like the resourceful Harry of old. But the feeling was short-lived, snuffed out by the sight of the bantam puller, pointlessly restored to his stool before the locked façade of Kaplan's Loans. There he sat for no earthly good reason, the living reminder of everything that was wrong.

Touching a desiccated finger to the bill of his nautical cap, he gave me his mechanical salute, after which he had the temerity to croak, "You is late."

This was more than the traffic would bear. Here was the two-faced creature himself, my uncle's functionary and my father's demon, the one who'd swapped my grandma for a box full of sparkles — and even in that he'd bungled the job so thoroughly that the cops wondered if the operation was queered on purpose. He had a nerve showing his prune puss around Kaplan's, instead of staying down whatever funkhole he'd made off to when I spotted him last.

"Late for what, you stinking nigger troll!" I shouted so that the whole farcockte street could hear me — let them hear! And when words did nothing to dent the puller's stolid composure, I spat full in his monkey face.

I prepared to stand my ground as he sprang for my throat. Together we would roll into the gutter, splashing blood on the cobbles, biting out plugs of flesh, and spitting teeth. Spectators trying to intervene would themselves be mangled. Meat wagons would draw up as bets went down. But while the gob of spittle slid snail-like down a crease of his stubbled cheek, Oboy remained unruffled. In fact, dabbing with a threadbare sleeve at his wrinkled punim, he actually looked to the cloudless sky like he thought it might rain. Then he leveled his sallow eyes at mine.

"Mistah Harry," he rasped, and a squawking sound came from his diaphragm, making me think he was about to launch into a speech. That a reticent shvartzer should suddenly let loose a stream of tortured diction was nothing new to me. Go ahead, I thought, do your worst. But laconic as ever, Oboy said only, "Mistah Harry, looka here."

He produced from his pocket what I had to assume was some instrument for settling the score with me. But it was nothing but an ordinary bobby pin, which he was holding forth like a prize I'd won for spitting in his face. While I tried hard to hang on to my anger, in the presence of such knuckleheaded irrelevance it slipped away. The shrunken homunculus had cheated me out of my moment. He hadn't even done me the courtesy of calling me hypocrite, of accusing me to my miserable face of running out on my father just like he had.

Or had he? Because, as I turned my head to hide the waterworks that were starting up in my eyes, I had another thought: with its cover blown, Kaplan's Loans could no longer front for anyone's funny business. You could credit Oboy with having, however inadvertently, bought the pawnshop a reprieve. Okay, so he'd secured it at the expense of my grandma's remains. But in playing broker to her posthumous mixed marriage, hadn't he also released her from a sort of Ellis Island of the soul?

And now, was it in some similar spirit of emancipation that he was waving this bobby pin under my nose? Like it was the key to the mystery of all his dubious motives? If for no other reason than to end his taunting, I turned back and made a grab for the pin, but the puller snatched it out of my reach. As I was shrugging to show that I'd had it with his stupid game, he hopped down off his stool. He scuttled over to the door of the shop and, lifting the python-thick chain, began to jimmy the giant padlock.

"Nix!" I told him, looking nervously east and west for lurking detectives. "Cheezit!" When he paid no attention, I stepped toward him and turned my back, making a feeble attempt to shield him from view. I nodded and grinned idiotically at the passers-by, a couple of whom responded with a knowing wink. At one point, turning enough to observe the puller's progress, I saw that he'd already sprung the lock. He was unwinding the chain — the sound bringing to mind the scene in "Captain Blood" where they release the galley slaves — and folding the lattice. I stood a hotfooted lookout as Oboy nipped inside the shop and tore the sheriff's notice from the window. In an instant he was back at the door, which he flamboyantly held open for me.

I might have stood there debating the issue if I hadn't been so anxious not to make more of a spectacle than we already had. So I hesitated only long enough to give the puller a put-upon sigh, then stepped quickly into the shop. Still, it wasn't lost on me how Oboy's ordinarily inscrutable puss — just before he darted forward to resume his perch — had about the liver lips an unprecedented touch of smugness. It was an expression that made me feel eerily as if everything that had happened to date was a part of some devious plan. It had all been by way of arranging a moment when I would walk into these off-limits premises by myself. A dumb idea, I put it behind me as I hurriedly shut the front door.

Then I wished somebody would tell me what to do next. Of course it didn't take an Einstein to figure that, in a place as stuffy as this, you might switch on the ceiling fans. And since the lights were attached to the fans, it involved no extra energy to shed a little light on the subject.

The shop was naturally no less a shambles than it had been the day before, a disorder that took my father's scrupulous chaos a step or two further. The thought of his upset merchandise was undoubtedly causing Sol Kaplan to turn over in his cell. So I asked myself where was the crime if the proprietor's son straightened up a bit in his absence. Even as I wondered why bother, I was already going through the motions. I was making myself useful — did I hear somebody say "for a change"?

At first, afraid that at any second I might be detained by the arm of the law, I worked hastily. I shored up the Saratoga trunks and the toppled Gladstone bags, stood the gardening tools at attention, sorted a shelf of items that were graduated in size from pipes to saxophones. I wound the clocks, plugged in the Wurlitzer, rebaled the scattered magazines and sheet music, stacking them in solid bluffs on either side of the aisle. This was more like it, I thought, and began to relax a bit. I took the time, as I righted the overturned bottles of patentless elixirs, to read their labels: one boasting certain spirit-banishing properties, another the dual attributes of shrinking hemorrhoids and restoring hair. I picked up a stray pair of opera glasses and looked through both ends, examined here a fallen jacket, there a sword in a tarnished silver scabbard, and thought: item, one shiny black clawhammer tailcoat, once owned by a preacher

301

said to have raised the corpse of a man who died owing him money; item, one parade saber with bronze hilt and serial notches, passed according to tradition from expiring father to surviving son at Manassas, San Juan Hill, Belleau Wood . . .

It didn't altogether delight me to find that I still had such amazing recall of my father's ledgers. Here was information that my already overloaded mind could have done without. On the other hand, it was maybe not entirely to my detriment that my head remained a depository for my papa's accounts, because when I looked in the narrow cubby that he'd set aside for his office, I saw that the top of his old wooden lectern was bare. The cops must have also confiscated his books.

So it seemed that, with my peculiar knack for remembering, I was in a position to render my father a service. Rather than let him come back from the pokey only to be crushed by the loss of his precious ledgers, I could duplicate them, almost verbatim if I wanted. With identical binders and a little speculation as to prices and rates of interest, I could make a virtual facsimile edition — I could even reproduce the crabbed handwriting that overwhelmed the margins like a flight of crows. Wasn't my penmanship at least the equal of my papa's for illegibility? With the exception of the crap acquired during my sabbatical, I could recite for the record the origin of almost every item I recognized and make educated guesses (such as who would know the difference) about those I didn't. I could invent what I couldn't copy from memory; it was my talent. But why would I want to do such a thing?

Why should I be a party to the perpetuation of my papa's legacy of woolgathering and outright lies, especially now when I had the chance to start from scratch? Because, with Sol Kaplan temporarily out of the way, I found myself possessed of a rare opportunity. Given the run of the place and minus the nuisance of my father's supervision, I could make some progress toward putting Kaplan's Loans to rights. There were worse ways of spending your time, I decided, than in taking inventory. If I applied myself, who knew but I might have the new books ready before my father was let out of jail. He'd return to find his accounts in apple-pie order. Every entry would be described with a pruned economy, each debit and credit column a model of sound commercial arithmetic. While I was at it, I might even make a few other changes.

For one thing, I would weed out this cash drawer stuffed with everything but cash, full of stale knishes and expired receipts for items that would never be sold. Such as this one — brittle as an autumn leaf, a moth flying out from beneath it — for a legless rocking horse, or this for a milking stanchion with crotcheted slipcover, a knotty-pine casket with contents unnamed. Later I would get rid of the worthless items themselves.

As I crumpled up the stubs and tossed them into a nearby fishing creel, I gloated over how quickly I had begun to get the hang of things. All at once I was coming into a wealth of practical wisdom. Flushed with complacency, my brain was discharging ideas the way cigars are handed out at a bris. Here was my birthright — the good head for business that had needed only a desperate enough hour to announce itself.

It was clear to me now that Kaplan's would definitely have to drop the loans for a while. No new merchandise should be taken in until this outrageous surplus had first been substantially reduced. For the time being we would become a (perfectly legitimate, of course) retail commodities outfit. In a few weeks, when we'd cleared sufficient capital to make it advantageous again, we could resume the practice of lending money. We could promote our competitive interest rates in the newspaper and on advertising fliers dropped from skywriting airplanes. You would see us compared favorably to our tight-fisted competition on hoardings and the sides of trolleys, on the sandwich board that Oboy might be induced to wear. Firmly established as a going concern, Kaplan's would no longer be prey to anyone's meddling. A certain once necessary evil — which you will notice that I'm not naming names — wouldn't be necessary anymore. In its final phase of reorganization, the shop would be proof against even my papa's excesses; this thanks to the balanced judgment and shrewd entrepreneurial instincts of his son. What with the coming war in Europe, we would make money hand over tochis — war, as I'd always been told, being good for trade.

And when Naomi, God bless her convex pupik, came back from St. Louis to find me an authentic mensch, when she saw how I'd become the bulwark of a reunited family, a breathing testimonial to the recovered pride and sagacity of the Kaplan men, we would be married. So what if we were next to being next of kin. Who's superstitious? If our son — I'd just realized that I wanted a son — if he should happen to be born with two heads, then so be it, we'd give him two names: Pete and Repeat, for instance; or Lucifer and Michael, like the bad and good angels, so the kid could have it both ways.

Again I congratulated myself on the inspired turn my thoughts were taking. Not pipe dreams but capable and mature deliberations, they were worthy of one whose feet were planted securely on the ground. Only to think such thoughts was to acquire weight and substance. My head overripe with momentous ideas, I had to cup my chin in my hands, propping my elbows on the blotter-topped counter for support. We would have a grand reopening complete with tricolor banners and balloons, a raffle in which customers would win what we couldn't otherwise give away. There would be shnaps and sponge cake like at a bar mitzvah, a rabbi to smash a bottle over the till — or so I was imagining when the door chimes pealed and a customer sauntered in.

He was a whip-thin old darkie with a courtly but weathered face beneath a broad-brimmed hat, wearing a dappled gray suit the texture of molting plumage. Tucked under his arm was a brown paper parcel that he carried with an exaggerated importance. I started to tell him we were closed, can't you read?, when I remembered that the notice had been torn from the window. I looked apprehensively over his shoulder, expecting maybe a signal from Oboy — patrolmen had seen the old man enter and trouble was on the way. At the same time, I figured, where was the problem? Just as soon as this character realized I wasn't my father, he would make his excuses and turn on his heel. It was the song and dance I recalled so well from that afternoon of the miscarried funeral.

But this one must have seen something other than my old, not-so-solid self; it was apparent already how I had changed. Or why else would he have politely doffed his hat, revealing a billow of hair like a scouring pad, and smiled a regular gates of horn? Having placed his parcel on the counter, he'd begun to unfasten a bow of shaggy twine.

Grateful as I was for the authority he'd seen fit to invest in my person, I was sorry to have to inform him — clearing my throat with a crowing noise that surprised us both — that he should save his energy.

"We're a strictly retail enterprise here at Kaplan's," I told him, trying on the argot for size, satisfied that it wasn't such a bad fit. "Cash'n carry's the long and the short of it, policy of the new management. Sorry uncle, no loans today."

I happened to notice that the brown wrapping paper that the old-timer continued to unfurl contained a book, *The Travels of Marco Polo* no less, its pages gilt-edged like Scriptures, its title embossed in copper on a dun-colored kid binding with a patina-green metal hasp.

Myself, I wasn't sure where in creation Marco Polo had traveled, but just looking at the book was enough to give you ideas. I could picture him at some juncture in his wanderings, about to cross a broad river where archers were poised for his protection on the forked tongues of dragons. I saw the trunks spilling silks and goblets and devil's inventions, the camels champing intelligently in their golden reins. I saw the whole caravan shimmering miragelike as it boarded a paddle-wheeled ark several parasangs long. Buff-skinned ladies were chained to their litters, their jeweled navels shining through lounge pajamas like beacons through fog. Sadly they played on their dulcimers and slide trombones.

"This here a rare edition," the old gent was saying, having totally ignored my caveat. His voice had a soothing bass resonance and his breath, as he leaned toward me over the counter, exuded a pleasant fragrance of gingery rosé. "It were salvage by my pappy from the wreck a the steamboat *Sultana,* long with sixty-leven white folk an a sho't ton a hemp. This uz famous, the city have ereck a stone which you can read it bout my pappy Mistah Hezeki Sledge. Well suh, the time have come when the book turn around an hexchange the compliment. What it done am it have save his natchl life. See that, tha's a bullet hole."

I was beginning to feel certain mutinous stirrings, unbusinesslike palpitations in the area of my chest. It was a kind of excitement that threatened to undermine the reputation for hard-headed professionalism I hoped shortly to enjoy. I nodded like now I'd heard everything.

"Un-hunh, and I'm the Rabbi Shmelke of Pshishke."

This tripped the old guy up, if only momentarily. During that lull I came to understand how, in business, your left hand might take liberties that the right need not know about.

As the old-timer began tentatively to resume his pitch, I slowly unfolded my arms. I sent the fingers of my left hand spidering down the counter toward a booklet of unstubbed pawn tickets. This, along with the rubber stamp and ink pad, I began to gather toward me. At the same time, with my right hand I punched a cash register key, the drawer springing open with a silvery *brrrng.* Looking idly in the till, the way you'd peer into a sack to see what was for lunch, I interrupted the old guy to offer him two bits.

His venerable head recoiled as if from the impact of such an insulting offer. "You be pull my leg or what!" he exclaimed. "I have you ta know this are a priceless hairloom, got gre-e-e-at sentimental valyah!"

As his frown intensified, his lower lip extended until it drooped over his chin like a sock in a wringer. "I is mos disappointed," he repined. "Course, in time like these whachacall-em hard time which it ain't never been no soff time down on Beale . . ." He inhaled as if to steady himself for the sacrifice he was called on to make, then presented his impressive set of ivories again.

"Time like these, I b'lieve I can see my way ta let y'all have this precious volume fo the picayune price a, shall we say, fi dollah."

My jaw dropped over the unnegotiable distance between five dollars and twenty-five cents. Any self-respecting merchandiser would have given the old bluffer the bum's rush out the door. But I told myself that this type of sparring would stand me in good stead for subsequent transactions — I needed the practice. Without further hesitation I came back with a compromise.

"A buck," I said, "take it or leave it."

Now he would know for future reference, and put the word out on the street, that Harry Kaplan was nobody's fool. He had the gift of driving a hard bargain; he had the horse sense. I dipped into the till where the jeweler's glass lay among loose change, and pushed back my specs to stick the lens in my eye. Now I wanted the visor, the rubber thumb, all the paraphernalia my papa had used to complete the illusion that he was what he pretended to be. The props made the man — this might have been true in my father's case, though in my own I was more convinced by the minute that I was born for this job.

Making a show of examining the old man's property more

closely, however, I made the mistake of actually examining it more closely. Through the lens I couldn't help but observe certain features I'd overlooked at first glance.

"Two dollah fitty cent," countered the old-timer, having chosen this moment to revise his expectations. But I was too absorbed in my scrutiny of his book to be distracted.

What I saw, when I'd unclasped and parted the covers, were crumbling mud-brown pages, water-stained and undulant as the lip of a clamshell. I saw how the print was aged to unreadability, the washed-out maps and drawings bled to apparition. I saw a pear-shaped hole several hundred pages deep, which I thought was less likely the work of a bullet than a worm.

I almost groaned aloud at how generous the bid of an entire buck now seemed. There was of course nothing for it but to retract my extravagant offer, the question being how to do it with a measure of diplomacy. Not that this crafty old codger, who was currently conceding unprompted to a buck seventy-five, deserved any special treatment. But I wouldn't want him to accuse me of violating the particulars of haggling, especially on this inaugural occasion. It wouldn't do that I should be taken for an amateur.

In an effort to override the change of heart my face must have betrayed, the old man had made his move. Already he was extending a shell-pink palm to receive his loan. A little flustered but still determined to back out of the transaction, I searched my mind for a way to get rid of him. Then I had an idea. Affably reaching over the counter, I took hold of his parchment-dry hand and gave it a hearty shake.

"Fine, fine," I assured him in response to an inquiry that neither of us had heard him make. "Always nice to see you, fairly makes my day. Next time bring the wife. And by the way, have you had a chance to read this? Well, so long. Ver farblondjet. Abyssinia."

My intention was that, confounded by my erratic behavior,

the customer would grab up his property and beat a hasty retreat. For a few seconds the old man did seem to be genuinely taken aback, but instead of fleeing the shop, he continued to stand his ground. He studied my face, evidently undecided as to whether I was pulling a fast one or just plain nuts. In the end, whatever his conclusion, he was suddenly all teeth again, returning my handshake so vigorously that the jeweler's loupe fell from my eye.

Then it was my turn to grow anxious, wanting to retrieve my fingers from the grubby warmth of his tenacious grip. No fooling, I wanted my hand back. But the old man hung on so tightly that you'd have thought he had hold of a leprechaun. He kept pumping my arm like he expected me to start spitting shekels.

"Young man," he announced, as together we seemed to be shaking on the deal, "it done look like you'n me is in bidness."

Later that afternoon I took in a battered bugle. It wasn't much, but the hepcat character who brought it in really handed me a laugh. He told me that he'd shaken it down, along with a peck of persimmons, from a tree where an angel was napping in Handy Park. This I recorded dutifully, entering the accounts on cardboard shirtfronts in place of the ledgers I planned to buy.

After the bugle I took in a lump of rusty metal that could have been a Cracker Jack prize, though the luckless veteran who pawned it guaranteed it was none other than the "Congregational Legion of Honor, awarded for bravery above and beyond the call of the wild." I was skeptical until he offered to throw in, as a bonus, Baby Face Nelson's trigger finger in a jar of alcohol. Then I paid a little more than face value for a pair of pennies, pinched (according to my customer) from the eyes of a famous dead hoofer. He boasted that he'd used them thereafter for the taps on his own dancing shoes.

I took in a tambourine made from a lynching victim's hide, a locket containing a curl of Shirley Temple's hair, some gold-capped molars that Casey Jones had lost in a brawl. I took in a hand-carved walking stick with its crook whittled into the shape of a serpent's head. The draggle-footed party didn't say so, but I thought it might have passed for the rod that Moses used to perform his magic tricks. Maybe this was stretching it, but that's what it put me in mind of — the magic rod the bashful prophet sometimes borrowed from his brother Aaron, the talkative one.